Oracles

OF AN
Ethiopian
Coffeehouse

Oracles

OF AN

Ethiopian
Coffeehouse

PAUL T. SUGG

TRUE DIRECTIONS
AN AFFILIATE OF TARCHER PERIGEE

iUniverse®

ORACLES OF AN ETHIOPIAN COFFEEHOUSE

This is a work of fiction. All of the characters, names, incidents, organizations, and dialogue in this novel are either the products of the author's imagination or are used fictitiously.

iUniverse books may be ordered through booksellers or by contacting:

iUniverse
1663 Liberty Drive
Bloomington, IN 47403
www.iuniverse.com
1-800-Authors (1-800-288-4677)

Because of the dynamic nature of the Internet, any web addresses or links contained in this book may have changed since publication and may no longer be valid. The views expressed in this work are solely those of the author and do not necessarily reflect the views of the publisher, and the publisher hereby disclaims any responsibility for them.

Any people depicted in stock imagery provided by Thinkstock are models, and such images are being used for illustrative purposes only.
Certain stock imagery © Thinkstock.

ISBN: 978-1-4917-7715-2 (sc)
ISBN: 978-1-4917-7714-5 (hc)
ISBN: 978-1-4917-7713-8 (e)

Library of Congress Control Number: 2015914664

Print information available on the last page.

iUniverse rev. date: 11/11/2015

Dedicated to my wife, Saule.

Part 1

AXUM

*M*orning sunlight drenched the streets of Axum, making the flaking white paint gleam over the concrete walls of its buildings as the city beckoned its inhabitants out to stroll about, attend business, or just exchange gossip in the morning cool. An occasional newspaper somersaulted across the street only to be tossed up by gusts of wind to kiss aged handbills on the walls and then fall over as if to caress wounds left by older bills that had either been torn or worn off, peeling off blotches of paint with them. The sleepy, ancient little town in the Tigray province of Ethiopia had now come fully alive but exhibited no mood of urgency in greeting the new day, as life would go on pretty much as usual. Axum, once a capital of world commerce in the first century, was now reduced to being a quaint ancient city at the base of the Adwa Mountains, whose sole claim to fame lay either in its towering obelisks or rumors that it actually housed the legendary "lost" Ark of the Covenant.

An Orthodox priest, or "abba," strolled down the dusty street clutching his jeweled, iconic Axum cross, feeling across it as he thought. Abba Befikuda (meaning "by God's will alone") cut a striking figure with his black robe flowing in the breeze. He noticed a small *awala nefas*, or dust devil, of about two meters in height, twisting its way incoherently down a side street, flinging a few large papers and other debris about in its minicyclonic activity. He mused at it, thinking it was a beautiful metaphor for other "dust devils," those that pester people, little pests from Satan's realm, or possibly figurative imagery for those other devils—insecurities that project those little voices of doom, depression, or inferiority complexes. Some might blow your way. But in many cases, unless one opens the door or walks directly into them, they aren't liable to mess up your hair much.

His eyes turned upward to see an azure collage of icy blue and aqua that tried to feel its way through thin stretches of clouds that overextended their reach, fizzling out at the sky's edge. He watched as an occasional breeze-turned-gust began chasing the wispy clouds across the horizon. Or maybe that was not his true focus of attention at all, for after noticing the beauty of a new day, his eyes seemed to peer straight through it all, revealing his contemplative mood, that his mind was clearly somewhere else, deeply concentrating on matters far more important than mere atmospheric conditions. He felt something in his bones, deep within his soul. His prophetic inclination began conceiving the notion that something or someone was on its way and would intersect his life in the near future. He began to feel a curious sense of anticipation, the way he did whenever a stranger, pilgrim, or some estranged person would be placed in his path by God's hand. He and his brothers had met several, several who believed they were on some course or spiritual walk but had either stumbled or been knocked about, staggering in an unclear pattern and needing to make greater sense of it all. He and his brothers would provide them with a sense of community and impart whatever insight they could to help those pilgrims chart or rechart a clearer course.

A camel's loud bellow jerked his attention back to the mundane. Mussie, a local merchant, was trying to get his camel, heavily laden with goods to be sold in the marketplace, to move from the spot where he had parked him outside a café. Camels still populated the ancient town despite the appearance of cars, which were mostly of pathetic Russian manufacture and all badly in need of spare parts and repairs. Camels and donkeys were still used either as pack animals or for human transport.

The camel, Wugat by name (meaning "piercing thorn in my side"), actually went by several names. Many, depending on how angry his owner was with him, were quite profane, and sometimes Mussie just called him the Antichrist. Wugat waited dutifully outside the café as his owner slipped in for his "morning coffee." His was a drink radically different from anything served in the coffee ceremony. Mussie and his friends liked to lace their concoction at least half and half with bourbon. Mussie (named after Moses, but whose name in Amharic actually translates into "one who is plucked from the water") liked to embellish a bit on the old biblical story concerning his namesake, inventing parallel scenarios regarding his own birth and childhood. He claimed that he too had been plucked from the water at birth and that the event so severely traumatized him that he was "forced to swear off water permanently" and opted for alcoholic beverages instead, the stronger the better.

"Hede, hede ... hede, hede," Mussie commanded. He began swatting the beast of burden about the flanks and buttocks with a switch in a futile attempt at getting the camel to move. However, Wugat refused to budge. Mussie's ire began to reach the boiling point, and he began to curse at the camel and hit him harder. Still the camel refused to move and even went so far as to raise its head in an act of snobbery, as if to crow and mock his frustrated owner's acts of futility. As Mussie continued to yell, the camel spat in defiance at his owner, let out a loud, guttural nuzz from deep within his stomach, braying into Mussie's face, and then proceeded to broadcast it around Axum. Mussie, now totally enraged, took the switch and prodded the camel, shoving it up his rectum, jabbing it a few times before pulling it out. But much to his surprise, rather than prompting movement, the camel responded by defecating the mother lode at Mussie's feet, much to the amusement of his friends hysterically laughing as they watched the spectacle unfold from the sidewalk. Mussie, not appreciating his friends' amusement at his expense, began swinging his stick, flinging camel dung at them. He proceeded to wander out into the street, shouting his laments toward heaven, asking God why he had been cursed with such an unruly beast.

The abba chortled, trying to hold back from erupting into loud, boisterous laughter as Mussie ran around swinging his switch. Befikuda quickly surmised that none of the four drunken sots would conceive of an answer to the camel dilemma. He decided it was time for him to intervene with the only likely solution.

He walked over to the beast of burden and patted him on the neck. "Wugat, Wugat, my large friend, why is it you torture your master so? I see he is administering the 'spare the rod, spoil the camel' school of thought, which has its place at times, but I know of a different remedy. I deem it necessary for these times when you are being so stubborn and really must move. I know your real weakness! I know of your sweet tooth and your love for the tangy nectar of pomegranates!" the abba said. He pulled a fresh pomegranate from his pocket. Befikuda had two more stashed away on his person, for the camel wasn't the only one in the street that day with a sweet tooth. The abba loved to crack a few open for a midmorning snack. He felt he could spare one for such a worthy cause. He cracked open the luring fruit and placed it in front of the camel, which nuzzed again with an approving tone, if not one expressing his sheer feeling of ecstasy at the very sight of his favorite treat! He quickly reached down and snatched up the section of pomegranate with his mouth from the abba's hand and began voraciously chewing up the delicious, fresh tangy seeds, extending his long tongue to lap up the juice that began trickling out of his mouth. He let off a higher-toned murmur that was more like a sighing nuzz, a sigh of pleasure, satisfaction, a strong indication that the abba's bribery was working. The camel gobbled up the pomegranate so fast, as if to inhale it. The abba laughed. "Oh, you really like that, don't you? Would you like another one? You would, wouldn't you?" He teased the camel, holding out a second pomegranate just out of the camel's reach. "Not so fast, Wugat. If you want this one, you have to walk with me over here, this way … that's it. Come now, Wugat, keep going, keep going, keep going," the abba coaxed. Befikuda cracked open the second pomegranate, prompting even more movement at a quicker pace, as the camel decided that the bribe was sufficient enough to give up his stubborn stand defending his fair chunk of the street.

"Look, I have succeeded in taming your beast!" Befikuda said.

Mussie stopped his rant toward heaven long enough to observe the "miracle" and then walked over to his camel, still thoroughly disgusted with Wugat but grateful to the abba for his efforts. He masked his attitude with a tone of respect and cordiality. "Thank you, Abba Befikuda. I see you have resorted to the sweet-tooth bribe." Then he sternly spoke to the camel. "You wicked beast, you should not pester this holy man for bribes!" Then turning back to Befikuda, he said, "I do appreciate you dislodging his sorry carcass from this spot, but you know I cannot afford to break down and give in to him, buying him off with a pomegranate or two each time he decides to be stubborn and unruly, or the least of my problems would be him putting me in the poor house, going broke buying him so many pomegranates!"

"I know, but it's getting late to get your goods to the market, and you needed to get him to move."

"Yes, yes, I know, and I appreciate that. But you know what he would do if I gave him all the pomegranates he wants? You think that load he dropped in the streets was big?"

"I know, I know, his contribution would fill the streets, dropping considerably more!"

"More than all the grains of sand in the desert! Not even Moses, my namesake, would lead the Israelites through all that. He would have prayed to God for a safer path!" Then, turning back to his camel he said, "Hede, hede … hede, hede. Let's go, you miserable beast. To the marketplace!"

Befikuda laughed and proceeded over to the drunken sots on the sidewalk still laughing at poor Mussie and his camel. The abba scorned them for having so much amusement at their friend's dilemma. He also admonished them for being drunk so early in the morning.

"So, you have amused yourselves so well at your brother's camel show and indeed at his expense? Then I think you should pay an admission fee!" said the abba.

"What fee is that, Abba Befikuda?" one asked.

"Take that shovel and this pail over there and whatever else you can find and clean this mess up—and clean it up now—to show all of Axum that you can do something worthwhile in your otherwise worthless condition!" ordered Befikuda.

The three obediently got up, somewhat slowly, and staggered over to gather up the tools and receptacle to dispose of the excrement. The abba walked away shaking his head as his thoughts returned to the prophetic mystery that had been weaving various possible scenarios in his mind. He mulled over them as he walked over to the apartment where he would meet his brothers for coffee. He would discuss the matters with Pastors Addesu (meaning "new one," as in "new one in Christ") and Tsegaye (meaning "by His grace"). Addesu had become a Lutheran pastor and Tsegaye an Evangelical, all three representing the three major Christian denominations prevalent in Ethiopia. All three clergymen had known each other since early childhood. Each had his own office in his respective church in a different part of town. Hence, they decided to purchase a centrally located place to meet each morning and discuss various issues of importance over coffee. It had been a three-bedroom apartment located in a row house building. It had a fireplace for cooking, a dining room, a bath and toilet, and a sitting or living room. They had converted it into their own coffeehouse. It was a warm, cozy place in terms of atmosphere. There was a suitable amount of furniture for sitting and discussing the day's topics while enjoying the coffee ceremony prepared by their wives. The rich smell of aromatic roasted coffee beans warmed the soul, loosening one up far more than a good dosage of valium. The syrupy, brown liquid gave off glints of dark rust, reddish brown, and amber as the rays of sunlight filtered through the steady steam while the server performed the long pour into the cups. The taste, so rich, more so than a thousand treasure chests of a thousand kings, was enhanced with the spices of cardamom, cinnamon, cloves, and granulated raw sugar, perking up a person's taste buds and gently, seductively caressing them as if to say, "Hello, good morning, and what's new in your life today?" The experience led one to savor the coffee with a reverence not accorded to mere tea, much less "tacky alcohol." Coffee, the drink of kings, intellectuals, merchants, and prophets, was a spiritual experience that enhanced the imagination and accentuated the thinking process to churn out gems of genius, whereas alcohol all too often churned out nonsense, particularly when taken in excess. However, coffee in excess merely prompted one to charge through life like someone with ADD in overdrive, accomplishing more in one morning than governments could ever accomplish in a year.

However, the three Ethiopian oracles drank coffee in moderation, for it was only one of the two main featured attractions of the ceremony. Conversation—honest heart-to-heart, soul-to-soul conversation—was the true activity that took center stage. No cell phones should be brought in, for the annoying tendency of younger generations to text message themselves into oblivion was an insult to these things of real importance in life. Technology had its place, indeed a wonderful place, but it was not here. Here, meetings of the minds matched with meetings for the hearts took place only in an atmosphere of total, complete, serene honesty.

Befikuda approached the row house. Flaking white paint gave way to spot jobs, dabs of paint, or mere whitewash to provide some resemblance of maintenance. A band of red paint covered the base of the building about a meter high to cover up scuff marks and other signs of abuse, such as splattered mud from the streets and other debris kicked up by passersby. A poster or two left over from Mengistu's Marxist regime still remained, his once blazing image now faded away as if to disintegrate with time along with the rest of the worn handbills. Bits and pieces flaked off, more than fading from existence but being blown into the dust bins of irrelevant history, like Mengistu.

He walked in, greeting his two friends, and then sat down, pondering over the prospects running through his mind.

"You've got that look on your face. We should talk about this as Tsegaye and I too have had some prophetic inclinations, nuances, or something. But first let us pray, giving our day up to God and asking for spiritual discernment and guidance on these matters," said Addesu.

The other two agreed and joined hands in prayer, blessing the nourishment they were about to take and those preparing it, as well as petitioning God for a renewed, fresh anointing of grace and clarity regarding the matters at hand.

As they began to imbibe in their morning coffee and cakes, Befikuda said, "I have had some sort of prophetic instinct or inclination brewing up from my spirit trying to tell me something, not necessarily a foreboding warning or anything but perhaps something more important. I have that same restlessness that I have had before, indeed that we have all had prior to something like this. It's a feeling of uneasiness ..."

"But not necessarily your own," broke in Tsegaye.

"Quite right," Befikuda quickly responded.

"It's as if you feel the discomfort, uneasiness, or pain of pilgrims of some sort headed our way," said Addesu.

"Yes, exactly," replied Befikuda.

"I felt the same way when I woke up this morning, as did Tsegaye. We already discussed this, but of course we wanted to wait for you to see what you thought, if again you shared these same thoughts and feelings simultaneously with us, as we have all been prophetically linked. We wanted to see if you concurred with us on these matters. Now that all three of us have concurred on this, I believe we have confirmation. Someone or something is headed our way," said Addesu.

"Some would automatically jump to the conclusion that it may be the biblically prophesied rapture, but this isn't it. The signs are not there for that. Secondly, too many get caught up in end-time prophesy that they seem to miss the importance or flat-out ignore other 'prophetic nuances' and indeed their real ministry of 'walking the walk for the talk of the talk.' They often use this as an excuse not to actively engage in the important work God has actually assigned them to do," commented Tsegaye.

"I agree," responded Befikuda. "This is one area of practically applied theology where we have all been on the same page regardless of denominational differences. In fact, many are so wrought up in that and other religious points as opposed to the calling of a faith-based relationship in Christ that they seem to intentionally ignore God's real calling for them in the first place and use such debates as an excuse to deafen their ears as a sort of spiritual anesthesia."

"With some, heavy anesthesia isn't even necessary. Mere Novocain would seem to do it," quipped Addesu.

All three laughed as they drank coffee and discussed the event they knew would come. Whatever it was to be, the three oracles of an

Ethiopian coffeehouse would be well prepared as always. They awaited it with great anticipation.

৵ও৹ ৹৹

The 757's roaring turbo jet engines produced a monotonous, droning hum that seemed to numb the brain in its hypnotic effect on Garret Holcomb, as he blankly stared from his window seat at the clouds passing by. En route to Ethiopia, his mind toyed with the notion that he was on a pilgrimage to Axum in search of the lost Ark of the Covenant. But was it a pilgrimage or merely a mad dash away from a perceived abyss, not necessarily a terrifying whirlwind but more like an empty void causing far more trauma—the emptiness of emotional bankruptcy in the estranged home life he had grown up in? He brushed back his dreadlocks and put in his earbuds, searching for the desired Bob Marley track on his new iPhone.

"No woman, no cry …" Bob sang out as Garret began to sway back and forth to the music, pretending to be the new Rastafari reggae king in the making, indeed the next Bob Marley. His disingenuous quest for greatness had led him from his white upper-class environment to smoking marijuana in the Blue Mountains of Jamaica. He banged around on guitar, bellowing Rasta style in a microphone while playing student at several colleges, bouncing from one to the other, much to the disgruntlement of his father.

Beside him sat another would-be pilgrim. He was retreating from the Bronx. Jamaal Abdul Meriweather was about the most obnoxious guy he could have sat beside. In addition to ordering way too much alcohol, he was constantly harassing the flight attendants, making sexual come-on after come-on, much to the irritation of all those surrounding him.

"I'm headed for Ethiopia! The motherland, dawg! How 'bout you, man?" Jamaal said, with slurred speech.

"Uh, same place, mon. I'm on a Rastafari pilgrimage. Headed to a place called Axum. I wanna get baptized by the Ethiopians in the name of Haile Selassie. Say, g-dawg, you wanna lay off or at least taper off on the booze a bit? You ever tried taking an overnighter and sleeping at 30,000-plus feet drunk? You wake up with the worst hangover possible. Trust me, dawg, it ain't pleasant, man. At least drink a lot of ice water. They say that helps clear things out a bit!" Garret replied.

"Oh, wow, yeah. Thanks, man—appreciate that! Really, I do. It's my first trip overseas, you know, so I'm really relishing this. Ain't all these stewardesses hot, man?"

"That's *flight attendant*, dumbass!" replied a flight attendant. Her irritation had reached the boiling point, as she was one of his objects of desire.

"Say what?" said Jamaal. He laughed. "Okay, okay, I guess I've been givin' these chicks a hard time!"

Garret smiled and laughed, shaking his dreadlocks. "To answer your question, *ohhh yahh, yahh, mon!*" he replied.

Jamaal went off about his desire to be the next Spike Lee, wanting to do a special documentary on the lost Ark of the Covenant and how Spielberg and Indiana Jones got it all wrong. He rambled on and on.

"You know that Ark of the Covenant was really brought from Jamaica by ancient Rastafaris from way back when who grabbed it out of Jerusalem, took it to their new home in Jamaica, and then like, you know, this dude named Many-licks, Meneluck, or something like that …"

"*Menelik*, the former king of Abyssinia, son of Solomon and the queen of Ethiopia," Garret corrected him.

"Yeah, yeah, that's the dude, that's the dude. He, like, you know, grabbed the ark and brought it back to Ethiopia or sumpthin'. Now, they say it's in Axum. I got to find a way to get in there and get it on film. I mean, like, the motherland got to take its rightful place in history and like *represent*. You know what I'm sayin'? And I know it's supposed to be my destiny to do it!"

"Well, wow, like that's heavy, mon," said Garret. He spoke in his best attempt at a Rasta accent. "Ya know, I don't know as you have all de details right in dat story, but you know, so much has been lost in de history, you may be right. Someone like you could set it all straight, you know. Me, *I'm a Rastaman!* Ya know, dude, like *rock, roots, reggae.*"

"Yeah, yeah, I know, I know. Man, that's cool. It's all good, dawg. You know like a man's gotta represent and all!"

"Yeah, it's all good!"

The two would-be pilgrims clamored on about their perceived destinies. The conversation droned on like the jets outside, driving surrounding passengers into a dull, listless state of unconsciousness as they tried desperately to wall off the drivel and put their minds in a safe haven somewhere else.

Each of the would-be pilgrims felt that he had been on some sort of quest for personal identity, when in fact they were running away from any real source of identity, indeed from any honest look at life for fear of all that it would reveal. Finally the topic drifted to more substantive matters. Jamaal's father was Clarence Meriweather Sr., a famous jazz trumpeter from the fifties and early sixties. He had played with all of the greats: Art Blakey and the Jazz Messengers, Dizzy Gillespie, as well as other legends like John Coltrane, the Elvin Jones Trio, and Charlie "Bird" Parker. His face would have been on the covers of countless platinum albums, but he couldn't get the heroin monkey off his back, which for all practical purposes wrecked his career. He blew out on his marriage with Jamaal's mother, leaving Jamaal at age three. Jamaal, born Clarence Meriweather Jr., deeply resented him for it and changed his first name as a result, but for some reason he still retained his last name. Maybe that was because deep in his heart he wanted to reconcile but couldn't muster up the guts to make the first move.

After his father left, his mother's addiction to cocaine grew worse. She became more abusive to him emotionally and physically. In addition, she began sleeping with a different man practically every night, which drove Jamaal into a rage. Many were physically abusive to him as well as his mother. When he was seven, he decided he had had enough and hit one of her many boyfriends in the back of his head with a hammer, hard enough to send him to the hospital. The police who investigated the situation called in the Department of Human Services, who promptly pulled him out of there and placed him in the foster home system. His anger and depression were so bad no one really wanted to keep him. Some foster parents, of course, just signed up to host foster kids for the money and could have cared less about the welfare of the child. Many in fact were worse than the environment he had been rescued from by DHS. He was bounced from foster home to foster home and largely learned what he knew from the streets.

Garret Holcomb was actually in the same emotional dire straits. Despite coming from an affluent background that seemed to be hell and gone from Jamaal's, he retreated away from the same type of disaster zone. Despite the physical presence of his stockbroker father, the old man seemed to be so wrapped up in work that he was emotionally walled off and was actually never there where it counted. This created an emotional schism, leaving Garret totally estranged, feeling completely detached. Garret's mother was a social debutant who seemed to be in search of the right coming-out ball that never happened. Instead, she drowned herself in gin and tonics, becoming a hopeless alcoholic, in and out of rehab centers so often they appeared to have revolving doors at 3,000 rpms just for her! The emotional bankruptcy created imprisoning, destructive paradigms that left both in emotional ghettos where no so-called lines of class distinction had any real bearing or importance and served as no excuse in life for the failure to deal with their issues. Both he and Jamaal grew up in a poverty of no love. Both were living proof that the poverty of love was far worse than the poverty of money. In this regard, they were a perfect match to be sitting beside each other.

"I guess we got more in common than we thought," said a despondent Jamaal.

"Yeah, surprising how abandonment can cut just as deep crossing racial lines. My dad had as bad an addiction as heroin—his job. Hell, at least he was so buried in Wall Street that he never had time for me. It's kind of hard to say which hurts the most, the pain from him not being there at all or the numbness of watching him walk through the house like a lifeless ghost, a shell of a dad, never being there where it counts at all but making a mockery of the whole thing—like I and it were a joke or something," responded Garret.

"I know what you mean. That's tough. Looks like we both had to raise ourselves when it came to being a man."

"They say it takes a man to raise a man."

"Yeah, it does. But when he ain't there, a boy's got to do what he got to do, find somethin' else. And a lot of times, that ain't gonna be good. Learnin' off the streets can be a bitch!"

"Well, why don't we team up, maybe cut costs and try to do this thing right," suggested Garret.

"Yeah, that sounds cool. I was thinkin' about something else too. Maybe you could do the soundtrack for my documentary, and we can launch both of our careers!"

"Sounds awesome! Yeah, let's do it!"

Garret drifted off to sleep. Jamaal's mind began to drift back to his early days in the Bronx. He drifted far back in time to the days of his earliest memories, the things that stand out with the brilliance of a shiny new toy or songs, whether lullabies or children's rhymes, with the bright, cheery tunes that find suitable homes in a child's mind. The shocking moments that terrify and wound may stick in the memory too, but more often than not, they are intentionally blocked out in defensive reactions, though their effects ripple through the soul and time eventually bring about emotional earthquakes.

Young Clarence Meriweather Jr. was three years old, sitting at his little table on a small chair, coloring in his coloring books. His father, Clarence Meriweather Sr., picked up his trumpet, sat on a stool, and began playing the most beautiful melody, so pure in tone with such an immaculate, righteous feel that not even the most inexperienced jazz aficionado could mistake it for anyone else's but his. It was a pure signature on his time and on young Jr.'s soul in a way he could never forget. Jr. looked up at his father, who was sporting his trademark fedora with the brims turned up. It was a jazzman's crown topping his rather well-rounded facial features, highlighted by his well-kept beard and moustache already showing the distinguished salt-and-pepper look that came with age and experience. The tunes would light up young Clarence's eyes with such a shine; you'd have thought an angel beamed straight through them. His whole face beamed in delight, lighting up the room in his glee as if the music alone triggered the gift of same in his spirit and soul. He cast an adoring gaze up at his father while the old man played on. When Dad finished, young Clarence Jr. would clap so enthusiastically he almost hurt his hands! Daddy would pick him up and toss him into the air, catching him, and ask him, "Did you like that, little Gabe, huh? You like that?"

Clarence Jr. would hug his father and run his fingers gingerly through his daddy's beard, then kiss him on the cheek, replying, "Yes, Daddy, yes! You play so good! You teach me, huh? Oh please, Daddy, please!"

Sr. would plant a loud, smooching kiss back on his cheek and say, "Someday, you gonna be jazzman too. But, don't tell yo' mama 'bout that. Let's just keep it our little secret for now!"

Jr. would just nod obediently and then hug his dad again. Then his attention would be jerked away by another man in the room, playing a trumpet too. The only thing that Jamaal could remember about him was that his cheeks would puff out like a bullfrog, and the man would make all kinds of funny looks at him with his eyes that would make Jr. laugh and laugh, much to the man's delight.

"C'mon, Gabe. Let's go, man. We got to get to this gig. Miles wants to talk to us, particularly you, about doing some session work. He's puttin' together this new album. He says it's the best thing since Bitches' Brew. We got to go, dude! Bye-bye, little Gabe," the man said.

"Okay, okay," he responded. Then he looked at Jr. and said, "You be good, little man. Okay?"

Clarence Jr. just nodded his head. He had no idea why they called him "little Gabe" or his dad "Gabe." His mother never referred to either that way. Also, it wasn't till years later that he learned the identity of the man with the bullfrog cheeks as the legendary Dizzy Gillespie.

Jamaal would cherish each of those memories, recalling each one, each time his father would play to him and then take off for a new gig. Then Jamaal winced as his memory approached the terrible climax: the night Daddy played but not so sweetly. He was very agitated that night. He merely said, "Good-bye, son," and then left for the gig and never returned. Jamaal stared blankly and then ordered another drink to numb the pain as he always did. Suddenly, Garret began moaning and groaning from a nightmare. He jerked forward, letting out an aborted scream and slammed back into the seat gasping for breath.

"What's wrong, man? You have a nightmare or sumpthin'? It's okay. It's cool, dawg."

"Same one I always have," Garret replied. "I keep seeing myself driving real fast, headed for a telephone pole head-on, and just as I hit, I wake up in sweats!"

"You want to talk about it or sumpthin'?"

"No … nah, just forget about it. I'll have another one of those though," he said, pointing to the whiskey and rye in front of Jamaal.

"Stewardess, uh, I mean flight attendant? Another one of these for my man here, please." He then turned to Garret and said, "Don't worry, man. This one's on me."

"Thanks, man," Garret replied.

The two toasted, drank up, and then drifted off to sleep.

☙ ❧

The plane taxied down the runway at Addis Ababa International Airport, making a rough, dull roar as the wheels made contact with the concrete and the pilot began cutting back on the engines and applying the brakes. The landing woke up both Garret and Jamaal, who eagerly looked out the window to catch their first glimpse of Ethiopia. They simultaneously put their hands on their heads, noticing the splitting headaches accompanying their hangovers. Moaning, they began fumbling with customs declaration forms. They filled them out with great difficulty and placed them inside their passports. They remained seated while others began to disembark from the plane. Then they stumbled off the plane, heading in the direction of luggage claims to wait for their bags.

The customs officer looked at both with a slight grin as he cleared them through immigration. The two pushed their baggage carts toward the exit, only to have their disposition worsened by the onslaught of cabbies calling out, "Taxi, taxi, mister?" Garret nodded to one and motioned to Jamaal to follow.

"Man, I hope I don't hurl in this dude's cab!" said Jamaal.

"Shoulda drunk more ice water. We will next time," responded Garret.

The cabbie took it easy on the two, noting their condition. Garret asked him to take them to a relatively modest-priced hotel, one with a restaurant. He complied.

"This one is nice—not the Sheraton, but at least it doesn't have cockroaches that can pick up your baggage and run off with it. Showers work too, with plenty of hot water, not like some in this price range. You'll come to appreciate that the longer you stay in Africa!" the cabbie said.

"Appreciate that," said Garret.

The two would-be pilgrims checked in and flopped on the beds, passing out in a state of misery.

❧❦❧

They awoke a number of times during the night, facing the time change's effect on their biological clocks. They had to force themselves back to sleep, suffering from jet lag. When they did finally get up, it was just a little past noon. They wandered around the hotel and surrounding neighborhood, strolling into a few kiosks that sold a number of cultural artifacts and souvenirs. They noted that few spoke English and none with the Rasta accent that Garret had expected. Jamaal, likewise, was shocked, particularly at the controlled giggles of the people they ran into, not to mention the woman who came up to him in desperation, trying to offer him her baby to take back to America!

They walked over to the Sheraton Hotel and sat in the restaurant, a little dazed from both the trip and cultural shock.

"Man, where's the bar in this place? Ain't no alcoholic, dawg, but I could use a stiff belt about now. Trip took it out a me, and—what's that language they speakin' here? Man, I ain't never heard nothin' like that before!" Jamaal said.

"I don't know. It ain't Rasta! That's for sure! Bar's over here, dude," replied Garret.

They strolled over to the bar and pulled up to the stools.

"What type of language they speak here?" Garret asked the bartender.

"Mostly Amharic. Some speak languages native to their area. For instance, in Tigray, they may speak Tigrean, but they have been making Amharic the national language here for some time now," he replied.

"No Rasta?" Garret asked.

"No Rasta." The bartender just laughed.

"Amharic? Where's that one come from?" Jamaal asked.

"It's our own. Probably the most ancient, truly authentic indigenous African language there is. We have our own script too. Here, check this out." The bartender held up a Bible in Amharic.

Jamaal and Garret gazed at the script with wide eyes.

"Whoa, man, that's some heavy stuff!" exclaimed Jamaal.

"What's even heavier is what it says," said the bartender.

"What's that?" Garret asked.

"It's the holy Bible and story of Jesus Christ. We totally reject Rastafarianism, as it is satanic crap. Christianity, indeed the Judeo-Christian tradition, goes way back to the beginning here. The Orthodox Church was one of the three original churches in the first century, before the white man in northern Europe in particular knew where this place was! I assure you, there are no Rastas here, not unless they are tourists on vacation from Jamaica!"

Garret looked at him in surprise. "You mean you don't baptize people in the name of Haile Selassie either?"

"No, we don't. Neither does anybody else. You can only be baptized in the name of the Father, the Son, and the Holy Spirit. Why did you come to Ethiopia?"

The two laid out their tales to him. He listened earnestly but actually focused on the real issue—the pain from emotional abandonment and their failure to come to terms with it.

"You need a real quest toward something, not running away from everything. You need some sort of real pilgrimage. They can help you with that up there."

"You been there?" asked Jamaal.

"Oh, yes, in fact all over Ethiopia. There is a lot to see here—a lot that needs to be healed, a lot that needs to be repented. Jesus came to save, not to condemn. Jesus came to the sinners like a physician goes to the sick, but people have to first see what they're doing is wrong and turn. To that end, they will talk to you in Axum, but they will never let you see the ark, nor do you need to. We see people from all walks of life. So have they. I am working my way through college, studying agricultural economics at the university. While here at this miserable job, I talk to people like you. I don't wall myself off from the sinners, the pilgrims, tourists, or whoever. But eventually, I want to make a difference in Ethiopia, in Africa."

"Man, that's so cool! Say, how do we get transport to Axum?" Garret asked.

"You can get a jumper flight to Axum. They leave every day. You check out that travel agency over there. They can hook you up."

After a few more drinks, the two rebels without a cause, clue, or a life stumbled over to the travel agency to make arrangements to travel to Ethiopia's epicenter of spiritual, mystical fascination—Axum.

⁓ ⊙꙰ ꙰⊙ ⁓

The small jumper flight touched down on the earthen runway at the Axum Airport.

"Man, this place do look primitive, don't it? I know I'm drinking alcohol here! Ain't no way I'm drinkin' the water here!" said Jamaal. He was almost in a state of panic seeing actual third world conditions.

An elderly Ethiopian gentleman sharing the flight with them looked at them and smiled. "Drink the bottled water. You'll be all right. Even drink the bottled water when you're in Addis. You don't have the antibodies we Africans have," he said. The stark reality was just one of the many simple examples that began to confront Jamaal with the fact that he was no African. He only had dark skin, and true African character, which truly defines one as African, has to come through experience and rite of passage, not through genes.

Garret just gazed outside. "Man, did you see those statue things stickin' out like the Washington Monument? I wonder what that's all about," he said. Jamaal just nodded his head affirmatively with a dazed look of fascination and amazement.

"They've been here two thousand years before Washington was ever born," said the Ethiopian gentleman.

"For real? Two thousand years? That's awesome!" replied Garret.

"Axum is an exciting, mystical place. You have to absorb it. I don't think you can do that on so much alcohol!" said the man. He looked at them through eyes of wisdom garnished by experience over the years. His black hair intermingled with gray and silver, giving him quite the distinguished look.

"You would do well to listen to this old *mzee*. I am his son-in-law from Kenya. In Swahili, *mzee* means *old patriarch of the clan*. It's his birthday today."

"Bottled water. Okay, that's cool. You drink that stuff too? You look pretty healthy. You carry your age well as we say back in America. And today's your birthday? Well, happy birthday! And how old are you, if you don't mind my askin'?"

"I'm 102, today, and I can still walk you into the ground if we go up into those hills you see over there!" the old mzee replied. He gave them a playful wink as he watched their jaws drop.

Jamaal and Garret just stared in awe at the old mzee.

"I thought everybody was just dying over here at earlier ages, and here you are 102 today? Is that for real?" Jamaal asked.

"Yes, it's for real, my son. Dying, yes we have that too, at all ages— too much they say. But Africa is an amazing place of dualities. Open up your heart and mind to receive and absorb it. Then you will see what it means to be African," he replied.

Jamaal and Garret just stared, then nodded their heads affirmatively, grabbed their baggage from the overhead compartments, and disembarked along with the rest of the passengers into a brave new world for both.

The next morning, the two adventurers decided to stroll around Axum after finishing breakfast at the Remhai Hotel. They marveled at the bathing pool rumored to have been the queen of Sheba's as well as the towering stelae, or obelisks, in Stelae Park. They asked a couple of shop owners about the Ark of the Covenant. They directed them to the Chapel of St. Mary of Zion, better known as the Chapel of the Tablets, referring to the tablets of stone God emblazoned the Ten Commandments on, which was placed in the ark along with Arron's staff by Moses. Jamaal began to gallop over in the direction in a fever, holding his state-of-the-art video camera he used to capture as much of the scenery around Axum as he possibly could. Garret ran to catch up with him, also eager with anticipation.

The guardian of the chapel viewed the onrush by the two in their quixotic chase of windmills from a distance. He laughed subtly, seeing the camera, and knew instantly what their objective was. He began to shake his head, thinking, *Here we go again. It's going to be another one of those days!*

The two approached the iron gate surrounding the chapel and began calling out to the guardian, who had begun walking away, heading back to the chapel.

"Hey, dude—dude, my main man!" they both yelled. It never dawned on them why he didn't and wouldn't respond to the word "dude." In fact, the guardian hadn't the faintest clue as to what "dude" meant, for it was not a popular pronoun in Amharic, and he spoke no English. Still, the two clamored on, yelling louder as if that would make a difference. Finally, the three oracles, on their way to morning coffee, noticed the commotion and strolled over to the chapel to rescue the guardian. They approached him and noticed the weary look on his face.

"Dananeh," said the oracles. They smiled rather sympathetically.

The guardian, desperately trying to maintain composure, grimly looked up at the three oracles. "Enezihen hulet mongoch wodeza endihedy adregelagn ras mitat honewebegnal" (Please take these two fools out of my face; they are giving me a headache)! he pleaded.

"Eshat" (Sure), they replied and then turned their attention to Jamaal and Garret. They could have been quite imposing with their tall statures, but instead their presence just reflected a noble stature, a peaceful demeanor. They stood solemnly, quite composed, reflecting a gentle dignity.

"Young gentlemen, you are tourists here in Axum? You been here long, seeing the sights?" queried Befikuda.

"Uh, yeah," replied Jamaal. "We just got here last night. Been checkin' the place out and all. I'm Jamaal Rashid Meriweather, and this is my friend and colleague, Garret Holcomb. I'm a film director doing a documentary on Axum and the lost Ark of the Covenant. We're both on a pilgrimage, you might say."

"A pilgrimage?" asked Tsegaye. "And if you could confide in us, doing us the honor, what pray tell is the nature of your pilgrimage or pilgrimages as the case may be?"

"Well, you know, I wanted to do a film documentary on the ark thing here. You know, be the first one to film it and all and put Africa in the limelight, put it in its rightful position. You know, we gotta make a true statement of Africa—who and what Africa is to the rest of the world. Wanna talk about how the Rastafaris millions of years ago brought the ark from Jamaica and all …"

"The Rastafaris—Jamaica?" said Befikuda with raised eyebrows in surprise. "You say millions of years ago? Reeeaalllly?"

"Well, you know, a long time ago. But anyway, I think, you know, like, it's a way for a brother to establish a link with the motherland."

"Me, I'm a Rasta-man. I'm into playing reggae music. Got my own band and everything! I want somebody to baptize me in the name of Haile Selassie in the ark so I can take my music to another level and provide Jamaal's documentary with soundtrack and all. I'm really into rock, roots, reggae. I mean, after all, I'm A Rasta-man, ya know, mon!" Garret said.

"Well, of course you are," responded Addesu, in subdued sarcasm.

"You have a lot to learn about Africa, about Ethiopia, before you can tell our story. You say you are a brother. I have heard African Americans say this, but a brother to whom? You are not our brothers yet, not till you have gone through rite of passage, and indeed that is something that has nothing to do with any baptism as you would think of it. Nor is it to be found merely in your genes," Befikuda said, motioning first to Garret then Jamaal. "First of all, you are in need of a real pilgrimage, but it would have nothing to do with the ark. You do not need to wrap your mind or arms around some Old Testament piece of furniture. You do need to wrap your mind and soul around something else. Tell me, young gentlemen, of what is the ark to you? Why do you seek the ark?"

Jamaal and Garret rambled on rather incoherently about their lives in a way that revealed deep pain and its possible source. As they spoke, the three oracles looked at each other, communicating the same message in their glances, that these two were indeed the event coming into their lives that they had foreseen. They knew they had their work cut out for them.

Tsegaye said, "First, forget the ark. They will never let you near it. It has a different type of significance today. You wouldn't understand."

"Secondly," said Befikuda, "you should come have morning coffee with us. You have never seen the famous Ethiopian coffee ceremony, I trust?"

"No," the two replied.

"Well, please accept our invitation, and we will discuss these things," said Addesu.

"Sure," they responded.

"You will learn much more from this than you would from the way you are going about things now," suggested Befikuda.

The guardian breathed a sigh of relief as the oracles led them away from the gate, allowing him to return to his regular duties.

They took them to the coffeehouse and began explaining the ceremony and its traditions. They introduced them to their wives, who were adorned in the traditional white, cotton *habesha quemas,* featuring the famous colorful embroidery around the edges, and the *netelas,* the white scarfs on their heads.

"Please turn off your cell phones. We engage in heart-to-heart, meaningful conversation here. You notice the instruments, all stooped in tradition. First, the servers take fresh green coffee beans and manually roast them in the frying pan, without the expensive roasters they use in Europe. Then they will waft the pleasant aroma around the guests for them to enjoy. By the way, you will take something like queen cakes? We also serve things like roasted barley, popcorn, peanuts, and coffee cherries. Watch the cherries though. Though we water down the coffee a bit for the last two drinks, the cherries will still keep you buzzing all day long!" instructed Befikuda.

"Uh, yeah, sure," the two replied.

The servers roasted the coffee and wafted the aroma over to Jamaal and Garret.

"It is intoxicating, yes?" asked Tsegaye.

"Wow, yeah," they responded, mesmerized by the mystical, spiritual essence of the ceremony.

"They will grind the coffee using the mortar and pestle, known as the *mukecha* and *zenezena*, respectively. Then it will be brewed in the *jebena*, the black clay coffee pot. They sometimes add cardamom, cinnamon, and cloves to the brew. Occasionally, they add butter and honey. Then it is poured into the small cups using the long pour," said Tsegaye.

As the server began pouring the coffee, the two guests stared in awe of everything they were experiencing, indeed honored to be a part of it.

"Now we impart wisdom and enlighten in Africa through telling stories, anecdotes, like parables," explained Befikuda.

"There are three drinks or cups of coffee in the ceremony: the *abol*, the *tona*, and the *bereka*. We will tell you three separate stories for each cup," said Tsegaye.

"In these stories, you will find much of what you are really looking for, much that you need to look for. You will find many answers and possibly many more questions will arise in your minds that you will have to find answers for. It will hopefully put you on a better track of intellectual and spiritual discovery," said Addesu.

As usual, they began with prayer. As each began to drink their first cup, the abol, Befikuda said, "I will tell you the first story called, fittingly enough, 'The Abol.'"

"Following that, we will have the second cup, the tona, which is slightly more watered down than the first, I might add, and I will tell you another story, which we shall call fittingly enough, 'The Tona,'" said Tsegaye.

"Then we shall have the third cup of coffee, the bereka, and I will tell you a story for that cup as well, which we shall call 'The Bereka' in keeping with the narrative of the coffee experience," said Addesu.

Part 2
THE ABOL

TOLD BY ABBA BEFIKUDA

*H*e gazed at the rosy-crimson hues at the earth's edge. The sunset always gave him a sense of peace, a time for reflection and a flow of relaxation signifying the end of another day. He sipped the coffee he had been nursing for about two hours. No sense buying a new cup. He still had this one.

His life was filled with riches, though by some shallow people's reckoning, he would die poor, lacking in the abundance of earthly riches that the walking dead valued over anything else and feverishly clung to when they saw everything else coming unglued in their lives. His riches were far more valuable—the experiences he had had in life, which far surpassed the others'. His experiences revealed far more guts and vision than his arrogant critics could ever claim.

Mulling over the most life-changing event he had experienced, he strolled across the street to a coffeehouse/bookstore, which featured not only a fine collection of books, used mostly, but also some French impressionist prints and a few sculptures as well. It was a cozy little nook for him to relax in and pen a few lines of prose or verse, pouring out his thoughts or just clearing his mind, spirit, and soul of what for all practical purposes were valuable gems of wisdom. However, without his artistic flair, transposing them into the written word to be preserved for safekeeping, they would eventually deteriorate, grow stagnant and stale, losing their brilliance to become detached fragments of compost in the catacombs of his mind.

He mused over those who died for the next iPad, the next technological wonder to come down the pipe. They were those who lacked any real intellectual grasp or understanding of technology, who had no discernment or proper philosophical orientation toward the same but felt that merely purchasing the latest high-tech gizmo made them high tech, the new cool. When, in fact, they were nothing more than whores of a zeitgeist machine, apparatchiks, caught up in the hustle and bustle of post-industrial society. They were becoming the epitome of Marcuse's One-Dimensional Man, and he had time for neither. However, the obsessive, compulsive technocrat wannabes did not spoil the wonderful rustic atmosphere of his favorite coffeehouse.

He sipped the last drops of his coffee, sat for a moment sucking up the atmosphere, and then decided to order another cup before writing. Ethiopian Harrar was on brew, his favorite. It sparked more vibrant memories related to the key central experience that largely defined his life.

He took out a moleskin pad from inside his coat and a fountain pen. He delighted in pen and ink for, "it is in the handwritten letter where ink clogs the inlets and bays of vowels and consonants that the soul of the writer is most honestly revealed," to paraphrase his favorite pen maker, Cleto Munari. Then he began to write.

The memories began to flow from his mind through the pen as if it were a supernatural conduit of the flow into a river of words pouring out onto the page. Sometimes just the joy of feeling a fountain pen served as a lightning rod, stimulating the very desire to write, connecting thoughts, the process of materializing the ether into concepts and phrases and then transmitting them to journal. He loved fountain pens; in fact, he collected them. But the pleasure did not stop him from wincing from the waves of agony that accompanied vibrant memories that used to plague his soul whenever he approached the topic in question. Each time he began, the agony coursed through him like a current from an electric chair. However, the current wasn't set on kill but merely various levels of torture that could and would kill him over time if he didn't deal with it right. And one of the last steps in dealing "with it right" meant to write it out and achieve closure.

He had survived the "electric chair" before. But he was older now and had other concerns, not the least of which was the cancer now eating away at his body. Doctors told him that it was terminal and even put a time limit on his survival, which he had beaten every time so far. "It depends on what surviving means," he said. "If I leave a memory or two behind me that changes the world, I will survive anything long after my flesh dies. If I know Jesus and not just know of Him and am right with God, I will live forever."

Now, as he began to write, the memories began to course through his mind. The more caffeine his mind absorbed, the more the stream became a torrent. Depending on how the rush translated into a cascade of words onto paper, he navigated through the torrent well, feeling the rush that he rather enjoyed—an eruption from spirit and soul. At the very least, it was an emotional release that could be loosely described as a literary climax. Although, most sex that he had experienced was never as satisfying as what he felt when he wrote. The women that darted in and out of his life were all too shallow, superficial to such an extent that they could never see, much less appreciate, what his experiences were or what he was really made of. They were too ethnocentrically anesthetized to appreciate cross-cultural experiences. They had no understanding of *mashambani* to truly understand the heart and spirit of Africa—or much of anything outside the next shoe sale at Macy's. Sex was not intimacy or making love, in contradiction to popular thinking in the West. It was all so empty, like the women he'd known—all except one, and her story never stopped running in his mind. Like a never-ending movie, it played to a captive audience of one, torturing him with the ending, but not this time. This time in writing it all out, finishing the book, which was not a mere novel but a testimony to his love for her, he would take the last step toward closure, enabling him to finally live in peace.

⁖⁖

It began with his first trip to the motherland—Africa. It's the motherland of us all, for it is where life began and certainly where his began and in a way where it also ended. All of us came from there. Some just migrated north and bleached out. Over time, all who "leave Africa" see the true African character denigrate, for Africa is not a mere continent or even a geographic place but a rite of passage. It leads to a new experience, an alternative universe and level of enlightenment. The more one strays from "the continent" is measured more by how one wanders away from the enlightenment, loses one's roots in the village in the cultural shock from the return and therefore loses a sense of what was gained. The voice of mashambani begins to grow fainter and fainter till it can hardly be heard at all.

He went there first as a Peace Corp volunteer and then through various development contractors, NGOs funded by the US Agency for International Development. His chief occupation was civil engineer, but he knew agriculture as well, as he had grown up with it in the Midwest. However, his real passions were writing, sketching, and music, the arts in general. He was very knowledgeable in all, had a passion for singing, and played the saxophone quite professionally. He performed in venues ranging from church choirs to jazz clubs. He could also handle guitar and bass, even the violin, which he took lessons for when he was younger, at the insistence of his parents. That probably explained why he never played the violin in public and often expressed his contempt for it, although some rumored that they actually heard sounds clearly resembling violin concertos from his room at night, which of course he denied.

He first traveled to Uganda prior to Idi Amin, but Milton Obote was no bundle of fun either, as he was quick to point out. He had worked all over east Africa, seen the Serengeti, and climbed Kilimanjaro. Africa had become his home, his first love. His soul was directed there. Spiritually, it was where he was born, and through a heavenly calling, he invested all his effort and passion there.

Uganda had gone through more than its fair share of civil war and political instability. First it was "King" Freddie Mateese and Milton Obote, then just Obote, then Amin, and countless other indigenous pariahs who economically cannibalized their own country while all the time blaming everything on the white man, making him the Judas-goat that Hitler made the Jews.

All of this paled in comparison to the massacres at the hands of Joseph Kony, probably the most lethal terrorist in the world. Kony was the heir apparent to run the pseudo "Holy Spirit Movement" of Alice Lakwena. This was nothing more than a satanically possessed witch doctor and a crazed band of rogues and thugs that tried desperately to disguise themselves as a liberation movement. It was anything but. In fact, they still practiced the same black arts of pagan religions, including performing the female rite of circumcision, which involved cutting the clitoris out of young girls and in some cases making them ingest it in a specially prepared soup "to become a woman." They would sing Christian hymns going into combat, but the ugly reality they engaged in made it all so hypocritical as to border on blasphemy, if not "crossing the border." One would do well to remember that even the devil has been known to quote scripture. However, he took it out of context so badly that Jesus had to set him straight.

After Lakwena's exile in Kenya, the movement drifted until Joseph Kony was tapped to take over the helm. He renamed the organization the Lord's Resistance Army (LRA). He immediately launched another ruthless campaign aimed at toppling Museveni's National Revolutionary Movement Government and thus seize control of the whole of Uganda. He also sought to take advantage of the huge schisms that divided Uganda, from tribalism to others probably more divisive, based upon greed, larceny, broken promises, and political rivalry, not the least of which found their roots in simple personality clashes.

Whatever the cause, the rifts inevitably turned into bloody massacres that never produced any real winner, only mass destruction and holocausts of which women and children were always the worst victims. ASA—Africa Strikes Again—shooting herself in the foot but also in her vital parts, somehow showing a brave resiliency to survive but not fully overcome. Her own internal strife sought to tear her apart, cannibalizing her own young. In this, Africa could not blame any outside forces. Although many tried to exploit the situation, they could not have done so if there weren't willing souls to oblige them. It set the stage for the greatest tragedy of his life.

But the worst tragedy can only take place if there is first the truest love, a love giving birth to joy and peace that becomes violated: the ravaging rape of the human soul, shattering the peace and stealing the joy. And only through the healing process can earthly love, joy, and peace be restored.

⊙⊙ ⊙⊙

Though he worked in a number of African countries, she kept pulling him back to Uganda. He met her in a little town called Serere where she was an agronomist at the Serere Research Station. She was slender where it counted and voluptuous where that counted. Her skin was smooth as silk and a much lighter tone than most Ugandan women. He later found out that it was because she was from the Tigray Region of Ethiopia and had been driven from her homeland by the civil war, terrorized by the DERG, the Marxist movement installed by the Soviet KGB that raped Ethiopia far more than anyone could ever claim Haile Selassie had done.

Her name was Brihan Abai, which means "light of the Nile." Her father, Abai (the Nile, masculine gender) saw "the light emanating from her eyes" when she was first born and hence named her Brihan, accordingly. As was Ethiopian custom, her last name was simply her father's name, hence Brihan Abai, the light of the Nile. She certainly was, in every sense of the term. When he first saw her, the sunlight hit her in a way that illuminated the edges of her hair, almost blinding him. Her eyes, haunting like a siren's song, drew him into a captivating trance, sucking the air out of his lungs, inducing a hypnotic state of paralysis. It stretched his senses into another realm so mystically that his feelings of pleasure didn't have time to catch up. It was beyond petty sexual attraction but the purest form of sensuality that touched his very soul. He dropped a hammer near her and walked over to pick it up as a clumsy way to find an entry point to introduce himself.

"Hi, how are you? I didn't hit your foot, did I?" he asked. In his mind, he was telling himself, *That was the most pathetic, lame attempt I could have ever used. The hammer didn't even come close to her—like she's never gonna pick up on that or anything!*

However, she made it easy for him. "No, not at all, but you are kind to ask," she said. Her brilliant, brimming smile emanated the light of God, clearly doing her namesake justice. "My name is Brihan. What is yours?" she asked. Her penetrating eyes revealed her keen interest.

"I'm James, James Mecklenburg," he replied.

"James, my I also call you Boanerges?'

"Why, why Boah-what? What was that?" he asked with a slight laugh.

"Boanerges. It means 'sons of thunder,' what our Lord Jesus named James and John. With so bold an attempt to try to meet me, I thought it might fit," she said. She giggled facetiously. "But I still found it charming, flattering actually. I've seen you before. You're an engineer working here? I must confess I've wanted to meet you."

He laughed. "Well, now with the formalities out of the way, I was wondering if you wanted to have coffee or tea or something? Would you like that?"

"Coffee, you say? Sure, I would love to, but tell me have you ever had coffee fixed the Ethiopian way?"

"No, can't say as I have. Do you fix it? Are you from there?"

"Yes. I am from Tigray Region, in the north, from a town called Axum. Why don't you come over to my place when you are done working, and I will fix it for you, traditional Ethiopian style?"

"Well, we will be working late tonight, working on the water supply. I won't be able to get to sleep if I drink coffee that late. How 'bout tomorrow—say, in the morning or around noon, perhaps?"

"Tomorrow will be fine. Around ten o'clock? Will that work?"

"It works!"

"Great. See you then, James!"

"Until tomorrow, Brihan. Say, what does Brihan mean?"

"It means light."

"Now that name fits!"

She smiled and walked off back to the laboratory where she was working. He took the hammer and proceeded back to the water tower under construction, with more spring in his step than ever before.

An African red bishop woke him the next morning with a beautiful melodic call, which he could hardly miss as it sang out directly outside his window, jarring him from sleep. He rose his head to catch but a brief glimpse of the brilliant red-and-black plumage flash past like an ornithological comet darting into the trees across the commons. He tried to roll over and go back to sleep. He was hung over from binge drinking with the boys after work. He didn't know whether he should hurl—or kill the little guys pounding on the inside of his cranium with sledge hammers, just above his eyes. Like two little mechanical German bell ringers from a clock, they came out like clockwork every time he had a hangover, circling to the frontal lobe, and began swinging their alternating assaults on his head like little Nazi Gestapo midgets dressed in funky Rhinelander costumes, hiding behind his skull, making it impossible for him to strangle the little bastards! He decided to just simply groan and get up. He had never thrown up on alcohol before and hoped that this wouldn't be the first time. He looked at the clock. *Nine o'clock*, he thought. There was something he was supposed to do. What was it, what was—? Just then, light reflecting off a passing car's bumper flashed before him and reminded him. "Brihan!" He had just an hour to get ready and to find out where on the compound she lived. In his glee yesterday, he forgot to ask; in hers, she forgot to tell him. He would have to ask Nkomo down at the canteen. He knew everybody there.

But first James would have to shower and lose the hangover. Losing the hangover was easy. He had been Special Forces and learned a trick or two overseas—breathe in some blasts of pure oxygen, and that would blow out the hangover, sobering up any drunk ASAP. They learned that one from "Pappy" Boeington's exploits in WWII. His famous Black Sheep Squadron would get hammered every night and then take a few shots of O_2 the next morning to sober up before going out on missions. James had a special tank of pure oxygen and a face mask just for that purpose. He struggled to get out of his BVDs but got them tangled around his ankles, took one step, and fell flat on his face. Apparently getting over the hangover would be easier than simply making it to the showers. However, he managed both successfully, got dressed, and headed to the canteen.

"Nkomo, Nkomo, gotta talk to ya!"

"What is it, Bwana? What has you running in here like your pants are on fire? Settle down, boss. Have some chai."

"No time. I'm supposed to have Ethiopian coffee at Brihan's place—you know, Brihan, hot-looking chick, works in the soil lab over there?"

"Yeah, yeah, boss, I know Brihan. You gonna hook up with that? Lookin' good, boss! No, you don't need no chai, not if you gonna be drinkin' that stuff! It'll light you up like a Christmas tree!"

"Well, first I've got to find the place."

"Easy. Go down that road there and second building on the left, first door."

"Thanks, Nkomo. Later, man!" James said, tearing out the door

"Luck, boss!" Nkomo yelled after him. "Hell of a way to start a beautiful Saturday morning!"

He ran for about twenty yards or so and then slowed down. The last thing he wanted to do was show up as a sweaty mess. Ugandan mornings were hot enough in a tropical climate to entice the perspiration out of a person, but he didn't want to show up on his first date drenched in it. He walked to the second building on the left and knocked on the first door.

"Come in. It's open," said Brihan. She was adorned in a traditional habesha qemis, the coffee server's dress, a white cotton dress, ankle-length, featuring bright embroidery around the edges. Her outfit was topped off with the traditional white scarf known as a netela, wrapped around her neck. She began preparing the coffee, washing and then roasting. The sweet aroma filled the room. It was intoxicating, like a natural narcotic. He inhaled it with gusto as she wafted it toward him as tradition dictated. As they drank the three cups, she explained the tradition and symbolism behind each ritual act. They engaged in long hours of discussion from art, music, and literature to just telling each other stories. Their souls entwined with their voices and stories. They developed the foundation for the bonds that would only grow stronger over time. Commitments are built, not merely spoken, based on cultivation of trust that develops over time, but true quality time, of which the first predicate is honesty—or it's all an exercise in futility. And there was nothing more honest than what was born here.

They were completely oblivious to the time. Hours passed, unnoticed, without care. The West views time in a linear construct, whereas Africa clearly does not. "My, well, will you look at the time. I really must be going!" is something one might hear in London. In Africa, that phrase isn't heard as much, for time here is defined in a more floating context—in a flow of priorities. After those other priorities are seen to, then one shows up at a meeting, and that meeting is then "on time," despite the fact that it starts two hours later than originally planned.

The priorities make all the differences in the world, and here the priorities were matters of the heart. Time could fly on eagle's wings, and no one cared. One should note that even in Western countries, when affairs of the heart take center stage, time takes a backseat, and the same attitude seems to apply.

"Are you hungry?" she asked.

"I'm not sure. I'm so wired on caffeine I don't know as I really have an appetite. Nkomo warned me about Ethiopian coffee. Said it would light me up like a Christmas tree. He was right! But that hasn't lit me up half as much as the company serving it! You're amazing, Brihan."

"So are you. But you will wither away to nothing if you don't eat, and it's practically dark, and you've had nothing all day but coffee!"

"Wow, you're right! Do you want to go to the canteen and have dinner—my treat?"

"A nice gesture, but something as special as today deserves something much better than the canteen, and I being your hostess would not think of you walking out without a home-cooked meal, which incidentally I already began preparing. Have you ever had *wot* bar-b-que and *ngira*?"

"Yes, I love it but can't find it around here!"

"Well, that's because this is your first time here as opposed to the rest of the Research Station Grounds. I'll fix you a home-cooked Ethiopian meal."

"Sounds great. Can I help you?"

"Oh, a bit, but you'll help mostly by staying out of the way," she said with a smile.

After dining, he helped her clear the table. The sun began to set, sending crimson rays through the window that glanced across her face.

Some would say that the beauty of the setting sunlight graced her. He would say that her beauty, particularly her eyes, graced the sunlight! No need to maneuver into a kissing position; it was a natural move for both at this point. His eyes kissed hers first, and then he cushioned her lips with his, which turned into a massaging grip as the two engaged in a long spiritual journey in just a few minutes, sinking into each other's souls, entwined by each other's spirit, becoming one. No truer intimacy has there been than what blossomed that day, blooming in the purity of a love well in the making beyond mere rapture of emotions, which christened their lives.

They continued to see each other regularly while he worked at Serere. They wrote letters to each other and stayed in touch one way or another during the times when he was called away to other parts of Africa on various assignments. However, the true love that grew drew heavier than any magnet. He returned and proposed. She quickly accepted. Then finally it was time to meet the parents in Axum.

⋘ ⋙

They came to Axum to follow tradition and pay respect. They had made plans without requesting her father's permission. But given new ways influencing Africa, particularly with a woman who had been out on her own as much as Brihan, this was not as lethal to the proposed nuptials as it used to be. Still, he was her fiancé now and at least had to pass her father's inspection, if not pay the bride price. Abai was not so much interested in dowry, however. He, himself, was an educated man. He had taught in Addis and had not only money from that but also owned several acres of land and impressive herds of cattle as well. He was more interested in James's spiritual level of development and upbringing, his philosophical outlook and areas many would consider the more esoteric aspects of life. But they were actually more tangible in a higher sense than the many other so-called tangibles some people ultimately placed more stock in. He was waiting at the Axum Airport with a rather reserved smile, trying to put the many ideas and thoughts away that can invade one's head in anticipation of a first encounter, or at least back in the proper files reserved in that special place in his mind. *At least give the poor boy a solid chance and meet him with an open mind,* he thought.

The plane circled the area before landing. It was a breathtaking panoramic view. Axum is laid out at the base of the Adwa Mountains in northwest Ethiopia. The plane circled over the hills and then began its descent onto an earthen runway. James noticed the unmistakable figures of the Cathedral of St. Mary of Zion and the towering stelae, the obelisks, that have long characterized Axum and alone have made it one of the most fascinating, mysterious cities in Africa (if not the world). The Chapel of the Tablets was also visible, where it is rumored that the lost Ark of the Covenant was housed. James was particularly fascinated with the obelisks.

"Brihan, the stelae—what was or is their meaning? When were they constructed and erected?" he asked.

"No one knows quite for sure on either count. They are judged to be at least two thousand years old. Some think that they may have been grave markings, but I don't know," she answered.

"Pretty large grave markings, even for kings," he remarked. "I think there was something more special in mind."

"I think you're right, but two thousand years ago? Who knows what it is. There has been a lot of activity over time, symbolism, answers lost with some of the history. Axum was the first true capital of what is now Ethiopia—an economic powerhouse of trade in the first century and one of the four major powers of the world in that sense! Not today though. Today Ethiopia is quite poor, but not as bad as in the eighties famine. We've come a ways but still have a long way to go. We could use you."

"Us, you mean—we're a team, you and I, and I intend to stay that way!"

"No argument here!" she said with a huge smile and then voraciously kissed him. She was excited and nervous in taking him home. She just hoped her family would approve.

As the plane taxied to a stop, she could see her entire family there to meet them, her mother and father, two brothers, and her sister. The immediate nuclear family generally held closer ties in present-day Axum despite the overall extended family systems predominant throughout Africa. Besides, the Axum Airport wasn't big enough to accommodate the entire clan anyway. She waved at them excitedly. They collected their bags and walked down the steps to the ground and off the runway area to the ecstatic embrace of the onlookers, curious with excitement. Abai extended his hand to James. "I am Abai, Brihan's father, Mr. Mecklenburg. I hope that you will be a fortress of stability, as your name implies, for my daughter's better welfare!"

"I see you've done your homework on the family name. Gonna give it my best shot, I assure you! Never been a divorce in my family for the three hundred or so years we've been in North America. I believe marriage is for keeps. I'll take good care of her. Someone as special as she … the intense scrutiny and concern coming from her parents is merited. I respect that," he replied.

"Father, stop!" Brihan insisted. "He's just gotten off the plane! Can't you at least wait till we get home before you interrogate him?"

"Yes, yes, Papa. There will be time for all of that later. Right now, let's just get them home, get them settled, and get him something to eat. You look hungry, dear boy! Are you hungry? Of course you are!" Mama chimed in before James could get another word in edge-wise.

"Yes," he simply responded.

"Good answer," said Abai, placing his arm around him. "I get a feeling about people. I've got one about you. Welcome to the family. If my daughter loves you, then that's good enough for me. Brihan's a level-headed girl. Not like some. I feel that if she has said yes, she knows what she is doing. She had plenty of opportunities at university, but something about them just wasn't right. But she has chosen you, so if she wants you, and you are a substantial young man who can support her, then why should I not give my blessing! More over coffee tonight. For now, let's just get to our place and rest a bit, eh?"

"Sounds, good, sir."

"Oh, forget the sir crap. Just call me Abai."

"Okay, sounds good." James felt a sense of relief.

Dusk fell upon Axum. Sounds of chatter and celebration filled Abai's house. A wedding was in the making! Ethiopian music played throughout the night. It was a festive occasion that brought in only a few close relatives for that evening, but the whole clan would show up at the bigger celebration planned for next day. The stress would be the first of many tests of James's strength.

Brihan awoke the next morning to a clatter of dishes and the sound of a chair or two moving across the kitchen floor as her mother began preparing breakfast. Her sister, Enku, stuck her head inside the doorway.

"Brihan, how goes it? You simply must tell me more! How did he propose, what's he really like … and above all, how does true love really feel? We didn't get a chance to talk last night, what with all the festivities! Tell me, tell me, oh you must tell me!" she pleaded. She was practically breathless, unable to control herself.

"Oh, Enku, my baby sister, settle down! I know you too want love, but be patient. It will come," Brihan responded. Her tone tried to project the older sister's reassurance.

"I'm not a baby anymore. I keep looking, you know, but I don't find much."

"It may just find you, Enku Abai, for you are the pearl of the Nile, the pretty one, and you are so beautiful in every way."

"In some ways, that's just the problem. Guys only want one thing!"

"Then don't give it to them! It's your choice! If you want true love, then look for something more real. Love is not a mere obsession but a communion of spirit and soul that goes the distance, stemming from a true faith. Real love is pure, despite what some say today. You have to look for the purity of heart, not the definition of pectals!"

"Oh, I know. Still, James is cute, isn't he? Some would say hot!" she said with a mischievous giggle.

"Oh, God, yes he is!" Brihan replied. "I hope he survives today with all of the relatives coming in, meeting everybody. He might go crazy."

James woke up, took his turn at the showers, got dressed, and walked into the kitchen to check on breakfast. After the usual amenities, he sat down with Abai and had morning coffee with his future father-in-law. Abai was reading the newspaper. The front page had an article talking about Alice Lakwena's exile in Kenya.

"Uganda's still bloody angry with the Kenyans over that madwoman. They want her handed over to the Ugandan authorities to stand trial. Kenya now claims some sort of BS about sovereignty, saying that she has the right to stay in exile in that refugee camp as long as she wants. Isn't there some sort of extradition treaty between the two? Uganda even tried an incursion across the border a few years ago, only to be driven back by Moi's Presidential Police Force. He didn't even have to send in his troops. His cops did it! Can you believe that?" Abai said with a tone of astonishment. "I mean, the woman is a bloody terrorist! Why would Kenya want to hold on to a terrorist? I mean, isn't there something in the Geneva Convention about that? Terrorists have exile rights? I don't think so! I think they have the 'right' to be extradited back to the country where they committed all of their crimes and pay for them!"

"Well, yeah, on the question about Museveni's army getting chased out by Moi's cops, yeah, I can believe it. They've always been pretty incompetent. They aren't going to deal with Joe Kony any better either, at least not for a while. I don't disagree with you on Lakwena and extradition either. After the Ugandan People's Defense Force (UPDF) defeated her at the Battle of Jinja, Alice 'left her restaurant,' hopped on a bicycle bound for Kenya. I think she ought to go back to see 'just how bad a cook she really was.' We saw a lot of her handiwork in Soroti."

"You an Arlo Guthrie fan too?"

"Yeah, saw the movie and everything."

"You can get anything you want ..." Abai started singing.

"At Alice's Restaurant ..." James chimed in.

"Excepting Alice!" both sang together in harmony and then laughed.

They began singing the whole song together while waiting for their breakfast. It was another male-bonding milestone. Abai had spent a few years in the United States teaching African literature at the University of Chicago, where he learned to like American music and saw the movie *Alice's Restaurant* when it came out in the sixties.

"I would have to agree with you that what has replaced this 'Alice's restaurant' is even worse. This Joseph Kony fellow is a nightmare. His band of lunatics is creating just as much carnage: looting, abducting children and turning them into child soldiers. It's an atrocity. It's one thing to watch your parents die; it's another to be forced to kill them yourself."

The two talked about random issues over breakfast. The communication between their eyes, more important than the words, revealed genuine respect and admiration. Abai would study James's gestures and movements. They began to develop the bonding that Brihan had hoped for. Abai began seeing James as his own son in the making, and James began seeing Abai as a father. Abai saw in James a passionate man about life in general. He could see that he would draw into a stronger fellowship, fill a gap that Brihan couldn't and shouldn't fill.

James's own father had passed years before. They had been close, and the death hit James hard. He had died from injuries sustained in the Korean War. His father battled with infirmities that sprang up from exacerbations of the old wounds, eventually developing cancer, which withered him away to nothing. His father had been the "old lion" staying strong, overcoming the pain until cancer finally took him in 1963, the same year James saw Kennedy assassinated on television. James, still reeling from his father's death, watched in shock and horror as the president's motorcade proceeded down through Daley Plaza in Dallas. Then he heard the shots ring out. The press played it over and over again, making James and the entire nation punch-drunk. The emotional impact of both left scars and a void James tried to fill with either being an overachiever or a binge-drinking party animal.

James served in Special Forces in Vietnam and then attended Ohio State. Growing up in Canton, Ohio, "Buckeye U" was the only natural choice for a young man. He received his B.Sc. in civil engineering, and then it was off to the Peace Corp, maybe to find himself, maybe to lose himself. Who knows? But now he had found himself in Axum, just a few days away from marrying the only woman he'd ever truly loved.

Abai felt genuine warmth in the man roughly fifteen years his daughter's senior. This was not the issue here like it might be other places, for women often married at much younger ages and to men at least that much older than they, typically in arranged marriages. More important, he sensed that James still desired the camaraderie of a father/son relationship, one at the mature point in their lives, where the interaction was to be more of a respectful, faith-based bonding of friendship, of soul mates, rather than paternal protection. The relationship desired now was one of respectful appreciation of well-honed wisdom and respect for each to be the captain of one's own ship at the same time. Both were old enough to make their own decisions, but both were wise enough to listen to one another and use each other as sounding boards as well. Most important, both found the unique comfort zone to be open with each other, a zone that would grow over time where they would be able to discuss practically anything.

Abai could empathize with James's loss, for he too lost his father to the ruthless Marxist DERG, now finally displaced after years of bloody fighting that exiled the whole family from Axum at one time or another. Now that Mengistu's bloody reign of terror appeared to be over, they were all settled back home again.

They had forgone the traditional mediator for the marriage, and there was no sense checking the family lineage back five generations as had generally been the custom in Ethiopia. It was obvious that James and Brihan were not previously related. Brihan hadn't been with anyone, not even James, hence the family's reputation was not besmirched, an important issue in Ethiopia, more so than other places. Given the tremendous destruction and psychological damage done by civil war and re-gathering of diaspora, the wedding received the blessing of all concerned.

The relatives came from all over Tigray, some one hundred to two hundred people in all. All brought dishes. There was plenty of njira and all kinds of wot bar-b-ques and stews: beef, goat, lamb, and vegetable. A huge platter was placed in front of the happy couple, covered with njira, spread out like a huge rice-flour crepe pizza of Ethiopia's favorite bread. Accompanying it were six wot dishes in their separate bowls, which were dumped out in separate pools of spicy ingredients in a circular pattern on the ngira. Chunks of njira were torn out, using the right hand only, and wrapped around mouthfuls of wot, then popped into one's mouth, exploding with flavor!

All ate till they practically burst open, then worked it off with music and dance, followed by more feasting. Toasts were made with Ethiopian beer, a form of nonalcoholic fermented drink made from barley. The wedding plans were made. The wedding would be a traditional Ethiopian Orthodox wedding held in the Cathedral of St. Mary of Zion in one week. James was given another place to stay until the wedding day. Then, in accordance with tradition, he would go to his bride-to-be's house, pick her up, and take her to their wedding.

It was Saturday. The wedding day had arrived! James was dressed in a white tuxedo matching the color of his bride's gown. He picked up his bride, as she would leave her father's house and join his. They passed underneath the traditional arch of lit orange candles in the procession to the cathedral. All the guests, particularly the groomsmen and the bridesmaids, began singing the processional *mezmer* (Orthodox traditional spiritual hymns or songs of jubilation) as the bride and groom entered the church and advanced toward the altar where the abba, the Orthodox priest, stood smiling, waiting to begin the actual ceremony.

The ceremonial cloaks and crowns were bestowed upon the couple, signifying the new king and queen of a new household. The crowns were made of a beautiful red velvet cloth, sewn fast around the cylindrical headgear (but with a rounded top unlike a fez), adorned with gold around the base of the crown, topped with a gold cross. The crowns also symbolized the crowns that they would lay at the feat of Jesus upon going to heaven, in accordance with Orthodox interpretation of scripture. The cloaks were made of the same material, christened with brilliant gold embroidery in the form of ancient Christian symbols trimming the edges, expanding outward, broadly covering the shoulders, all held together by a single gold clasp at the neck.

As the abba began his sermon, the onlookers couldn't help but notice how Brihan glowed in her bridal gown. She was so radiant a bride! James noticed that she was even more blinding than the day he first met her. Her inner beauty, the loving purity of her soul, generated a magnetism that in turn emanated a mystical twilight that could be felt by the entire church, blessing each one as it gently caressed them. This was her day! Enku looked on with teary eyes, bubbling with glee for her older sister. Her mother, as expected, was a sobbing mess.

The couple exchanged wedding vows and placed the rings on each other's fingers. The abba bestowed his final blessing upon them and pronounced them man and wife. As James kissed his bride, the entire church erupted in the closing wedding mezmur. Once outside, the women erupted with ululations, the traditional high-pitched cry with flittering tongues so common amongst African women, their ultimate cheer and expression of rapturous excitement and ecstatic, enthusiastic approval!

With the wedding over, the real party began. Food, music, dancing, and toasts carried on throughout the night, leaving all, particularly the happy couple, thoroughly exhausted. This was the biggest reason why James and Brihan decided to wait a day before leaving for their honeymoon. In parting with Ethiopian tradition, they would leave for a honeymoon rather than spend three days in the husband's house, as he didn't actually own his own home, much less have one in Axum. Nor was any relative on his side of the family living in Axum for him to use theirs. Hence, he and Brihan would fly to another location. First, a jumper flight to Addis. Then they would board another flight to the honeymoon location: Arusha, Tanzania, in a five-star luxury hotel where one could step out onto the balcony of the bridal suite and take in a beautiful view of Kilimanjaro.

This was something they had planned for some time, both having a mystical fascination with the mountain. They also decided to wait to consummate the marriage till they checked in, if for no other reason than the wedding and celebration left them too exhausted to enjoy anything, including making love.

The Ethiopian Airways flight touched down at Arusha International Airport. The new bride and groom gathered their carry-on luggage from the overhead compartments, still reeling from the exhaustion of the wedding festivities. James had wanted to pack everything in suit bags and hand luggage that could go carry-on. But no, Brihan wasn't one to travel light, much to James's frustration. These were at least some of the few quirks that they had to adjust to over the years. But being in love, true love, means you have to live with those random idiosyncrasies, for if one is truly in love, it has become a galvanized, welded bond between two souls, forging more the just the trivial sense of commitment so popularly spoken of on today's talk shows, a serious commitment of dedication to walk life's path no matter how thorny and go the distance. But one should remember that the thorns are the external abuses from the many blows life throws at the couple in question, not the actual blows they might physically throw at each other. That sacred bond of trust must be protected from such petty, violent outbursts, for once violated, it is extremely difficult to rebuild. Likewise, the dishonesty of betrayal is as equal a violator. Adultery is living a lie and then trying to cover it with half lies. One who lies merely seeks to hide the truth, it's often said, but that still implies that one is still cognizant of truth's existence in the first place. But one who tells half lies to cover greater lies no longer seeks to hide the truth but has conveniently forgotten where one put it and tries to blur lines of distinction so badly as to develop a spiritually lethal indifference toward the real things of value in life, preferring instead to walk in a void of moral anarchy completely bankrupt of a genuine soul.

James and Brihan knew this all too well. This was probably why Brihan had not married earlier, nor had James. They both sensed a lack of honesty in their past relationships, the type of which they found in each other. It was the firm basis for a love that would clearly go the distance.

That beautiful night in Arusha, so starry lit, was more than a postnuptial sexual interlude but a rapture of emotions, of intertwining intimacy kissed by the magic of the night. As if graced by the Southern Cross above, they made love to each other, unleashing their passion, bestowing an anointing of grace on each other that blessed their consummation, giving witness to yet another miracle—the miracle of a new life conceived.

This became particularly evident approximately a month after the honeymoon. Morning sickness kicked in and with it all of the quaint symptoms to add such a colorful touch to their apartment's décor. Brihan made a beeline for the toilet. This wasn't exactly what James had expected so soon, and he rightfully showed concern. However, after a test at the local clinic, confirmation of the pregnancy turned anxiety into joy. It also prompted orders of soda crackers and mineral water to be placed at Brihan's bed stand to soothe her symptoms. They decided that if the baby was a girl, they would name her after where she was conceived, Arusha; if a boy, James Abai Mecklenberg.

⁓ೣ⊘ ⊘ೣ⁓

Time passed, and both labored and loved. Their love grew even stronger as their new relationship grew. Brihan grew as the child within her did, all occurring normally throughout the gestation period. James placed his head on her womb, feeling the young one kicking inside. The two discussed whether the child would be a football player or dancer by the little bumps they felt. He massaged her and looked over her protectively as a man would. She tried to work as long as she could, as she was dedicated to the cause her work furthered. He, the same way, pursued his career with all due diligence but with the nervous apprehension in the back of his mind about Brihan's better welfare as the pregnancy continued. *She should quit,* he thought, *go on maternity leave or something.* He made regularly unscheduled trips to the soil science lab to check on her, which always brought a smile to her face. He still continued to worry, despite her assurances that all was well.

In time, she did go on leave, not just because of his insistence but because it dawned on her she needed to take care of two people, not just one, rather than save the planet in the next few months. If she wasn't responsible to take care of the person most in need of her, her own child-to-be, how was she to take care of all of Africa, much less the whole planet? She remembered her mother saying, "Don't tell me your plans for global conquest and how you will change the world with a sink full of two days' worth of dirty dishes!"

Mama along with Enku came to Serere to be with Brihan in the last trimester. James wondered whether he would lose his sanity, but Abai came down from time to time, keeping things on an even keel. Their bond was a healthy one, which helped foster a greater sense of peace of mind, despite the three women hovering around all of the time. James appreciated their presence actually, for his relationship with Mama was actually quite good in comparison to many other son-in-law/mother-in-law relationships he was familiar with, although by no means perfect or as good as the one developing with Abai. Not to mention the fact that they made things much easier on Brihan, the most important factor of all, giving him more relief from anxieties as the birth approached.

Abai had a secret he had not told James about. He desperately wanted to see his first grandchild born. Boy or girl, it made no difference. The walls of his heart were growing paper thin. He was not as young as he used to be and didn't know how much time he had left. What time he did have he would dedicate to his family, particularly James and the new grandchild. Brihan's younger brothers had entered university now and didn't always stay in touch as much, sowing their wild oats, but they still kept in contact with home enough to show respect. Still, he loved the companionship he had fostered with James, and the feeling was mutual. He didn't want to break the news about his heart just right now, as he knew James would possibly go into depression, having lost so much before, and he didn't need that with the worries of upcoming fatherhood.

Abai went out on a stroll with James one Saturday morning. He brought along some seeds and breadcrumbs to feed the birds. James noticed the weariness in Abai's appearance, particularly his face.

"Are you all right? I mean, everything okay with you? You don't look so good."

"Oh, I'll be all right. Just a little winded," he replied.

Abai gave his usual confident, reassuring smile. Still, James kept a close watch on him. They sat down on a bench by the side of the road for a breather. Abai took the seeds and breadcrumbs from his coat pocket and tossed them onto the ground in the direction of some Asian orioles and other golden orioles jumping around the side of the road searching for food.

"They're gorgeous, you know—the orioles with their brilliant yellow-gold plumage and black top, or these with the black around the eyes like a mask and the black wings with white tips. They migrate here during the winter months, as it's always warm here. They and the golden weavers dart past you, and it's like the sun exploded before your very eyes with their brilliance, catching the light just right!"

"Yeah, but this supernova doesn't make you go blind!"

"Almost," Abai laughed. "It almost blinds you to other meaningless details of life that can cause so much anxiety but reveal their total existential, lack of importance in the long run. My, they're simply gorgeous though. Take these small sunbirds, for instance—so little but so startling with the effervescent rush of energy they exhibit and inspire. Such energy simply radiates from them, from their beauty, the ultimate colors of life! Take this one, for example," he remarked, pointing out the little ornithological wonder darting around a chrysanthemum blossom, dipping its long beak in to sample the nectar. "Check out the luminescent, dark green back and head showcasing the brilliant ruby-red plumage just under the beak covering the neck. A rather glorious-looking bib, is it not? Simply magnificent!" he marveled. "The beauty of this continent is matched only by its horror. With so much glorious escapades of life surrounding us, it's almost unbelievable how we manage to blow it all up in a bloody inferno."

"I've seen my fair share of blood. I don't need to see any more. No one does, but evil is real. It's not mere ideology that produces violence. A lot of those nasty events just head your way. Though there are efforts we can take to make the place better, trouble will always come. You just have to be ready for it."

"True. But one must also consider Sun Tzu, who said in the *Art of War*, 'Wars are battles of moral courage, fought, lost or won in the temples of prayer prior to the first shot fired on the battlefield.' Jesus tells me my ultimate temple is in my heart and soul, where my prayers originate with sincerity and from where they count the most. There has to be, first, a righteous foundation and power of discernment behind and guiding any true ideology, belief system, or design of a decision-making paradigm. There has to be a solid point of moral clarity matched with ultimate conviction to see visionary implementation through to its completion—producing total realization, full fruition of ideals, ideas, etc. First and foremost, one has to be right with God, the only true way to achieve inner peace from which enlightenment from a spiritual quickening comes from. Only when you have that peace and are no longer spiritually dry does the spiritual fire burn hottest, for any dryness that cracks spirit and soul is far worse than anything that merely parches the throat. Son, how dry are you still? How much peace do you have? What is the status of your temple?" Abai asked.

"I don't know exactly. It's getting better. Uniting with your family helps—helps a lot, in fact," he said, putting his arm around Abai. "I still wrestle with some issues, about Jesus, God, all of it."

"I know. The bonds between a father and son are an imperative as well if the boy is to fully grow into a man. You were shattered. War shattered you as well, like it shattered me. But both of us need each other, and the healing will continue. You're stronger than most. You don't need any psychobabble crap. You just need what we have been developing. You need God in your life. You need Brihan. She needs you, and so do I."

James smiled and asked if Abai had more birdseed. Abai reached into his coat pocket and gave him a handful. James tossed more out toward the orioles and weavers as both men smiled, enjoying the warmth—warmth of the sun, companionship, love, and the beauty surrounding them, enhancing their inner peace.

As the due date approached, the Mecklenbergs moved into the new three-bedroom house that had been built on the research grounds near the canteen, which featured a fireplace, living room, two baths (with workable showers), and a kitchen equipped with all of the basic amenities. Mama and Enku bustled about the house tending to Brihan's every need. Occasionally, others showed up, well-wishers or just children bringing dishes of food. The couple's popularity made the event one of the most anticipated in Serere.

One Saturday evening, Brihan began feeling contractions. She already had one false alarm exhibiting Braxton-Hicks contractions, which only simulated labor. Still, this time people began taking all of the necessary precautions, as the approximate due date had already passed by a few days.

Mama tended to her most closely, given that she was a retired nurse. Her father had been a doctor. Noting that she was such a fine, healthy baby, he named her Tena, meaning health. He also felt in his bones that this one might pursue a career in healing, unlike her older siblings who showed no interest at all in their father's chosen profession. Her saw in the name "Tena" someone not merely healthy but someone who would manifest healing amongst others, both by personality and education in the field.

This grew more apparent as Tena grow older. She began showing maternal signs of character, trying to take care of others, sometimes to the point of going overboard. She sometimes meddled too much in the affairs of others, to the point of aggravating the aggrieved parties, who didn't so much suffer from perceived infirmities as much as young Tena was looking for acceptance. However, being Daddy's girl, her father imparted wisdom. He did not just "school" her as teachers so often do. She developed the type of balance enabling her to engage in friendships that headed any codependent personality off at the pass, much less Munchausen bi-proxy. Tena became a nurse working alongside her father as casualties mounted up in the Ethiopian Civil War in the late seventies. Her medical skills were extensive, even going so far as to perform "meatball surgery" when casualties racked up so extensively that there were not enough doctors to tend to them.

Her influence spread over to Enku, who had just finished her first year of medical school. Enku anxiously assisted Mama Tena, timing the contractions awaiting the birth. It became clear that this was no false alarm but the real thing! Accompanying Enku and Mama were two midwives. A doctor had been summoned from Serere and was on her way. However, if she failed to show up in time, the present crew was more than capable.

Outside, James sat on a wooden chair, waiting anxiously with Abai and Nkomo. Abai stood out in the yard looking up at the sky, whistling, which he always did to detract from the nerves. Inside they heard moans, groans, and sporadic chatter from Mama Tena and her crew. The doctor finally arrived, greeting the gentlemen outside, speaking in reassuring tones before going straight into the bedroom-turned-makeshift-delivery-room, like was so often the case out of necessity in rural Africa.

Inside, Mama Tena wiped the perspiration from Brihan's brow as the hour of birth drew nearer.

"Oh my God!" Brihan cried out in agony after another contraction had passed. "We agreed to name the baby Arusha if it was a girl, but either way I think we should name it Kilimanjaro. I feel like I'm passing the entire mountain!"

"Just relax and get ready to push when I tell you to," Mama said. "I went through an extensive labor with you too, and we both turned out pretty good. You're doing fine. It won't be much longer now."

Outside, James was cringing. Abai strolled around the yard. Nkomo lit up a cigarette.

"I've been through a ton of tough situations: armed combat, disaster relief after tsunamis and hurricanes, you name it. Even taken on enemy and killed 'em looking into the whites of their eyes, but never anything like this before. In those other situations, I had a handle on things. I could act, at least had control of the issues, but not here! Here, I can't do anything but sit here and listen to her scream!" James lamented.

"That's always the hardest part," Abai said. "Physical pain isn't as bad as the nerve-racking torture some events put a person through, and the more nerve-racking variety is made worse by the feeling of helplessness you experience when you are forced to confront the fact that not only can you do nothing but you realize just how little control one has over anything in life's circumstances in general. Such events strip away the illusion of control, making human beings feel most uncomfortable."

"I've seen that, particularly in combat. Certain physical elements, yeah, you might control that, but at the end of the day, the outcome, the sum of all fears or agonies, you really don't," James replied.

"It would appear that there are too many unchecked variables, things one can't calculate into simple finite equations to make life that simple. It appears that much of life consists of too many mere random events, precluding one's capacity to predict outcomes or even get a solid grasp of the issues. However, not all is merely a series of random occurrences.

There is a God. He is eternal, and He is supreme. But He has given free will. Humans make their own choices as to whether they want to follow God's path or their own. Love means not being a control freak or dictator, codependently trying to manipulate others, but being confident enough to allow freedom of choice rather than making everything a walking, talking, controlled robotic extension of your own personality. Actually, the ones who reject God are the ones who become the control freaks and have to have all of the answers, really just saying they want all of the control—the secularists, the demagogues, communists, fascists, totalitarian, and authoritarian types. And of course they say they are doing it all in the best interests of others when they never are. They're just trying to do it in the best interests of themselves, to salve their own insecurities. When humans take their own path instead of God's, look out. Things begin to float in a moral anarchy, and human activities in particular become quite unpredictable and indeed on their own become quite random. It is in the fallen universe, in the climate I have described, that whole series of random events float in a sea of uncertainties. But there are answers, answers above and beyond mere intellectual grasp, answers that are found in a higher realm of knowledge."

"Where?" James asked.

"In the realm of faith," Abai replied. "And faith is all you have right now, so go with it."

"Still, it's tough."

"Oh yes. Not even with the greatest amount of faith does one stop being human! You don't think they're scared in there? I guarantee you they are. She's also got the physical pain to deal with. But Brihan's got faith—*strong* faith. I can also assure you of that as well. When it comes to the miracle of birth, medical science can only do so much. At the end of the day, the outcome one way or another is in God's hands. And remember, the day may not be just a twenty-four-hour day. Eventually, all things committed to Him work together for the good, for His purposes."

"Well, my faith is only so strong. I'm still having questions about God, all of it, but closer to reaching that point we've talked about."

"I know. Take your time. You'll get there and for the right reasons."

Nkomo rattled something that sounded like bottles in his duffle bag. "Ya know, boss, one of the things that goes through every man's mind about this time is worry about you. You worried 'bout whether or not you gonna be a good daddy or somethin'. You know, any man can sire a child, but it takes a real man to be a daddy to his child and raise dat child. Women can't do it alone. Some think they can, but they wrong, boss. Some women forced to do it, because the guy run out on her, y'know, or dis, dat, or the third thing somewhere over there dat he not handle and took off, but still she gotta find some kinda man to be role model to raise dat kid, or nuthin' gonna turn out right. Some of my best days not in Nairobi, or Kampala, but herding cattle with my daddy, listenin' to him. He taught me much. I got six kids, one wife, and we doin' pretty good. Ya know, boss, I been your friend a long time now. Know you in some ways better than you know you! You gonna be a fine daddy! Don't let no crap 'bout that add to your worries. Okay, boss?"

"Yeah, okay, and thanks, Nkomo."

"I agree with Nkomo," said Abai.

"Still, used to drink a lot before. Not so much lately, but I don't think today is a good day to quit!" James lamented.

"Well, certain things do have their medicinal value," said Abai.

"I could go for a good bottle of scotch right now!"

"Well, boss, I anticipated that," said Nkomo. He reached down into his duffle bag. "That's why I brought this twenty-year-old, aged, blue-label scotch whiskey, ice, and glasses. I got some seltzer water and mix too, if you like!"

"Where did you get twenty-year-old scotch out in the bush, Nkomo?" James asked, with ultimate astonishment.

"Oh, you know, boss, I got connections who got connections who got connections. This is Africa. Y'know how it works," said Nkomo with a big toothy grin.

"Yeah, I know, but I don't think anybody knows quite like you do, Nkomo! I thought your speech sounded a little slurred! You been hittin' 'dat ding' already?"

"You betcha, boss, but Nkomo still know what the hell he talkin' 'bout. You good man, bwana. You do okay bein' daddy. Don't you worry there!"

"He sure does know what he's talking about! Mr. Nkomo, sir, will you commence pouring as I put together some makeshift facsimile of a bar here?" Abai said, with raised eyebrows, grabbing and setting up the coffee table.

"Certainly, bwana!"

As the men began to drink (rather lavishly), the night came to an end as the sun began to unmask itself from behind the trees on the horizon, its red rays illuminating the scarlet blossoms of the flamboyant flame trees below. James was on his third scotch and soda when he heard Brihan's anguishing cry, a cry not only of pain but of joy, as it was soon followed by gasping laughter and tears at the same time. Moments later, the luster of a baby's cry echoed across the dawn horizon. Arusha made her debut in triumphant fashion.

"It's a girl!" Enku yelled. She came screaming out of the house to embrace the guys anxiously waiting outside. Enku leapt into the three, crying, hugging, and kissing all. Inside, Mama Tena, the doctor, and midwives tended to Brihan and the baby.

James, himself sobbing, said a quick prayer to God, a God he was still uncertain about but to whom he was thankful to nonetheless. He ran inside and spoke to a midwife coming out of the bedroom. "Can I see her now?" he asked. She motioned toward the door with a beaming smile. James walked in.

"The mother and baby are fine," the doctor said.

"Come over and see your daughter," said Brihan. She was exhausted but still smiling, in fact glowing.

James walked over, lifted up Arusha from Brihan's arms, and beamed a smile at least as photogenic as Brihan's. Tears streamed down his face. He said, "Hi, Arusha honey. I'm your daddy!" Then he gently kissed her on her tiny cheeks and forehead. Arusha cooed softly then cried again as her lungs had not quite yet adjusted to the harsh cool air rushing into them. As the cry wafted over the dawn, it lit up Serere as the sun's crimson and scarlet hues lit up the sky. With the dawn of the new day came the dawn of a new life. James's faith had grown dramatically. But all faith will be tested sooner than later. And his was to be tested in the future above and beyond anything he could have possibly imagined.

♦♦♦

Time passed, and Arusha grew into a darling young girl. Indeed she was Daddy's little girl who loved to tug on James's newly grown beard. Fortunately, he did not wear glasses for her to grab in her toddler years. She marveled at everything she experienced. All was new!

Grandpa came to visit as much as time, transportation, and finances would allow. Arusha was a particular delight to her grandfather. He would toss her in the air, spinning her around, totally neglecting his failing health. He took her out on walks, pointing out this and that. He and Grandma Tena would buy her gifts and sweets, spoiling her as much as possible, as this was a grandparent's prerogative.

Arusha grew a fascination with the colorful birds on the research grounds and often sat on the same bench with Abai that he had earlier with James. She would reach into Grandpa's coat pockets and toss seed and breadcrumbs to feed them. Sometimes Abai would tease her, beckoning her to grab some "birdseed" from his coat pocket only for her to find a brand-new toy there instead! Her eyes would widen with delight, becoming electric with excitement with the discovery of her new treasure. She would squeal with delight, hugging her grandpa around the neck, asking, "Is this for me, Grandpa!"

"Of course it is," he would reply.

Then she would almost strangle the old man with her bear hug, exclaiming, "Oh thank you, thank you, thank you, Grandpa! You're the bestest grandpa in the whole, wide world!" The love and adoration almost seemed to heal his withering heart—almost. However, whatever his heart lacked physically, Arusha made up for in spiritual and emotional uplifting. He would have given his life for her on the spot at any time. He would tell her all about the various species of beautiful birds and flora, about birdcalls and nesting habits, which Arusha, being a gifted child, soaked up like a sponge.

James would come around a bit later—always on time, before Abai would try to toss Arusha up on his shoulders and walk back to the house straining himself, his heart in particular, for more than it was capable of standing. Only through a miracle did he survive the one time he tried. On that occasion, James went into a conniption fit seeing the lack of color in Abai's face as he lowered Arusha to the ground. Abai then spent the next twenty minutes coughing and wheezing, trying to gasp for breath. James looked after Abai's health more than Abai did.

Arusha developed a love for her grandfather, clearly adoring the old man. She too noticed the symptoms and would ask what was wrong with Grandpa. Being a child, she could not fully comprehend the gravity of his situation and status of his health, despite being gifted. These involved matters of the heart and life that her innocent eyes were not well trained enough, from seeing life in general or sufferings, to fully appreciate and understand.

James, ever watchful, paid very close attention. He took over various physical tasks from Abai, giving that look of understanding in a mere glance, which Abai acknowledged as long as it was not overly obvious to the others. Not that either of the two women lacked suspicions. Quite the contrary, they knew all too well but tried to wall off the depressing details from their immediate attention. Still, they picked up on the nuances and acted in proper accord, respecting Abai's feelings and wishes so as to not draw undue attention and spoil the moment.

Abai was not actually in a state of denial, though his antics made it seem that way. He was more than aware of his situation and knew there was really nothing that could be done about it; not even a heart transplant would save him. His condition was rather rare, exhibiting complications and symptoms that would make any such operation extremely high risk with an almost certain 95–100 percent chance of fatality. Not only were the walls of his heart paper thin, so was his aorta. X-rays earlier had detected a condition later verified by a CT scan at a hospital in Cairo—an aortic aneurysm dissection, a tear in his aorta, but not one extending clear into the abdominal area. Still, this type of ailment was often a "widow maker," and he was fortunate that the tear that also extended up into his carotid artery had not taken him already. He had gone to Cairo to get checked by a better physician and have tests run on him using equipment that didn't exist in Addis at that time. He traveled there under the guise of a business trip so as to keep Tena in the dark. Doctors discussed a highly experimental procedure with stints, but given his age and other factors, it was seen as too high a risk with extremely high chances of permanent paralysis from the waist down, as blood would have to be cut off from the spinal cord for as much as twenty-two hours. Additionally, he faced a high risk of permanent kidney damage, forcing him to be on dialysis for the rest of his life, not to mention the problems of risking stroke caused by atrial fibrillation, which would be terminal. He had no desire to spend his remaining time, short as it would be, as an invalid being wheeled around by James in a wheelchair, deprived of enjoying the vibrancy of life as he knew it, almost comatose on drugs to the point of hardly feeling anything at all, in terms of the excitement and joy that he wanted to experience on walks with his granddaughter, no matter how trying they were on his heart. That was not staying alive at all but merely existing in a stale, stagnant, gray, dull nightmare of living hell. His heart would beat but with no life. Gone would be the walks with Arusha or accompanying his field hands into the hills above Axum to graze his livestock, feeling the sun and wind on his face and breathing in the intoxicating mountain air. He had lived life with joy and gusto, despite tragedies he had triumphed over. He would face death, which was inevitable the same way, with the same dignity that he had life. Learning how to face death was equally as important as any lesson learned about life. Indeed it becomes the most valuable lesson to be learned in life. Abai was in his eighties now and had lived life to the fullest. He had been a guerrilla fighter giving Mussolini's troops hell in the Ethiopian mountains at age fifteen, met Haile Selassie, and survived famine, the Ogaden War, and civil war. He had taught on three continents, published poetry, and farmed in the same lifetime. His faith was his strength that carried him through. And his faith would carry him across the greatest divide in life, into the waiting arms of Christ at the throne of God. He would brief everybody about his condition in time. *Until then, why bother them?* he thought.

James was more intuitive than the rest. He knew pretty well what was wrong. Brihan suspected but walled it off from her mind. Mama Tena stayed in complete denial out of her fear about the man she had grown to deeply love, despite marrying him in an arranged marriage years ago.

Back in Axum, Abai asked Tena to make him chai and sit down and talk with him. He told her how much he dearly loved her and thought this the best way to break the news. He explained everything as Tena took his hand.

"I know about this," she said. "I certainly know you as well as you do, and you know me as well as I know myself. We have become one over the years. The aortic aneurysm dissection—I wasn't quite aware of that, but I certainly suspected it. I have contacts in Cairo too, you know. We have both been adjusting to the inevitability of the situation. But remember, I am a nurse and have a duty more sacred than the Hippocratic Oath—to take care of you, making you as comfortable as I can."

"We should break the news to the others," said Abai.

"Yes, of course. They already suspect as well. Also, we must be sure that you take your blood pressure medication daily. You can't miss an interval. That is the key, particularly given the aortic tear, so it doesn't hemorrhage into a full-blown hematoma. That presents more danger than the heart itself."

They took several morning walks together, watched his salt intake, and tried to keep him healthy and strong but not overtax him. They broke the news to the family members, who didn't know whether to be depressed or merely relieved, for knowing for certain even when the news is bad news is much better than living in limbo, agonizing over bits and pieces, fragments here and there, leaving open opportunities for the imagination to run wild, creating excessive anxiety as the demons of uncertainty play havoc with the mind and emotions. Their faces donned masks of despondency, behind which lay sorrow and the questions of how to deal with it and Abai himself.

Abai woke up one morning and stepped to the window, peering out at the hills above Axum. Sensing that his time had come, he decided to accompany his field hands into the mountains to watch over the flocks as they grazed. He took the car out to the farm and then proceeded to walk up into the hills with the boys. Near the summit, he sat down on a flat rock. From this vantage point, he could see all of Axum and far into the distance. He took in the vast expanse, experiencing a special joy, a joy that is defined in terms of the liberation by inner peace from all the cares in the world. He smiled as he watched his livestock feed on the grass. It was a blissful peace he found, liberating the soul, allowing it to fly freely without restraint, leaping out carefree! No anxiety or stress to weigh him down—just freedom, peace, a rapture of inner joy that warmed all over. His thoughts could travel the great expanse of space and time, his psyche caressed by mental images of his beautiful songbirds, of loves lost and gained, engaging in more than just a daydream, sailing down a metaphysical concourse, a stream flow of consciousness that left him aglow.

He observed the clouds sailing like Spanish galleons across the sky, their sails picking up rays of sunlight that seemed to propel them even more than the wind itself. He felt a strong ray of agape love reach into his innermost being, beckoning him to steer one of those galleons to his final home. He breathed easily for a while as he sensed his immediate surroundings fading away. He wheezed a bit and then took one last breath, closing his eyes, "just to rest them a little," he said to himself, and then commandeered one of those galleons of his own, headed for the gates of the New Jerusalem. His head slumped forward as he dropped his walking stick. It rolled downhill, tapping the foot of a teenage boy herding the cattle. The boy looked up to see Abai's whole body slumping forward, sliding down off of the rock.

"Mr. Abai! Mr. Abai! What's wrong?" he hollered out.

He called out to the others, who immediately ran over to tend to their boss. They even sent their most fleet footed to town to summon help. But of course it was all too late. Try as they might, neither the doctors nor Tena could catch up with Abai's galleon in the sky.

James seemed more rocked than anyone by Abai's passing. Abai was yet another person he had grown attached to who had died on him. He had taken another chance and opened up his heart, revealing his inner most soul to Abai, something that scares most people (although few seem to admit it), establishing true bonds of family and love, leading down the healing path that had been shattered once again. In a case such as his, prior existing medical reports to inform and thus help one prepare for the inevitable are an exercise in futility given damage inflicted by the constant battering ram to the soul, which is almost irreparable. Each person's pain is somewhat unique, and whereas one's own may be equally as traumatizing as others, each still shows unique idiosyncrasies, limiting the extent one can identify or empathize with it. Common experience helps others relate to it—similar tragedies, etc.—but only God knows the soul, its inner depths and the depth of pain, fear, or other infirmities a person truly suffers. Rather than play psychiatrist, many are better off just being a friend, brother, or sister, serving as a conduit of God's love to wrap around their soul during the times of trial. How close or how tight may differ, but a true friend is sensitive enough to know when to lend a shoulder and when to back off, granting that extra space required. It was a job where no "psychobabblist" need apply. James would have ripped his heart out had one arrogantly tried to intervene with his "advice."

James often closed his eyes and just shuddered. He felt lost, not just the mere sense of loss. He was dazed and looked at Brihan and Arusha playing in the yard with fear. How would he be able to put it all together to be the man they needed as husband and father, particularly when the emotional shock of still another loss locked him up in a virtual state of paralysis, unable to talk about it with Brihan?

He wanted to crawl into a bottle of scotch and die, but Nkomo wouldn't let him. He'd cut him off at the bar and often lent James his shoulder. Sometimes he would talk to James, but mostly he would just listen, which James needed the most. Other times he would literally catch James as he collapsed in grief. But at least this was a sign that James could actually begin to feel again, hence a positive sign that he was honestly starting to face the stages of grief.

Over time, he began to adjust and accept Abai's death, as did Brihan, who was devastated by grief as well. Her spiritual sense of discernment prompted her to give James the space he needed. She had other family, making it easier for her to rebound, but he did not.

Arusha understood that Grandpa had died, that there would be no more walks to watch the pretty birds or toys to magically pull out of

Grandpa's pocket. There was no more Grandpa to toss her up in the air, teach her about the birds, animals, and flora, no one ever again like him. She would see his loving eyes in her mind and just cry. It was a bit easier for a child due to the lack of understanding and full comprehension of death, which can wrench the emotions out even further. Her innocence served as a barrier to the anxieties that tortured her father.

Eventually, James could talk with Brihan about it, each finding healing in their embrace. On many occasions, Arusha would jump on them for a family hug. The Holy Spirit embraced them all as they became conduits of the healing power of God's love to one another.

⋅ಇ ಇ⋅

The drums of war began intensifying in the north, as life went on as well as could be expected in Serere. More contracts came in that kept James busy in the Soroti District—everything from water systems, to roads, to telecommunications. Occasionally, he traveled around east Africa on various short-term assignments. Brihan expanded her career to include other areas of development above and beyond soil science and agronomy, sometimes including relief work. However, she disdained "more relief," as it all too often became a substitute for development, actually retarding Africa's long walk to freedom.

"Food aid relief has killed more people than it's saved. Only if there is an absolute devastating situation, where immediate deaths will occur without it, should relief be the policy, and only when there are no domestic sources of food production available or when it will not economically disadvantage the local smallholder farmer production, inhibiting them, indeed putting them out of business! Otherwise, they are moving us backward, merely polishing the shackles that keep the poor enslaved to poverty and trying to make them complacent with being driven further into an underclass with more brightly polished shackles! No one needs their shackles polished! They need them totally, completely removed! To remove them, Africans need to adopt a new paradigm, one that rejects the nonsense of entitlement mentality and puts in place one that sees them as entrepreneurs waiting to happen.

Better then to teach them how to fish to feed them for a lifetime rather than merely give them a fish, which only feeds them for a day!" said Brihan.

James raised his eyebrows a bit, hearing Brihan uncharacteristically take off, giving a fire-breathing Sermon on the Mount regarding development issues. Generally, she was someone who was more focused, reserved, and coolly collected. "What has you so on fire about this tonight?" he asked. "We both not only feel the same way but have talked this over before. But you're really riled up tonight for some reason. What makes today any different? Something happen? You dealt with this in the Ethiopian famine. What makes today different? What's up?"

"Oh, I'm stressed out a bit, and they're calling on me and some others to do some relief work that the government could and should be doing with all of those MONGOs in Uganda, and we're right in the middle of testing out some new hybrids, in the critical phases no less, and we just can't spare the time. Besides, we come up with this and better-value chain construction, and we'll do far more to help the poor than this relief *dedebe* ever will!" she fumed.

"MONGOs? Dedebe? What're those? Do I really want to know what those little quips of yours mean?"

Brihan laughed a bit. "MONGOs stands for My Own NGO, which is becoming the leading industry in Uganda, which are totally worthless, nothing short of muzungu siphons, sucking money into their own salaries, nice cars, and homes, never really doing anything to develop the smallholder farmers' self-reliance and hence not doing anything to promote economic development in the first place. Dedebe means watered-down cow manure in Amharic. It doesn't even rise to the level of real thing, good for nothing!"

James, drinking a Coke, erupted like a volcano and then promptly fell off the couch in a fit of laughter. The Coke spewed all over the floor, but at least the volcanic eruption saved him from choking to death. "Well, Museveni talks a good game, but how he delivers is another question. A lot of agencies—the same way. We just do the best we can, keep slugging it out and hope for a better day. To paraphrase Ferris Buehler, normally it takes a million years to compress a lump of coal into a diamond, but that's where politics and geology differ. You shove a lump of coal up a politician's ass, and they'll crap a diamond in ten minutes."

Brihan laughed, went over to the couch, and sat down beside James.

"Hey, listen, I've been summoned away to Nairobi on a two-day conference. Why don't you and Arusha come with me—once you're done with your tests, that is, and then we'll head down to Mombasa for a little vacation, stay at Diani Reef in a nice hotel and relax, chill out a little. We could use some more time to ourselves," James suggested.

"Oh, I don't know, James. They've called me away to go work in northern Soroti District and up around Lira to help with the Acholi refugees from the north."

"What? Are you nuts? No way in hell! There's nobody to sit Arusha. They're all away on holiday leave, and that place is a hell hole—a war zone! You're not going up there!" James yelled. He spoke in a demanding tone, bordering on hysterics.

"Oh, I can handle it." It was Brihan's best attempt at a reassuring tone. Trying to settle James down wasn't convincing, as Brihan wasn't exactly convinced herself. "The government assures us that Kony's troops have been driven further north and there's no real danger for the time being. And besides, we'll just be up there a week!"

"The government's assurances! Now that's dedebe, and you know it! The government is totally incompetent and hasn't been able to handle this rebellion so far. Kony seems to have outmaneuvered them at every juncture! The government has made all kinds of promises before, worthless reassurances. Just ask Kony's victims how legit Museveni and the UPDF have been with any of them!" James yelled.

Brihan bristled and stormed out of the room. She knew deep down that James was right, particularly given the circumstances.

"Look, it's not up to you to save all of Africa. You have a child to think of now, not to mention me, your husband—we are a family. Remember what your mom said about the dishes in the sink. That was a figure of speech. You have to handle the more important responsibilities first," he said.

"I know your concerns, but I have friends that are going into the IDP camp. I feel I should do something. We are supposed to be pulled out of there if Kony makes a sudden move south," she yelled back.

"And what if inclement weather hits and your transportation goes down? I can guarantee you Kony's won't. Not to mention the fact that nobody knows how far south he is now. UPDF's intel is a discombobulated mess. They're morons. They don't know anything at all. Brihan, kiss this off and come with me to Nairobi and Mombasa. Let them—let someone else, someone who doesn't have a child—do this! Better yet, just let the NGOs who are funded to handle this handle it! Let them use their own personnel. Brihan, don't make me forbid you to do this. I'm real close!"

Brihan arrogantly walked out of the house. James headed in the direction of Nkomo and a bottle of scotch. Brihan's stubbornness would be her undoing. A few days later, she packed up enough clothes for her and Arusha and proceeded to join the team headed north.

James sat disgruntled in the easy chair, sharing another drink with a disbelieving Nkomo after she left. Both found it inconceivable that anyone would risk her child on such a venture, given Kony's reputation.

"That one's a stubborn one, she is. I hope that in her great delusions of justice she don't end up shootin' off her battleship mouth only to end up sinkin' her rowboat ass, 'cause I think that all it gonna be if Kony show up! He has guys that can cover that terrain. I know that place well, myself!" said Nkomo.

"Dedication's one thing, but this is an obsession," added James. "This is the first major thing that we have really crossed swords on, I mean, this bad. I suppose I could have just physically grabbed and incarcerated her and, like, tied her to the plane headed for Nairobi, but law enforcement has a tendency to frown on that sort of thing."

"Nah. That don't work for you. She made her own choice. Nairobi would have been a better one." Nkomo let out a loud sigh.

James grimaced and poured another drink of scotch. He had been a soldier, as had been Nkomo at one time, and both still had a soldier's instincts. He had a good mind just to grab an AK-47 and go up there. However, the Ugandan PDF would most likely catch him at some checkpoint and put him in jail for who knew how long. He nervously prayed to Jesus for Brihan's safety. He still had made no firm commitment to accept Him as his only Lord and Savior yet. Still, he hoped she would return unharmed, with Arusha in the same condition. He had to fight the queasiness of the uneasy feeling he had. He tried to fight off the demons of self-doubt and those who tried to whisper in his ear, "It's your fault! You should have stopped her!"

James swore at them, screaming in his half-drunken stupor, "It's not my fault! You can't tell her anything!"

"Settle down, boss! No, it ain't your fault! Nobody's saying it is, nobody I can hear anyway. Maybe some of those little self-doubt demons talkin' at cha, but you just got to kick them out of here. You know what the Bible say: resist the devil, and he will flee. Just ignore that crap. It'll go away. Settle down, boss. Nkomo's right here." Nkomo, his truest and most trusted friend, tried his best to reassure him. "You want another drink, or maybe you had enough? What do you think?"

"Nah, I've had enough. Thanks, man. Hey, I'll be all right. Why don't you go home to that pretty wife of yours and get some sleep."

"You sure, boss?"

"Yeah, I'm sure, go ahead. I'll be all right. See you tomorrow."

"Okay, boss," said Nkomo, putting his arm around him. "Stay cool, man."

James passed out in the chair after Nkomo left. Summoning God for a miracle was one thing, but even the most devout Christian should be aware that praying for a miracle does not give one the license to act so blatantly irresponsible as to constitute a mockery of God and put Him to the test, evidenced by deliberately walking in harm's way. God does not respect a Christian witness acting as a "false hand of providence" as opposed to a godly commission for which there may still be sacrifice. Indeed, one can walk away from a miracle, refusing the protective hand of God with the disingenuous nature by which one approaches God regarding the petition in the first place. If a person is bound and determined to heedlessly walk into destruction, despite scripture, which instructs you to avoid certain calamity, don't expect a miracle. God has given free will, including the freedom to walk out of His protective guidance.

James was a military tactician from way back. Brihan was not. He could tell by some of Kony's moves his intentions were to drive straight south, further into the Soroti District. Then he would move onto Mbale, Jinja, and then Kampala itself. Brihan had been foolish. She had not listened to wise counsel and was moving instead into harm's way. In turn, she may have just walked her way out of the protection of divine providence. James had to attend the conference in Nairobi, for it was mandatory. Brihan's gallivanting north was not. It was a mere request for volunteers, volunteers that would not get the necessary backup and support they were promised.

✤✤✤

Joseph Kony strolled through his camp with an arrogant swagger, his mind ablaze by a form of spiritual poison that locked his spirit, soul, and mind in an evil, deadly form of prison. Shockwaves and sparks of electricity from obsessive, compulsive thoughts intermittently flashed within him, charging a current that coursed through his body like a tractor beam further gravitating him into the dark side. It was the cardinal root of perversion, a catalyst that released a deadly, addictive concoction, manifesting itself in the spread of evil and delusions of grandeur throughout every aspect of his being. It led him to enjoy the most perverted activities of bondage, sadomasochistic sexual violation of women, and torture. He particularly delighted in violating those of extreme innocence in their early teens and even younger. These he would violently ravage, raping their souls more than their bodies, leaving them wailing mounds of flesh, like burned-out, twisted fragments of metal after a bombing raid. He delighted in the illusion that after his sexual conquest, he had "totally defeated them." But this was true only if the victim actually surrendered her soul in submission to Kony in the midst of her humiliation. But many, despite humiliation, did not, keeping control of their souls and even in their hatred of him trumpeting a cry of "victory" in that it was they who held the moral high ground, making them superior to the rapist that had sunk so deeply into the rectum of hell that he actually confirmed his own surrender. He was just too blinded by spiritual darkness to see it.

In addition to the aforementioned sins, the man and his generals not merely engaged in but delighted in torture. They not only forced the female rite of circumcision but dismembered their prey, sometimes just maiming them, other times murdering them. He cut the lips and breasts off young girls he abducted. He tried anything to break all of his abductees psychologically and steal their souls, to make them mindless, robotic apparatchiks. He tried to reconfigure them into a mass of obsequious sycophants, instruments of death that would kill on his command, pledging total loyalty to follow him into the gates of hell. He would force them to kill their own parents and immediate family members in attempts to convince them that there was no turning back, that they had crossed the Rubicon, leaving only one course left: to follow Kony. He sought to infest them with lethal propaganda to ensure a force of slaves totally committed to fighting for him, given the want of any base in a justified cause.

His objective was to obtain power in Uganda by any means possible. He launched his campaign to topple the Museveni regime. It was rumored that Museveni's UPDF had actually opened fire with automatic assault rifles at point-blank range and not dropped anywhere near the casualties they should have. No one had an explanation for this. It was clear Kony had received no miracle from God. Some claimed it was spiritual warfare by satanic forces going up against less than spiritually committed UPDF troops. At the very least, it was mused that the lack of genuine faith and adherence to a godly walk by the Museveni regime left them somewhat short in "earning" miracles from the Almighty to blast through the vales of spiritual darkness even with AK-47s. Others said it could just as easily be written off to total incompetence and lack of aim by the Ugandan military. Who knew? But through it all, Joseph Kony marched his way to hell step by step, believing that he was possessed by spirits who channeled through him to all of Africa. He thought he was some sort of spiritually incarnate prophet of dead apostates from ages past, in total contradiction to any Christian teachings. However, he chose to stay conveniently oblivious to his blasphemy as he marched with scorched earth intent, torturing and abducting defenseless children along his crusade for the Antichrist to Kampala. In his way was a defenseless IDP camp in northern Soroti District. They were meaningless chattel to Kony, except for the former child soldiers who had escaped his lair to find refuge and possible redemption amongst the other war-torn refugees. For them, there would be no mercy. As for the others, he couldn't care less, except for the more attractive females he would try to impress into service as his brides, and if he happened to pick up some additional soldiers, so much the better. The rest he would discard as so much refuse and ensure no leaks or witnesses to the government, press, or anyone connected to the International Criminal Court, which had already indicted him on thirty-three counts of war crimes and crimes against humanity.

⁓ ⊙⊙ ⊙⊙ ⁓

Brihan, though an agronomist by trade, was called on to help the resettlement. Most of the promises never materialized, including the ones made about accommodations for the volunteers. There were no provisions or housing accommodations of any kind, not even tents, but more promises were being made by fast-talking government officials saying that the tents and food had only been delayed but would arrive *shortly*. The place was a madhouse, the operation a complete fiasco. Brihan was already kicking herself for buying into the line sold by her supervisors and government officials. After resettlement, the agronomists were to conduct a survey and construct a game plan for an agricultural scheme as an overall effort to enhance sustainable rural livelihoods. The operation was a total pile of chaos that hadn't been thought through at all. Government planners had made too many vast assumptions and were too shortsighted, leading them to draw too many premature conclusions, not to mention the most unrealistic timetable she'd ever seen. Resettlement presented far too many complications and problems than anyone had anticipated. Serious planners would have given far more time for resettlement and the necessary resources to house, clothe, and feed the refugees before even beginning to define study parameters to come up with a solid game plan that would actually implement an agricultural scheme of optimal economic scope and scale necessary to provide for and sustain the inhabitants. Nobody did, however. This was a mere political stunt at best, designed for public relations and the benefit of politicians and other indigenous pariahs who syphoned the aid into their own pockets. They either put the cash directly into their offshore bank accounts or sold off the in-kind aid and deposited the money in the same manner.

The whole mess left Brihan disgusted. But her disgust soon turned to terror as she noticed a huge cloud of dust on the horizon, an ominous warning of the oncoming nightmare. Armored personnel carriers and a multitude of foot soldiers appeared out of the clouds. The child soldiers advanced forward in a robotic form, distinguished from actual zombies only by the look of hate emanating from their eyes, perverted by torture and propaganda. They descended on the camp like a plague of locusts armed with AK-47s. Hell had arrived!

Mortar shells exploded within one hundred meters of Brihan and Arusha. She stood paralyzed in shock, as did most, amidst the carnage, followed by horrendous screams of terror and agony as limbs and sinews of children and other hapless victims flew past her, painting her and the surroundings in splattered blood. Horrified officials quickly commandeered the vehicles, fleeing the scene heedlessly neglecting the fate of the others, leaving behind defenseless women, children, and the infirmed, stranded to become ravaged by the oncoming hordes. Cars, jeeps, and trucks lurched over potholes and hills, tearing through bush in a cowardly exodus as Brihan and the others screamed for them to come back. At that point, the whole world appeared to be a mental institute, and the lunatics were running the asylum.

Brihan immediately chased after Arusha, who began to run aimlessly in a mindless race to some sort of perception of a safe haven. The child reacted to the stimulus of fear by charging out in any direction that she perceived to be a retreat from harm's way, regardless of whether it offered any true sanctuary or not, reflecting the true nature of a child, to flee in panic in a wave of fright that overwhelms the mind: just get out of there—run. Run anywhere. *Just run!* The terrified child just wanted any shelter from the storm that would offer an emotional, psychological safe haven, just wanting the evil, the terror, to go away. She ran without any sense of direction, fleeing as they all began to do, in mass hysteria. Brihan fortunately caught up with Arusha, snatching her up and flinging her on top of her shoulders.

"Now hold on tight, like you use to do with Papa and Grandpa," she instructed.

Arusha obeyed, clinging tightly around Brihan's neck in a panic-stricken grip as Brihan dashed into the nearby forest in a vain, futile attempt to hide from Kony's henchmen.

Mortars began pounding the camp. It was as if all time and space were ripped apart in the eruptions of fire and shrapnel in such an explosive force that tore the ground apart, sending trees and torn flesh hurling up into the sky atop plumes of flame that seemed to reach up, cursing the sky and all around it. Plumes of black-and-gray smoke bellowed up, broadcasting body parts, twisted fragments of metal, and other remains in a sickening, bloody rain of death from the point of impact. The ordnance seem to rape the ground the way they tore it apart as they pummeled into it in as deranged a fashion as Kony did his victims.

Child soldiers, Kony's cannon fodder, advanced into the camp indiscriminately shooting the defenseless, helpless refugees. They were followed by the older soldiers and commanding officers. More disgusting than the carnage of war itself was the fact that the attack had been ruthlessly staged on an IDP (Internally Displaced Persons) camp, which was a temporary collectivity of shattered souls desperately seeking refuge from the same war, some surviving on Sunday meals of termites and salt, who merely begged to see the light of day in their lives once again. They were part of a wounded nation reaching out in a fledgling spasm of pain, trying to grasp the brass ring of a democracy. Nine times out of ten, they only found it to be a sick merry-go-round leading them to revisit the same type of desecration to the soul again and again.

Kony's sick bastards actually delighted in seeing the ghastly expressions of bewilderment and shock on the faces of their victims, further delighting in their pitiful outcries of anguish, not the least of which were screams of, "Why, why?" as they shot them at point-blank range. If the bodies could be stacked up into funeral pyres, they would light up the night for miles around, as the demons of hell screamed loudly in joy, delighting in the atrocities and further enflaming the obsessive ambition of Kony and his whores of war.

The older soldiers began fanning out around the camp and surrounding territory. Young boys between ages eight and fifteen were taken to an open space and ordered to sit on the ground. The ongoing cries of women being raped could be heard throughout the camp. Still, occasionally there were sporadic sounds of gunfire as Kony's troops continued to indiscriminately murder hapless victims, particularly if they came across any former child soldiers who refused to return into service for the LRA.

Brihan held Arusha tightly, hiding behind brush overgrowth amongst a thick grove of trees. Kony's troops began tromping through the forest in search of any fleeing refugees. So far the government was unaware of Kony's exact location, dangerously miscalculating his moves and how far south he had gone. He had no desire to let anyone escape and tip them off. The government officials fared no better than the refugees they had left behind. Kony had encircled the area the previous night, cutting off all roads of escape. The fleeing vehicles ran headlong into roadblocks manned by soldiers aiming rocket-propelled grenades at them. Kony's boys opened fire, blowing the vehicles off of the road. Kony gave strict orders not to leave a single leaf or fern unturned. Everyone was to be found and rounded up. Child soldiers prodded through the forest in Brihan and Arusha's direction. Brihan held her hand tightly over Arusha's mouth as the child trembled with fear.

Then something potentially more deadly began to slither down from a tree, headed for both. It was rather large snake, silver blending into olive green in skin tone, of about twelve feet in length. It came upon the mother and child and instinctively began to rise, opening its mouth to reveal the jet-black interior from whence it got its name and exposing its dangerous fangs dripping with the most lethal venom on planet Earth. It was a black mamba extending two-thirds of its body, almost nine feet up in the air, capable of resting on the remaining one-third coiled up on the ground. It was the most terrifying stance one could imagine. Brihan screamed as the snake's head reared back to strike a lethal blow. A single strike could inject approximately 250 mg of toxin, with the lethal dosage being at minimum 150. The venom would course through a person's veins and in thirty minutes or less constitute an "extreme medical emergency," so field books said. Translation: death would be imminent. Any strike above the waist would give the person maybe ten minutes instead of thirty, particularly if it hit the carotid artery. At least 1,000 ccs of antitoxin would be required immediately to save the victim, and out here, there was none to be found.

The scream attracted the attention of one of Kony's soldiers, who immediately turned and fired off shots from his AK, cutting the snake in half. Unfortunately, the scream gave away Brihan and Arusha's position as well. Killing the snake was a mixed blessing. The soldiers seized Brihan and Arusha. Once submitted to Kony, they would suffer a far worse fate. To have died by snake bite would probably have been the real blessing, a far more merciful death.

The child soldiers surrounded them; their gaze communicated all that needed to be said. Their sergeant, a lad of about sixteen, motioned with his gun barrel for them to get up.

"Thank you for saving us," Brihan said. She was making the best attempt at establishing some sort of cordial dialogue to avoid further provoking their captors to the point of making any rash reactions.

"It's a little soon for that, until General Kony confirms who and what you are," he replied.

"Still, I thank you anyway," said Brihan.

"You don't look like a Ugandan. Your skin is lighter tone, your facial features—you are maybe from Ethiopia?" the sergeant asked.

"Yes, from Tigray Region, Axum to be exact," she replied.

"Axum. I use to be from there, long ago. Now I don't know where I am really from, nor do I much care anymore. Let's go," he ordered. His tone was stone cold, not speaking with any booming voice of authority but one of total indifference toward them and indeed the entire situation. It was totally despondent, not reflecting any emotion at all. He was just nonchalant, following orders, and seemed to show disgust with everything about life in general.

They marched back to the camp, and the soldiers handed Brihan and Arusha over to Kony. Kony looked at them and found both Brihan and Arusha desirable. Arusha was now just past her ninth birthday, and that was old enough for Kony, particularly in the event that Brihan refused to be another one of his brides. He walked over to Brihan with a lascivious smile. "Who are you? You don't look like a refugee here. No, you came from somewhere else. You are dressed too good, look too good, healthy to be one of them. Who are you? What are you? Where are you from?" he asked.

"I am Brihan. This is my daughter, Arusha. We have come from the Serere Research Station, volunteers to help out with this mess that you have largely created with your insane war. I am an agronomist, so why are you keeping us? What need have you of an agronomist? We don't know anything about war or explosives and such. We can do you no good. Why not just let us go?" she replied.

"I don't want to tip off the government as to exactly where I am. No need to give them any tactical advantage. How do I know you wouldn't tip them off as to our whereabouts?" His eyes cast a strong look of suspicion.

"You don't think that they're going to find out soon enough? We know some people made it out. What's to stop them from using a cell phone? Even though there are blackout zones, there are countless other means, including some with ham radios who could have gotten the message out. Word travels fast around here, faster than you think. I'm willing to bet that sooner than later, Museveni, with all the incompetence of his regime and military, is going to zero in on you, particularly with this bloody fireworks display you have created, which had to have been picked up for miles around! I guess one could say you really know how to make an entrance!"

"The government cowards were caught at roadblocks and executed by my soldiers. I doubt if anyone actually made it out alive to communicate with anyone and give our position away," said Kony. He sneered arrogantly at them.

"You mean murdered, don't you, you bastard! Did you even stop to think that some of them were equipped with CB radios to communicate with? Incidentally, like I said, we are just volunteers, trying to help those whose lives you already butchered. They were helpless, forlorn refugees who barely survived your prior onslaughts, not government troops. This is an IDP camp, not a military installation! You had no cause to attack them; indeed, you have no moral cause—period! You have already lost this war, even before you see your final military defeat. You lost it the day you began with the most evil premise for going to war, putting one insane foot after another. You could never win! Your military battlefield 'victories' like this one are slaughters of defenseless men, women, and children who constituted no threat or even a symbol of the government. You have no moral cause. You lost the moral high ground the day you started, your rhetoric being nothing more than an empty, false oracle featuring a primitive lexicon and all of it amounting to nothing more than political masturbation! It's all maggot-infested rot, and you are doomed to lose. You who claim to be the rebels, who claim some self-righteous cause of indignation against the 'evil of the government'—you, yourselves, are the evil! You have no ideology but a bad, false political religion that has already died by a terrible case of rickets of its own faith! You project so much more evil through the sewer that runs through your soul than Museveni it's pathetic, and though he's no choir boy, he looks like a cherub or seraph in comparison to you! You cannot and will not attain any moral high ground, hence, your guerilla campaign will not win the hearts and minds that it requires to even sustain it, much less prevail in a war of attrition. You lack what you need to mobilize your masses. They will never rally around you. Look at your troops! You are relegated to child soldiers! *Children, mere children!* Where are the able-bodied young men to fight for you and serve as the bulk of your army? Your indoctrination will never take the place of a valid moral point of clarity, codifying an ideology that attracts the support of real partisans. No one supports you. You will soon be wiped off the face of the earth like the pestilent scum you are!" Brihan roared.

Kony cursed, hurling slanderous insults at Brihan. "You just signed your death warrant, bitch, except for one possible exception to the torture we will put you through sending you from this world. You have the option of becoming my bride, submitting to my every sexual desire any time I want it—any way I want it!"

"You mean *whore*, don't you? You want someone to be a mindless sex toy and submit to you, be your slave and feign adoration and reverence to you? Grovel after you as if you are some sort of god! I already know a real God and His Son. I would only date you if I was too lazy to commit suicide but desperate enough to consider slitting my wrists!" Brihan retorted. She would face Christ as a martyr before submitting to Kony. Besides, it would be far worse for Arusha to see her mother actually concede defeat rather than die courageously. Brihan was willing to die for her convictions standing but would never go down on her knees by submitting to lies or prostituting her soul. "I have Christ within me. You can murder me or my daughter, but you could never kill our souls!" she said in defiance.

Kony went ballistic. He slapped Brihan and grabbed her by her crotch as she fell back. He forced his mouth upon hers and then violently stripped her bare. He psychotically bit her breasts and other body parts until he drew blood like a vampire. Then he threw her into the hands of two of his soldiers who delighted to take part in the desecration.

Still she remained bravely defiant, knowing full well the fate that awaited her. She responded with the courage of a lioness. "What? You're so weak, *like a woman*, that you have to have three assault me? Aren't you such a big, tough man! What, you can't beat up and rape a woman by yourself? Or will you have to have help with that latter part too?" She mocked him and spat in his face.

Kony screamed as if every spirit from the caverns of hell raged within him, charging out from the darkest part of his inner sanctum. He punched her with a closed fist, cutting her lips, blackening her eye, causing a cut to bleed, then threw her to the ground and proceeded to viciously rape her while his henchmen held her limbs. All the time he demanded that she verbally dehumanize herself, renouncing her Christ, and concede to being the worthless, vile, sexual ragdoll she had described earlier as the true object of his desire. Kony desperately tried to break her, but he couldn't and went further insane seeing the futility in trying to render her spiritually bankrupt where he could impress her into service as a fallen demimondaine—his sordid, ignoble courtesan. She resisted and resisted, despite being raped repeatedly. She screamed in anger and horror, gritting her teeth at him. When he finished, he motioned to his other henchmen, who had her as well. When they were done, Brihan lay dazed, barely conscious but still with her soul intact, having never surrendered where it counted most.

Kony ordered one of his subordinates, "You are Karamojong. Show her how you kill people the traditional way!" The soldier smiled sadistically. He pulled out his machete, which he always kept razor sharp just for this purpose. With quick, sharp, decisive blows, he began dismembering Brihan: first her toes, then feet, legs, fingers, hands, and arms while all the time keeping her alive, as this was a skill handed down for well over a thousand years. Her breasts and genitals went next. All the parts were placed around what remained of her in a circle. Kony grabbed a can of lighter fluid, dousing her and her body parts with the flammable fluid, then flicked open a lighter, igniting the flame, and tossed it onto Brihan.

"Now, watch yourself burn to death!" he growled smugly.

She burst into flame. The screams did not last long as she was already half-dead from excessive bleeding. However, Arusha's would not subside. She began to run aimlessly away from it all, screaming hysterically.

"Shoot her!" Kony ordered.

One of his henchmen armed with an assault rifle aimed and shot three rounds through the child's back, dropping her lifelessly to the ground. All of hell's demons howled with delight. However, given Brihan's spiritual resistance, they had lost in ways they were all too spiritually dark to see.

The eldest of the child soldiers who found Brihan in the forest observed the sadistic torture. He had had enough. He ducked out of sight and proceeded to vomit while trying to steady himself against a tree. Tegene Tefere had also been from Axum. This woman was blameless in every way. This was not a political movement but a madhouse. He had been abducted by Kony at age ten and turned into a child soldier. His name, Tegene Tefere, meant "protector" (Tegene) and "one who is feared by his rivals" (Tefere). His surname aptly described his father, Tefere, a mountain of a man who fought off an entire patrol of the Marxist DERG in Ethiopia singlehandedly when they attacked his family's compound. He took out several with a .45-caliber pistol and then with a machete, taking at least two bullets as he hacked the invaders of his compound to death. He sacrificed his own life to give his family time to escape.

The family sought refuge in Gulu, Uganda, where Tegene's uncle lived. As is custom, a man's wife becomes the wife of his brother in the event of his death. They all lived together until Kony showed up. He made Tegene a soldier and forced him to kill his uncle-turned-father and his mother, in addition to his new father's other wives. This left Tegene's mind twisted and confused. He was supposed to be the protector, not the murderer. What was he now? He didn't know. He only knew that he fought for Kony out of fear, but the feelings now racing through his body, not the least of which were nausea and repugnancy at the acts of torture, far outweighed and surpassed the fear. It was time to leave. He kept vomiting as if trying to expel the shame, hatred, and guilt that swirled inside him like a sickening kaleidoscope of emotions. Once done, he could barely hold himself up. However, he was clear-minded enough to decide that he and two other friends he had made, themselves abductees, would escape. They would find the prime opportunity, he figured, and make a break for it.

He approached his two friends, Alemayehu (meaning "he has seen the world") and Feleke (meaning "it sprang," as in crops spring up), and told them of his plans for desertion. The two had also witnessed Brihan and Arusha's murders and were still shaking, petrified in fact by the spectacle of the macabre. They seemed relieved to hear Tegene's plan. They too wanted out but were afraid to even tell Tegene about it. They looked up to Tegene like a big brother but wondered how he would react. He had been somewhat erratic, particularly over the last few months. Would he back them? Or would he be in another mood and act like the soldier, turning them in, which would lead to punishment if not death? Tegene was their leader. He had been a soldier with Kony the longest of the three. When he told them of his plan, they felt a temporary relief. However, it would be replaced with the anxiety of formulating the right strategy to ensure a successful, clean getaway. Otherwise it would all be for naught. They would be shot by either the guards or Kony himself. The risks were high but a necessary price to pay given the costs of remaining with Kony.

They spent the next couple of days laying plans for the escape. The key lay in distracting one of the guards in particular, long enough to slit his throat, quietly enough so as not to draw attention from the other guards. Then they would commandeer a vehicle, put it in neutral, and push it just long enough to be out of earshot range from the camp. Then they would start it up and travel northeast toward the Kenyan border and take safe haven in a refugee camp there.

But they needed a real distraction. *What would it be?* Tegene thought. It had to be something that would captivate the guard's mind so totally that he would be unaware of the sixteen-year-old Tegene sneaking up on him with a knife. The guard's name in question was Okello. He was about twenty-five, older and stronger than the three combined. Tegene knew Okello had a critical weakness he could exploit: lust—deep, perverted lust that grew even more perverse the more he hung around Kony. That type of sexual disease was infectious without physical contact or fluid exchange. It radiated from the inner perversion of the soul and spirit of anyone who opened up that door and wallowed in it by thought, word, or deed. Those who decided to stay with Kony lowered their spiritual drawbridge, leaving the psyche an open target, overwhelmed, causing a mutation, a perverse sexual addiction that delighted in the rawest form of debauchery and sadism. Okello had been totally drawn to the dark side.

There were three young Acholi girls about the same ages as the boys. The eldest, Celeste Okulu (born near or on the way to the river), was about to reach her sixteenth birthday. She and the other two, Miriam Akot (child born during the rainy season) and Geneviève Anyanyo (born at sunrise), had been abducted and impressed into service as "sexual aids," concubines for Kony and his staff. Okello had long made advances and sought after the eldest, only to be rebuffed. Tegene talked with the three girls. They had developed a kinship during their captivity. Celeste listened intently. Tegene told her to lure Okello toward her, making him think that she was offering him sex. Tegene would be hiding in the brush with a Special Forces knife he had procured that almost appeared to be a Roman short sword. Once she locked Okello into a tight embrace and put her mouth over his, Tegene would step out and kill him, this way doing it without Okello so much as uttering a sound to give them away.

"Just for insurance, I have an Italian stiletto switchblade knife!" Celeste said, revealing the knife. "I'll keep it in my sleeve, reach down his front to make him think I'm going to unzip his fly, then I'll eject the blade into his gut or, better yet, feel his chest and plunge it directly into his heart!"

"You are not a trained killer, Celeste! You may be able to pull it off, but it's very risky. If you fail, we will all be caught and shot! I assure you, I will be there," Tegene replied.

Then they waited for nightfall to carry it out. Miriam and Genevieve procured some extra provisions, stealing a couple of backpacks, and kept them well hidden until the anointed time. Alemayehu and Feleke likewise managed to stealthily snatch a couple of Gerry cans of petrol, placing them in the ditch by Okello's vehicle but still out of sight where he would not stumble onto them. The vehicle was a used old Soviet manufacture UAZ 469, all-terrain vehicle with a mounted KPV 14.5-caliber machine gun that Kony managed to purchase when the old Soviet Union "filed bankruptcy" and began unloading military equipment for hard currency. He picked it up with a little help from Al-Qaeda. The KPV was a heavy-duty machine gun that would come in handy should they encounter trouble in their escape. Some would refer to it as a light artillery piece. All was set for the critical moment that would either spell out their deliverance or doom.

The night came. It was overcast. The rainy season was due. The absence of moonlight created a dull, dark canopy, the atmosphere an eerie soliloquy that seemed to cast a comforting dark blanket of anonymity, hiding all that wished to remain unseen below. If the six brave children pulled this off just right, they might make it far enough away to be free of danger. Once the rains hit, the roads would deteriorate, quickly turning into chasms and or washboards that would slow Kony's vehicles down to approximately five miles per hour. Potholes would emerge from the rains that could break the axel of a pickup truck or demolish the suspension struts.

Tegene took his position in the bush, perfectly hidden. He saw Celeste walk up near the vehicle and begin to proposition Okello.

"You could have me now if you wanted," she whispered in his ear close enough for her hot breath to caress his skin. "I won't tell Kony. You have begun to appeal to me. If you prove yourself to be the big man where it counts that you claim you are, there are two younger ones, fresh, that you can have as well!" The vibrations of her whisper licked his eardrums, sending the tremble all the way to his loins.

"I will show you how much of a man I am! Come here!" he stammered. "We are far enough away from the others that no one will hear you. Be as loud as you want. I will like that very much, even the look of fear and intimidation in your eyes as I take you, and I will take you—rough style, the way I know you like it! Even if you wanted to resist a little to make it more exciting, no one would hear. We are too far away from them for that."

"Oh, I was counting on that," she said. Her seductive tone hid her deception well. "No one will hear, so come here and show me how much man you really are!" She grabbed the back of his head and forced his mouth onto hers.

"Oh, you want it bad, don't you?" said Okello. Her aggressiveness both startled and further aroused him.

Tegene gritted his teeth as he witnessed the seduction. Even though she was playacting to carry out the plan, it tore him up as deep down inside he loved her. *She really is turning it on and has that bastard's sense of perversion, grabbing him by the throat amongst other places!* he thought. He watched as the whore-mongering sack of trash growled like a lion attacking his prey, proceeding to rip off her blouse in his attempt to take her. It drove Tegene into a state of rage. The time to strike was now, if for no other reason than because he couldn't take any more and wanted to rip Okello's body apart!

However, Celeste took out the stiletto firmly in her hand as she began feeling from his crotch up to his chest. *Oh, no!* Tegene thought. *I told this woman not to play the hero, but there she goes!* Tegene stepped from the shadows wielding his knife, slipping it quietly around Okello's throat, and slashed him to the point of almost decapitation. Celeste, simultaneously with Tegene's assault, pressed the eject button, extending the blade between Okello's ribs, ripping through his lungs and heart. The man died instantly without so much as a whimper, just a look of shock and disbelief on his face, falling to the ground. Blood exploded from him as if it were crimson exhaust from a rocket propelling him through the gates of hell.

The six children commandeered the UAZ vehicle, placing it in neutral as planned, and pushed it down the road about one hundred meters, with Feleke, the smallest, steering a relatively steady course. The getaway had been successful and silent thus far, hence no need for the KPV. They dispensed with the machine gun, both to lose weight and avoid drawing undue attention from UPDF soldiers who were bound to ask more than a few questions of children looking like an assault squad coming into any given village. Then Tegene jumped behind the wheel, turned over the ignition, put it into the proper gears, and stomped down on the accelerator, tearing down the road en route to freedom. But the real journey to freedom meant to make the journey back to a real life, a journey that could take a lifetime in the healing process to get over the hatred and damage done in a massive spiritual assault that blew jagged holes through psyche and soul. But the first step had been accomplished. The road was now open. Over time, they would make the real journey home to a state of peace of mind and wholeness. At the very least, they would arrive at a place they could live with and hopefully considerably more—to reach a point of restoration of the love and joy that had been robbed from them.

Rains began to pour down during the night, washing out some of the roads they had wanted to take. Hence they stayed on the road to Mbale, headed southeast to Tororo, and then crossed over the border into Kenya. They were met at the border by guards who questioned them extensively. The children convinced them that they had been abducted by Kony and forced to fight for him. They had no desire to stay in Uganda, for fear that Kony would take or retake any given village they found sanctuary in and murder them. For the girls, it would be worse. The border guards let them pass, recommending that they go to a first-aid station set up for refugees in Kitale just for that purpose. The guards stood appalled as Tegene described the assault on the IDP camp. He told them of the Serere volunteers who had been massacred along with the officials. The border guards informed their superiors, who in turn informed the Ugandan officials. Eventually the news got back to Serere.

When Nkomo heard the news, he dropped his head, banging it on the table with his hands clasped behind his neck, and cried out in anguish. He sobbed and wailed for hours. He just muttered, "No, *no ... no!*" He was in a state of shock. Even after the real pain and anguish had run its course in Serere, the community was never the same, incapable of being functional again. Brihan and Arusha in particular had become such a beloved part of Serere that the people at the research station would continue to experience breakdowns. At the very least, they all walked around as though they were stumbling through phantom pains brought on by an amputated appendage for months to come.

Nkomo also dreaded James's return and having to break the news to him. After seeing the toll Abai's death took on him, Nkomo knew that this would be mega-fold in comparison. He feared James would lose all control, possibly to the point of taking his own life. Worse yet, he might resurrect the Special Forces warrior inside himself, hunt Kony down, and kill him—kill him in a mad frenzy in the most brutal way possible, which would release destructive mechanisms within James, creating a worse injustice in what it would do to James than the justice in ridding the world of Kony. He would almost be beyond redemption, except for the one answer that James would find more difficult to accept given the magnified level of hatred and insanity that would erupt from hunting down his nemesis and slaughtering him. No doubt James would kill him, for James was a far better warrior than the little tin Caesar, psychopath pretending to be a general. But would James remember what Abai told him regarding Sun Tzu's *Art of War?* Would his temple be in proper order to achieve justice from the hunt, much less heal James or even provide him with shelter from the grief and issues he would have to face from the deaths of his wife and child? Moreover, would it bring either one back? It wouldn't matter to James once he heard the news. Nkomo knew the course James would take. He would hunt Kony down and terminate him with prejudice. To quote Shakespeare, "Cry 'Havoc!' and let slip the dogs of war!"

֍֎֍

James returned from Nairobi completely unaware of exactly what had happened. He flew into Entebbe Airport, seeing the same hustle and bustle that characterized most airports. He stood with baggage in hand, puzzled that no one from the research station had been there to pick him up and drive him back to Serere. He got a taxi and told the driver to take him to the Imperial Hotel. Nkomo had a cousin named Julius who worked there. He could find out from him what had happened and possibly get in touch with someone who would come down with a car and give him a lift back. He wasn't sure if Brihan had completed her work at the IDP camp, so he wasn't surprised when they didn't show at the airport.

Once at the Imperial, a young boy offered him a newspaper. The headlines of the *New Vision* read "Massacre in Teso." His eyes locked onto the headline as his blood vessels began twitching in his temples. His gut grew tight as he forced himself to read the article. It did not list the victims' names. He desperately tried to cling to hope. *Maybe they made it out alive,* he thought. "They had to, they simply had to!" he murmured to himself. He was in a state of shock, which temporarily fought off the alarm and panic that accompanied thoughts of the contrary. He couldn't and wouldn't accept the notion that they had been killed.

He stumbled into the bar at the Imperial Hotel for an engagement with a good bottle of scotch, preferably one at least ten years old.

"Got any ten-year-old Dewar's?" he asked the bartender.

"Yeah, costs though," the bartender replied.

"No problem. Cost doesn't matter. Just bring on the bottle, man!" James said.

"You got it. Tough day?" the bartender asked.

"Let's hope not," James replied.

Down at the end of the bar, a drunk, bent over, his head buried in his arms on the bar, all but passed out, blurted, "I know dat voice, man." Barely lifting his head off of the bar, he slurred out, "Dat you, James? Sorry I didn't pick you at the airport, boss! I got—detained. Bartender, gimme another!" Nkomo demanded.

"I told you, you've had enough!" said the bartender.

"Hey, man, my cousin, y'know—he, like, own this place, y'know, man? Now, give me another whiskey!" Nkomo grew even more demanding.

"Who do you think told me to cut you off? Besides, Julius don't own this place. He's only the manager," said the bartender.

"Aw, hell! He's the black sheep of the family anyway!" Nkomo laughed, holding up his own hand, looking at his own skin.

"Black sheep? Seriously, the black sheep? That's rich!" the bartender said. He casted a sarcastic look with a wry, humorous smile. "Now I know we got to cut you off!"

"Give it to him, on me. I'll take responsibility for him," said James. "We'll stay here tonight. He won't be on the road or anything."

The bartender begrudgingly nodded his approval and poured both scotch on the rocks.

"I'll take care of you, Nkomo," James said. "I wondered why you didn't show up at the airport. Now I know. You heard from Brihan? She and Arusha back from their quixotic chase of windmills yet?"

There was a deafening silence over the bar. Nkomo, his head just off the bar, sat paralyzed, his eyes fixed straight ahead at the mirror.

The bartender just lowered his head and stepped back, turning away from James.

"You gonna take care of me? Who da hell gonna take care of you once I tell you?" responded Nkomo.

"Tell me what? What happened?" James demanded to know.

Nkomo staggered over to him. "They ain't comin' back, boss," he said, choking on grief. "They … ain't comin' back, boss—damn, I'm sorry. I'm so, so … sorry. I'm sorry, boss—boss!"

"Nkomo, what, what—what?" James grabbed Nkomo and lifted him up off of the floor in a state bordering on uncontrollable hysteria.

Nkomo just kept muttering the same words, pitifully, over and over again with tears streaming down his face. "I'm so sorry … sorry, boss, boss, I'm so sorry!" James released his grip in shock. Nkomo collapsed down on his knees, then sprawled back, resting his back and head against the bar sobbing. The bartender took the newspaper and pointed to the headlines with a serious look on his face that reflected remorse as well. He also showed fear, fear of what the news would do to the hearer and the pain that it would inflict. Julius came into the bar.

"You're James Mecklenburg?" he asked.

"Yes," James replied.

"You'd better sit down. I have some bad news for you. Your wife and daughter were amongst the casualties. All those from Serere were murdered. I'm terribly sorry, Mr. Mecklenburg. If there's anything we at the Imperial can do …"

James broke into a fit of rage, interrupting him by grabbing him by his shirt and throwing him over the bar. He screamed in uncontrollable rage, splitting tables in half with single blows and took out the walls with a series of round kicks. He went berserk, totally, completely berserk. Nkomo sat on the floor, his back still resting on the foot of the bar, wailing in agony, horrified, watching as the worst of his anticipated nightmares played out. He raised his hands over his face crying at the sight of his best friend's self-destructing episode, at the agony and anger blasting out of James's soul that seemed to burn the whole bar down like radiation emanating from a nuclear explosion. It took fifteen Ugandan policemen to hold him down, as just five or six weren't enough. He had already thrown them over the side railing out onto the street. Once wrestled down, James just screamed and cried in the greatest outpouring of grief anyone had ever seen. Nkomo crawled over to him, crying, and carefully put his arms around him. James just nuzzled into his right shoulder and sobbed uncontrollably. The police cautiously loosened their hold. Julius explained everything to them. The cops just shook their heads in remorse. Julius poured enough scotch down him to subdue James. The police asked Julius if he wished to press charges. He declined, given the situation and knowing James would pay for all the damages. "But," he asked, "who will pay for the damages done to James from all of this?"

Nkomo looked up at Julius, staring through his own tears, and projected a look as cold as steel into his eyes. "Kony will, with his life!" he muttered grimly.

After James consumed a whole fifth of whiskey, they got a room at the Imperial to sleep it off. James transferred money from his Barclay's account to the hotel's to cover damages and pay for a week's stay at the hotel. Julius knocked on their door, temporarily interrupting their binge drinking long enough to check and see if they were still alive and the room relatively intact.

"Why don't we just move the bar into our room while it's under renovation?" James suggested.

Nkomo quickly nodded his approval. "We'll look after the booze real good, cuz!"

"Yeah, I'm sure you would. No, I don't think so. Drinking up all the inventory might be considered embezzlement by our auditors. Besides, we need spirits for our other customers, and I don't want the guilt of being responsible for your deaths by alcohol poisoning!" said Julius.

"Probably a good idea. Wait—you can die by alcohol poisoning? It's not poisoning—never killed me before!" replied James.

"You're Special Forces. You're tough! You developed a tolerance!" said Nkomo. His speech was just a tinge more slurred than James's. "I'm running out of words—you talk to Julius. You can talk better than me."

"I'm about to correct that right now!" declared James, lifting a new bottle of scotch to his mouth.

"You two ever stop to figure you got a drinking problem?" asked Julius.

"What the hell you talkin' 'bout? We go out. We drink. We get roaring drunk. We fall down. We pass out without hurling all over the place. So, what's the problem? Ain't no problem. You see a problem, Nkomo? I don't see a problem!" responded James.

"I can't see a damn thing, much less any problem," laughed Nkomo.

"I'd say we got this thing down to an art and a science! What do you think, my brother? Do we know how to do this or what?" James said.

"You betcha, boss! Hand me that damn bottle."

"Oh, Sweet Jesus, protect us!" prayed Julius. He began shaking his head and walked out of the room.

The two passed out, then woke up, then drank till they passed out again. They spent the rest of their time getting kicked out of as many bars in Kampala as possible. They drank to overcome the pain, as most do, always hiding from something, the real issues causing the pain in the first place. We're not talking about mere social drinking here. No, quite to the contrary, we're talking about heavy-duty, stinking binge drinking, four sheets gone to the wind, head in the gutter, blast-their-ass-into-next-Tuesday drunk! Eventually, they found that the pain was still there, the reality of the situation hadn't changed at all, and the grim consequences of living life in an imperfect world still had to be dealt with. James pondered over the issue of reclaiming the remains and a proper funeral, dealing with his in-laws in Axum, and above and beyond all, avenging the deaths of his wife and child. He asked Nkomo about heading up to the northern Soroti District, to the IDP camp and at least finding the remains to return them home, either to Serere or Axum for a proper burial. Nkomo doubted if it was even possible to enter that territory, as it still could be under LRA control, and government troops might cut off access in or out. Getting around potential government roadblocks would be the most difficult problem, particularly if they were going to head up there equipped with what James would have him assemble—enough hardware to mount a minisiege of Anzio.

"I won't need that much," James said. "Probably a couple of the new M-20s with laser sights, couple of latest-model AKs with plenty of ammunition. I don't intend to keep them on single shot! Also, we might need a couple of RPGs for distraction. The real big bang will come from the C-4 we're gonna use. Also, get either a couple of those Rambo knives or just machetes. Russkie Spetznatz have those ejector knives; they could come in handy. Two crossbows and—you pretty good with a blowgun? I've seen you use that before. What do you dip those darts in? We need that, definitely."

"Special concoction. Don't worry. It'll work!" responded Nkomo.

"I know you can get all that stuff, right?"

"No problem, boss, you got it. The C-4 will take a little time, but it can be had," Nkomo assured.

"How much time on the C-4?"

"Two or three days, a week tops. The rest you could have tomorrow. I got IOUs I'm pullin' in from all over this half of the continent on everything from intel, arrangements, passage, and equipment, IOUs from a lot of places, ex-pats included," Nkomo replied.

"Start contacting them," James instructed.

"Way ahead of you, boss!" Nkomo's tone reflected his smoldering hate.

"I don't have to ask you how much you're gettin'. I know you're acquiring enough for both of us," James said. His words reflected the sentiment he shared with Nkomo and a bond with the man who literally had James's blood in his veins. It was the tone of assurance in knowing each would go the distance for the other. Both would make the journey to the ends of the earth, to hell's gates if necessary, to stalk Kony down and terminate him with prejudice.

Nkomo looked at him and smiled, the type of smile one would expect on the face of the grim reaper. "They murder Brihan and Arusha, who I loved almost as you, just differently, like a sister, and Arusha, like my own daughter. They also hurt you, my brother. They do all that—they hurt Nkomo. They make my own wife and kids cry. They hurt me. They make the angels cry. They make Nkomo cry. Nobody does that and gets away with it! Nobody! No question about it, boss.

We gonna git 'em! Africa's been playin' games with bastards like that for too long. Rest assured, boss, you know Nkomo's with ya. We gonna take his sorry ass out!"

The bond between the two was a blood bond, both spiritually and literally. Both were the universal donors, O negative, who could give blood to anyone but only receive blood from someone of the same type. Over the years, they had been in scrapes where emergency blood transfusions had been necessary. They were the only ones present at the time whose blood could be used for the other. The two had become brothers. Nkomo had lost one child to AIDS. The child had contracted it through a bad blood transfusion at Mulago Hospital in Kampala. He contemplated suicide, but James pulled him out of it. James reminded him of his other children, not to mention his wife. James would have taken them all in and married her as Nkomo's brother in accordance with tradition, had he been called on to do so. But James convinced him by just giving him someone to hold onto, showing that life was still worth living and to take it one day at a time. The had each other's six. Now James, with no Brihan, no Arusha, or Abai, hadn't any real family, his own in America having already passed. Nkomo was all James had now. And now he would march with James to the four corners of the earth to track Kony down and inform him in no uncertain terms his day of atonement had arrived!

The key was not in acquiring the necessary military hardware. That was easy. They key was in formulating the right strategy, the timing and overall ground game necessary to distract Kony's troops and isolate him. If they could isolate or out-maneuver him into a corner, a secluded compound for instance, accompanied by just a few soldiers, no more than ten, then that would work. They could take out at least five with unique small weapons, such as crossbows and blowguns, before the rest knew they were under assault. Then semiautomatics would take out the rest of Kony's entourage. All guns would be left behind as they moved in for Kony's execution. That's what they made machetes for.

⚬⚬ ⚬⚬

The UPDF ran into ambush after ambush. However, eventually Kony was pushed out of the Soroti District and forced to retreat northward. Nkomo overheard locals working for a faith-based NGO, World Vision. They spoke of "spiritual mapping" they had done. They clearly, firmly believed that satanic spiritual warfare played a huge role in Kony's strategy and that his mix of pagan religions and apostate ritualism that he tried to spin off of Christianity, clearly warping its doctrine out of any proper context, bankrupt of righteous character, rendered this religious whore to become an open target for Satan whether he actually, consciously called on him or not. Kony's heresies were not limited to religious faith but also to political ideology and military strategy. To say the least, he didn't market himself well to locals. More and more people began walking out of the grip of fear to take a defiant stand against him. They were valuable sources of intel. This reveals a critical flaw in so-called revolutionary movements that amount to nothing more than roving gangs of thugs led by false messianic personalities suffering from the worst forms of narcissistic personality disorders. A true revolutionary movement can never believe that the ends justify the means. The beginning premise must be justified itself, or the case can be argued perfectly well and still lead to a false conclusion. More than a mere logician's warning, this generally serves to be the key root of the ideological bankruptcy that begets holocausts and war itself in the first place. Attempts to implement a failed ideology to military strategy will result in a failed praxis. Amongst other results will be the alienation of the general populace and failure to attract true partisans to take up the cause, as Brihan had predicted before she died. Pseudo-revolutions create enemies rather than partisans, undermining the whole effort, contributing to intelligence leaks and ruptured supply lines and thus sow the seeds of their own demise.

Nkomo, in particular, could take advantage of those leaks. He was also not unaware of the important role spiritual warfare played in Africa in general, not just in the effort to defeat Kony. He discussed the matters intensely with World Vision's personnel.

"Africa's past and present feature too many episodes of the supernatural invading the realm of the natural, or temporal, to dismiss our conversation as mere superstition. Such events, particularly when replicated time after time, confound scientists and those who feel that life can be summed up in finite equations, too narrowly defined in parameters of thought that completely disregard the prospects of spiritual warfare's role in determining the outcome. Their arrogance prevents them from deviating away from their closed-off ephemeral worldview, which imprisons their mind to have any concern for their own eternal fate, much less the role of supernatural entities in their lives," said Musoke, one of the project managers. He continued, "By identifying the spiritual forces of darkness at work and in what parts of Uganda they appear to be most active, namely in the vicinity where Kony tends to roam the most, we are able to more clearly identify our objectives in prayer, calling on God's forces of righteousness to bind demonic activity in those areas and break the spiritual darkness. We deny Kony of what he needs the most on a number of fronts. As satanic forces are not omniscient, their activity would be limited to demons, not Satan himself, and to a specific geographic area and persons at any given time. Therefore, if the bound area is liberated by heaven's call and conversely bound by God's protection, Kony's troops will be rendered powerless, incapable of lasting against better-equipped UPDF or even local militia."

The other worker, Mutende, added, "Perhaps just as important is the function of the Holy Spirit in its role of spiritually quickening the spirit, soul, heart, and mind, further strengthening the undaunted resolve of an African people who refuse to let the precious voice of freedom die. This rises up partisans against Kony and those who will work with government troops to get rid of him. God's voice coming as a powerful whirlwind, felt in the heart more than audibly heard by the ear, liberates masses who had been enslaved, paralyzed by fear by forces of darkness. Their chains are broken, their gripping fear disintegrates, their paralysis overcome, and a tidal wave of courage rises up in their veins, powering legs to walk and arms to fight back against Kony, if armed only with a hand plow and five acres of land. Liberty first requires the spiritual quickening to stimulate the dynamics of freedom within a person to make him or her come alive to win the battles in the temples of prayer prior to the first shot fired on the battlefield. This is necessary before any human speeches can resonate. The partisan must first individually make that choice, to see the champion within himself or herself respond to God's call for justice before partisans can all rise up as a force and move beyond mere military campaigns to build a nation. Any band of partisans, much less a nation, that refuses to do so refuses to be led. And one cannot lead a nation that refuses to be led."

"That is true," Nkomo acknowledged. "My brother in the cause and I intend to go after Kony and eliminate him. I assure you we have skills to do so, to isolate and kill him. You want to throw in some prayers in there for us? 'Cause, sometimes you know, God calls on a champion to draw a sword more than in just the spiritual sense. Ecclesiastes is pretty clear on that topic."

"Quite true," said Mutende. "Your heart has to be spiritually right, and for a combat soldier, that doesn't mean to consider all forms of killing to be a sin. Even Jesus only used the Hebrew word *RotzeaCH*. He never made reference to the word *MotyaMal*. The thing is, you have to be committed to the right principle and exact that cost, use your skills in a specific fashion that extracts the target and the evil, dispensing with the bacteria trying to kill the body. That doesn't mean you go crazy and extract a thousand eyes for an eye. You get me?"

"I read you, bwana," replied Nkomo. "What we need is your prayers and any people you got that we can get intel from."

"No problem on either account," Musoke said.

"You know where Kony is now?" Nkomo asked. "Most people think he been driven back, you know, but nobody, including Museveni, know actually where he is."

"We've got a general idea. He's actually left Uganda. He seems to be drifting back and forth between Sudan, northeast Congo, and the Central African Republic. He's taking advantage of the chaos caused by the civil war up there in Sudan. Everybody's so busy fighting each other that he just seems to slip through everything; nobody's got time to pay any attention to Kony. He's mostly just trying to rummage through the country in search of food. He's been pretty badly beaten up, doesn't have much left. Listen, we've got people up there, contacts in all kinds of places from here to Yei and Juba, who can give you a more accurate lock on where he is. They can also help you with supplies or shelter. You know, they can accommodate you while still protecting your anonymity. That you need more than anything—to be able to get in and get out without attracting any more attention than need be, particularly when you get to dealing with army roadblocks from one side or the other, SPLA or the government. If you're carrying a lot, they will happily lighten your load."

"You need something of a distraction. Those troops are going days without eating. You need something to isolate Kony from his troops," added Mutende.

"Food would make a good distraction," replied Nkomo. "It would make a very effective weapon, more so than the gun or sword at the outset. I understand that they are hitting UNDP relief camps and storehouses, sometimes even killing ex-pats in search of food and other supplies, like medical supplies. Once distracted, a few well-placed rockets or grenades could send them flying off in separate directions, forcing him to divide his forces long enough for us to make our move."

"You may not need that much, depending on where you find him. If he's hiding out near the Jur River, you might use food to lure his entire remaining army across the bridge. They may be so focused on getting well fed for the first time in about a month that they won't notice you or care about Kony. But life is unpredictable, so be well equipped just in case. If you have to keep them over the bridge, then use your explosives, maybe to blow the bridge and isolate him from his army," said Musoke.

Nkomo took a deep breath and said, "Okay, you line us up. The rest we'll handle. In terms of local authorities yelling about ex-pats running around the place with guns and all, let's just say this conversation never took place, and I was never here, if that makes your situation any safer—politically, legally, I mean."

"Don't worry about it or us. Nobody has any love for Kony, and the government would really like to see him go away," Mutende replied.

The plans were laid out. The necessary provisions were procured, and James and Nkomo gathered in more intelligence feedback as it came in. Kony's location was identified. Nkomo used his contacts to pull in the IOUs and greased a few palms to be able to clear borders armed, without so much as drawing a hint of suspicion much less arrest. Then the two set out to avenge not just the deaths of Arusha and Brihan but all those lives Kony had destroyed. This was unfortunately a situation where justice would be achieved only when blood was paid for with blood. If Kony wanted forgiveness for his crimes, he would have to pray to God for it. James was too human, by his own power, to grant it.

⚹⚹⚹

They set out, bound for Gulu and then would cross the border into Sudan, meeting with Musoke and Mutende's contact in Juba. Kony had retreated to a town on the Jur River in southwest Sudan called Wau. Wau had already seen more than its fair share of war. Wau meant "City of Fire" and lay in the middle of territory claimed by the Dinka, Nuer, and Shulik. It was a virtual no-man's-land, an area contested over for years, and in the most recent conflict, it had changed hands repeatedly between Khartoum and the SPLA. Much of the town had been flattened by war. Kony parked most of his army near the one bridge that crossed over the Jur River to give an escape valve. Control over the transportation logistics provided the escape route to retreat either into Congo or the Central African Republic. Additionally, should he choose to escape, he could blow the bridge and provide a serious obstacle for anyone chasing after him. The chaos in the area had given him a cloaking device, as every soldier in the area, including any UN peacekeeping forces, were so occupied with the ongoing war that no one had time to dedicate to the hunt for Kony. However, that same chaos and logistics would prove to be a double-edged sword. A small contingent led by someone with Nkomo's influence could slip thorough virtually invisible to Kony and be lurking in the bush ready to pounce on its prey at a moment's notice.

James and Nkomo acquired a couple of Land Rovers as opposed to military, all-terrain vehicles, like a UAZ or Humvee, so as to be less conspicuous. They also contracted three larger trucks, or lorries, and drivers to move tons of food up the west side of the Jur. The lorries were to bear the logos of either the UNDP or some other NGOs involved in relief work. These were the lures to be parked on the west side of the Jur Bridge, just outside of Wau. They would be near the bridge but just far enough away to ensure drawing the entire army over there and leaving the bridge free and clear for the rest of James's purposes. The drivers would keep a safe distance, abandoning the trucks and hiding in the bush before using RPGs to land some grenades close but not too close, thus promoting the illusion of an attack that had forced the trucks off the road and made the drivers flee their vehicles. The drivers would commandeer a Land Rover about a hundred meters from the bridge as a getaway vehicle for the drivers once the attack had been staged, to beat a fast path out of there. James and Nkomo would place C-4 plastic explosives underneath the bridge attached to the girding. The food would be too irresistible to attract merely a few soldiers. Several if not all of Kony's remaining army would charge across the bridge toward the convoy, driven by their ravenous hunger to "steal the food." After most had crossed the bridge, James would set off the C-4, trapping Kony on his side of the Jur, with hardly any support at all. James and Nkomo would then move in on Kony and whatever entourage he had left for the kill.

James was totally focused. In this mode, he was a perfect killing machine. He was Achilles without the heel. His mind, well-tuned for this, worked in a perfect synergy with motion and terrain to become the most effective weapon in combat. However, the soul is the most effective weapon for justice. Nkomo occasionally glanced over at James with that question running through his mind. After it was all over, would it truly be all over? Or would James wake up at 4:30 in the morning fighting this war and countless others raging within him in a cold sweat for years to come? Would he merely execute Kony or unleash the fabled dogs of war in the form of post-traumatic stress disorder, butchering himself as well? Nkomo put it out of his mind. Going into a fight, one had to be single-minded, clearly focused on the objective at hand and force the rest into the shadows, or you wouldn't come back at all. Regardless of the potential outcome, Nkomo would fight side by side with his brother to the end. James would do as much for him.

They arrived ahead of the food convoy and found the bridge completely unguarded. They stealthily waded into the water by the bridge and set the C-4 in place, then got out of the water, became the shadows, and backtracked to their vehicles to wait for the proper moment.

The food convoy reached the west bank of the Jur, about fifty meters or so from the bridge. The drivers cut their engines and quietly got out of their trucks. They took cover in the bush a safe distance from the targets and opened fire with the RPGs, being careful not to hit the trucks or inflict any damage on them or their cargo. The drivers nodded to each other then took off for the Land Rover safely concealed in a wooded area some distance west of the bridge.

Kony's guards woke up, startled by the explosions. They asked each other, who had fired the RPGs and at what. Many came running down to see what happened. Their eyes widened as if to eclipse the rest of their faces when they saw the food trucks.

"Relief trucks!" one exclaimed. "That means food and medical supplies!"

Scores of Kony's army, practically all remaining, awoke to the clamor and proceeded to charge across the bridge in a storm of desperation, given that many hadn't eaten in two or three days. Supply lines had been severed. There had been no support coming from anywhere. Kony's army was literally starving to death in a war of attrition. Child soldiers lacking the maturity of adults quickly lost faith. Those who hadn't just straggled off no longer cared about Kony's objectives as hunger, despondency, fear of starving to death, and the pains of lost loved ones began to churn inside of them. Only the fear of being caught by government troops and the possible consequences kept them from leaving. The guilt and shame that accompanied vivid memories, images of home demurred by the atrocities they were forced to commit seemed to rape their very consanguinity and lashed their emotions like a cat-o'-nine-tails whip. It left them bewildered and confused. The only thing they knew for sure was that their bellies burned with hunger. The assault on the food trucks became a free-for-all. Only about five aids remained with Kony. It was better than what James and Nkomo had hoped for.

As the children broke open the crates of fresh fruit, bread, matoke, groundnuts, and canned food, including meat and other delicacies, tearing into it before any officers could take inventory, James sat quietly, observing the carnage, waiting for the precise moment. He watched with somewhat of a benign form of reserved sympathy. He felt a form of ill-disposed, congruous benevolence, despite his many qualms about this army. An oxymoron? Perhaps. But if ever there was a true moment for this paradox of emotions, this was it. He really felt no ill will to the children, as they were victims of Kony too. James merely wanted to isolate Kony. He saw what appeared to be the last of the stragglers cross the bridge for the food. It was enough to give Nkomo and him sufficient odds to carry out the rest of the mission. He hit the button on the detonator, sending out the frequency that set off the C-4.

The explosion was a little more than they had anticipated. "Ehhhh— better to go long on the amount of C-4 used than too little," said James. "This way we're sure not to leave any of the bridge standing. Don't want to allow any of the troops to cross back over the bridge and throw a fly in the ointment!"

Concrete girding, iron, and steel railings flew up into the nighttime sky, with the rest of the bridge collapsing into the river, submerging into its depths. The children only looked up momentarily. Some thought that maybe Kony had placed mines that accidentally went off, triggered by something. Others just jumped in surprise or sat stunned. However, given that they had just latched onto the first real food in months, none really cared about the bridge, given their higher priority. They quickly went on about their business, gorging themselves on glorious, glorious food!

James removed his shirt and smeared dull, dark facial paint across his face and applied it more generously around his upper body and back to dull any possible shine from the moonlight that would give them away. Additionally, he put on green camouflage paint around his face. Not only would it blend in with any visible foliage but would cast a horrifying specter in Kony's eyes before he died. Nkomo applied the same. James put on his Special Forces beret and muttered, "Death before dishonor!" Nkomo nodded. The two made their way up the east bank of the Jur toward Wau, the City of Fire, to burn Kony to the ground.

Kony, having been awakened by the noise, ordered one of his subordinates to restart the campfire near his tent. He sent two of his personal entourage to see what the commotion was all about and ordered that if there were indeed food trucks to procure as much as possible for him. That left only three others with him, two adult officers and one twelve-year-old. Those were better odds than either James or Nkomo had hoped for.

James motioned for Nkomo to take the left flank as James moved in from the right. James and Nkomo decided to stash their assault rifles and chose instead to go with two crossbows, a blowgun, and machetes. Given the lack of personnel accompanying Kony, there was no need for the M-20s. Better to keep an economy of weapons and the operation sleek, maintaining the top priority—expediently, with calculated precision, eliminate with as little fanfare or disturbance possible, avoiding an onrush of Kony's troops down on them.

Kony stepped back behind the tent to relieve himself. Once he was out of sight, James and Nkomo fired razor-sharp arrows from crossbows, hitting both adult officers in the neck, tearing through both sides, rupturing the carotid arteries and jugular veins, killing them instantly. Nkomo picked up the blowgun and fired off a drug-tipped dart, hitting the child's neck, rendering him unconscious before he could even turn and notice the fate of his adult superiors. James and Nkomo darted through the campsite, quickly grabbing the bodies and flinging them into the bush. They stood lurking in the shadows waiting for Kony to return.

Kony came back, only to find his remaining entourage missing. *They went out to get some food perhaps?* he thought, but he had given no order for them to do so. He called for them, but they did not come. He turned around to look in the bush to see if there was any sign of his errant insubordinate soldiers. When he turned back, he saw the most imposing figure he'd ever seen with fixed eyes of steel staring right through him above the flickering firelight. Kony, both perplexed and startled by James's advance, didn't know what to make of him at first. But what he was staring at was the worst possible sight Kony could have ever laid eyes on. Nkomo stepped out of the shadows into the firelight as well.

"Who the hell are you?" Kony muttered at both.

"The angel of death," James solemnly replied, his eyes not wavering from his target. The tone was not to be mistaken for lack of resolve or hate, for James had an ample supply of both. He would operate from a coolly collected resolve to methodically release that anger in the most efficient manner possible, inflicting as much pain as possible, extracting revenge or merely just avenge. To him, the two were now one and the same!

James motioned for Nkomo, who threw Kony a machete. James then motioned to Kony to come to his side of the fire.

"I'd like to know who a man is before I fight him. Who are you?" he asked again.

"You want to know who I am? Tell me, did you know the names of everybody you slaughtered at that IDP camp in Soroti District? Did you even know the names of the Serere volunteers, including the Ethiopian woman and her child? You raped her and slaughtered her. You shot the child. Her name was Brihan, and her child, Arusha. They may have been nothing to you, but they were everything to me!" James retorted.

"Brihan and Arusha—yes, yes, I remember them—collateral damage. Who were they to you?"

"Collateral damage, my ass! You practically wiped out a defenseless IDP camp. It wasn't even a legit military operation, and even if it was, this took place after the fact of combat where you raped and purposely murdered them! They were nothing to you, but they were more than the sun, the moon, and all the stars in the sky to me. They were my wife and child! Blood must be paid for with blood! Prepare to die, you bastard!" James roared.

Kony stepped from behind the fire. He looked at James's Special Forces beret and the tattoo on his shoulder and began to feel more than a bit queasy. James's eyes intently tracked Kony's movements.

Nkomo stood by with arms folded, broadcasting a look of stone-cold anger-turned-hate.

Kony took a few practice swings, slicing the air. Nkomo laughed, mocking the little Napoleon. James gave a half smile and then took his own machete and slashed his own chest diagonally without flinching. He smiled even broader and took a proper stance to engage in combat.

Kony moved to his left. James countered by moving to his as the two began to draw a circle of engagement, a circle of death for one of them. The tension grew so thick you could cut it with one of their machetes maybe, for it was way too intense to cut it with an ordinary knife. Kony made the first move, trying to swing crossways, which James expertly countered, knocking the machete back, practically out of Kony's hand. James began to glare and smile at him. Kony tried a thrust only to have it repelled and countered by James's elbow to Kony's face, breaking his nose. Blood streamed from both nostrils down across his mouth, pouring off his chin. Kony tried to wipe it off, but more continued to flow as if the very pigments of his facial skin were changing to crimson. As he staggered back, his eyes went wild with rage, and he vaulted off his heels into a wild, tragic lunge at James, throwing a clumsy roundhouse swing with his machete. James ducked the move and then slashed the muscles of Kony's right shoulder, gave him a snap kick to the solar plexus, and flew into a round kick, landing it firmly on the right side of Kony's face, fracturing his jaw and cheekbone. James darted to Kony's right, slashing his knees, severing his anterior cruciate ligaments (ACLs), and moved behind Kony, taking a backswing and severing his posterior cruciate ligaments as well. With the same swipe, he hacked Kony's patella ligaments, totally depriving Kony of his legs. Kony dropped to his knees, screaming in pain. James moved in and slashed his chest as Kony continued to scream, screams that began to turn into pitiful cries for mercy, begging James for that ration of humanity Kony had refused to give any of his victims. Kony should have directed his petitions to a higher authority, for James, being only human, was definitely the wrong person to ask, given James's disposition. He had no time to listen to disingenuous pleas from someone as despicable as Kony, someone who only wanted to save his own skin, lacking any true remorse, totally unrepentant, showing all the sincerity of a bottom-feeding lawyer in a plea bargain for a serial killer with a DA. Forgiveness was not amongst the top ten on the Special Forces warrior's to-do list for the day.

James began to methodically dissect and torture Kony, stabbing into his pressure points and jabbing glowing-hot wooden embers from the fire into the wounds, sending searing jolts of pain through him, like current from an electric chair, with the current set on torture rather than kill, to drive Kony into a fit of delirium.

Nkomo stared at what was becoming another specter of the macabre. "C'mon, boss! Get this over with. Finish this clown and let's get the hell out of here!" he pleaded to James.

James didn't heed. He struck Kony with the butt of his machete firmly enclosed in his fist, knocking him flat on his back. James contemplated cutting his arms and legs off but chose something else instead. With one blow of his machete, James ripped Kony's zipper and button out of his pants, completely exposing his genitals.

"Not much to brag about, are they, Kony?" he sneered.

With one swing at his crotch, James castrated Kony's pathetic excuse for organs he had used to desecrate Brihan with and tossed them into the fire. Then James, as swiftly as a surgeon, opened up Kony's chest and severed his heart free from his chest. He reached in and grasped it with one hand and simultaneously bent over and drew in a mouthful of Kony's blood. Then he spat it into his face while crushing the amputated heart in his hand and threw it into the fire, all quick and expedient enough for Kony to see before he faded from this existence and woke up in hell. As a final playful gesture, James decapitated his enemy and kicked the head like a football, where it ricocheted off three trees.

James stood up, drenched in Kony's blood, and let loose with a roar that would rattle the graves of Africa's ancestors, with a crazed look in his eyes. There was silence now, dead silence. James stood gasping for breath from an emotional eruption that approximated Vesuvius spewing flaming, hot lava in the destruction of Pompeii. Nkomo just stared at him in horror.

"C'mon, Nkomo. Let's get the hell out of here!"

Nkomo just shook his head. "No, no ... boss, no—you kill a man—like that ... I ... Nkomo walk another way! You kill a man like that, you not accomplish much. You kill a man like that, I walk another way!" Nkomo lamented in fear of what James seemed to have become and what he would become, afraid that the door James appeared to have opened would only allow the demons from hell reprieve and possibly shut the door to his own sanity.

"Well, to hell with you then!" yelled James.

James staggered out of the camp, blood drenched, not feeling much like a saint or avenging angel and terribly nonchalant over whether he was sinner. Nkomo just thought for a minute and said, "Aw, what the hell!" and proceeded to walk behind James, following him to the Land Rover. James's soul was tortured but not beyond redemption and needed an exorcism in the form of love and companionship in his hour of crisis. Nkomo walked up to James, who was bent over the car, resting his head and arms on the hood.

"I'm here, boss," Nkomo said gently.

"Well, boss, what do you think? Time to go?" James asked.

Nkomo smiled gently but still kept a look of seriousness in his eyes. "Boss, what the hell you think you accomplish up there, huh? What the hell you think you just do, huh? You think you accomplish something up there? Yeah, you rid the world of Kony—you accomplish justice there. But what kind of justice you do for you? You kill a man like that—set a whole slew of demons out of hell's gates. Look what you've done to you! You just stuck a stick in a mud hole and shaken up all kinds a poisonous snakes with the spiritual energy you release today. Kony, that bastard, he dead. You paid back a blood price that had to be paid with blood, had to be answered, but there was no honor achieved in the way you do it. You makin' demons howl with delight with the madness and evil you release inside and outside of you. You had just cause to kill him, but did you lose it all in the way you kill him? You save the world from Kony, but who gonna save you from you?"

James took a Gerry can of water and washed Kony's blood off his body. "The water cleanses me physically from the blood. But what will wash away the filth in my soul?" James asked.

"Blood already been shed for that: the blood of Jesus. I'll be here for you always, you know that. But that blood waitin' for you now," said Nkomo. "You just got to make that choice, because God gave free will. He don't impose. Love not like that. You got to choose—you got to make that decision. Like Mr. Abai said. You remember all that? You need all that stuff now. You need to go up to Axum. That thing they have up there—that Ark of the Covenant thing? You got to check all that out and come to terms with the deaths of three people from up there, Brihan, Arusha, and Abai. I'll go with you if you want, you know. You know Nkomo. I'm with you to the end!"

James clasped Nkomo's forearm as Nkomo clasped his.

"Okay, but for right now, though, let's just go home."

They took off in the Land Rover, headed back for Uganda. However, the journey through grief and healing would be a lot longer one.

⚬๑෧ ෧๑⚬

James and Nkomo mulled around Serere for a few months, basically laying low. Reports of Kony's death were starting to filter back to Uganda. However, they were "filtered" with misinformation, mostly from the LRA claiming that Kony was still alive, that only a doppelgänger had been killed and that the LRA would regroup and launch a new counteroffensive.

"Doppelgänger, my ass!" said James. "It was him, and they know it!"

"Doppelgänger? What's that?" Nkomo asked.

"A double," James replied. "A double that's used to pose for the real thing to throw off would-be assassins like us!"

"Man, ain't nobody gonna make a double dose of a sick bastard like that. But y'know, boss, something about all this BS comin' out from all angles tips a guy off on somethin'. We kind of suspected but never talked about it until now. Don't sound like all this propaganda crap just comin' from the LRA. It seems to be comin' from other sources. It's like, maybe Kony was convenient or somethin' for some other bastards with political intent. Then he go crazy on them, out of control, and not be able to control him anymore, like Frankenstein's monster, and he become more than just a little bit of an embarrassment to people, people local too-not outsiders, not *muzungus*. Rumor has it he got a lot of financial help from Africans living abroad and some local politicians who don't like Museveni. That diaspora, as they call it, not considered to be foreigners by us. They still Africans who just usin' money from the outside. They lose their roots, and some do. Then they muzungus too—outsiders. But I don't know. Maybe they just like corrupt pariahs here. In that way, they not change at all."

"I'm sure conspiracy theories abound, Nkomo. Some days, particularly when you checkin' that stuff out, you da boss, not me!" James said.

"We both the boss, boss, particularly over that bottle of scotch we knockin' off!"

"Damn right! That sucker doesn't stand a chance against us! You know, whether it was Kisi Besigy, other political interests against the president, or even Museveni himself who wants a convenient war to serve as a distraction and rallying point, a type of counterpoint to have people rally against Kony and attract disingenuous support for himself so he can buy time to either build this country or rape it and get away with it— who knows? We've seen stranger things happen in Africa. Africa is a land of exciting mysteries!" James said. Though being facetious, there was a hint of seriousness in his tone. "Either way, I don't give a damn! The man was a monster who took everything I had, like he did to a lot of other people. We know he deserved to die! I killed him for everybody. What you're hintin' at is that though a lot will appreciate it, there are some, some maybe in high places, that won't. We better lay low just to see how the wind is gonna blow on this thing. Then I'm off to Axum. This thing up in Ethiopia, I got to do by myself. Only I and I alone can confront this one. This battle is strictly mine."

"I know, boss. You know I'd go with you if you wanted, but this thing, these demons, they all yours. You got to confront them on your own. I was hoping you'd see that, for your own sake."

♦♦♦

James pondered over all of his past situations, the death of his father, Kennedy, Brihan, Arusha, Abai, his experiences in Vietnam, those things that stuck a blade in him and twisted it. He mulled over those sparks that ignited more flames, sometimes flash fires. Other times they just left smoldering coals that refused to burn themselves out. At times he sought to use them as sources of motivation, but they were false sources, false motivations. Genuine motivation has to stem from a healthier perspective, a more valid context of how one views the past. It requires that a person unchain himself or herself from the past to be free to walk in the present, much less set proper goals to advance into the future. True motivation must move a person toward something not running away from fears, a positive conquest of adversity and not a panic-driven negative retreat.

He took a leave of absence and drove a newly acquired Land Rover to Ethiopia. He drove in a relative state of peace. His route took him through Kenya, where he stopped off at two of his favorite places: Lakes Naivasha and Nakuru, where thousands of flamingos habituated. He always felt a greater sense of peace there, like cleansing saltwater rather than mere chicken soup for the soul, something that spoke to him of purity, preservation, substance, and cleansing, as if it alone could rid him of impurities.

He witnessed the winged ballerinas of white alabaster and cream-sporting pink highlights and black tips strut across the aqua-blue mirror that had become their stage for an unchoreographed spectacle. Sunlight graced the mirror, brilliantly illuminating its vibrancy, revealing contrasting shades of aqua, cyan, and indigo as it cascaded down across the glassy water, then gently danced on the ripples of Lake Nakuru's shoreline before darting ashore, disappearing in the trees. The scenery spoke with such imagery, as if light moved the objects more than the gentle breeze, which wafted up the brine of the salt lake into his nostrils. He closed his eyes and inhaled as it acted more powerfully than any man-made narcotic, streaming away cares and tensions, leaving him in a blissful state. All muzungu baggage must be discarded, as Africa has no tolerance for it when crossing through this rite of passage. Its flamingos are the ballerinas who suddenly spread their wings, triggering a flash of pink, turned magenta, turned crimson as they took flight into streaming rays of sunlight, leaving the concourse on a brief semicircular flight pattern before landing fifty yards from where they embarked. It all spoke to him in a mystical experience unparalleled by anything but a direct encounter with Almighty God.

He watched the landing of new, smaller ballerinas, donning pink plumage. The greater and lesser troupes interwove in their dance amongst one another. The lesser flamingos, with brighter pink plumage, danced intermittently with their larger cousins, the greater flamingos, bending over so gracefully to snatch tasty morsels out of the salty brine waters.

His feet sank in the sandy salt-crusted marsh as he photographed with his eyes, having no need of a camera, for like Karen Von Blixen, the colors of Africa were vividly etched in his mind, his soul, his spirit. He was reminded of a line by Bob Seger in his classic "Traveling Man"; only Bob didn't get it quite right. He talks only of women he has known in the past. But in comparison to this, where one sees a mural of agape love painted by God's finger, if Bob's little affairs are all he has to make him a wealthy soul, then Bob has to be the poorest guy on the planet. It was the experiences like this at Lake Nakuru, etching indelible impressions on his mind, that truly made James a wealthy soul, albeit tortured, but still wealthy nonetheless.

He traveled north, taking the highway through Nyehururu and around Mt. Kulal into the Turkana Region. He drove through the semiarid terrain, the dry red-clay soil dotted with acacia thorn trees and a bit of sage-colored brush amidst the bleach-blond grasses that rolled out to the bluffs in the distance, stretching out to meet a radiant blue sky at the horizon. As dusk approached, the sunset stretched fiery orange bursts and red trails that seemed to reach down and nourish the red-clay soils with enhanced coloration, making the whole terrain give off a foreboding but spectacular display. The rustic beauty produced a tranquil-like alcohol-induced effect, which intrigued him as he was stone-cold sober. Glints of scarlet hues, chards of light intermingled with natural sunlight rays, caressing his face, all of which seemed to give him a greater sense of clarity and settled comfort. He crossed over the border and got a hotel room at Mega. From there, he traveled northward and west to Addis, Bahir Dar, Gonder, and finally to Axum. Once there, his first stop would be the cemetery, then his in-laws'.

⁕⁕⁕

James stood over the graves of the three people who had meant the most to him in his later years: Abai, Brihan, and Arusha. Having been recovered by the Ugandan government from the IDP camp upon Kony's retreat, Brihan and Arusha's bodies would have been interned in a mass grave along with countless other unidentified victims. However, Nkomo's wife had identified the bodies and had them placed in separate body bags for burial next to Abai. James had been unaware of the events, having been in a dazed, drunken stupor much of that time. Many thought it just as well for him to stay back in Soroti, or even Kampala, for fear of what his reaction would be once the bodies had been identified. Even so, he did pull himself together to attend the funeral. The funeral, closed casket, had been a private one with only family, which included not only James and his in-laws but also Nkomo and his family.

Now, James stood emotionless over the graves and placed flowers at the headstones of each. His silence was more an absence of words and emotions choking on the gripping paralysis like one would experience from the early stages of cardiac arrest, due to his inability to deal with the grief, as opposed to a reverent silence in respect of the dead. He wanted to feel! Oh, how he wanted to feel again and unload it all! Part of him wanted to jump in the graves and hug all three, and part of him wanted to just run. But all of him knew he had to come to terms with this, or he was already dead before going into the grave, a lifeless ghost that would just float through this existence, never carrying on with the goals that the family had championed and never doing any justice to their lives. That wouldn't be what any of them would have wanted. He had to recover and carry on, for their legacy deserved at least that much and more.

He drove to Mama Tena's house. His mother-in-law came out to meet him. The two just looked at each other, their eyes reflecting an ocean of emotions. As if the tide came in, they fell into each other's embrace and cried.

"Welcome home, son. It's been too long."

"I know. I couldn't. Not at least till I took care of unfinished business."

"I heard about this. I knew it was you. Gruesome as it was—he deserved it! He deserved it!"

"Yeah, I kind of went—a little crazy. I don't think I picked up any of his demons. Hell, I've had too many of my own to the point that I don't think there's room for any more. Still, I've got to deal with all of—"

James completely broke down in midsentence and just sobbed. Mama Tena, the one who heals, just held onto him with a teary-eyed look of sympathy. She was the first step in the healing process.

Enku came out. She was home on semester break. She hugged and kissed James and then motioned for them all to come inside for coffee and cake. Abai's sons were still up in the hills tending to the cattle, carrying on with the family tradition. The three sat down to relax, chat, and begin restoring the warmth of family as a healing balm, like the balm of Gilead to the vicious wounds that left them all ragged from the torturous events of the past.

Daybreak brought bright glints of sunlight into James's face, stirring him from sleep. It had been a restless night, like all had been since Brihan and Arusha's deaths. He had been running on a pure adrenaline rush from stalking Kony and the drive to kill. Once that had been accomplished, the limbo and lethargy set in, which accompanied chronic depression, weighing him down like a ball and chain. He glumly stared at the blue sky through the window above his bed for about fifteen to twenty minutes, staring, just … staring. Any number of thoughts wished to run through his mind, but they would have to get in line and wait their turn. He just stared. It was too early to think, regardless of what time it was; it was all too early. He had just woken up. He … just … stared.

Then he spontaneously said, "Time to get up," and roused himself out of bed. He didn't bother to shower or shave, just put on his clothes and slipped into a worn pair of boat decks and walked into the kitchen.

Mama Tena stood in the kitchen by the coffee pot on the stove. Seeing his condition, she motioned for him to take a seat.

"Have some coffee, straight—no whiskey or scotch this time. You need to perk up a little this morning. How do you feel? Hangover?"

"Yeah, a little. Polished off a bottle of scotch in my room last night after everybody went to bed."

"I know. Not much gets by me in this house. It's okay. Not that I mind. But I felt you needed some pretty strong coffee this morning."

He sat down for breakfast, observing the vapor raising up from his hot coffee.

"It's Harrar, a different kind of blend than what I normally get—not quite like Yergachef or Sidamo but still quite good," said Mama.

"I think it's the same blend Brihan served me when I first met her. She did the whole thing, the entire coffee ceremony for me," recalled James.

"She was special. We all loved her and Arusha. We were all hit hard by the murders. You have to get over this and move on like we all have to do. Life is for the living."

"Yeah, that's assuming you have a life worth living. You first have to be alive, feel alive. Not like this. I don't feel very much alive, rather dead inside. Don't worry. I'm not contemplating suicide or anything like that. I'll plow through it; it's just that my soul and spirit feel dead. I'd like them to come alive again."

"There is someone that can help with that. The same person incidentally who taught Brihan the coffee ceremony—how to do the long pour, the whole thing."

"Who's that?"

"The same abba at the cathedral who performed the ceremony for you two. He's just returned from Jerusalem. You should talk with him."

"Why not? Wouldn't hurt."

Abai's sons, Adamu (born of the red earth) and Azmera (harvest), entered the dining room, shaking James's hand and embracing him. They exchanged morning pleasantries and sat down for breakfast.

They had both gone into agricultural fields, one majoring in agricultural engineering and the other ag-business and agricultural economics. Both had enough elective hours in animal husbandry and such courses as agronomy to be aptly qualified to take the family business up to the next level, with some exceptions—the exceptions that could be filled by James and his expertise and experience. Both the boys spent a great deal of time up at "Abai's Rock," sometimes talking about him and what he taught them, sharing the wisdom the old man imparted or just contemplating on their own. Other times they just left flowers or some other relic on the rock, making it a shrine of sorts to Abai's memory.

They discussed irrigation with James and water harvesting, recommending that he go up into the hills with them to graze the livestock. They impressed the notion upon him it was not just to be seen as "the place where Abai died," but where, indeed, the old man became alive. It was his favorite place where he received great inspiration for his poetry and took down notes, as well as found it fitting to be the place where he took his last breath, peacefully with dignity. What Abai had found invigorating up there, James would too. He might even feel Abai's presence up there, have that spirit reach out and touch him or hear the voice of God in his heart. Either way, he needed something to distract him from wallowing in the grief while providing a healing balm at the same time.

They also talked of plans to expand the agricultural business of the family, making it more profitable. They needed his help and guidance in this. Besides, all would be great to reestablish intimacy and strengthen family bonds to help James heal, for the last thing he needed was to tuck himself away in isolation.

James agreed, but first he had to contact the abba at the Cathedral of St. Mary of Zion, he told them. Depending on when and how long his meeting with the abba would be, he'd join them in the hills later. James's appetite began to perk up, and he asked for a second helping. Mama Tena smiled. This was a good sign.

James pondered over the topics he had discussed with Adamu and Azmera. These ideas were very appealing to him. Possibly he would extend his leave of absence from Serere. Outside of Nkomo and his, there wasn't much left for him there anymore. He needed both his immediate family and something new at the same time. He continued to think about it as he passed by the Chapel of the Tablets on his way to the cathedral. He nodded at the guardian of the chapel.

"Dinaneh," he greeted him.

"Dinaneh," the monk relied with a smile.

James just looked at the chapel where legend held that the lost Ark of the Covenant was located. Was it really there? Did it really possess the power some claimed it had? He wondered about that and all the mysteries surrounding the ark that people talked about. These were questions that the abba could probably answer. Did he need to touch it to be healed? What power could and would heal him? He proceeded to the cathedral. Hopefully he would find answers there.

⁂

He approached the doors of the cathedral, somewhat intimidated by its architectural stature. He stood motionless for a few moments, wondering whether to knock or just open the door and walk in. Then he shook his head. "Of course you just walk in. Who's gonna hear you knock in a cathedral this big? Besides, you always just walk in."

He opened the door and stepped through the archway. He looked upon the grandeur of the sanctuary, the ornate door, and memories raced through his mind, memories of Brihan and their marriage. He closed his eyes and just shook for a few moments. Then he opened them and proceeded to force himself to look at the place of love, inhale the quaint, pungent aroma of incense that lingered in the wood, the walls, the ceiling, not just the air. He forced himself to stand up to the inner fears and muster up the courage to face his inner demons and look at the palace of his nuptials.

He walked around a bit and spotted a person dressed in black robes, knelt over in prayer. Abba Atatafe (one who chronicles) got up, crossed himself, then turned around to see James standing at the back of the church.

"Good to see you again. I've been expecting you, James," said Abba.

"How'd you know I was coming? What, some sort of prophetic inclination or somethin'?"

"No. Cell phone!" He held up his new Motorola phone. "We're no longer in a blackout zone! You're mother-in-law called. Amazing stuff, this new high technology!" he said with a beaming smile. "How are you doing, my son? I understand you've been going through some rough times. In fact, you've been going through some rough times throughout most of your life. I'm aware of your involvement. Don't worry. Everything you say here is safe, covered by priest/parishioner confidentiality."

"Think I need to jump into a confession booth or something?"

"You need something more than confession. You sure don't need condemnation. You need understanding. You need counseling of a special type. Most of all, I figure you just need someone to talk to. If you want advice or feedback, I'll give it. In God's gift of free will, He decided He wasn't going to impose. Things with human beings must first start with a free-will choice. So, if Abba Father God has decided He will wait for you to choose Him and He will not impose, at least not at this juncture in the biblically prophetic timetables, why should Abba Atatafe? Who am I to do what God says He won't do? If you make that choice to enter into a fellowship with me, then you are the one who opens up that door. Then it's all fair game for me to comment or advise on. First question we have to face is, do you really want to be here?"

"Yes, I do. I've had my qualms with God, the church, on a lot of things. But what Mama Tena advised was spot on. I need to do this. I want to get over all of this crap inside of me."

"Spot on? What does that one mean? It's a nuance or something I haven't heard before."

"Uh, it means right on—or accurate, hits the point exactly, the nail on the head if you will."

"Ah, yes! Spot on! Very good! I like it! Okay. You want to come to my favorite spot in this place—besides the sanctuary, of course?"

"Sure."

"Then follow me." He led James to the library in the back of the cathedral. Amongst the numerous bookshelves and tables were two cushy, high-back chairs facing each other, by the window and separated by a small coffee table.

"Welcome to the true intellectual center of Ethiopia, if not all of Africa!" Abba Atatafe said. "We have more volumes here than about anyplace around, including the university in Addis. This is not the only floor. But I like this place over here by the window. The stained-glass row at the top adds something as the light filters through it. Then there's the clear glass, where full sunlight comes in and I can see out. It's a nice place to read, daydream, or even take a short nap!" he said with a wink. "Abai loved this place too. We spent hours talking over everything, having chai or coffee and cake here by the window. He got his inspiration up in the hills, but he did most of his actual writing here at that table, just right over there."

"It's a very nice place—serene, peaceful. I like it."

"Good. Would you like some queen cakes and tea or coffee? Surely, you'll have something with me?'

James nodded his head in approval, not that he was particularly hungry, but he didn't want to seem impolite to Abba, who was offering such warm hospitality.

Abba summoned one of his attendants to bring the refreshments and then sat down with James in the chairs. They were the most comfortable pieces of furniture James had ever sat in, leather-bound, old, well-cushioned. He just sank into it. It was as if the chair just hugged him, welcoming him to take a momentary reprieve and just sit a spell. There was a time and place for more Spartan environments and a time and place for comfort and relaxation, particularly while one read or just contemplated. James commented on that point.

"You ever tried taking a nap in something like a hardback wooden chair? There's a difference between piety and going sadomasochistically insane," the abba said.

James nodded with approval. This was a priest more human than some he had known. This was a guy he could relate to.

The attendant came with a tray, with a brown Betty full of black tea, creamer, sugar, and some cakes, along with matching cups, saucers, and dinner plates. He placed the tray on the coffee table in front of them. The abba and James thanked the young boy, who smiled and went on about his duties. The two munched on queen cakes while savoring the tea.

"You know the monks at the monastery at Lake Tana love the green tea. It has no taste! I never really cared for it. They seem addicted to it though, swear by it!" Abba Atatafe displayed a look of puzzlement, which also reflected his clear disdain for the tea.

"They say it's healthy for you, though."

"There's a study coming out around every corner claiming something's healthy for you, then another one around the next corner vowing and declaring it'll cause cancer and kill you. A lot of things are rumored to be healthy. People have been drinking this black tea with cream and sugar for years and have lived just as long as those monks in the monastery," Atatafe responded.

James and Abba discussed James's disposition in general terms. He told Atatafe about the business prospects with the family agricultural interests, about Adamu and Azmera's vision and how they wished to incorporate James in it. Atatafe thought this was good. Then James asked him about the ark.

"What about the Ark of the Covenant? Does it really have the power many here associate with it? Can it do me any good—heal people and stuff like that? What if I were to touch it with all sincerity? Would it heal me like some say?" James inquired.

"Ahhh, the ark, the ark, the ark … the ark. Everybody who comes here wants to either see or hear about the ark. Tell me, of what is the ark to you? Why do you seek the ark?"

"To get healed, set free!"

"Set free from what?"

"Set free from all of this garbage inside, from the anguish inside, from all of the pain."

"You need more than a little absolution. You seek full redemption. An old antique piece of Old Testament furniture isn't going to do it. We don't stake faith in the ark itself, for it has no real power, particularly on its own. We concentrate on Almighty God, Abba Father God, the only person or entity with any power. The ark was only a means for Old Testament Jews to relate to Him, a form of vehicle of sorts that He manifested His power through for Israel to experience some sort of one-to-one contact with Him. That all changed with Jesus Christ. You don't need the ark to communicate with God anymore, and He alone has the power to cleanse, to heal, to redeem," Atatafe replied.

"So how do I contact Him?" James asked.

"Through His Son, Jesus Christ. You have to accept Him on your own free-will submission. Until then, you're too unclean inside to start traipsing around the Chapel of St. Mary of Zion, or the Chapel of the Tablets, as we call it. Besides, they would never let you or anyone else in. Jews, for instance, would never let someone like you, particularly in your state, go near the Holy of Holies. That's the whole thing with the Old Testament covenants. You had to do so much to purify yourself, what with all washing and rituals, etc., etc. The fact is you can never make yourself clean enough or good enough on your own to receive God's grace. The beauty of Christ is first in understanding that God accepts your presence before that, taking you exactly as you are. You can only be cleansed by the free-will submission to Jesus Christ and His presence brought into you by the indwelling of the Holy Spirit. But you have to truly, honestly make that choice and understand it, understand what it means, such that you know what it is and can truly say to have fully embraced it as your choice. I think you probably need some time to think about that—time with me, the boys, time in general."

"Yeah, I know. But I know I've got to get over this."

"You will."

"What significance does the ark have now?"

Abba cleared his throat with a soft "hmmm." "It has significance in a different way. But it's a little early in your Christian walk to get into biblical prophecy. You haven't even read the Bible in a while. You need to concentrate on something more basic than that, or neither the ark nor its future will have any significance to you."

"Prophecy?"

"End-time prophecy. That's a little confusing for new believers. We'll get into that later."

They finished the tea, and Abba walked James to the door and said he'd be there anytime. James felt that ten o'clock in the morning would be good as a general meeting time.

"I'll keep it open until you decide otherwise, till God and you feel I've led you about as far as I can," said Atatafe. "And come by anytime you want. I'll have the boy fix you tea and cake, even if I'm busy with something else."

Abba Atatafe walked back inside the cathedral and returned to the library. James strolled down the street, glanced up at a bar, thought better of it, and then strolled on past. He didn't need the booze right now. He was looking for something else and moving closer to it, day by day, one day at a time.

ᴔ⬮ 🙰ᴓᴑ

He approached his in-laws' house and saw Adamu and Azmera in the front yard.

"How did it go?" Adamu asked James.

"Oh, okay. Just starting out, you know," replied James. "We'll just see where it goes. He's a pretty cool guy. Nice library! I could use a place like that to sit in, read, write, you know, keep a journal. We talked about that—writing it all out as a part of the healing process."

"I can think of something else that would help. Going up into the hills with us, just to wander around up there and sense what Father did. You don't have to herd cattle if you don't want to; just go up there and breathe the mountain air," recommended Azmera.

"That's good because I don't think I'd be very good at playing cowboy. Never done that before in my life. I'm an engineer!"

"You'd get the hang of it in no time, once you got started, probably better than us! We had others do it, to be honest. However, you really don't need that as much as you need the peace and serenity that you could find up there. The mountain air does wonders, you know," said Adamu.

"You think I'll find Abai or even God up there?" asked James with a smile.

"You can find God anywhere. You can feel Father's spirit. Deal is you might just find you up there," responded Azmera.

"Good point. I'll go."

Later that day, James accompanied Adamu and Azmera up into the hills where they herded the cattle to graze. The mountain air was indeed intoxicating, quite inspirational in fact. The sky up there was so huge and so close. The clouds, like the puffy galleons Abai saw, cruised across the sky like a whole fleet of ships, embarking from their respective ports, setting out to their own destinations. James looked at them and thought, *What is my course now? Everyone has a destiny. Wonder what mine is.* He pondered over it, and for now that was enough. He helped herd the cattle but mostly just explored the mountainside, checking out the wildflowers, the panoramic view of Axum and surrounding environs, and most of all, Abai's Rock. It was a shrine but of a different type, not one that had to be so revered that one dared not touch. Rather, it was a shrine with a different sort of reverence, one that, like Abai, invited a person to sit and contemplate, to be touched and that wanted to touch others, a place that availed itself for someone who wanted to be healed and touch his or her soul with loving reverence, the way Abai did. It was an inviting place that prompted one to sit down and obtain the enlightenment that it had provided Abai, bestowing the same blessing to others. This was a more fitting tribute to the man. This is what he would have wanted, for even Jesus beckoned the infirmed to extend their hands and touch Him to be healed. Abai would do no less and always sought meaningful interaction with the lives he came across, whether student or family.

James sat on the rock and just gazed out over the landscape, freeing his mind as Abai did, letting the cool wind whistle through him, blowing away distractions to his peace. It was as if it was the voice of God coming in the form of the Spirit gently caressing his troubled mind, his troubled soul. In fact, maybe it was, all beckoning him to pursue what started that day, to stay in Ethiopia and begin the voyage home.

Adamu approached him and asked, "What do you know about irrigation, particularly bore-hole well irrigation? There aren't any rivers or streams near the plots we want to irrigate that have the sufficient discharge or flow to give us the water we need without causing too much stress on the water sources for others. Other riparian settlers (those next to, adjacent to the water source) are going to yell, particularly if they can't get enough for the livestock."

"Interesting question. First, do you have the computations necessary to determine your overall evapotranspiration rates for the crops in question, soil filtration rates, slope, calculations for surface run off—run Penman's equation or anything like that? You've talked about some crops. Some sound like specialty crops not necessarily grown in this area before."

"We've decided on the crops, know the filtration rates, and began working on Penman's equation to figure that, along with rainfall, the overall irrigation water requirements. The source is the overall issue," responded Adamu.

"Well, let's complete all the calculations so we know for sure. As for the water table, you know the depth and yield?"

"Depth is located at about twenty-eight meters (roughly eighty-five feet). Yield seems to be high."

"Okay, we want to avoid diesel fuel because of the cost, namely obtaining the quantity we need over time for a diesel pump. I can maintain any pump. Hell, I can make the parts, but I know of an appropriate technology pump that can suck up the water from those depths, and we can actually operate on a superior economy of scale. Let's determine how much we need. Then I can build what we need to get it."

Adamu and Azmera smiled. They were organizing a co-op to move their products, wellness herbs, and power vegetables. They also were considering dedicating some land to jatropha weed. Over time they could produce a biodiesel fuel capable of running any diesel engine without any petroleum additives, which would be very lucrative.

James listened to their ideas and smiled as well. He could help put all this together. They were going to take the family business to the next level. Perhaps by losing himself in such a worthy enterprise he would actually find himself. Maybe it would take him to that next level he so desperately sought after.

The next morning, James sat just having breakfast and coffee with his mother-in-law and Enku. They engaged in casual small talk, and then James got up and said, "Time to see Abba Atatafe." He strolled down the streets with a bit more spring in his step than before. He nodded and greeted the guardian of the Chapel of the Tablets and proceeded on to the cathedral where Atatafe was waiting for him at the front door.

"Good morning!" Atatafe greeted him in English

"Dinaneh!" James replied in Amharic.

"I'd like to continue improving my English. Could we converse in English?"

"I'd like more work on my Amharic, actually," replied James.

"Ah, we have an impasse here. Nothing insurmountable, I don't think."

"Bedsides, your English is virtually impeccable, particularly in comparison to my Amharic!"

"You really think so? Or are you just saying that?"

"No, no, really. It's actually quite good. Better than native speakers I've known, in fact!"

"Really? You really think so?"

The abba sounded genuinely excited. It meant he had achieved native fluency in six foreign languages, the others being Tigrean, Amharic, Russian, Italian, and Greek. He could read Hebrew as well and even get by in Arabic but not with near the proficiency of the others. When James heard this, he was rather astonished at the abba's linguistic skills. More importantly, Atatafe was knowledgeable in a number of substantive areas, making him capable of talking about matters of importance relevant to the true areas of concern, rather than those who merely babble on in different languages with the arrogance that they are cross-cultural and knowledgeable when in fact those types are little more than ignorant tourists.

The abba was equally impressed with James's skills, language fluency, and background. The abba particularly admired James's extraordinary musical talent, given Atatafe's deep appreciation and fondness for music. As the talks were going pretty deep into James's soul, they agreed to keep it in English. After some brief warm-up discussion to break the ice of a new day, they got down to business.

James discussed his past and how that made him to a certain extent much of what he was. There were positive elements of drive and negative hindrances that explained the overachiever and party animal. The real issues finally came up, starting with the loss of his father, war, his lascivious nature, and the horror that kept him from becoming whole, from being able to love and let go.

Abba Atatafe grasped the key central issues throughout the discussion. He could sense the currents of James's soul. In general terms, he told him that he needed to embrace the faith-based relationship and approached the topic from different angles from what James had heard, and that made greater sense to him.

"Look, on the evil in this world that you lament, you need to realize something. God gave free will to the human race. Love doesn't mean not having to say you're sorry, but what it does mean is that you can't confuse it with being a controlling, manipulative codependent. You have to give someone that freedom to choose. Humans took a choice in their paths of life—something else besides God. People are responsible for the evil that people do. Love means not being a dictator to us in this very temporal, ephemeral world. But humans have that choice, and choices you have options on, but consequences you don't. They are realities that we must confront and cannot run from, one of the biggest of which is Judgment Day, the ultimate Day of Atonement standing before God. That's where He has ultimate control. There will be the time when this era of choice is eclipsed, and at that point, people will have to stand one way or another and be counted and held accountable.

"Now on this issue of your emptiness, God can fill that empty cup. But you have to invite Him in, and that means you have to accept His Son, Jesus. You say that you were born in a hospital some years in the past, in the fifties?"

James nodded.

"Not really. It says in Jeremiah 1:5, 'Before I knew you in the womb, I knew you.' You were born at the beginning of time when God breathed you into existence in the form of a purpose in heaven, before He breathed that purpose, that life into your mother's womb giving true fruit to your parents' conception. A purpose in heaven is much more than a purpose as seen on earth. It contains your entire vision, who you are, and the potential to be actualized as to who you will be, your destiny. Once you are conceived, you are then born into the world of natural sin. Sin is actually defined as the estrangement from God, not merely doing some dirty deed. In fact the issue that makes the deed dirty is in fact that when one commits it, one estranges himself from God and does so more and more each time one does it. It is breaking with God's word and covenant with us. However, that continuity can be restored, and indeed the whole purpose in life of anyone is eventually to choose that route, which enters into a closer oneness with Abba Father God in a loving, interrelated communication and overall experience, a personal relationship with God that grows closer and stronger the more one advances down that Christian walk. It's the reinstatement and furthering of that divine continuity, if you will, with the Father. Whenever we are separated from this, we wither and die like a plant pulled up from its roots where it receives its nourishments, where the water along with the soil bring the nutrients to its roots and foster the growth to full maturity. Sin is an opaque wall of darkness that humans on their own cannot see through. Once you give your life to Christ, He smashes that opaque wall, and the light shines through. Whereas before you could not see in darkness, now in the light you can. On that light of God cruises the Holy Spirit, the third dimension of God's character who ushers in the second dimension of His character, His Son, Jesus Christ, into your soul. It is Christ's presence within you that actually converts you. No human being can do this; only Christ can. We can only lead you to Christ. You have to make the voluntary decision to accept Him, or He won't enter into your being. Once He does, then and only then are you a Christian. The love overflows, and the healing process starts. Your cup not only becomes filled, in that other half that was empty, it floweth over, as scripture says.

"Something unique also happens. With the indwelling of the Holy Spirit, a spiritual quickening takes place, bringing that vision out of dormancy, out of that closet of a spirit you had before being born again, when all was dead, transferring it to the forefront of the conscious mind where it now becomes alive and can be visualized and actualized.

As you actualize it in its full potential, you discover more of who you are. You walk down a path that leads to that closer oneness with God. You become more whole, complete. Your cup is more than filled; your life is full, full of true prosperity—wellness, wholeness, and sufficient resources to live well and prosper. Your cup flows over to bless someone else as you have been blessed. You are free from these chains that bind you—free to love once more. There are other things that happen along that path, things that we will talk about later. But for now, you just digest that, and I will digest what you have told me, and we'll talk more about it tomorrow."

"Sounds good," responded James. "I'm still really curious about the ark and what you said yesterday. Does it really have power, though?"

The abba thought for a moment and said, "Yes and no. We don't stock so much faith in the ark but in its only source of power, indeed our only source as well: Almighty God. Abba Naroud, a major figure in our ecclesiastical community, puts it aptly when he says that the ark still has power, 'but it is not the power of the ark that matters to us. In the teaching of the Ethiopian Orthodox Church, God is the reigning king, the only source of power in the universe, the one and only Creator of all existing life. God Himself is our source, and he alone possesses light and power and grace. Since the ark today contains the ten sacred words written by God, the gift of His Holiness cannot be diminished within it. Today His grace still rests upon the ark. It remains holy and significant.' I say it has some power just by virtue of the fact that it contains those tablets touched by God's finger and even the slightest residue from that alone would give off some power, or vibes as you in the West would call it. Is throwing yourself upon it going to heal you and provide you with what you really need? No. You need to overcome a lot of things and reach a proper understanding of matters, come to terms with the past. You're going to have to climb over a lot of mountains and go through a lot of valleys. Only then will you learn anything. God still performs miracles but ultimately to reveal His glory, to let people know who He is, people who otherwise really can't see in front of their faces come to terms with that issue and embrace Him as the God of love that He truly is. Besides, if you have to live life through miracles, you are not showing that you have much faith in the first place, because having God do it all by miracles actually requires less of a walk by faith than it does to do things without miracles but knowing God still has His hand on your shoulder."

"True," acknowledged James. "What about the ark's power when they carried it ahead of armies going into combat?"

"That was primarily during Old Testament days, before God removed His presence from it at the end of the reign of King Manasseh, leaving only the tablets there, with that residue of power I mentioned earlier. Manasseh was one of the most corrupt kings of Israel and was eventually seized by the Assyrians. People got the ark out of there so it wouldn't be taken. Then they brought it here, for safekeeping. Nobody figured either the Assyrians or the Babylonians later would come this far with their campaigns of military conquest. However, there is one battle that you should know about. It occurred in 1896. The Battle of Adwa during the first Ethiopian/Italian war. The Italians had earlier negotiated a treaty with King Menelik, the Treaty of Wuchale, in which there was a highly disputable Article 17 in the treaty. You are a military historian. You know about this battle?"

"I'm familiar with it," James replied. "The Italians, under the command of General Orati Barateri, attacked Menelik's army with 17,800 plus troops, artillery, etc. and got obliterated. The clause in question seemed to say different things between the Italian and Amharic translations. For all practical purposes, the Italian version said Menelik had to conduct all foreign relations through Rome's Ministry of Foreign Affairs, rendering Ethiopia to nothing more than a protectorate of the kingdom of Italy. The Amharic version said he could use the Italian ministry if he wished. Italy sought to impose this interpretation by force—hence the war."

"Quite correct. Our troops had been routed in a series of campaigns, winning only one battle at Amba Alagi, pushing the Italians back to Tigray, around this area for all practical purposes. Both armies were losing out in a war of attrition. Supplies were low. Our boys were living off of the land, and as the supplies of local smallholders, or, as they were seen back then, peasant farmers, exhausted, Menelik's forces would have given up, and his army disintegrated. The Italians themselves were on their last rations, with only five days' worth of rations left. Barateri knew this and told his officers of his intention to retreat on March 29. His officers virtually went ballistic, claiming that Italy would rather lose thousands in a winning cause than regroup, which would be seen as a retreat that would further erode morale both amongst troops and at home. They convinced him to go after Menelik and crush him in one final blow. They sadly miscalculated. Menelik assembled a force of 120,000 troops under the command of seven separate officers. Menelik was going to break camp on March 4 until spies from one of his generals told him of the Italian advance. Menelik had his generals position his armies, all 120,000, strategically in the mountains, along with artillery to meet or ambush them. We had either stolen or purchased arms in the form of rifles, Hotchkiss, and Maxim guns from the Egyptians, French, or other European suppliers.

"On the day of the attack, the Italians had divided their forces due either to poor maps or incompetency of command over several miles of terrain. General Albertone's brigade was to position themselves on Mt. Kidane-Mehret to give them a tactical vantage point. He parked his army on the wrong mountain. Upon learning of his mistake, he sought to correct it by redeploying his men to the correct mountain, moving them directly into the line of fire of one of Menelik's generals. Eventually they were obliterated. Other brigades tried to rescue them but couldn't reach them in time. The various Italian brigades, one by one, were scattered about and systematically annihilated. The battle was over by noon that day. Seven thousand Italians were killed, fifteen hundred wounded, and more than three thousand taken prisoner, including General Albertone himself. The Italians were forced back to Asmara."

Abba took a drink of tea and cleared his throat. "Now, what has that to do with the ark? I would remind you that though huge in number, we had just gone through a severe famine. Our troops were not merely relegated to living off the land, off of peasant farmers, but doing so at a time when there was hardly anything for anybody to live on period. Most of our equipment was antiquated, except for a few Maxims. It has been rumored that they took the Ark of the Covenant into those hills with them, and that helped them defeat the Italians. Was it the power of the ark? Or was it the numerical superiority? Given our troops were malnourished and demoralized, we still won. The Italians were totally confused going into combat, walking into a treacherous mountainous campaign. A European army totally obliterated by an African army handing a European power its worst defeat since Hannibal. Did God act, creating confusion in an army that had won successive victories with only one prior loss, only to be obliterated by a totally demoralized army—albeit superior in number? Or did He have to, given the incompetency of the Italian army in preparing for the battle? Another look at this would say that the mere presence of the ark provided spiritual inspiration to give our troops strength where they had none, despite numbers and terrain. Our troops were all but starving to death. Who knows? The latter probably fits better than most theories. Perhaps the spiritual power of God, which may have been moved through the ark, unleashed a wellspring of courage that moved the army. We know the glory left long ago, but still there is some spiritually prophetic significance to the ark. Your healing will have nothing to do with it, however."

James pondered over the history of the battle for a moment. Then he remarked, "Menelik decided not to chase them totally out of Africa but settled for an abrogation of the treaty and Italy's recognition of Ethiopia as an independent sovereign state, but he gave them Eritrea in the process, something Eritrea has never really forgiven the Ethiopians for. He felt that to totally humiliate the Italians would have backfired, giving the Italian military more support for their war, as mere humiliation would quickly turn into hatred and a massive call for all of Italy to rise up and obliterate Ethiopia. The backlash would actually turn into rage, further fueling the home fires as opposed to a loss like this, which eventually would serve to weaken home support for the war, leading to protests and eventual withdrawal. On that point, Menelik was right. The Italian prime minister was forced to resign. Menelik didn't bring on another Italian invasion that would have forced him to fight another campaign in the middle of the rainy season with no supplies, still in the middle of a famine, and hence a war he would be doomed to lose. As it was, the loss fueled Italian sentiment to support Mussolini when he invaded again. But at least Menelik's strategy held them off thirty years as opposed to fueling anger that would have brought about Ethiopia's annihilation within a year!"

"That is quite right," replied Atatafe. "Fighting a war has a strong spiritual character to it. I remember Abai speaking of Sun Tzu and the status of one's temple."

"Yeah, I remember that. He talked to me about it. He was absolutely correct."

"Another down side to our victory, according to local historians, is how this fueled a traditional arrogance promoting the isolationist and conservative strain deeply rooted in our culture, which further empowered those who blatantly refused to adopt any new technologies or promote any new innovations, even in a way that would enable us to adapt to the inevitability of modernization and still retain our cultural identity. Modernity is inevitable. The question is how do you adapt to its innovations within your society and not lose your culture or sovereignty? Technology applied right empowers. When applied wrong, it is not appropriate technology at all and can shatter the entire social structure. The real major problem comes in dealing with the extremists at both ends. They say that the traditional extremists won out and destroyed much of our country and its future, retarding our development where otherwise we could have played a much more effective role in the development of Africa with our sovereignty intact far more than we have. This plagued both Menelik and Haile Selassie for years. Indeed, many feel that this attitude is one of the things that led to our decline as a world power at the end of the first century. Such things in life always have mixed blessings. So was the ark something that played a major role in all of this? Whether the ark was involved or not, humans still possess that free-will thing, and how they run with it makes a big difference. How you run with God makes all the difference in the world. So as Abai asked you, what's the status of your temple? Only Christ can heal that, and then you sort through the rest through contemplative prayer."

"How do I give my life to Christ?" asked James.

"Just a simple prayer and mean it when you say it," replied the abba.

"I'm not totally ready to make that plunge but a lot closer," James said.

They embraced and parted until the next time. James left, no longer caring about the Old Testament ark but looking to something quite higher.

James continued to work with his brothers-in-law, staying at Mama Tena's during that time. They computed the irrigation crop water requirements for the selected crops and determined both depth and yield of the water tables. James had learned of an irrigation device for pumping up water that did not require a diesel pump: an oxen-driven suction pump developed in Bangladesh at the Rice Research Institute there (better known as BRRI). Developed in the late 1980s, the BRRI pump was a four-cylinder pump driven by oxen attached to a central shaft (by yoke or lever), which drove a simple crown wheel and gear system. The action in turn operated the cylinder and pistons, producing discharge. The pump had been effective pumping water up thirty meters from tube wells. They only needed to produce a crown wheel 1.5 meters in diameter, which powered the two 30-cm drive wheels (constructed in gear design with teeth). The drive wheels operated the crankshaft, which in turn operated the pistons in leather-lined buckets, providing the suction power operating through the suction manifold to draw water at lower depths than what most non-diesel pumps were capable of managing. The crankshaft was to be made from 3-cm-diameter mild steel, readily available in most parts of Africa. The lever attached to the oxen yoke could be made of most any substance of the strength of bamboo.

Adamu and Azmera liked the idea. Appropriate technology need not require every aspect of Western technology, until such schemes reached a higher economy of scale meriting more capital-intensive devices. It was a good way to start and economize. They decided on using furrow irrigation at first and would consider emitter drip systems later down the road. They developed and deployed the system.

James observed the water expediently flowing through the furrows. "Works. Eventually, you want to shore up application efficiency, which is extremely low with furrow schemes. You're gonna eventually lose a lot of water in surface runoff, amongst other losses. There are other innovations we'll have to deploy for water harvesting so we can continue growing in the dry seasons, multiple-cropping schemes, etc." he noted.

Adamu and Azmera heeded James's instructions. They often took notes and retained all of James's sketches and diagrams of various appropriate technology devices in files.

Working on the farms out in the fields or in the machine shops was healthy for James. It enabled him to occupy his mind with productive, useful ideas rather than dwelling on misery from the past. He was a part of something that helped strengthen a healthy continuity with the spirit of Abai, Brihan, and Arusha. He was involved in a family activity that not only prospered them but spawned economic development that blessed the surrounding area as well.

The long strolls up to Abai's Rock continued, which also provided a serene healing environment. James would just sit and contemplate, chewing on a blade of grass or a stick while looking out over the Ethiopian countryside. Down below, Adamu and Azmera proceeded to irrigate the fields again. James observed the water flowing through the furrows from above. The water, gleaming in the sunlight as it raced through the furrows, appeared like silver ribbons expanding across the fields. He was more than inspired by it. He gazed at the silver ribbons unfolding as if they were pushing out all impurities, the evil from the world, nurturing the plants and enabling them to reach their full potential yield. They cured the parched dryness to let the wellspring of life unloose itself to the world. It was cleansing and nurturing, and observing it was a spiritual epiphany. He pictured the real streams of living water soothing his spiritually parched soul, moving through his veins and arteries, flushing out the toxins inside and providing restoration. The intercessory power of the Holy Spirit would bring that water, Jesus Christ, into his life. God was beckoning him closer. James knew it was time. He returned to Axum, going straight to the cathedral, and met Abba Atatafe and told him of his decision. Abba beamed a smile that would light up the world. Then he grasped James's hands and led him in the sinner's prayer. James truly received Jesus Christ for the first time. James's eyes widened, and he exclaimed how he felt like a huge tonnage of weight had just been lifted off his shoulders and chest. Abba just laughed with James, both reveling in James's newfound joy!

"This is a good beginning," said Abba Atatafe. "We'll work on the rest of these issues one at a time, one day at a time."

"Okay, great. Off to a great start though, huh?" responded James.

"The greatest!" replied Abba.

⚬⊙⊙⚬

In further conversations with Atatafe, James and the abba discussed the value of prayer, deep contemplative prayer, and about writing as a way to pray. In these types of prayer modes, a person is forced to go above the mind into a spiritual transcendence directly in the presence of God, to identify the deeply rooted spiritual issues that are the key roots to the problem. Then, in writing, one combines the experience of drawing from the heart with a keen intellectual focus, prompting the thought process to further develop and organize relational patterns, revealing greater clarity and a sharpened perspective on the matter and thus more effectively communicating them to God. Such writings are of great assistance to someone like the abba as well. Obviously, the point is not to illuminate issues for God's benefit but for our own and open us up more honestly in a prayerful relationship with God. In this way, we voluntarily remove all the stops and little dams inside us built from instances over time to allow the cleansing flow of the Holy Spirit through us and begin that juncture of the healing process. "Besides," Atatafe said, "God likes clear communication just like anybody else does. Why should we deprive Him of it? Now what you have to realize is that now that you have accepted Christ and confessed your sins and asked for forgiveness, which of course has been granted, you need to call on Him to accompany you into this journey into your past. You need to realize that your soul was ripped, or shall I say raped out of you, in each of these experiences you went through. That part of your soul still lays back there in the middle of that ring of burning fire those experiences created. For instance, Vietnam and those flames burn too hot for you to just traipse through them and embrace that tattered portion of your soul on your own. You need Christ to show up and quash those flames with the mere raising of His hand and lead you into that inner sanctum and embrace that hurt, tattered part of you. That war was brutal on your psyche. Southeast Asia is one of those rings of fire burning, smoldering possibly in the catacombs of your mind, something you tried to bury away but never dealt with. You need to quash that ring of fire first and foremost so that you can walk into that area and embrace that younger James Mecklenburg in combat fatigues and retain that healthy part of you again. That warrior is still a good man and needs to be cleansed from the agonies of combat, embraced as the noble soldier that he is, victimized by war and by his own government, as you have indicated. It wasn't his fault that he was there, but he is still ravaged by war. Bring him back inside of you again. Tell him it's okay and reunite with an important part of your essence that's currently stranded, calling out, waking you up at 4:30 in the morning in post-traumatic stress disorder in cold sweats. The war's over. You triumphed over its brutality. You have nothing to be ashamed of. You did what you had to do. The smoke of war singed him, but his character is still intact, wounded but not dead. You need to call upon Christ to walk with you and merely raise His hand, quash those flames, and join Him in that embrace. You need to forgive yourself for what you have done to you. You'll also have to forgive the others who have hurt you, including Joseph Kony."

"That's not going to be easy," said James.

"Oh, it's impossible in these cases without God. You can't do it alone. By your flesh, you can't do it alone; you don't have that strength. Only He can give you that strength."

"Forgiveness, forgiveness! Big issue! Been a warrior a long time. This forgive-and-forget business isn't something I can really buy into."

"Well, one, you're going to have to, and two, who said you have to forget? I think if one interprets scripture properly, you're not supposed to just forget. Jesus forgets your sins once confessed, but He's God. You're not. That's not the point for us. Think of it this way. To forgive is the decision to begin a process of sorting through the aftermath of what is being forgiven and secondly, a gift to ourselves, not necessarily others, because to quote Anne LaMotte, 'Forgiveness is giving up hope of

133

having had a better past.' As such, I see forgiveness as not the obliteration of history but the acceptance that it occurred, and the decision to move forward not allowing it to chain us in the past, to reconcile history moving forward, taking into account new circumstances. You learn from history. You neither obliterate it nor allow yourself to be shackled by it," Abba Atatafe explained.

Over the next few months, James and the abba went into contemplative prayer, traveling deep within James's past. Jesus showed up each time, right on time, spreading light in James's soul and psyche where there was darkness, walking with James by the hand and quashing all the burning rings of fire, whereupon James would embrace more and more of himself that he had left behind. He embraced his father, Abai, Brihan, and Arusha in the process. Over time, he managed to forgive all those who had hurt him, even Kony. As he released them, he released himself from the past as well.

The work with the family served as a one-two punch along with his sessions with the abba. His production of biodiesel fuels, other crops, and the rest of the family business prospects provided an environment where God could not only talk to him but one where James listened as well. It was a walk that revealed revelations of a purposeful life, a positive healing track that would lead beyond mere restoration but continued strengthening, fuller growth, and stronger continuity with God. He journaled on all of these topics, applying scripture to all—healing, agriculture, economic development—revealing the overall essence of healing agape love fleshed out in practice. He would write it all out, achieving more peace each step of the way.

On a morning walk up to Abai's Rock, James began coughing far more than usual. Adamu gave him a handkerchief. James began coughing up blood. Adamu looked at him with grave concern. They sat on the rock and discussed this new development. James traveled to Cairo, where he was diagnosed with cancer. Only facilities back in the States would be able to provide him with the necessary treatment he needed. He telephoned Nkomo and told him he was returning to America. Nkomo came up to Axum along with his wife to talk with James and give support. They had a lavish party at Mama Tena's house as a send-off. The whole family was obviously sad to see James go and vice versa. But all recognized that the mission James had set out to accomplish was completed now. Many had survived cancer with proper treatment, and the family clung to rays of optimism that he might return. But deep down they knew that this could and probably would be James's last stay in Africa. They might have to travel to America if they wanted to see him again.

When James boarded the plane, he waved good-bye not just to family but to Africa. He knew he would not return except in his memories.

Over the years, James kept in contact with Nkomo and family. Nkomo came to America to see him occasionally, as did Mama Tena, the guys, and Enku, but not as often as Nkomo.

His memories, pen, and journal along with his favorite coffee shop were all he had now in terms of earthly possessions. But the agape-centered peace he possessed was an eternal gift, a possession far greater than anything else and something he would carry across the great divide. That was a given, stemming from his salvation, which left him well centered. Now, back in the present, he sat in his comfortable high-back chair and finished writing. He sipped the last few drops of coffee, trying to breathe past the cancer, but it was difficult. He looked at the final lines in his journal and smiled. It was complete—the story finished and closure totally achieved.

He felt at peace and very, very tired. He sensed his own surroundings beginning to fade away. However, cancer had not won, for he had triumphed over life's adversities in general and indeed over life itself. His was a life well lived. It had been his dance, and the choice to end it and move on was his, made with dignity.

He took one last breath and, like Abai, proceeded to close his eyes, "just to rest a little." His hand slumped lifelessly off of the armchair and dropped the pen to the floor, his head slumped forward to his chest.

"Hey, James, closin' time, man. You wanna 'nother cup for the road? James … James?" the barista said. He walked over to James's body slumped in the chair. "Hey, James—James? You okay, man? Hey, John, he's not breathin'! Call 911! We got an emergency over here! James may have had a heart attack or somethin'!"

The EMTs were too late, for try as they might, none could pull James back from his final destiny. Having attained the peace he long sought after, he commandeered his own galleon, as had Abai, sailing toward paradise. He disembarked to walk into the arms of Brihan and Arusha outside heaven's gates. He looked up to see two other figures turn around with beaming smiles: Abai and his father.

"Paradise awaits," said Abai. They all embraced and then took their first step as a family into eternity.

Part 3

THE TONA

TOLD BY REVEREND TSEGAYE

*H*e walked up the path approaching the old cabin, logs and mortar hammered together by dedicated arms and heart years ago. It was falling apart now, showing signs of age and neglect, almost a shack. But to Peter Van Hampton, it was so much more in ways beyond architectural grandeur, ways that mattered most. It was a living monument to the courage of a man who survived the Normandy invasion and to his passion for fishing. He had built this cabin. "He" was his father, now passed away.

Inside was the hearth where father and son warmed each other in better times, the times before the schism between the two that threatened to tear the family apart. The fireplace still looked inviting. Over in the corner was the boy's twin bed, the springs within still good after all these years. As a boy, Pete slept on the ground, camping out any number of times, but his dad got him some springs in the bed anyway, wanting to make sure Pete got a good night's sleep so he could get up "bright-eyed and bushy-tailed when the fish are biting" the next morning. The boy, now a man, realized that it was he who had built himself a rock-hard bed to sleep on throughout adolescence and somewhat beyond.

In another corner, by the window stood a sink and wash basin. No indoor plumbing here—only water from the stream down below that they washed up with, which they then poured down the drain, and it expelled the water directly onto the ground outside. It was a Spartan cabin but in many ways the most comforting place he could remember. Only their torrents at each other made it otherwise. An old leather couch, an armchair, and a table with a few chairs around it seemed all that remained in the cabin, that and a haunting personality, as if the cabin still had a life of its own. Its soul, its persona, still emerged from the walls and beams, bringing both warmth and ominous despondency. It seemed to speak out to him, echoing memories, some nightmares from the past.

"You stood the tests of time well, serving the purpose you were built for," Peter said with a smirk. "But now look at you now! Though a monument to what I loved and much of what I hated, you're starting to fall apart!"

"I'm still here though," it seemed to say. "With all the crap you put in your system, will you be able to say as much in your later years? Will you fare this well? Architecture always withstands the winds of time, telling stories about you long after you're gone, and I'll still be here long after you're dead."

"Aw, c'mon, it's not as if you're the Library of Alexandria or anything!"

"Oh but I have volumes to tell, stories to reveal—the stories of your life included," the atmosphere, the soul of the cabin seemed to echo back to him. There was a voice he seemed to hear—nothing audible but a voice in his heart conveying a message, a message he could feel more than hear. The soul seemed not merely confined to the cabin but to the entire summit of the hill. It was this place, the place where he largely grew up and learned lessons of life, love, and hate, how to fish and how to hunt.

"And how much of my story is there in you and how fair? Can you recollect it all accurately, or has the old man's bombastic control mentality scarred you so bad as well that everything becomes an extension of the old man's prejudicial bias?"

There was a silence now. The place, the cabin, refused to answer him, possibly just assessing the situation, pondering over the question, or maybe just waiting for another voice to speak to the young man's heart. It could have been his father's persona, or his ex-girlfriend-turned-estranged-wife, or more likely the voice of God wishing to speak to him with a powerful but gentle sound, like a brook rushing through his soul to give him peace. His mind became distracted by other thoughts, however.

He had violated the sanctity of the cathedral during high school by taking his girlfriend up there along with a few of his usual vices and lascivious thoughts. He picked that spot to get even with his father, whom he was infuriated with after an argument. He and the girl walked up to the cabin, got high, and then had sex, giving up their virginity in lust and revenge rather than in love. He would show his dad, a pastor who counseled him against premarital sex. It wasn't the embrace in a loving rapture, experiencing true, beautiful intimacy in a communion of souls like on a wedding night. This lust that they masked as love was merely a frenzied eruption of anxiety that in the long run actually destroyed any hopes of intimacy between them. They'd had sex for all the wrong reasons. They were eventually married, but the special essence that kept his mother and father together for so many years was never there. The marriage crashed into divorce in five years.

Still, the cabin weathered the stain, not having been as scarred by it as by the tremendous fights between him and his father over one of the most critical issues of that day, the Vietnam War. His draft number was twenty-one, and without a solid standing of an academic career at a university, he was on his way to the rice paddies of Southeast Asia with an M-16 in his hands. He was still wreathing in memories from both the war and the exacerbation it created of a schism well in the making. The cabin seemed to remember too. He could sense it. It was in the smell, the feeling from the old timbers. But there was this other feeling in the cabin, a presence he had known before. He felt it tug on his heartstrings, beckoning him to reconcile the issues. It was that voice he heard from someone unmistakable, from that incident on the battlefield near DaNang, which was to be his last in Vietnam.

He had blown it in college—too much partying until 4:00 a.m. and sleeping until 4:00 p.m., he missed classes and flunked out. He majored in the revolution of the sixties, which showed its lack of sincerity, dying out in the seventies from a bad case of rickets of its own faith. The Left became nothing more than a movement of con artists, upper-middle class white kids who became the self-made prostitutes of their own school of pseudoideology, postmodern philosophical puppets, many of whom failed to grow up only to become the cheap, superficial, obsequious masses of liberal sycophants, apparatchiks zombified from a steady diet of political crack candy launched from David Axelrod's zeitgeist machine. He soon found himself on a chopper heading into combat, the bloody drama of the unknown. His mind drifted back to the days of combat.

⚬⚭⚬

He stared out of the chopper as its blades played a monotonous, droning hum of a song that left him all but comatose. It was to be one of his last battles, he hoped. His nineteen months in Nam were about up. He sat with his right shoulder propped up against the chopper fuselage wall, cigarette burning in his mouth, taking slow drags. He blankly stared, not alive but not dead, just functioning like a burned-out combat machine, his psyche numbed by combat fatigue and total indifference. All were the makings of a good dose of post-traumatic stress disorder. The second lieutenant was fresh out of West Point, so eager to earn his place in the annals of heroes. In other words, he was the type of overly ambitious, careless young officer who got a lot of troops killed.

"Name me the two types of troopers on a battlefield, Sergeant Van Hampton!" he bellowed out with enthusiasm. The correct answer was supposed to be "the quick and the dead."

Van Hampton replied, "Generally, here, it's the poor and the minorities, Lieutenant, because they're the only poor bastards that couldn't get a 2S student deferment to avoid this fiasco!" He lit up another cigarette without so much as moving or showing any facial expression change whatsoever.

"That is a lousy attitude! Keep it to yourself and don't infect the rest of the troops with it!" the lieutenant ordered.

"Lieutenant, permission to speak freely at cha for just a minute, *sir?*"

The lieutenant grimaced and replied, "Granted, but make it quick! We'll be at the LZ soon."

"Lieutenant, I've forgotten more about armed combat than what you ever learned at the Point. Nineteen months in this hellhole. Most of these guys here have seen almost as much as me. All of us a lot more than you. Now you can tout your rank all you want to, but here's the deal. You want to get out alive in this one? You want to accomplish your mission? Tell you what—keep focused, keep it wrapped tight but not too tight, keep your wits about you, and listen to us about going into this. We know a lot of their tactics, whereas you don't. Get the job done. Don't try to be some hero. Heroes of that type get everybody killed. Just get in, get the job done as expediently as possible, and get the hell out of there once we call in backup to stabilize this area."

"Thank you for your advice. When I want it, I'll ask for it! Until then, I have rank for a reason. You had rank once, several times in fact, and now you're back to being a sergeant again. What happened? The fact is you're undisciplined! What exactly was the last episode that got you demoted from lieutenant?"

"Bustin' another West Point asshole in the mouth and breaking his jaw! He really didn't want to press charges. The broken jaw was his excuse to fake lockjaw with the help of a doctor friend he bribed. It got him his ticket out of here! Me, the MPs threw me in the stockade for a while. Higher-ups decided to press charges and bust me in rank."

Van Hampton just stared at the second lieutenant, who just looked back and then looked outside, eagerly anticipating his first outing in Vietnam. Van Hampton just shook his head. *This guy could get everybody killed*, he thought. Peter would do his job and get himself out of there, killing who he had to kill and operating according to his own orders as opposed to the wet-behind-the-ears lieutenant from West Point.

The choppers approached the landing zone, coming in hot. Wind tossed the branches of palm trees that waved through the breeze like the hair of a beautiful woman, windblown, as she strolled down a beach. The sky was a radiant blue, the surf deeper in tone, displaying shades of aqua that flowed through the water and seemed to shimmer through it. The sunlight drenched the sea before the light flooded up onto sandy beaches in the direction of the village-turned-armed-NVA-encampment. The beauty of the scene was about to change, shattered by the oncoming conflict.

Air-to-ground missiles fired out of the choppers, bursting forth, blasting trails of fiery orange-and-red exhaust en route to their destination. Lookout towers disappeared upon impact as the rockets hit. People scrambled as they began pummeling the ground. Helicopter gunners began laying down a blanket of death as soldiers and some civilians who weren't fortunate enough to get out of the way were spun around and tossed on the ground in a bloody display of acrobatics. Enemy soldiers ran for cover as alarms sounded. Many took cover and immediately sought to fire back at the American cavalry charging into their lair. Machine guns still kept blazing out of the choppers as they landed and troops charged out to take positions. The explosive sound of destructing percussion all but terrorized the young lieutenant, whose grimaced look turned into a half-open mouth flashing pearly whites and eyes generating fifty thousand volts of electricity as he approached his rendezvous with destiny.

Van Hampton put his hand on his arm. "Stay cool. You'll get through this. Just keep your wits about you. I'll see you through. There's no shame in listening to a non-com now, not in combat. No one at the Point is looking. Stick with me. We'll make it. Got it?"

The young lieutenant nodded affirmatively.

"Git some, git some," a machine gunner yelled, gritting his teeth, as if the only way to survive the insanity of war was to develop an insane hatred, gripping your weapon and gunning it till it quit. "Git some, git some of my screaming hot lead," he yelled and then just started screaming, calling the enemy by any number of names designed to reveal their pedigree. Van Hampton looked at him and moved on. He had seen it all before. Nothing much surprised him. In fact, he had seen more maniacal crap than this, on both sides of the conflict. He just moved in the direction of a depression in the ground next to a fallen tree and got ready to shoot.

"Lieutenant, lieutenant! Where the hell is he?" he said. He positioned himself and began surveying the enemy's position. Snipers were up in the trees and many more in the bush. They had to be taken out. They were already dropping American soldiers in their tracks. The best tactic was to try to outflank the enemy moving to the right. Moving straight in looked like a trap. The enemy was forming two jaws about to snap shut. Van Hampton motioned to some of the others, who recognized his point immediately. Move to the right and flush the enemy out, forcing them into the other jaw, and catch both in a crossfire with other Americans who had landed far to the left who could come up on the enemy's left flank. They could obliterate them in about an hour. Moving straight ahead was suicide. Unfortunately, that was just the young lieutenant's strategy. He proceeded to move forward, yelling "Take 'em, take 'em. We have numerical superiority! Storm the ramparts, you young heroes!"

Storm the ramparts? What the hell did he think this was? Storming the Bastille in nineteenth-century France or trying to take a medieval castle with ladders, being concerned with the possible vats of boiling oil pouring down on you in the tenth century? Numerical superiority could vanish quickly if you led all your troops into an ambush going up against tripod machine guns! He yelled at the lieutenant to move towards him and get down fast!

"Get down, Lieutenant! Get down and stay down! Belly crawl in my direction. That's not the way to work! Get down! Get down now!"

It was too late. Machine-gun fire cut the young lieutenant into pieces, dropping him lifelessly to the ground. Others who obeyed his orders were getting cut into mincemeat. Van Hampton belly crawled over to a dead soldier who had a grenade launcher. He grabbed it and then made it back to the tree just as machine-gun bullets whistled past him. He opened fire on targeted positions, blowing the enemy out of their strongholds. He turned his attention to the snipers and proceeded to gun them out of the trees. He and two other patrols grabbed a few M-60 machine guns and a couple of M-20 recoilless guns and proceeded to the right, getting behind the enemy, who was already proceeding forward to mop up what they thought was the full strength of the American force.

Van Hampton, now in command, ordered his men to position themselves and open fire. They mowed down the NVA caught by surprise.

A bitter firefight ensued between the NVA and the other American battalion that had landed to their left. As Van Hampton predicted, the NVA was now caught in the snare and being obliterated. Then something in the distance caught his attention. More enemy soldiers and combination of Viet Cong and NVA began moving across an open field heading in their direction. This was bad news. So far, he and his two patrols had not been spotted by the new enemy force, which appeared to be quite superior in number. In fact, they came pouring out of tunnels. A whole division of enemy troops was about to descend upon them. Van Hampton grabbed a corporal who had a communications pack on him. He feverishly got hold of their home base and called in the coordinates for an air strike, or this was going to be Dunkirk all over again.

The air strike soon appeared and began dropping napalm all over the place. Van Hampton raced back to his original position along with his patrols and jumped into a ravine as the liquid fire gel starting erupting all over the battlefield and then some. The two patrols scattered around him, but a wave of napalm fire ate them alive. Van Hampton looked in horror, not just at the flaming bodies but at two remaining canisters of napalm spinning backward, coming out of the sky, headed straight for him! Some desk jockey must have blown the call on the coordinates, probably some ass with "military intelligence" (which he always considered to be a contradiction in terms) who had them drop some of their payload to close. He grabbed the body of a dead soldier and put it over his head, squatted down in the ravine, winced, and feverishly prayed. The napalm hit, racing over him and the area in a wave of gel flame, virtually toasting the body over him, which protected him. It was the last duty for this fallen hero, to protect another American soldier from dying—from his own military's friendly fire. When it was over, everybody was dead. There was nothing left of the NVA camp, of the Cong, NVA, or the Americans, save him. If the objective was to secure the beachhead, he guessed that the mission had been accomplished. There was nobody there but Van Hampton.

He strolled around aimlessly and lit up a cigarette. Dusk was beginning to fall, the sunset casting an eerie red glow over the blood-soaked battlefield. He walked up to a rather inconspicuous spot, a small hilltop rising out of the bush just past the enclave. Here was a ready-made campfire left over from the napalm strike, a few logs from fallen trees still burning. He parked himself on a rock, staring at the glowing embers. As he gazed into the fire, smoking his cigarette, he noticed movement just on the other side of the hilltop. A wounded NVA sergeant stumbled into the clearing, grimacing with pain from wounds. Van Hampton braced, his hand on his M-16 as their eyes met, but for some reason he did not open fire. For some reason, he found an exception to the general rule of kill the enemy and just observed him. The NVA sergeant just sat down opposite Van Hampton, looking at the fire. His wound appeared to be a flesh wound but still could be serious if not treated. They just stared at each other for a few moments in an uneasy stillness.

"Smoke?" Van Hampton offered.

The enemy sergeant just shook his head no.

"The wound—bad? You need a doc or something? You speak English?"

"I speak some. No, not that bad. Not bad enough to be put in a POW camp," he replied.

The two looked at each other some more. Then Peter broke the silence again.

"For some reason, I don't think I'm supposed to kill you. I sure don't feel like it. In fact I don't feel like doing much of anything anymore. Something or some voice, like inside me, just giving me that notion that, not this guy, not today, for some reason. I don't know why! Between the two of us, we've blown up everything else around here! Why not you? I don't know, I don't know, I just don't know … For some reason, I just don't feel like killing you right now. Guess you're lucky, huh?"

"Guess so. I saw you. For some reason, I not feel like killing you either. Don't know why. Maybe same voice?" the enemy sergeant replied.

If the situation were reversed, in terms of the wounds, would he still feel that way? Van Hampton thought. He couldn't trust him, nor could the NVA trust him. But there was some force that he felt was stronger that maybe he could trust. He continued to stare at his enemy and wonder what was next.

"I had position to kill you. Saw you, my gun ready as you walk up here, but thought, *Hell with it,* and didn't shoot. Don't know why either. Then I feel my gut hurting and saw blood. Wound in the side. Not serious, not good either," the enemy replied.

"My name's Peter, Peter Van Hampton, from a little town called Pella, Iowa, USA. And you?"

"Tran, Tran Van Loc, from Hanoi."

"Tran. You let me take a look at that wound? I got some stuff over there. We have—or I should say had—a medic. I maybe can get some antibiotics, stiches, or something and treat you a little. I know something about that from being out here and dealing with medics in armed combat."

"That would be most kind. You would do that?"

"Yeah, why not? Hopefully this is my last battle. Then I should be headed home and out of here. But you never know what the higher-ups are going to pull!"

Peter walked over to Tran, who tossed his AK-47 aside as a show of good faith. Van Hampton inspected the wound. It was a flesh wound, but out here in the jungle in a tropical climate, it could be prone to infection, which could get serious if not turn into gangrene. He got some medical supplies from a fallen medic and treated the wound. He hit up Tran with a few hypos of morphine to kill the pain and then stitched up his enemy and bandaged the wound. Van Hampton offered water, but Tran suggested an herbal tea, the ingredients for which he had on him, that would hydrate and bring about a few healing remedies at the same time. Peter made the tea over the fire with a few cups. Then both drank and shared a little about their lives. Tran's father had been an artist whose creativity was castrated by socialist realism, the dogma handed down from Marxist-Leninism when the Communists took over North Vietnam officially in 1954. His father became depressed and eventually a drunk, painting drab paintings of ghostly figures as if to depict the bareness of his own soul. Tran had no love for Communism himself but like Peter was drafted into the conflict by Hanoi. Peter shared his life with him, about the schism with his dad, a reformed pastor, and how he was just angry at everybody, particularly Washington and Lyndon

Johnson. Both looked at each other and smiled with sardonic laughter. Neither one really wanted to be there. Neither saw sense in what was clearly a senseless war.

"Tell me about your father's faith. I too was a Christian. The Communists tried to beat it out of me, but they failed."

"Can't help you much there. I've been rebelling against it for so long. Educated in it but not the one to school people in it."

"That is unfortunate. I would like to hear more. Communism is a false, political religion that has already died by a bad case of rickets of its own faith. Christianity still alive, maybe more than you think."

"You mean a North Vietnamese Communist is going to witness to me about Jesus?" Van Hampton laughed. "Hell, my own dad couldn't even do that!"

"I'm not a Communist, not in any deep sense, only mouth the bullshit to keep alive. My dad, he get drunk—he beat me. I didn't get along with him either. We have something in common but for different reasons maybe."

"I keep thinkin' I ought to reconcile the schism when I go back. After all this insanity, you really got nothin' left but family in the long run. I mean, what's it all worth?" he said, motioning to all of the destruction surrounding them.

"Heal it before he dies. My own father, he died a year ago because of the bottle. I got some people left if I can find them. This war—crazy! I know our ideology is a lie. Your country don't know what it's doing over here! It all worth nothing! Nobody right when everybody wrong, and nobody wins when everybody loses, most of all the children."

"Yeah, that's right. And here we are stuck in the middle," Van Hampton acknowledged.

He and Tran sensed an airy, mystical quality to the twilight fast descending. Something was in the air. If he could grasp it, it would be a catalyst to the inner peace he lacked. He just knew it. It was that same voice, or person maybe, something that beckoned him, but he couldn't quite understand it all. Whatever it was, if he and Tran could obtain that peace, they would achieve the only victory coming off a battlefield that any soldier could.

Morning came and along with it the sound of choppers approaching the scene. The two woke up, and Tran, noticing the choppers, nodded to Van Hampton and proceeded to go.

"You take care of yourself, Tran. Hope you find your people back in Hanoi when this war is over. Better run before the enemy shows up!" he said with a smile.

"But I wonder who enemy is. Maybe real enemy is bankrupt ideology and war itself," he replied.

"Maybe," said Van Hampton.

"You take care of yourself too, Peter. Safe trip back home," said Tran. Then he waved and disappeared into the bush.

Reinforcements showed up and picked up Van Hampton, taking him back to his home base. He was debriefed then given some R and R in Saigon. However, his hopes of going home were soon to be dashed on the rocks of military bureaucracy and orders for one last excursion into armed combat. He felt that somewhere some of the higher-ups were out to get him. That was probably true, but nonetheless he was soon to be headed back into the field.

His battalion was already engaged in a horrendous firefight against the NVA. He no sooner took two steps after jumping out of the chopper into tall grass when a mortar exploded, sending burning shrapnel into his chest and driving a broken piece of propeller into his back. The last thing he heard before transcending upward and onward was the medic yelling, "Get another chopper down here and some blood. This guy's chest is makin' like Mt. Vesuvius on me! C'mon, man, hang in there, hang in there. Quick—I'm losing him!"

⁂

The next thing he saw were the most beautiful fields and streams exhibiting the most intense, beautiful colors he had ever seen. Birds flew by in radiant colors, some luminescent, others flashing brilliantly colored wings and swallowtails that gently brushed up against his face as if in a loving caress, totally unafraid of his presence. Suddenly a person sat down beside him, munching on something. He cracked open a pomegranate, looked at him with a smile, and offered him some. It was a person he recognized but looking a little different than pictures he had seen before.

"What's happenin' with you today? Welcome to paradise! Things not exactly like you expected?" he asked.

His speech was very conventional, colloquial in fact to Peter Van Hampton's part of the country.

"What—you were expecting the King James Version or something? You don't talk in the King James Version. I didn't even talk in the King James Version during my ministry on earth. Hebrew and Aramaic actually, and you don't speak a word of either, do you? *Well?* I figured you'd be more comfortable with this. Also, in terms of appearance, I'm not exactly thirty-three anymore, you know." Jesus smiled at him. "Don't bother to get up. You're not going to be here long."

"How'd I get here?" Peter asked.

"Well, first you were born. Your father led you in something called the sinner's prayer, which you said but never meant. You had this love/hate relationship with life itself, flunked out of college, and then got blown up on a battlefield in Vietnam and died. That's a quick synopsis of it all. However, we've decided you're going back."

"Why did you let this happen? Aren't you responsible?"

"Oh, don't give me that load of nonsense. Listen. We gave you bozos down there free will. Yeah, you're Our children, but you still act like bozos, allowing yourselves to be influenced by this rebellious angel We threw out of here at the beginning of time. Free will, that's what love is all about, not codependency where you develop a control-freak personality claiming to be rescuing this person or that from himself or herself, much less hedonistic lust, like all of you seem to think down there, with the exception of a few. You say you want to go your own way and listen to Charles Darwin? You do that, and We take Our hands off of you clowns and let you hit a brick wall, which you do every time. Don't blame us. The blame's with you! You chose the route of natural sin, not us. Humans need to take responsibility for their own foul ups and failures. Most of the time, this responsibility thing you only fake at best. It's almost amazing the way you say that you don't want to believe in Us until things go wrong, and then you believe in Us when you want to blame Us because of your lack of guts to face your own lack of character. I'm particularly amused by these self-proclaimed atheists; they're a rather comical lot. They shook their angry fists at God when things didn't go like they planned and unleashed an angry, futile diatribe they had the audacity to call a debate at Us, which they invariably lost (and will always lose), and in their humiliation they decided to cop out with a denial tactic to anesthetize themselves from their new self-inflicted pain by denying that We exist and called themselves atheists. Ever ask yourself a question? Why would they be humiliated for losing an argument with someone they claim doesn't exist in the first place? Through the back door these fools actually seem to confirm that We do exist, and what's more, We are exactly Who scripture says We are. Now, in your case, you have some major corrections to make. You're getting a second chance. Don't blow it, kid!"

"I'm going back to the battlefield?"

"Only long enough to be medevacked to a hospital and then back home. And by the way, don't call this reincarnation. It's not. You're going back to the same body you got blown up in—after this death hiatus. You're just getting an opportunity that most people never get. Make the most of it."

Peter wanted to ask Him about reconciliation with his father, but Jesus's smile preempted him. Jesus spoke softly, "Hopefully you will in time, time enough for both of you to learn a few things. But again, it's your choice."

The young man opened his eyes to see the medic leaning over him with a delightfully astonished look on his face. "Welcome back to the land of the living. You're lucky! I almost toe-tagged you! You're on your way to a Saigon hospital, in line for a purple heart."

⚬⚮⚬

After the war, he had returned home, shutting virtually everybody out of his life. It wasn't just the war that disturbed him. It had only exacerbated that which already festered in his soul. He would wander downtown in his little quaint Dutch community in south-central Iowa, just sitting on the park bench in the local square. It was a colorful, beautiful, idyllic little town quite proud of its Dutch heritage, founded by immigrants in the 1840s. He occasionally just sat in the local bakery having coffee and pastries, such as Dutch letters, with the almonds and almond paste. It was probably the biggest thing he missed overseas. He often dreamt of Jaarsma's Bakery and the pastries there. But when he returned, things did not live up to his fantasies. Coming back home was difficult. He found that either he couldn't connect or they couldn't. He stared at the people as if they and Pella were all part of a movie that he watched but couldn't interact with. It was as if he could scream and no one would hear. He felt like he was in an alternate universe, unable to connect with anybody or anything. It was all so cold, so detached. Indeed he felt he was coming detached from reality. In their idyllic little community, suffocating in their little small-town paradigm, they couldn't relate to what he was going through, the cauldron burning deep down inside him. Occasionally he did scream, which only worsened the situation, as he frightened people around him, particularly children, which he deeply regretted. Was his declining mental health alienating him even more from people, or was it the inability of people to understand mental illness and the stigma it casts on the mentally ill that caused the alienation? It was probably a combination of both. He would often tell the children, "It's okay. I really don't bite," and offer them some pastry. Sometimes they took it, sometimes they just walked away looking, staring at him. Since people knew him, it wasn't a problem like it would have been in a larger city. No one accused him of improper advances toward the children. He just wished there was someone who could truly relate to him and the post-traumatic stress disorder he was going through. He only wanted one thing: for his country, at least his hometown, to love him as much as he loved it and truly appreciate the fact that at least one time in his life he spilled his guts to provide them with a blanket of freedom that they tucked themselves in bed with every night. No one was going to hurt them because of people like him that stood the line and took bullets and napalm in their place. He wanted them to just reach out to him and help him heal. Every time he got the same rhetoric from the Veterans Administration, it became more and more clear that the old adage Nam vets had heard was true: World War I produced the Unknown Soldier, but Vietnam had produced the forgotten man.

He stumbled through his little town's festivals, from high school and college homecomings, staring at all the floats and pretty homecoming queens to the big one in spring that made the little town famous around Iowa: the Tulip Festival in May. There, the town's population swelled from eight thousand to almost one hundred thousand in one week! He would show up earlier on Saturday morning for the parade, sometimes even in the rain, awaiting the event that he had cherished with his father as a little boy. But then again, he just stared, the magic gone out of it and the terror creeping in by all of the people that crowded in on him, making a drone sound and stinging hum in his brain that wouldn't quit, that wouldn't quit … that just wouldn't go away! It was suffocating! They were suffocating him! He couldn't breathe! He struggled to breathe. His heart began racing. All these people … all these people! Why didn't they just go home—just go home! Oh, he just wished they'd all leave! That sound—that hum! It just grew louder and louder, like it was tearing his mind apart. He wanted to scream, but he couldn't—it would scare the children, the children … it would scare the children … he didn't want to hurt the children … it would scare the children!

He grimaced, his arms locked around his waist, and he began to twist back and forth, shaking, gritting his teeth. He was all locked up inside, ready to explode. He ran. He just ran … through the crowd, sometimes knocking people down who were in his way. He just ran, as people looked on astonished with frowns on their faces—frowns that looked judgmental. He didn't care. In fact, he hated them. He ran away from it all until he reached a safe haven, an alley where there were no people at all. He stood there and just shook, sometimes his body going through convulsions and his head hitting the wall. He began to scream, screams that were somewhat muffled as his throat was too locked up to the point that it choked off the full luster of a good primordial scream. Uncontrollable profanity came out of his mouth, and he found himself with uncontrollable ticks and convulsions. He knew that there was no real reason for him to feel that way, that it was just Tulip Time, but it just wouldn't quit, it wouldn't quit … it wouldn't quit! Being exposed to as much napalm and Agent Orange as he had left him with what was later diagnosed as Tourette's syndrome in addition to PTSD. No one understood it in Pella, not back then. The alienation left him in a state of misery that could only be cured by getting the hell out of there.

He went back to college, getting a degree in agricultural engineering at Iowa State University. He found counseling there with other vets that helped him deal with the situation. He was going to build now, not kill. He was going to scrub his soul clean from all that had rotted in it since adolescence. He spent years overseas at it, to no avail, still feeling like a filthy rag inside. His father never understood what he was doing, and neither did anybody else. Development was a life, not a mere career, and seemed to dwell in another universe from here. Nobody here at home could relate to him or what he did at all. They had no realistic context to apply anything he said into a framework that they could assimilate and understand, as they were dying in entrapment, entrapment in the stale, stagnant, dead paradigm of their locale. For them it was life as usual. For him, this life as usual was a death sentence. Thus, home was no longer home at all but a mere passing weigh station in his life, which nobody "at home" even wanted to understand. They were riveted to this place like a prison and couldn't leave if they tried, and they hated him because he could and did.

That was a long time ago, but he still had to shake the battlefield memory from his head and his first few months back home. Memories of his temporary stay in heaven would never go away either. You don't forget something like that. He felt that same voice tugging at him, beckoning him. He walked around the cabin, debating whether or not to open up to it or even give it the time of day, when he stumbled across some old relics. An old Orioles baseball cap lay on a shelf in the corner. He had loved that hat when he was a kid, as well as the team, and the bird—most of all the bird! He had a passion, some would say obsession, with brilliantly colored songbirds, fascinated at their flight and thrilled with their ability to defy gravity all on their own, while humans were earthbound without technology. That was why he originally rooted for the team despite their mediocre standing in the American League, until the heady days of Brooks and Frank

Robinson, who propelled the Orioles to a World Series win in '66. Peter smiled at the hat. Right next to it were two pictures of him, one in the Sudan as a volunteer for the Peace Corp and the other when he worked for a USAID contractor in Ethiopia. The latter had him with his arms around three of his best friends, Ethiopian engineers who had made a dramatic impact on his life.

He paused as he remembered another bitter fight ensuing in the cabin over his choice of direction. It was not just the choice but also the fact that he sought to merely use this to cleanse his soul, short of the one way to cleanse it, the way his father recommended, which was why he rejected it. His father told him he needed to make his own choice for Christ, a born-again, faith-based relationship without which confession was merely parroting religious rhetoric without any meaningful, cleansing effect. This addressed the only true spirituality there is, going above and beyond the practice of empty, dead religiosity to embrace a loving relationship with God through Christ. Pete stormed out of the cabin saying bitter, cruel things intended to hurt.

It wasn't until he got to Ethiopia where he worked alongside the three Ethiopian Christian engineers that he decided to make the plunge. They were outside the embattled generational feud that raged with flames too hot for him to listen to his father. As he pondered over it, he allowed his thoughts to drift him back into the past again.

⊱⊰

It was a bright, sunny day in the Tigray Province of Ethiopia. He was working in a machine shed equipped with a few lathes, a punch press, and a milling machine. They were constructing various forms of appropriate technology for farmers as well as doing some maintenance service on various cars and other vehicles. The Soviets had supplied farmers with Yenisei and Donn combines, which were poorly constructed and always breaking down. There was always a lack of spare parts.

"These things are junk! Nothing but junk!" Peter said exasperatedly. "We never have spare parts and have to jimmy-rig everything or make our own!"

"They don't even have a decent supply chain in the Soviet Union. What makes you think anybody in Moscow would put one up here?" replied Dejen (meaning foundation or pillar) "They're getting condoms for parts, and the hospitals get nuts and bolts for condoms or in place of feminine hygiene products. Wonderful GOSPLAN. Their ideology is crap, and their industrial might even more so. Ever tried fixing a threshing unit with a condom?"

"Nah, and I don't know many women interested in using a gear shift to keep from getting pregnant either or handle that other matter you just mentioned. Heck of a revolution for the DERG to imitate," Peter responded.

"Too bad we can't get good John Deere. Nothin' runs like a Deere, like you say in America. I went to school at Illinois, not far from the Rust Palace, their corporate headquarters in Moline. Used to work with them in the fields. Give me Big Green over the Reds any day of the week," said Dawit (David).

"Better not say that too loud, or their spies will get you," said Amha Selassi (meaning "gift of the Trinity"). He was laughing, but his tone showed that he was speaking the truth in jest.

"Let their revolution fix their own combines and tractors, and we'll see how long that lasts!" Peter replied. The other three just nodded.

The revolution couldn't sustain anything, much less technology. What Peter wasn't aware of was that trouble was headed his way. The revolution was indeed going to grab him and his fellow engineers to fix more than combines. There were military vehicles and armaments that needed repair, and his expertise would come in handy. After having sworn off using technology to kill, he was now going to be called on to repair and perfect the operating status of that same type of weaponry to enable others to do it, which was going to be just as bad. Peter, more so than the others, was also aware of the particulars and details of small-arms fire, assault weapons, tanks, and the rest to be able to keep any weapon of war functioning, not to mention support vehicles.

He had been developing a close friendship with the Dawit, Amha Selassi (who they called Selassi), and Dejen since arriving there months ago. However, he had also been seeing an Ethiopian woman and her family. He thought of marrying her someday but didn't know whether he was ready, or she, particularly in terms of dealing with his Tourette's. What he didn't know is that people such as her didn't see the Tourette's, only the strength and purity of his heart. People who have had to face struggles often see more than just the petty exterior and learn to appreciate the person for who and what he or she is and what he or she can do. They care more about how that person can help them in a reciprocal relationship, as the greatest enemy is the poverty and deprivation that threatens their children's lives, far more than a case of Tourette's ever could. The reciprocation develops a stronger bond that can go the distance far better than something developed through Internet dating services. Still, he was cautious. His first marriage didn't work out too well. He didn't want to go through that hell again.

The village had also harbored Tigrean rebels, known as the Tigrean Liberation Front. Whereas he had not joined up with them or developed any close alliance, he was aware of their presence, and occasionally he and his brothers had provided them with assistance. The battles between the DERG and the TLF had been vicious. The DERG had decided to settle the issue with them once and for all.

One evening, DERG troops in a commando raid entered the compound and kidnapped Peter and the three others. They took them back to the DERG command post some kilometers away from the village and laid out their ultimatum.

"You probably wonder why you? Why are you here?" said the DERG colonel.

"Thought crossed my mind," replied Van Hampton.

"Our friends the Russians have not been faithful in keeping up the supply lines to us, particularly when it comes to spare parts for our trucks, personnel and assault vehicles, not to mention the tanks. Our sources tell us you have had the same problem and have been proficient at remanufacturing engines and making the spare parts on your own for your equipment. This is most ingenious of you. You have heard it said that an army must march on its stomach. It also must advance on well-repaired vehicles and tanks too. As a cook maintains the stomach, so you must maintain our equipment. We need engineers such as you. Unfortunately, Addis doesn't see it that way."

"Why don't you try another memo? Your socialist bureaucracies seem to thrive on that stuff. Maybe some dumb bastard just didn't get the last one!"

"That's quite funny. You are a comedian. We deal with funny guys like you all the time!" He nodded to the sergeant standing next to Van Hampton, who promptly struck him with a rifle butt.

Van Hampton winced with pain but didn't fall over. He just glared back at the colonel and said, "You just bought the farm with that one. No way in hell I'm going to help you out now. You kill me—you're still screwed! No engineers, no maintenance. Better treat us with kid gloves or we pull a sit-down strike!"

The colonel looked at him and replied, "Oh, we figured that. You are too strong and brave to threaten with your own deaths. However, how are you at letting the entire village get wiped out, including your wives and children, or your girlfriend and her two sons, Mr. Van Hampton? Here is the deal. We are going to attack the village soon. It is a TLF holdout. We intend to be quite thorough. In fact, if you don't help us, we will massacre the entire village, every last man, woman, and child."

"You feel you have some claim to the moral high ground with that?"

"According to Marxist-Leninism, morality is quite relative. Anything is moral so long as it promotes the socialist revolution. The ends justify the means. However, if you help us, your loved ones will be spared, and we will do our best to merely hit the military targets and kill only the combatants."

"Your ideology! It's bullshit! I even know a North Vietnamese Army sergeant who says the same thing. Nobody won Vietnam. They're going back to capitalism as fast as they can fly. Their socialist narrative is utter crap. The socialist ideology has failed, and if the ideology fails, your revolution fails, and you have truly lost the war where it counts no matter who takes the capital city's flag, so to speak. You're going to find that out the hard way in Addis whether you like it or not."

The colonel just stammered and shuffled his feet in controlled anger. "You want to see everybody there dead? The only way to keep them alive is for you to help us!"

Given the ultimatum, the three begrudgingly decided to help, not to further the DERG but to save as many as they could from extermination.

The guards left them alone at night. Where were they going to run off to? The blackmail would be sufficient to ensure their continued work, much less keep them from escaping. It didn't stop them from talking amongst each other and making plans, however. The guards were unaware of the fact that Peter could speak fluent Amharic. They were discussing the battle plans for the assault on Peter and the others' village. The whole promise of sparing the lives of the innocents was a total lie. It was all a ruse to get them to fix the equipment.

Once everything, particularly the UAZ vehicles, were in prime working order, the DERG forces would leave the outpost and hit the village with everything they had. They would attack without mercy, taking no prisoners and shooting the wounded on the battlefield. Their plans were to massacre the entire village and not take chances. Once they flattened the entire area, they would return to their base camp and keep the engineers hostage for the remainder of the war, continually perpetuating the myth that their loved ones were alive and would be waiting for them at the war's end.

Van Hampton said nothing as he munched on some njira and wot. He waited till the guards walked away to sneak a few beers on duty and then quickly made his way to his brothers who were getting ready to turn in for the night.

"You know how we all said we couldn't trust them? That the colonel lied through his teeth, more than being just a little suspicious looking?" Peter asked.

They all nodded their heads.

"Well, we were right. They never intended to spare anybody in the village. They're going on a scorched-earth policy. They're going to kill 'em all. I've got an idea."

The three drew closer and listened intently.

"We sabotage the tanks, mounted machine guns, and any other light artillery pieces they have. We'll also sabotage their UAZ 469 vehicles to either breakdown about the time they get to the village or during their assault. There are some chemical solutions we have the ingredients for. We can line the inside of the guns with them. They'll blow upon firing and detonate the shells inside with them before the shells make it out of the guns. It's a combination of magnesium and phosphorus compound. They try to use their guns—the whole thing explodes: guns, and all. Their tanks will blow as well when they try to use the big guns on them. Everything will go up in smoke. We need to break down a couple of vehicles, at least to make it appear that they won't run so they will leave them behind—one for you guys and one for me. I know something about demolitions. You don't. Now, given how much they actually have here, it'll be risky enough if just I do it. You get involved, and you just doubled the risk that we all get blown up."

The others agreed.

"So, what you are saying is that once we sabotage their equipment, they leave. Then we make the vehicles operational, and we three leave. You're going to stay behind and blow the place. When and where do we meet up with you again?" said Dawit.

"What about any remaining guards?" broke in Selassi.

"Okay, first the guards. They only leave four guards. They aren't a problem because they use the opportunity to party hearty, as we say, and get drunk. Also, some prostitutes from another village generally will show up and more than occupy their time. As long as they perform their services for the DERG's troops, then the DERG doesn't wipe out their village. Lucky for the girls, the DERG hasn't determined whether or not the TLF is using their village as some sort of strategic hamlet like ours. I assure you the guards won't be a problem. The only issue is figuring out just how much ordnance they have stored here so I don't get blown to kingdom come. I've already procured enough explosives, including C-4, to strategically place the stuff then hit the button and take the whole place out as it is."

"Okay, the plan works. And where do we link up with you again? The shop back in the village?" asked Dawit.

"Well, the TLF ought to eat them alive when the DERG's equipment blows up on them. Assuming that the DERG assault force is either totally obliterated or the remaining survivors captured, that might work out. It would be good not to take chances. To stay on the safe side, you know Mt. Kidane-Mehret? We're not too far from there. It's one day away from here and far away from any possible other DERG activity. It's actually TLF territory for now. If I'm not there in two or three days, come looking for me."

"That works. We'll meet you there. Hopefully we don't have to come looking for you though. If we do, the odds of you being alive when we find you won't be good!" said Selassi.

"Well, it's the best play we've got. Otherwise, the village is dead, and when they don't need us anymore, so are we!"

The three acknowledged Peter's point, and then all tried to sleep—with one eye open and one eye shut.

The actual attack had been planned to take place the next week. However, a few miscues here and a few there regarding equipment maintenance, and the attack was postponed for another two weeks. This gave the four musketeers ample time to sabotage the DERG's guns and set the rest of their plan in motion regarding the rest of the camp. The prostitutes, indeed the guards' favorites, had been in the camp intermittently. Peter and Selassi talked with them one night when they were leaving. The girls, all about sixteen, hated the guards, the DERG, and the desecration done to their bodies. They agreed to slip something to the guards that would guarantee their inactivity. They would be drugged well enough not just to take them out of the picture but waylay them for about two days. All was set in place.

On the morning of the attack, the colonel thanked them for their assistance in a mocking tone.

"We'll do what we can to spare your loved ones," he said. His was so transparent, his tone so disingenuous, it was nauseating.

"We appreciate that. I assure you we did our part," he replied. Peter acted well enough to win an Oscar at the Academy Awards. His nonchalant manor was the perfect cloak of deception.

The colonel smiled. Then the DERG force took off en route to the biggest military disaster of their lives. Once gone, the prostitutes showed up, and the party began. It took about fifteen minutes for the drug to work, and the guards were out of commission. Selassi, Dejin, and Dawit picked up the girls and drove them back to their village, which was on the way to Mt. Kidane-Mehret.

Van Hampton just looked around, surveying the area for one last time. "This is one combat op I'm really going to enjoy!"

He had put together a makeshift detonator that would work. He wasn't quite sure if they had determined all of the explosives and armaments there were in the depot, but he had a fairly good assessment, enough that he felt he could take the risk. What he couldn't know was that the DERG had dug some tunnels and created an underground chamber to store rockets and RPGs. Given the massive explosions of C-4 combined with ordnance above the ground, it would rip the ground apart and set off the rest. He had parked his vehicle far away from the camp but not perhaps far enough.

He crouched behind a safe spot and hit the detonator button, setting off the chain reaction of explosions. Unfortunately, the whole camp went up—guard quarters and all. The ground opened up, and flames erupted as if hell reached up in one last gasp before it all blew into oblivion. The truck was tossed about a hundred meters, Peter about twenty meters as he was crouched behind a mound of dirt, giving him some protection from the shock waves of the blast. He lay unconscious but not dead. However, there seemed to be no one to tend to him. His situation was quite dire.

⋄⋰⋰⋄

He winced as the sunlight blinded him. He struggled to consciousness. He couldn't move his arms to shade his eyes with his hands. He had no concept of time, of how long he had been laying there. He wondered if he was paralyzed but then felt pain in his ribs. That was a good sign. He managed to turn his head slightly to see the heat-generating waves across the terrain, playing optical illusions on him. The air seemed to move in waves like an ocean across the dry terrain. He lay there, stretched out, barely breathing, with a slight wheeze. He couldn't wait for the sun to go down. But then that would bring on the cold darkness of night for which he was ill prepared. Nonetheless, he was soon to get his wish. He passed out again just before dusk. He came to again, just long enough to see a brilliant canopy of stars, the Milky Way galaxy stretching across the sky, casting a more brilliant display than he'd ever seen in his life. He stared and contemplated how big a God his father had but that he had never made the move to fully embrace himself.

He muttered a prayer, asking for God's help to see him through this, admitting that he hadn't actually made the plunge yet like he should but was still searching. He just asked, begged for just a little mercy, a little grace to see him through and maybe pull him out of this mess. Then he passed out again.

He came to the next morning, still flat on his back. It was quiet, except the sound of the wind blowing over the scene of desolation. Dazed, he stared out at the horizon. Amidst the blur of heat trails and wind gusts, he thought he saw a figure, maybe a person moving toward him. He didn't know … he just didn't know … he … just … didn't … know. His throat was parched. He dreamed of fantasies where he would just lay in a cold snow-fed stream in the Rocky Mountains with his mouth open, letting the water run in it and quench his thirst! Then he slipped from consciousness once more.

The sound of pans clanking together woke him up. He detected motion just to his right, up above his head. He noticed a canopy overhead that shielded him from the sun. As he further regained consciousness, the sensations of feeling once again began flowing from his extremities, unimpeded to his mind. He felt a pillow of some sort underneath his head. He noticed that his head was elevated slightly. He heard the sound of a fire, sticks and embers crackling nearby, but it was not a huge campfire, only a smaller cook-fire.

"Here, try to drink this," a voice said. "Don't try to move too much. Just raise your head a little and take some sips. Drink slowly now. You're pretty badly beaten up but not too bad—just some broken ribs. Fortunately, nothing else is broken. From the contusions, it doesn't seem that you have serious compound fractures or jagged ribs trying to pierce your lungs. I believe they're just cracked, maybe a little more than that but not too serious. I bandaged them up fairly well. Looks like you'll live. Drink some more of this tea—slowly though."

Peter took some sips of tea. His Good Samaritan laid his head gently back on the pillow. Peter managed to glance up and saw a boy about sixteen, his appearance bearing some likeness to someone he had seen before. The lad was Ethiopian, maybe Tigrean. He bore the look of someone indigenous to that part of Africa, but there was something about him. Peter couldn't put his finger on it.

"Where the hell did you come from? Who are you?"

"Hell had nothing to do with it. I'm originally from Cyrene, but I'm actually from all over this area. My name is Markos, Mark as you would call me," he replied.

"Cyrene? That a village? Never heard of it! But here's the deal: if you can get me back to health again, as far as I'm concerned you're a heavenly answer to prayer, an angel from God!"

"Uh, wouldn't quite say an angel. You may be talking in the figurative sense. But who knows? God moves in mysterious ways! Let's just say I'm a servant of God and saw somebody in need, and God and I thought it would be a good thing if I helped out since I was capable."

"Sounds good to me."

"You rest now. We'll let that tea take effect," he responded, wiping off Peter's forehead with a cool, damp cloth.

When Peter woke up again, he observed Mark preparing some other nourishment.

"Here, drink this. You'll probably like it. It's cold. Go ahead and drink a little more, as much as you want. I think you can handle it now. It'll help keep any fever down."

"How'd you come up with cold water out here? It's not as if there's a fridge out here or anything—nor electricity even. I pretty much blew it all up."

"Well, first I boiled it to make sure it's okay, and then let's just say I know a few things about keeping things chilled out, not the least of which is leaving it out all night to cool when the temperatures drop and then insulating it to retain the cool temperature of the water. I've got my ways."

Peter drank the cold, cold water, which quenched his parched throat. It felt like heaven!

"Ah, that's good. My throat has been *so* parched, like a whole desert backed up in there!"

"Well, you've been flat on your back, immobilized for about three days! A person gets pretty dry in that situation. You know the old biblical story about Jesus and the woman at the well? He told her of water that she could drink and would never thirst again, the water of everlasting life. She asked about the messiah, and Jesus told her she was looking at Him. Then Christ told her everything about her life, and He hadn't ever met her before. She was stunned. She believed. It takes a miracle of sorts for some people to believe. 'Oh what a wicked and perverse generation it is that always has to see a sign.'"

"My dad was always talking about Jesus. I didn't listen much."

"It's not about the generational conflict between you and your father that blew up in smoke in that cabin above Lake Red Rock near Pella, Iowa. It's about you actually seeing a full life in your limited years on this planet, getting saved and coming to terms with all the things that grieve you in addition to concerns about the afterlife. It's about you and Jesus Christ—nobody else involved, not your dad, not anybody else save you and Jesus, the only path to God the Father. It's about you becoming saved and getting over this pain. Tran tried to tell you the same thing in Vietnam. Then you can see fit to heal the schism between you and the old man back in Iowa. If not, it'll metastasize worse than a cancer and gradually eat you alive until the day you die."

"Well ... what? How did you know about that ... about Dad and all? In fact, how did you know I'm from Pella, Iowa, or about Vietnam and Tran? How could you possibly know? I must have talked in my sleep or something."

"Oh, you would be surprised how I know some things."

In fact, Peter hadn't talked in his sleep at all and actually never went into states of delirium either. He had been out cold.

"Who are you—Jesus or something making a divine appearance, providing me with an epiphany or something?"

"No, I'm just His servant, Mark. Epiphanies? Yes, God uses His saints, who are technically any true believers, to provide epiphanies to people by word or simply just by the encounter where something strikes you and you just see it. Here, drink some more of this tea. It'll replace all the salts, minerals, and vitamins that you have lost in your ordeal. I also have a little wot and njira for you when you are ready to eat that as well."

"Thanks. Can I have a little more water first?"

"Sure. Then drink some more of the tea."

Slowly but surely, the saint nursed Peter back to health. The tea was unbelievably effective. He began regaining his strength over the next few days. There was no sign of his other musketeers showing up. He figured something had happened preventing them from returning. He spent his time mostly sitting upright and talking with Mark about various topics. Mark had told him that he had lost his own father at an early age. He and his mother had moved to Jerusalem for a while. Then he had decided to come back to Africa. Peter went into his own life as well.

Occasionally, Mark lifted Peter up to take walks for therapeutic exercise to regain his strength. Peter went from leaning on Mark to using a crutch Mark had made for him. He began thinking a lot on what they had discussed. He knew he owed God a debt he couldn't pay himself. He needed to get closer to Him. He would discuss this with Selassi, Dawit, and Dejen when they reunited. They were believers, and he found them to be good sounding boards for ideas at the very least.

He woke up one morning to see Mark packing up his things. It had been almost two full weeks since he blew the compound, then days being treated by Mark alone.

"Your friends will arrive soon, today in fact. I must be going. There are some other things that I need to get on with. You're healthier now. You're going to make it."

"I've been thinking about a lot of things. I want to thank you for everything you have done for me. I still don't know how you could have known all the facts and details about my personal life that you did. Amazing!"

Mark just smiled. "You helped Tran on the battlefield. Thought you could use a little grace in your own life too. There, your friends are here—in the Land Rover coming!"

167

Peter turned and saw the three headed his way. He waved enthusiastically with his free arm, the other resting on the crutch. Then he turned around to say something to Mark, but he was gone. Astonished, Peter looked around for him, but he was nowhere to be seen. It was as if he had vanished into thin air!

Dejen hollered out to him, "Peter, you survived your demolition derby, I see! The crutch—you badly hurt?"

"We couldn't get to the mountain on time because of battles between the DERG and the TLF. The DERG has been temporarily pushed out of the Tigray Province. Don't know how long it'll last, though. We made it to Kidane-Mehret and you weren't there. Nobody had even seen you," said Selassi.

"Not hurt too badly, not now anyway. Mark fixed me up. Say, where is that kid? Did you see him? He's a kid about sixteen. He was just here!"

"What kid?" asked Selassi. "There's nobody here but us. The whole area has been flattened out with nothing for anybody to hide behind. If there was someone with you, we'd have seen him, at least the truck leaving. How long ago did he leave?"

"He was just here! Just now, and he was on foot!"

"Well, then we would have definitely seen that!" responded Selassi.

"Well, there's no way I could've fixed myself up, not in my condition. And this tea here. I don't even know what this is. Nor did I have the ingredients to make it. Explain that. I'll tell you what—this stuff works, though!"

All were amazed and didn't quite know what to make of this situation. They all hopped back in the Land Rover and proceeded back to their village, talking about all the events that had passed. They didn't know quite what to make of the situation. The DERG force had, as expected, been obliterated by the TLF while making their fatal assault on the village. Van Hampton's girlfriend and family were anxiously awaiting his return. After a happy reunion, Peter decided to go to Axum to a clinic to get himself checked out. The other three decided to accompany him.

When they arrived, they went to the marketplace to grab a few supplies. Walking past an artist's kiosk, Peter noticed an icon.

"Who's that picture of, that face on the icon?" he asked.

Selassi looked at it. "Oh, that's the artist's rendition of St. Mark, you know, Mark the author of the gospel of St. Mark. He is the patron saint of the African Church and was eventually martyred, being dragged down the streets of Alexandria. They are all painted by that man over there. He is a very prayerful man. This is the image he says God put in his heart of St. Mark, of all of them actually."

"You're kidding! That ... that's a spitting image of the kid who helped me! No kidding. That's ... *Mark!* Oh man, you don't think ..."

"Who knows?" said Dawit.

"He said he was from the village of Cyrene. His father died, and he and his mother moved to Jerusalem. Now he was back here in Africa," said Peter.

"Cyrene? There is no village around here called that. Cyrene. That's the name Libya and other parts of North Africa were referred to about two thousand years ago. Nobody calls it that anymore. Indeed, after Mark's father died, he and his mother moved to Jerusalem and purchased the house that had the famous upper room where Jesus appeared after his resurrection. She was a Falasha Jew. He later returned to Africa and founded the church here, basing it in Alexandria, which became the hub of the church for all of Africa," Dejen said.

"Man, I tell you. I swear that's the guy!" said Peter.

The old artist who owned the kiosk just smiled. "You are not the only one to see him in our time," he said. Then he winked and beamed a smile wide and bright enough to light up the kiosk.

They discussed the need for Christ in one's life. Peter mulled over the issues and then decided it was time to make the plunge. They prayed together, and Peter accepted Christ in his life for the first time.

∘⁕∘

He had accepted Christ. But being born again didn't mean that everything was going to be perfect from there on out. He still had to climb over mountains and go through valleys he had put between himself and the people who truly loved him. He still had a lot of reconciliation to do and bridges to rebuild.

He came back to the States a few times, only to make a few sporadic phone calls to his father. Both men sputtered at the topic they wanted to address but hung up the phone short of a full embrace of the truth, their need of forgiveness that would lead to mended hearts and reconciliation. Pride always seemed to get in the way of honesty, confession, and redemption. Soon after the last attempt, the old man died.

Peter thought of all of those attempts. How had his dad come into possession of those pictures? He hadn't given them to him. He held the pictures in his hands and then hurled them into the wall in anger and frustration, shattering the frames. The wind blew through the empty cracks in the mortar, and the cabin creaked and moaned, as if grieving from another wound inflicted on it, more from the rage storm than the shattered frames.

"Why couldn't you have just learned to accept me for who I am and understood me? Why couldn't you come to appreciate it and just tell me you loved me?"

"But wait a minute!" the cabin seemed to say. "He did tell you, and you tried blurting out the same. That's why it really hurt, because you two did love each other but played this hit-and-miss game trying to communicate it. Who are you to doubt the sincerity, you who sought to use meaningless psychobabble crap to cleanse your soul and other futile means, merely anesthetizing yourself to pain and sin itself, not to mention responsibility? Both of you two were too embattled, fighting yourselves as much as each other, to be able to see it."

The inner voice's pull grew stronger on his heart, beckoning him to the leather armchair his father used to sit in. He walked over and sat down. He found a piece of paper, folded, sticking out between the cushion and the right armrest. He took it out and unfolded it. It was a message to him from his late father. The handwriting showed signs of the tremors brought on by Parkinson's disease, which had claimed his life but not his soul. The young man read it slowly.

Son, I always wanted to sit down with you one last time here. I wanted reconciliation in the worst way. I guess our stubbornness and pride always got in the way. But I always knew sooner or later you would come back here. So I left you this note so hopefully we can still get some closure on this, this schism between us. Boy, mission work, charity or aid, like the Marshall Plan—that I understood. Having a job with steady income—that I understood, as that was out of my generation. But this consultancy work and development was like an alien planet to me. Son, some people from Africa, Ethiopia to be precise, dropped by the church and left me these pictures of you and took time to explain to me what it is you actually do—the work with the farmers, villagers, blacksmiths, and whatnot, and now I understand. I am very proud of you and what you have done. I heard that you are born again now. They led you to Christ. Good for them! You were always too angry to listen to much of anything I said. But I understand your expression of faith by word and deed. I always felt that introducing people to a living Jesus Christ was more important than trying to convert them to a religion. I always emphasized that myself. I preached from a pulpit into people's hearts, and you preached from an irrigation ditch. You've had your own ministry, and I have to respect what God has led you to do like you have to respect what God led me to do. I forgive you for everything in the past. I ask for your forgiveness where I've hurt you. I love and respect you more than you could ever know. You are my son. Godspeed. May God go with you, lift up His countenance upon you, and give you peace.

Love,
Dad

He crumpled the note in his hand and stumbled out the back door to the small plot where his father was buried. His throat was choked up so badly he could barely breathe. "I love you, Dad," he stammered, "and I forgive you too. I always respected you, and that is what really hurt. I never felt you respected me, but you did. You just didn't understand all I was doing. How could you? Nobody else around here does. You weren't going to be any different, not without being there. You were the best man I ever knew, certainly the most honest. God, I miss you, Dad!"

He winced with pain as his heart broke and mended at the same time. A consoling hand came across his heart, and he felt the onrush of peace sweeping through him, a peace he had never known before now, except when he had made peace with Christ in Ethiopia. But the commission he instantly received was to come here to this place to reconcile, and this rapture of peace made him feel complete now. The voice he heard or felt was the voice of God. The cabin never spoke on its own, of course. That was the hand of God prodding his soul, stirring up things he wanted to deny, releasing a torrent rapture of conflicting emotions from brilliant, vivid memories, memories so thick he had to wipe them from his face, but not as vigorously as the tears he could no longer fight back, now streaming from his eyes.

Part 4

THE BEREKA

told by Reverend Addesu

*T*egene Tefere looked at the matatu park, watching all of the drivers taking a smoke break, talking with one another while the runners, boys that worked with them, went about hustling up business. "Nairobi, Nairobi, Nairobi, Nairobi!" they yelled out to potential customers wanting to risk riding the time-honored transport of dubious distinction. Others hollered out their destinations as well, in efforts to stuff as many people in a large VW van or vehicles like it as they could. There is an old rhyme: "I don't know many men alive that passed on a hill doing 105!" It doesn't seem to resonate with matatu drivers, nor does the concept of preventative maintenance even when facilities are available.

He mused over the spectacle, the people—from vendors, to customers, to drivers in a swarm, a thriving little metropolis it seemed, all in itself. Feleke hopped up on the wall and sat beside him, munching on some roasted corn. The two gazed at the scene, thinking in the back of their minds about their future, more immediate than long range. What were they going to do? Both saw the stay in the first-aid camp as being temporary, and neither liked the prospect of being tossed about from one relief agency to another, nor the prospects of being set up with families. Often times, the family divided up the children and went their separate ways, and more often than not, they treated the newly adopted refugee kid like a pack mule, not necessarily a loving member of the family. They had been together for so long; they were all family now and couldn't fathom being separated, particularly over long distances where there would be no hope whatsoever in meeting each other again. The girls in particular had become more than a little attached to the guys, and though they were capable of some self-defense, they saw the boys as their protectors and best hope to get out of the current situation, in addition to the affection they had developed, which was anything but casual. Separation anxiety would take on a whole new meaning here, as, emotionally, they were as about as attached as Siamese twins were physically.

They had talked about gathering their belongings and heading out to somewhere ahead of the administrative directive that could separate them, but where? Tegene had talked about heading back to Ethiopia, to Axum, to home. Feleke and Alemayehu had thought about it as well. But what about the famine and strife up there? Could one be certain of actually coming home again? Tegene's family had been wiped out. Feleke's and Alemayehu's—who knew? They had lost communication with their loved ones and had no idea if they were alive or dead. What would Axum be like, or Lalibela, or any other part of Ethiopia? They hadn't seen it since civil war all but obliterated the entire country and exacerbated the famine that constituted a holocaust of millions. They lived a rather listless existence.

They walked back to the small hut where they were housed and met Celeste. She offered Tegene a cup of millet porridge. He took it and began eating it. Her eyes communicated more than just affection for Tegene but were also inquisitive.

"What are you thinking in terms of us getting out of here?" she asked. "There is something new in the wind. I heard the councilors talking about it. It had to do with relocation."

"Part or all?" Tegene asked in earnest.

"All—in fact all of the refugees from the northern Uganda area. They are all being moved."

"To where? Did they mention that too, I mean more of an exact location?" Tegene further pushed.

"It is just somewhere in the Acholi area, I believe. I couldn't quite get the exact district but somewhere there. I can't believe that they want to send us there. They think Kony is finished. I don't believe so, not till I see his head on a plate!"

"Acholi! Don't they know what is going on up there? It is not safe. Nobody knows where Kony is, if he is alive or dead. We know that his army is still active, still active trying to recruit child soldiers like us!" said Tegene.

"Children younger than us are walking twenty kilometers, perhaps more every night, trying to avoid abduction. They are stealing them every night!" said Feleke.

Tegene nodded. "These people know nothing. The whole world is crazy. We are all we can depend on now," he said. He looked into Celeste's eyes, who looked back into his, displaying total affection now, the questions having been answered. She knew that he would see them through, and even if they succeeded in sending them back to Gulu, he would devise some plan to move them out of harm's way. Being with Kony as long as they had been, they were good at scavenging, without getting caught no less. They would be able to come up with the necessary provisions to survive, even until they were adults if need be. They turned in for the night, mulling over the new news. Tegene just sighed on his bed and thought, *No news is good news*, then drifted off to sleep.

The next morning, the camp officials broke the news to them over breakfast. Joseph Kony had been chased out of Uganda. The entire country was considered safe by the UN refugee organizations and governments around the world, all of which had no clue as to what the nightmares remaining were and how they lingered on, not just in the minds of those traumatized there but in the abduction of children forced into becoming child soldiers. The children were all headed to another makeshift IDP camp, in Gulu of all places!

Tegene just chewed on his chapatti like a cow chewing its cud, totally expressionless. But behind the stoic face, his mind churned with bitter disappointment. They would have to get out of there and head to some place of refuge. Wherever that place was, they would have to find it, figure it out, and flee. Gulu, particularly over the long run, was not an option, not for them. Kony's guerrillas were bound to come in and spot them at some point. That would make escape far more difficult. They may as well have had a price on their heads, the way Kony would hunt them down for retribution. If not him, Okello had many friends, some who wanted revenge.

Alemayehu looked at him and just chortled. "This is such a load of crap!" he said. "What are you going to come up with? Us going to Gulu? If we do, we don't stay there long. You don't, that's for sure. And if you go, we all go!"

"You don't have to tell me twice!" he replied. Tegene just shook his head and thought about creatively procuring supplies and how to get to a vehicle once they got to Gulu and move east and north to reach a safer place, safe from Kony. *Creative procurement.* He liked that phrase. He first heard it from some other locals stealing from NGOs. It was a much better choice of words than stealing, as stealing was so very negative, albeit accurate, but very, very negative! Creative procurement. *It sounds so much better,* he thought. Besides, stealing and scavenging were the only things he knew. It was the only life he had known since being abducted by Kony years ago.

The camp officials told them what to pack and what they would be supplied with. The rest they were "sure to get" once they got to Gulu. That was a laugh. The UN, governments, and many NGOs generally shared one thing in common from what he had seen: incompetence. He would bring his own tools and materials, things they wouldn't find, and get what all six needed. He, Feleke, Alemayehu, and the girls packed up after breakfast and got ready to board one of the transports en route to Gulu.

⦿

The hot, dusty weather of the dry season brought scorching temperatures to the north. The bus rolled into Gulu amidst chaos. People scrambled around the scene like excited chicks across a farmer's compound. Many looked into the buses and other forms of transport, staring at the refugees as if they were all actors in a play or part of a circus troupe.

The buses parked, and the agency personnel instructed all to file out of the buses and congregate in the open space in front. Tegene tightly held to Celeste's hand. The rest, Feleke, Alemayehu, along with Miriam and Genevieve, huddled close behind with all the walls of people, stranded refugees off the bus pressing in. The six tied to thread through the crowds, indeed the entire stressful process of lining up without being separated so they would be more likely to be placed in the same area of the IDP camp. It was a loud commotion that drew the attention of all of the townspeople who came to observe the spectacle.

The field was a football pitch with makeshift goals made up of poles nailed together at the ends. Tegene looked at them, as did Feleke and Alemayehu, and smiled, smiled as their minds left the scene temporarily to drift on more pleasant memories of days they played football together in Ethiopia.

A whistle blown by a rather important, distinguished-looking man, appearing to have authority of some sort, snapped their attention back to the present. He was someone with the local town council welcoming them to Gulu. He seemed like a pastor who always guaranteed his congregation a good twenty-minute sermon, even if it took him an hour and a half to deliver it! It was hot, the wind dry, and the old windbag even drier. Still, they all clapped for the local official once he was done, which brought a smile to his face and relief to the refugees that he was done. Standing in the heat listening to the would-be president of Uganda was as pleasant as root canal surgery without the Novocain. After all the pomp and circumstance, the refugees were shown to the camp.

They trudged up the gently sloping hill to the place designated for them as a pseudo-facsimile refuge. It was a miserable spot in what was becoming a nightmare of hell. The camps, though temporary habitats, were part of an ugly reality that left permanent scars, wounds that habituated within the heart, spirit, and soul that could plague a person for life. The war in northern Uganda had gone on too long as it was. The scars were as deep, filthy, and disgusting, full of rot and poisonous debris as the open sewers that ran through too many African communities, which appeared to be infected, vicious cuts of human waste and rotten food, on a continent screaming out from poverty that made life unbearable to most in affluent countries. Tegene looked at it all, immediately sensing the metaphor, and shook his head disgustedly. It reflected the misery of those abducted to fight as child soldiers, not to mention the horrors of young girls impressed into service as concubines.

What those running the IDP camps were either unaware of or indifferent to was that the horrors of rape at the hands of Joseph Kony were no worse than being raped in the so-called safe havens of the IDPs. Better than 60 percent of the women in IDP camps had reported being brutally sexually assaulted every year. This was a statistic that had been conveniently kept from NGOs and the press by the government.

Tegene made sure that all six were together. Nobody really set them up with adult supervision, which was just fine for them, for in many circumstances some adults tried to take advantage of the young girls. Tegene lay on his bed roll, resting a moment. Then someone came by with mosquito nets to protect them from malaria at night. Tegene and Celeste put them up over all the bedrolls as Feleke and Alemayehu prepared the cook-fire, and Genevieve and Miriam began preparing the meal.

The six of them, like an extended family, ate the meager provisions of their dinner. Some families that had been there longer were dining off of roasted termites with salt. Tegene just looked at them and shook his head. Termites were not seen like fried ants or locusts, which are delicacies. Termites were seen as the poor man's poorest dinner, a most disgusting substitute for cassava, matoke, groundnut sauce, and beef stew. How long would it be before they would eventually be reduced to the same diet? He had no desire to stay there that long to find out.

Celeste sat beside him, snuggling up close but not too close, and not looking at him directly, letting her body language communicate for her instead. Tegene took notice and cast a sly, quick glance in her direction and then just smiled.

The sun began setting, and they all just sat around the fire listening to the chitchat in the nearby vicinity, which revealed all of the gossip in the camp. Many talked about child abduction, about the nightwalkers. These were the children from smaller surrounding villages and compounds that were extremely vulnerable to the LRA's raids. In they came, making the long trek to Gulu to avoid harm. They walked a path that was fraught with danger, leaving them exhausted, too exhausted to concentrate in school the next day. They were little, terrified children, gray ghosts to the rest of the world that took too much time to become aware of their fate, indeed their importance as God's children.

In they came, walking, without any Moses to lead their exodus from horror. They stretched out their simple mats on the floors of places such as "The Ark" in Gulu, set up by churches to take them in for the night. Tegene bristled at the conversations he overheard. He even went so far as to tell Feleke and Celeste to "shut up" so he could hear more clearly. If he was going to eavesdrop, he was going to make sure he got the facts.

He looked into the fire rather stoically. He and Celeste remained there after the others turned in for the night. She moved in a bit closer. Tegene responded by putting his arm around her in a rare display of affection, which surprised her, prompting not just a mere smile on her face but a rise in eyebrows.

Tegene Tefere, the man of steel who never showed emotion but rather a battle-hardened exterior that seemed to creep inside him and pervert if not fossilize all there, was showing he was actually still capable of being human after all. He was sixteen going on thirty. So was Celeste. Both had weathered enough tragedy in life to age them far above their years. Celeste didn't know how far to push any romantic ventures. She knew he had feelings for her, deep ones actually, but the tortured soul chained them all captive, preventing any outlet. The situation was tricky. If she didn't respond at all, he might feel rebuffed, turn angry, and possibly react violently or turn away from her completely for months, which she didn't want. If she came on too strong, he might bolt, freak out in a sensory overload and run, feeling pangs of anxiety. She decided just to sigh and rest her head on his chest. She looked up to see his eyes looking back and smiled at him.

Tegene had wanted her. He had no qualms about how many had been with her. He was concerned with how it may have affected her. He once heard her say, "Men spend nine months getting out of a woman and the rest of their lives trying to get back in one!" The men she had known were Joseph Kony and his henchmen. She had been his courtesan, and he had passed her around to his generals. She developed the assumption that men were incapable of feeling anything except sadism. She had known nothing else until she met Tegene. Despite the harsh exterior, she sensed something underneath. But maybe that was a myth. She had toyed with the idea and then saw confirmation of a soul in him as they scavenged together to survive. Extreme times brought out different dimensions of character in a person, revelations of and about him or her that would otherwise go undetected. This was the most extreme sign of affection he had ever displayed; he had actually just put his arm around her! She began to snuggle even closer and stroke his hand. He responded by gently holding and caressing hers. She wanted to kiss him but was afraid that it would spook him like an untamed animal in the wild.

He had discovered his glands a few years back and was quite aware of the fact that at his age they were like the cup that runneth over but didn't dare act on them. She had been Kony's, and to do so would have been suicide. Now he remained reserved and accepted her casual advance, enjoying the warmth that gently caressed and kindled his own emotions. The two just sat there by the fire, letting spirit and soul intermingle, developing a base for a true intimacy most people never know.

⚬⚭⚭⚬

Not far from Gulu was the village of Obim. In a compound just outside the village Bartholomew Adenya and some other members of his family sat nervously around the fire, looking out of the corners of their eyes at any possible movement, tracking any sound to see if evil lurked in the bush. It has been said that "simply because you're paranoid, doesn't mean the bastards are out to get you!" Indeed, the specter that came lurking their way had shown proof time and time again that the bastards were out to get them. Conversation in tones of low murmurs ranging from idle chitchat to serious discussions passed the time in vain attempts to keep nerves steady as people inwardly quaked with fear. On the outside, they sat in an uneasy stillness like the quiet in the eye of the storm, trying to hide their fear, as if showing signs of fear would attract dangerous predators that could sense it and move into attack, like lions sensing fear in their prey. However, lions merely want food for their pride and appear to show more of a moral cause than Kony. His predators stalked unsuspecting children in the darkness of the night and operated from a false pride, spawning an evil darkness almost unparalleled anywhere else on planet Earth. The sound of crackling embers surpassed the volume of those surrounding the fire who spoke in muffled tones, difficult for anybody to pick up standing more than a few feet away.

Many in Obim sought to congregate atop Obim Rock, a rather huge rock formation outside the village that had been famous in the area. It was high above the small village of Obim, and from there they thought they could ensure more protection from the LRA, with a superior vantage point to spot marauders in the distance. It had become a makeshift IDP camp atop the rock. However, this particular family chose to stay at their compound to protect the livestock from cattle rustlers. They were caught in a horrifying conundrum, to protect their children from abduction or death from hunger if they lost their cattle and livelihood. It was a closely calculated risk either way.

Bartholomew Adenya (Adenya meaning "open the way" or "path") poked at the fire, glancing to the hut where the children slept, with a huge sense of uneasiness. His eyes cast a loving cloak over them as he thought about the day each was born, about how much he loved them and strove to provide a better life for them, including an education to open a path to the future for them. He feared for them and would give his life for them. He and his neighbors had already lost three daughters to the LRA: Celeste, Genevieve, and Miriam. They had not heard from any of them. They had no knowledge of their whereabouts or if they were even alive. He felt pangs of guilt as he poked the fire, even though it was not his fault. He had gone out to check on the cattle that night. He had carried a machete with him as he was prompted by sounds from the herd indicating the presence of a predator of some sort. The cries of his livestock subsided, however, only to be replaced by his children's screams. The cattle had merely trumpeted warnings of LRA marauders. They had grabbed Celeste, kicking and screaming, and proceeded to drag her away with them. Bartholomew Adenya, being a well-read, literate man, had read H. G. Wells's *The Time Machine* in secondary school. The LRA reminded him of the Morlocks, Wells's apelike troglodyte creatures fearing light of any kind, craving darkness, dragging humans away down below for food. However, unlike the Eloi, Celeste turned out to be anything but ineffectual as she would demonstrate in the future. He struck one of the soldiers in the neck with his machete, killing him. He charged into the rest in a furious but still futile attempt to rescue his eldest daughter. A burst from an AK-47 put bullets in his hip and leg, dropping him to the ground in anguish. He tried to reach out to Celeste as the other LRA marauders laughed and mocked him as they dragged Celeste, who was screaming at the top of her lungs.

That was three years ago, but the memory was too fresh in his mind, and the bullet wounds had left him with a limp when he walked. He sat with his brother, Geoffrey, by the fire. Each took turns taking catnaps throughout the night as the other watched over the compound and the herd of cattle. They were a little better armed now than then: a twelve-gauge shotgun, AK-47, and a .22-caliber hunting rifle in addition to machetes. Tonight they would come in handy.

A patrol of LRA henchmen stealthily made their way toward Obim and some of the surrounding compounds. They stalked through the night, mostly in search of food, as rations were running low. It they could find some additional material that could be shaped into child soldiers, so much the better. They came upon the herds outside the compound where three years ago they had stolen Celeste. Some of them were in that raid and remembered not only Celeste but her father's vigilance as well. Three, in particular, had no love for him at all, as they had been close to the LRA soldier that had been killed.

They slaughtered one of the cows immediately for a kebab. They were ravenous, both in terms of hunger and revenge, and desperately sought to satisfy both. They moved into the compound and stealthily crouched, trying to scope out the terrain. The LRA commander raised his hand and waved forward as a signal to advance, not seeing anyone tending the fire. The five deranged assailants walked into the middle of the compound. The commander pointed to the remaining four to divide into groups of two and search out the thatched-roof huts. There were no signs of remaining occupants. Perhaps they had gone atop of the rock for the night like many others and had merely left this convenient fire for them to cook their kebab and feast. *But that seems too good to be true*, he thought. He wanted to make sure. He didn't suspect that a bunch of uneducated peasants from the bush would be armed and present any significant danger. He was wrong on all counts. They were not mere peasant farmers, for that very phrase makes too many derogatory assumptions and implications that fail to accord farmers the true respect and dignity they deserve. They merely owned small holdings of land and hence, were "smallholder farmers" not "peasants." Secondly, these very intelligent smallholders were armed, poised, and ready to strike!

As the soldiers tried to enter the huts, they were greeted by gunfire. The first soldier walked into the children's hut only to be met by two shotgun blasts. He virtually exploded from the chest up, his head all but disintegrating. As his torso and midsection fell directly backward onto the ground, his partner, too close behind him, literally flew backward from the impact of the blasts, out of the doorway about two meters, landing at the feet of his commanding officer. At the other hut, the two invaders were met with a fury of machine gun bullets blasting out of an AK, dancing from the impacting rounds as if they had uncontrollable St. Vitas before they spun around dead. The commanding officer, with a look of shock on his face, opened fire into the hut where the shotgun blast had erupted, only to be killed himself by fire from the Kalashnikov coming from the other hut.

After the brief but deadly firefight, Bartholomew staggered from the hut and dropped dead on the ground. Children came out of their hut screaming in terror. Geoffrey ran over to his brother, who had heroically given his life for his family. His wife came out wailing, as did her sister. The rest of the night was pierced by ululations of grief and mourning until the dawn.

❧❧❧

News of a failed raid in Obim reached Gulu in a few hours, as Obim lies only about twenty kilometers away. However, there were no exact details or names mentioned, just that a raid to scavenge for food and abduct children had been averted, with all the LRA soldiers involved being killed. Celeste's eyes widened with alarm when she heard about it. Tegene, chopping wood with his machete, paused long enough to look up, sensing something was wrong.

"Celeste, everything all right? You don't look so good," Tegene said, moving over to her.

"Obim village—it's not far from here … *my village*. That raid last night; it took place there. I've got to go back there to see what happened, see if everything, everyone, my family, if they're okay."

"Go back? I know you want to, but you haven't been back in so long, not since they took you. There have been any number of raids there and several places around there. Why now? What's so different about this raid that you suddenly have this compulsion to go back home? If you do, you open the doorway to possibilities to get yourself taken again if LRA soldiers are still patrolling the area. Just because some were killed doesn't mean they took out all in the immediate vicinity of Obim. We know how they work. Kony still has an army, be it beaten up, but still an army, and they are not going to quit making raids until he is dead or they are all wiped out. This would be worse than suicide for you if they recapture you. Celeste, the risks are too high right now. Let's make a plan, obtain a truck, weapons, other provisions. Then we go back—together. I'm not going to let you accidentally slip back into Kony's hands."

"I would rather die first!"

"You just might if you get caught. And what they do to you first will be worse than death, I am telling you. But I don't like either prospect. Look, we make a plan and then go. I know your stubborn streak. I won't allow it otherwise!"

"You won't what?" Celeste yelled. She was fiercely showing that defiant stubbornness Tegene mentioned.

"Listen, woman ... or should I say girl, because you are not talking like an adult, one who is using common sense! I'll stop you if I have to! I finally have found someone in my life who is ... real. I am not going to lose you!"

"Someone who is real ... someone who is real? Is that all?" she said. She looked up at him, flashing a mischievous smile, and gazed at him with probing eyes. "Do you see anything else in our relationship—feel anything else?"

He just smiled. "Yes, but I won't tell you unless you promise me you are not going to Obim on your own or just with the girls! You should not go out of Gulu, at least not for now. You are safe here. Kony isn't likely to stage raids in a town this big anymore. He is only hitting the smaller, more defenseless villages like Obim. Places like that, that's where all trouble is now."

"Okay, okay," she said. She just nodded and then walked off in search of Genevieve and Miriam.

Tegene just grimaced and looked around, shaking his head, totally exasperated. "Fool, crazy woman!" he muttered.

However, once Celeste had her mind fixed on something, there was no stopping her. She mulled around some scheme or loose set of plans in her mind to get to Obim and satisfy her angst regarding her family and siblings. She told Tegene she and the girls were going for water. He nodded. Then she, Genevieve, and Miriam grabbed Gerry cans and proceeded over to the sole water source for the entire camp. If there was a line, so much the better. She could use the time to discuss the plans with the other two who were also from Obim. They too would be concerned about their families.

Miriam's father had been a pastor for years. An LRA raid had left him mutilated on the right side, his leg and right arm partially amputated and leg completely gone, but still he continued to preach, his inner strength surpassing his physical disability, serving as an inspiration to all, particularly his daughter. She knew that without tests there are no testimonies. By faith she would brave what had happened to her to impart greater hope and vision to others suffering. She could identify with their pain and her voice, truly the genuine article. She couldn't to be mistaken for a phony talking disingenuous nonsense. Her words were salt, nurturing, of substance. Now she hoped that faith would see them through, keep them strong through trials and tribulations. Such strong faith cements will and unites mind with an undaunting spirit to provide the strength they needed to surmount the obstacles they would face. That type of courage would be needed. It bred a type of leadership element to help coordinate and bring about a sense of community together, to rebuild the sinews of shattered community and lives that had been devastated by the war. It was a leadership element that could be introduced with a tone of subtlety, something that a woman could pull off even in a strong patriarchal society. It might even be welcome, given the government's inability to protect the outlying rural villages.

She felt a deep calling in her heart to return home someday and help her father's ministry. But was it a true calling? Or was it a reaction out of fear and her desire to seek a safe haven, anyplace but where she found herself at the moment? Was it a fear for her loved ones and just her desire to see them again? Or did she really have a calling and the inclination to the discipline and commitment such a life would demand of her? She struggled with it. She knew that home was anything but a guaranteed safe haven. Possibly what she craved, what so many craved, was that psychological, emotional safe haven or perception of one, a place that existed in her own mind rather than any given piece of geography. She wanted that enclave of emotional security in her own soul and psyche from harm that was actually existential to geography and physical environment. It was that place that many run to, to shut out the torment, including those memories that would linger on after the LRA had been eliminated. Possibly losing herself in the Lord's work to assist her father and rebuild her home was a way to heal, to erase the memories or at least reconcile the past. All made her very keen on Celeste's idea.

Genevieve just nodded. She looked up to the other two like the younger sister to older sisters but not without an independent flair of her own. She had been born in a village near Ft. Patiko, a former slave-trading port built by the Arabs long ago and later taken over by the British. The site had been hit by the LRA numerous times. Hence, her father moved them to Gulu and eventually Obim, where they had other relatives. However, moving away from the former slave fortress of the past did not protect her from the slavery of the present day, as she was eventually abducted by a raid on Obim. She felt empathy and sympathy with all abductees. She showed her practical side in this discussion.

"You keep talking about going to help, but on the practical side, what do you actually intend to do? How do you plan to even get there, much less help? What do you intend to do? Do you really think we are going to turn into combat soldiers and fend off the LRA if we encounter them, depending on how many soldiers there are in any one given raiding party, which we are still likely to encounter? The guys were taught how to fight and were made into soldiers. They taught us to be concubines. What are we going to do? Preoccupy them by spreading our legs while some hero appears out of nowhere and kills them?" Genevieve asked.

The other two laughed.

"Well, there are some in Kony's concubines who are more dangerous in sex than the guys are with guns. They give something that no soldier can get rid of and no bulletproof vest can protect them from. Who's the deadliest of combat soldiers of them all?" Celeste quipped.

"Fortunately, that's not us! We have not acquired HIV yet, and I don't intend to and certainly don't want to go back and run the risk! What if we are captured, abducted, again?" said Miriam. "Genevieve makes a good point. What do you actually intend to do?"

Celeste thought for a moment and then replied, "We can just give them hope, help those move to Gulu until the war is over. We can help take care of our brothers and sisters. At the very least, we can relieve their minds that we are alive. It is time we went back. I was going to tell Tegene that the major reason we didn't go back before was shame. We were ashamed! Now we have to see past that shame and return. I think he knows that. But he perhaps was referring to something else, something deeper. We still feel shame. We seem to have become so numb to fear we seem to ignore it, but still, it lingers on deep within us. But he was asking what the true motives were. Was it fear? He has said often enough that we still feel shame, as do the guys, even though none of us should, as we have been victims ourselves. But still, the shame lingers. We can't seem to shake it! He asked what's different about this raid, what's different now, as if to ask what's different in us," said Celeste.

"What is different in us? Where have we changed? We know, but we have been bustled around so much in panic we have not had the time for this inner reflection, to discuss this, properly look at it. We are no longer just naïve young girls from the village anymore. We have changed, but it is because of our relationship with the guys, and they have changed because of their relationships with us. The relationship has helped us all over the shattering of our lives by Kony," said Miriam.

"It is because of the blending of our spirit and soul," said Celeste.

"Because … we love them! Because we have finally found men in the form of boys, not monsters, who see in us something different besides whores. We have people who genuinely care about us for the first time since we were abducted. Through love we are beginning the long process of healing, and so are they," said Genevieve.

Her beauty in simplicity bit through the frail vales of denial, and her clarity, surpassed only by her honesty, brought smiles to the faces of the other two. Maybe they were overcoming the shame. Maybe Tegene was trying to get Celeste to admit that she loved him, but maybe not, as desperately as she wanted to hear him say it to her. Possibly returning home was not going to be of major help to their families or even safe. But maybe, she thought, *it would relieve some anxiety and provide some closure that we're looking for in other ways. Maybe it would salve more wounds and provide more of that psychological safe haven in the catacombs of my mind that would help us navigate through the days ahead.*

Celeste and the girls discussed some facsimile of a plan to go to Obim just for a while and leave a note for Tegene and the guys, who would be sure to understand. Then they would grab a matatu for Obim. As it turned out, the guys would not be so understanding. In fact, they would be furious, particularly Tegene!

190

At daybreak, Celeste arose and quickly gathered her things. She quietly glanced over at Tegene to see if he was still asleep. He appeared to be. Then she hastily left the hut and met Genevieve and Miriam by the cook-fire.

"The matatu leaves for Obim in twenty minutes. We have to hurry," instructed Celeste.

The other two nodded.

"Shouldn't we leave some sort of notes for the guys or something? I mean, we shouldn't just leave without them knowing where we have gone. We do love them and would like to come back to them. You don't leave your loved ones high and dry," said Genevieve.

"Besides, they may think that we have been abducted by Kony and might do something rash that could get them killed," chimed in Miriam.

"I left Tegene a note and told him to tell the other two," replied Celeste. "Now let's go."

The three bustled off in the direction of the matatu park and proceeded to travel southeast toward Obim, not knowing they would walk into a funeral for Celeste's father. That news hadn't reached her, only that the LRA had once again come to her village. She thought about it all with nervous anticipation, not knowing exactly what she would find.

Tegene awoke only to find the note and went ballistic. He stormed out of the hut and roused the other two, yelling at the top of his lungs. Feleke and Alemayehu were equally enraged as well as shocked that the girls would act so irresponsibly. Fear was no excuse for their actions. They had all been afraid before but had been battle hardened by life's successive blows and had learned from experience not to act so impulsively.

"What the hell was she thinking? She wasn't—none of them were!" yelled Tegene. "They had no clear information of what happened there, of where Kony is! It was more than irresponsible. It is plain insane, close to suicide. They don't even know if there is a village left. The reports have been too sketchy, incomplete. They have just made themselves into targets—open targets!"

"We have to go get them," responded Feleke, "for a number of reasons, not the least of which is that we are all well known. It's not every group of soldiers that kills somebody like Okello, steals a vehicle, the women, Celeste, who was one of Kony's favorites, and then we collaborated with the government. We may as well be on some sort of wanted poster in Kony's army, if they had them. They'll torture the girls to find out where we are. They knew we were all together."

Alemayehu agreed. "We have to find them before Kony does. If he finds them first, they're finished. He'll kill them eventually. If they're lucky, he'll merely kill them quickly. If not, well you know."

"We know, and we won't let that happen," said Tegene. His eyes were defiant, looking toward the horizon with a focused rage. More than angry at Celeste, his blood boiled at the thought of Kony touching her again. His thoughts about Kony and the social decay he represented, like an infestation of termites into the foundation of a building, it could cave in society if not checked. Everything Kony represented was a poison extending from beyond the physical torture he had inflicted upon his victims and society in general but constituted a spiritual dry rot, a virus worse than AIDS that tried to destroy society at its very soul. It all fueled Tegene's hate for the LRA, prompting him to toy with designs in his mind to bring the entire LRA down, if only he had the command of sufficient numbers to do it! But alas, he lacked the means. However, it was an obsession that burned within him, and at the very least, he would lay down his life for Celeste. He would kill anyone, particularly LRA, who would try to harm her.

Tegene struggled to get through his daily chores, his mind ablaze with thoughts of what would happen to her and of what life would be without her, thoughts he struggled to shut out of his mind. Then he began preparations to go to Obim. He discussed plans with the other two.

Feleke at fourteen was actually older than Alemayehu by one year, though one couldn't tell by looking at him. He was smaller than the other two but quick on his feet. Alemayehu was tall and slender with strong arms. A very stealthy lad, he was always in trees and could climb up most anything, including walls, always finding little crevasses to dig his hands and feet into. The three made an excellent trio for stealing most anything. All were quick and silent. They had to be to have survived their ordeals. Tegene told them not to worry about the truck. Cash would be a necessity, to purchase petrol if nothing else. Perhaps they could break into one of the kiosks or stores in Gulu at night and rob the cash register.

"I'll get the guns. I already know where they are. You two hit the grocery stores in town. Take the backpacks with you. Get the cash first. Then grab as much food as you can," Tegene instructed. The other two nodded in agreement. They separated to begin setting plans in motion.

Tegene arose in the predawn darkness, using it as a cloak of anonymity to make his way, unseen, to a bar he knew of. It was a popular hangout with most truckers in the area, many of them drinking practically till dawn and often just passed out there, not moving a finger till morning. Gulu was on the end of their runs, and they used the break to party with gusto. He approached the bar in a pantherine fashion and peeked over the ledge through the window. The drivers were all passed out and seemed to be snoring loud enough to drown out any noise from the outside. He made his way over to the truck and climbed into the driver's seat. To his delight, the keys were left in the ignition. The driver's carelessness was Tegene's fortune, for time was of the essence in grand theft auto. Tegene turned over the ignition and drove away nonchalantly and quietly, with no fanfare.

Back at the camp, Alemayehu and Feleke waited with the other necessary supplies. They fidgeted about in anxious anticipation, wanting to get this show on the road. Tegene drove up and stopped, put the truck in neutral, and got out. He silently motioned for the other two to get in the truck while he went into his hut and got all the weapons he had been previously gathering over time. He emerged with two AKs, an Israeli Uzi, .45-caliber handgun, a shotgun, and three machetes tucked into his belt. He had two full ammunition belts and several clips bundled under his armpits and cradled with his forearms against his chest.

"There are two more ammo cases inside," he said.

"What the hell are you going to do? March on Kampala?" exclaimed Feleke.

"Shut up! As crazy as the girls have been, who knows what they may have gotten themselves into!" he responded.

"True. But tell me where did all this come from?" asked Alemayehu.

"Oh, I've been collecting, a few from here and there. Hid them so nobody would know until we really needed them," Tegene said. He flashed a big toothy grin and walked back to his hut.

The other two just glanced at the cache with astonished, wide eyes.

"Okay, let's go!" said Alemayehu.

Tegene returned with the remaining ammo cases and tossed them into the back of the truck. He jumped in behind the wheel, put the truck in first gear, and drove off in the direction of Obim Village. As daybreak fanned out across the sky, bursts of radiant color illuminated the horizon with fluorescent orange, scarlet, and magenta, projecting rays of red and golden light that streaked through deep purple and gray clouds as darkness continued its retreat. The dawn's sunburst gave a sense of hope and peace to Tegene as he drove. *If there is a God*, he thought, *hopefully He smiles on us today. Hopefully, the girls will be all right.* He gazed at the morning glory unfolding before him in the sunrise, took a deep breath of courage, and drove on.

⊰⊱

At Obim, the scene was dreary, with families in mourning but otherwise trying to carry on with life as usual. The matatu pulled up to the small row of buildings and shops. Celeste, Miriam, and Genevieve disembarked, gathered their things from atop the vehicle, and proceeded to walk in the directions of Celeste's family's compound. It didn't take long for them to realize that the danger had struck closer to home than they thought. People's looks of surprise and in some cases joy at her return quickly gave way to sympathy. She looked back at them puzzled but began adding up the signs and quickened her pace to the compound.

She walked past the outer parameters of the village about fifty meters past the last kiosk and walked through the gap between the brush, which marked the boundary of the compound. The brush was planted in a convenient rectangle around the property, with gaps at the front and back for entry. The brush was Africa's picket fence, serving the same purpose little white picket fences do in America, demarcating land and providing the decorative safe feeling around home and family. It depicted the same sense of idyllic tranquility of the home, like one would see in Europe or America—it was home! Celeste's heart swelled with emotion as her eyes welled with tears taking it all in. Little chicks scurried about, feverishly bobbing their heads up and down, pecking at kernels of maize that lay scattered on the ground under the watchful eyes of their mother hen. They felt safe and secure. Unfortunately, Celeste did not, for beyond mere appearances was a despondent gloom in the atmosphere, a wave of anxiety that seemed to roll in at her. The peace of the compound had been shattered by the attack and aftershock still lingering on. It was as if the compound groaned and wreathed in agony, reflecting some sort of persona of its own—a person in grief over a loss.

Her mother walked out of her hut and straightened immediately as if struck by lightning at the sight of her eldest daughter. Her eyes widened with surprise as she erupted in jubilation and tears. Celeste stood shaking, overcome with emotion herself.

"Mama," she meekly cried out through tears. Then she yelled, "Mama!" and ran toward her. Mama immediately snatched her up with her big arms.

"Matoto (child)!" she cried out. The two clung to each other, weeping. They exchanged greetings, saying how happy they were to see each other over and over again.

"I knew you were still alive—I just knew it!" Mama said.

Celeste reacquainted her with Miriam and Genevieve, as Mama could hardly recognize them from the young girls in the village they were when they were abducted. She immediately embraced both and instructed her other children to quickly run and inform their parents that their daughters, who were believed to be dead, were alive and well and, most importantly, home!

"You take some food now, yes? Come sit, and we will fix something," Mama said. She clapped her hands, summoning Celeste's other siblings, who yelped with joy at her sight. They ran in and hugged her. Mama instructed them to fix some groundnut stew and *matoke*. She told someone to slaughter one of the cows for fresh meat for the stew. She figured she would need more for the wake anyway.

"Did you hear about your father?" Mama asked Celeste.

"Hear what? I know that there was a raid on the village. What about Papa?"

"You haven't heard. I thought you came back because of him."

"Yes, we did. We came back to help him and you, Mama, not to mention others."

"Oh, child, oh my sweet Celeste …" She began gently breaking the tragic news. "You can't help your father anymore. He has passed. Your father was killed, murdered saving your siblings from the LRA. He died heroically. Between him and your uncle Geoffrey, they killed all of the marauders, but he was shot in the process. We will be burying him tomorrow. The wake has in effect already begun. This has been terrible. This whole war has been terrible. It is insane. We are all devastated but feel joy at the same time that you have returned, alive and healthy!" She grabbed Celeste, who burst into tears. Genevieve and Miriam just hung their heads and began to weep.

Celeste had tried to dismiss the nightmarish thoughts that had been running through her mind, that her own family members might have been among the victims. She knew it was a possibility. She stoically stared in a daze intermittently throughout the day. She was in shock over the death of her father, which contributed to the confusion she muddled through. It crossed up her feelings, which seemed to collide in a six-way train wreck, exploding at an intersection. Despite thoughts that it was possible, it still caught her off guard, as death of a loved one inevitably does.

Genevieve and Miriam tried to console her, giving her proper space to allow her to deal with it. She helped her mother prepare the meal for the wake and then later proceeded to greet all attendees who came by to pay their respects. Her lips quivered as she approached the casket. She ran her hand over her father's body and gently caressed his face. She bent over and kissed his forehead, saying, "Jojoka malo, jojoka malo, warwate kuca" (Farewell, Papa, farewell, Papa, I'll see you on the other side).

The funeral proceeded according to traditional Acholi custom. Dancers gathered to engage in the Mwel Awol, the traditional funeral dance. The women gathered in the center of a circle just in front of the gravesite. The men danced in the outer circle, surrounding the women, with shields and spears. Drummers began playing the syncopated rhythm, sometimes throwing in and expanding into diverse polyrhythmic beats and feel. African rhythms often deviate from the straight form so popular in Western music to embrace nonstandard forms of rhythm that maintain a continuous flow, leading the audience and dancers to sway with varied time structures to a rhythmical symphony of syncopation. Many in the procession and crowd sang with the dancers. Following this part of the funeral ceremony, Bartholomew's body was lowered into the ground. Some would say gone but not forgotten, but that is not exactly the Acholi way.

Following the burial, the family gathered back at the compound. Geoffrey stood outside the hut blowing on a horn whittled out of the horn of an impala killed in a hunt. As the horn blast sounded, Mama, being the matriarch of the clan, began chanting his name over and over again, holding an oiled leaf and egg, calling his spirit back into the house. Then the family proceeded into the hut, which remained dark, and sat around calling and chanting his name, telling him that they still loved him, that his deeds were heroic, and that they wished for him to enter the house and forever dwell there amongst them, where he would hear every conversation, bit of laughter, and tears of sadness. Though he was seen to be in another world, they considered the universe to be juxtaposed so that his presence would still be there in the hut if he chose to enter it. They even left his favorite dish at his spot at the table and a chair for him, where he used to eat and discuss family matters and other business. Though some of the young who were accustomed to more modern ways might reject the supernatural aspects of ancestor worship and possibly ancestor worship itself, still they respected this as an Acholi tradition and a symbolic remembrance of someone passed and a sentimental way of feeling that the lost one's presence was still among them and would still be felt. The ritual at the hut was to be performed three times that night and then again at dawn the next day when the cock crowed.

Celeste began assisting Mama around the compound. There was a major discussion amongst the relatives about the inheritance of property, as legally women had not obtained the right to inherit property. However, given that in this case Mama was his wife and not his daughter and was more than fit to handle the business, the elders decided to allow property transfer into her hands, with Geoffrey overseeing the whole operation and having the ultimate responsibilities that Bartholomew had exercised as father. He would actually herd the cattle along with the boys. Celeste and the girls just sat dazed, wondering what to do next.

They didn't have to ponder long, for a truck began rolling into Obim on a cloud of dust. The occupants haled an old man sitting in a chair, tipped back against the wall of a kiosk, and in essence held him in a stare that projected both anger and disgust. Tegene asked him about Celeste Okulu and her whereabouts. The old man just pointed in the direction of the compound, advising them to tread lightly, as her father had just died. He also warned them that failure to do so might anger her father's spirit, who might return as a *cen*, an evil or warlike, avenging spirit, and harm them. Tegene thanked him and informed him that they would enter respectfully, that they were merely worried about the three girls, as they had left without providing any suitable explanation. Given the war, they were afraid that Kony might have intercepted them. The old man nodded with a wise smile, humming his acknowledgment if not tone of approval.

"They are there," he said, still pointing in the same direction.

A cen! Really? If her father was to become or send back a cen, he would probably haunt Kony and the LRA responsible for his death and daughter's abduction. If there were so many cens about from the holocausts at Kony's hands, how come the cens hadn't killed him yet for his sins and desecration of Uganda, indeed most of east Africa? Tegene thought. Who knew? He was too tired from the drive and recent events to think about it. He just wanted to find Celeste and talk with her and wrap his arms around her.

They drove the truck to just outside the compound. The weapons and ammo had been well concealed. Still they didn't want to chance the prospects of someone rummaging through the truck, looking for something of value and just happening to stumble across them. Tegene got out of the truck, instructing the others to stand guard over the cargo as he walked into the compound in search of his beloved Celeste. He ran into her brothers and asked about her, whereupon they pointed to the back where she was with the cattle, watching over them. He walked through the compound and into the bush where the cattle grazed and saw her standing on the outskirts of the herd.

He tried to keep his temper—but no! He began to let her know that this wasn't the way to work!

"You just traipse down here to Obim, risking everything, and you leave a mere one-line note of utter bullshit, totally lying to me, doing the exact opposite that you promised! What the hell were you thinking?" He caught himself before he really launched into a tirade. "My condolences about your father. I know it's tough for you now, but I had to say something. It isn't as if you left with the knowledge that he had died and were returning for the funeral. Kony is all over the place. I was scared to death about you and had to say something."

"I'm sorry. I'm sorry I lied to you and betrayed your trust. It was a stupid thing to do, but it happened to work out in another way, with father and all. You say you had to say something, because you care?" she asked, actually wanting him to say more.

"Yes, I do. Of course I do. I have told you this. More on that later. We stole a whole armory's worth of weapons just in case, along with a truck we creatively procured. We should stash them somewhere."

She gave a little laugh. "You were going to take on the entire LRA?"

"If I had to," he said. His tone was stern, resolute. "For you, I'd die. Practically done it for other things. You are the first thing I've found actually worth dying for!" he said, looking down, pawing at the ground with his feet. He looked up at the horizon.

She gazed at him, no longer even giggling but looking upon him with a tone of respect and loving adoration. *He would die for* me, she thought. He had actually said that, the closest thing to "I love you" so far. But to actually hear this much from him and so definitely stunned her with admiration and gratitude. A smile crept across her face as she continued to look at him. He looked back and smiled briefly.

"I'm sorry I took off so impetuously without really talking to you or planning it better. It was dangerous. You're right. I didn't know Papa had died. It was reckless for us to think that we were going to just come in here and save the village from itself. Then when we got here, we found out that the casualties included Papa. It has been very emotional for us, like a roller coaster without the amusement park. The ups have been seeing Mama and letting her know that we are all still alive, and the downs, well, you know."

"I know. We ... we now have the rest to deal with—namely, what do you still have to do here? We can't stay her long. The LRA is still in the area, in retreat, but still around and desperate. We have to stick together."

"Yes, Tegene," she said softly. She continued to gaze at him with alluring eyes.

He sensed that she loved him. He loved her. Some day he would have to come to terms with the battle-hardened exterior to be able to say it.

She thought for a minute and said, "I should stay here for a while, a few more days anyway, just to help Mama out and my brothers and sisters. Then, I don't know. I don't want to go back to the IDP camp in Gulu, but we can't stay here too long either. They could come back if for nothing else then to scavenge for food. I should help my family readjust to this new situation. My uncle Geoffrey will take over most of the duties pertaining to the livestock. Mama will continue tending to the fields as she has always done."

"We are not going back to Gulu. We should try to make it to Ethiopia. I know a place, Axum. It is more stable now. I was wondering ... Celeste, would you go with me to Axum? Kony will never find us there. I have talked with Alemayehu and Feleke about it. They agree. Of course, we're from there. But you, you are Acholi, from this place. This place is your home. Are you willing to leave home and go with us?"

"Wherever you go, I go, for that is home. Home is supposed to be a sanctuary, safe. This place is not safe, not now. This place is not home. Home is where you go; home is with you. With you, I am always home."

She wrapped her arms around him and held him tight.

"I feel that way too. We are our own home, our own house. I was incomplete without you, and you without me. Now, I feel whole. We are both whole now!" said Tegene.

⊶ෙ⊷

Alemayehu sat nervously in the driver's seat of the truck, casting an occasional glance back at the weapons cache. He pondered over the situation, thinking this could be a nightmare. First, the truck was stolen. Second, the guns were stolen. Third, the guns were simply there, automatics and a shotgun no less! This could raise a number of questions if they were discovered by the wrong people. Yet, still, there was the prospect of Kony's patrols coming back. If that was the case, they would still need the guns and possibly a lot more. Tegene had talked about going to Ethiopia. Alemayehu thought this a good idea. He just knew things had to move. He wasn't one to just sit around reacting to something. He wanted to move. He felt that reacting just got him into trouble and in many cases rather dangerous situations. However, as Tegene was quick to point out, Alemayehu felt but often didn't think, and his impetuous nature could get him into worse spots. Hence, Tegene convinced him that just because someone did due diligence in planning, it wasn't being reactionary or mere inaction but a responsible measure to ensure success as much as possible when the person did act. Tegene was always good at that, and some had rubbed off on Alemayehu.

Alemayehu meant "he had seen the world," and not much of what he saw of it looked too good. He was disillusioned, disheartened, and bore a very negative disposition.

"You look hungry. You should take something," Genevieve said, offering him some chapatti and a bit of stewed meat. "And don't say you're not. I know you," she said with a smile.

"Do you now?" he replied with an amusing smile.

"Yes. Here, have something to eat. You have that look in your eye, as if you are far away, but the horizon seems to look very bleak to you. Your face is—how did my teacher put it? Ah, yes, despondent. Your world sometimes appears bright with vibrant colors, but so often lately it appears to be a depressing, dull gray. You once painted with a love for life, you said, but now you think that if you painted at all, from within it would all be dank, dark paintings of misery."

"If I could paint at all. I almost feel that that gift has died within me."

"It hasn't. I can tell. It may be asleep, in a state of dormancy, my teacher once put it, but it could be resurrected, brought back to life. I see it in you. I love you, Alemayehu, and I can see this in you!"

He turned his head and looked her in the eye. "Love can be a dangerous thing, particularly at times like this with people like us. I have killed so many. You love me in spite of that? You can love someone like that?"

"I was a whore. Sex was mean, sadistic, and methodical. You are still with me. I know you love me."

"You are and were no whore! You are a victim! It was not your fault. You had no choice!"

"Neither did you! Kony forced you into combat. It wasn't your fault either. I love you in spite of all of that; I love you because of your strength in not totally losing your mind and heart despite it. You still have a conscience. You are still strong, and you will paint beautiful, vibrant horizons and sunrises again!"

"I know this much. I can lead us out of here along with the rest. I know I can build a new life—with you. You help bring a spark to my life ..."

"A new dawn!" Genevieve broke in. "You need a new dawn. And dawn needs someone with sight to see it and build the rest of the day."

"Yes. And where do you think I can find that new dawn?" His eyes softened as he smiled at her.

"Did I ever tell you what Anyanyo, my Acholi name, means? It means born at sunrise—at dawn. I am that new dawn! I could be that new dawn for you! You can be my warrior and eyes for a new future.

You have seen a world of hate, war, and agony. You can see another one too. It is time that you began to seek another world with me. I can help."

"But one cannot see in darkness. One needs a new light—a new dawn as you say. You are that new dawn. I have always known it. Will you come with me to Ethiopia? Will you be my new dawn and light up a new day in my life? I only want to see it if you are in it with me to share it. But we need Ethiopia and something else to consecrate it all. I am not sure what that is, but we will find it all together. We have something that goes the distance—a real love. In that regard ..." he stammered, trying to move his mouth past the pain that had choked off these same words before, "I love you too."

She nuzzled up to his cheek. "I have wanted to hear those words from you for so long!"

She kissed him lightly on the cheek. He kissed her lips and then her eyes with his own. He put the food down and held her. Then they embraced tightly, as if holding on for dear life.

Just outside the main hut, Feleke sat whittling a stick of wood. He wondered how much longer they would stay in Obim. His name, "it sprang," was fitting in a number of ways that all characterized him. First, "it sprang" meant "quick, fleet-footed, sometimes mercurial." He sprang. He moved often. In fact, like Alemayehu, he wanted to get the show on the road. This had been conditioned in him by years of fear with Kony, and now these sensations only spiked as his freedom from the LRA was a little too new for him to absorb with ease. At any moment, he felt, he would have to use that same knife to plunge into some LRA bastard's gut.

Secondly, "it sprang" also characterized his rural upbringing, as crops sprang out of the ground as they farmed, and he was a man of the land. He longed for the days of his father's farm, of tending the crops and herds of goats and cattle. It had all been so peaceful, paradise in fact, before war blew it all to hell. First it was the DERG, and then after his family ran to Uganda for some perception of safety, Kony showed up. He longed for the days when he herded cattle with his father in the tall grasses underneath a big blue sky that seemed to stretch forever. His father would call him over to a clearing and bid him to sit with him by a campfire and would show him how to whittle with a knife, cutting miraculous toys and figures from a stick of wood. Feleke's eyes would widen as his father would show him how to work with wood. He showed him the same love and guidance as he showed him how to work the land, for a man who can use his hands such would never go hungry. His bounty here would be measured not just in the sense of agricultural economy, albeit important, but in the family legacies and stories that told the world who they are/were that would live on through generations and that way ensure their immortality, regardless of any belief in ancestor worship. But that was so long ago, even though the memories were so bright they could gravitate his mind away from the current misery. They seemed like yesterday.

Now he felt dead inside. Aside from those wonderful memories, he felt his soul had been so badly wounded by Kony that nothing would spring from it again. He growled, trying to sift through the soil of his conscience to see if there was fertile ground for a new crop of ideas, or had his imagination vanished along with hope of a new, better life?

Miriam walked up to him. "What are you carving?" she asked.

"It's the beginning of a necklace for you," he replied.

"You're making that for me?" She was excited, for this was one of few instances where he intimated something of affection. Most of his talk was stilted but cordial. But lately he had been showing signs of humanity toward her, that he liked her—a lot, which she rather enjoyed!

"Oh, I like it already. Here, I have something for you. I know you like knives. Here. Do you like this one?"

It had a rich ruby-red handle with a marble finish to it. The trim and butt were bronze but polished and shined as if gold! It was not a small penknife but a larger buck knife about ten centimeters without the blade extended. Feleke looked at it as if it were more valuable than all the gold and silver on earth!

"Miriam, you got this—for me? I will carve us out a whole new life with this one. It is the most beautiful thing I have ever seen—almost! Where did you get it?"

"It was my father's. He gave it to me to give to you. I told him about you. He would like to meet you. When you carve, you don't merely whittle—you are an artist. Things grow, seem to spring from your mind. Your imagination makes them grow, and then you sculpt them out of wood! It is amazing to watch you work."

"Nothing much grows there anymore. I feel like it's a barren wilderness in there, like much of the land I used to farm with Father, but I can't grow anything from this soil. I feel that my life, like it, has become a scorched earth hell."

"I know how you feel. I feel dried up inside emotionally, spiritually too, like the rain that once brought life has now been choked off. The rain has became bitter tears—until I met you. Now I feel that it is fresh. I am feeling a sense of renewal. You have put your life on the line for me like no one else has. I feel there is still something of life still stirring in you."

"Indeed, a rainy season to give life to me again, so the crops in the field will spring up again."

"My name is Akot. Do you know what it means? It means born during the rainy season. I am that rainy season to your life. You see the new life that can spring up for both of us. I will be the water for your soul, and you the growth for me, the foundation to grow a whole new life for me!"

He looked at the knife and smiled. "I said this knife was about the most beautiful thing I have ever seen." Then he looked deep into her eyes. "But you, my gift from heavenly rain, my love, are the most beautiful!"

Her heart jumped into her throat. She gently stroked his hand. He embraced her and locked his lips upon hers and voraciously kissed her again and again as the actual rain began pouring down. The rainy season had begun. The rain drenched both of them in their embrace, not that either one cared. They had been dry long enough, for way too long.

⋯⊙ ⊙⋯

The rains came, growing in intensity with each second. The gentle downpour began to unleash a deluge of rain, pounding the ground in a torrential downpour. It bathed the earth, nurturing the ground, streaming, jetting down slopes and crevasses, making new rivers along the way as if to cleanse the earth of all impurities. Tegene stood out in the middle of it all with arms outstretched, his head tilted back, raising his face upward toward the sky. His mouth was wide open, trying to drink in all of the rain heaven could dish out, his shirt unbuttoned, fluttering behind him like a cape as he tried to mystically bathe himself in heavenly rain to cleanse his soul. This act held greater importance for him than mere soap and water on his skin. He tried to let the percussion of the raindrops force the thoughts from his head and simply let his mind go into free wheel in peace. This was far more desirable than staying in a shelter with a hard roof, for the deafening sound of rain hammering in the convective rainstorms that hit Africa's rainy seasons sounded like machine-gun bullets, bringing back too many memories of combat. Hence, such shelters were no shelter at all, not from the real storm that plagued him. He felt that the soaking downpour in fact was. Celeste clearly did not understand.

"Come in out of the rain, Tegene! Come over here to the shelter by the fire so you don't get cold and wet," she said.

"No fire can warm me like that in my soul here in the rain itself," he replied.

She looked puzzled, then smiled and said, "Well, you can keep me warm. I'm getting cold!"

He slowly walked over to the shelter, a lean-to of sorts covered by thatch. It dulled the sound of the rain somewhat, but only to the extent that it made the "bullets" sound far away, not totally absent. He held her as she snuggled up to him. He nuzzled and rubbed his face gingerly against hers, but still there was tenseness to his embrace. She noticed he didn't shiver a bit, and his eyes looked far away.

"Where do you go at times like this? Where do your eyes and heart take you? I feel that you are not with me but somewhere else, somewhere far away. I know in the long run they belong to me. But at times like this they belong to something or somewhere else. You are far, far away. Tell me, where and what is this place?"

"A place of pure peace, of running water, with just God and me. I have never wanted anyone else there. It is where there is no war, no death, no pain, no hate."

"And no love? Is there no love there in this place?"

"There has been peace, but no love, at least no romantic, human love that can be lost and hurt—no love of that kind, only of another, above and beyond what you refer to, until now."

"What do you mean?" Celeste asked.

"I know that there is a God. I feel His presence and love there. An abba that I once knew called it agape. It's a place where I go where He has me in a better place to talk with Him and listen to Him. He has my full attention in the waterfall. There I hear His voice, where the water is so clear and sweet, and around it are flowers in all kinds of different hues and colors. Birds fly by, nesting up in the mountains. It is a crystal-clear waterfall, a crystal waterfall high up in the mountains where no one is there but God and me, and no one can find me if I don't want to be found—a safe place. The water falls down over six tiers, like one I once walked through many years ago. I walk behind it and lean on the cool, wet stone face of the mountain, the wall behind the crystal waterfall, and just gaze at the water. I watch the drops drip off of the lush green plants and ferns that run across the rock face, outlining rocks, cracks, and crevasses in its formations.

"Then I take a deep breath and step directly into the falls. You would think that the pressure of the water would knock me down and drown me, but it doesn't. Even though the entire waterfall is over three hundred meters, it doesn't. It bounces off of six ledges, six tiers, which takes something off of the force of the waterfall, but still it pounds on me, and I stand, facing upward into the water blast, my arms stretched out, letting it pound and wash away the impurities in a cool, rejuvenating wash. I step all the way through it and feel the tingle, the rush. I am renewed! My head is clear, my conscious even clearer. I have been cleansed, and all remnants of war are too far away to bother me now. But if only it would last! It doesn't. I feel the need to go there again and again in my mind. I try to return to it in prayer and afterward in my spirit. I feel the sensation again and again, the heavenly rain falling down upon me, cascading through my soul, pouring down in spiritual dimensions of my life as I seek greater clarity of it all, to all of the experiences—both the good and the bad. The voice of God comes not in a booming voice audibly but in a quiet whisper inside. But I can sense to power of it all, more powerful than the gale-force winds of a hurricane. It comes to me with a tone of peace, confidence, and reassurance. Even if I have sinned, I know that His hand is still upon me and it is going to be all right. But, still I think He is telling me something else, something else that I need from Him that will make it all complete. But I am not sure what that is. Still, here, I feel I can bear my full soul to Him, to the whole universe from my darkest recesses of sin to the highest joys of my life. I walk out of there and become a brand-new man, at least for a while. I stand in the pool of water in front of the falls and lean my head back with outstretched arms, rejoicing at how beautiful life can be in comparison to how dull, grungy, and filthy it looks at other times."

Celeste listened intently, looking at him with eyes of intrigue as he spoke, describing the effervescence rising up inside him as all the impurities in life seemed to be flushed out of him, of the zeal and ecstatic feeling rippling through him in an indescribable rush of sensations she longed to feel herself but had never experienced before. The complete loss of inhibition, standing unabashedly naked, opening up one's soul completely to God was breathtaking, something she desperately sought but could not fight through the pain and shame to do so, possibly until now. She was also awestruck at the revelations Tegene had shown. She was indeed moved at how revealing and open he had been, more so than she had ever seen from him so far.

She looked out at the fields being drenched in the rain. Not far away was a depression in the field, just past a couple of small mounds, that was quickly turned into a pool of water in the downpour, with lush green brush and plants on the bank. A tree stood, leaning over the plants, its longer branches forming an arc hanging over the pond. Its leaves went from dancing up and down in the rain to becoming a waterspout, as the branches seemed to combine into a solitary path for huge drops that turned into a waterfall, pouring off into the newly formed pond. Celeste got up, took off her clothes, and proceeded to step out of the lean-to. She reached out to Tegene and took his hand.

"Come," she said. "I see a waterfall."

He stripped off his clothes and walked with her into the pool of water in the middle of the field.

They stood gracefully in the cold rain, gazing into each other's eyes. Water streamed down their bodies as they moved closer, holding each other in something beyond a mere sexual embrace. The engendering interlace of spirit and soul, a form of communion, was far beyond that. It was stripping oneself more than in any mere physical sense and was a deeper spiritual revelation for both of them where the layers of shame, pain, guilt, and degradation came off, the type of cloaks that had normally been glued to them regardless of any physical garments. They truly stood naked before God and each other, revealing their souls and leaning their heads back to catch the rain in their eyes and mouths, rinsing the tears from their eyes, their souls, feeling as free as the beautiful snow-white egrets that lofted out of the ponds, flying almost effortlessly into the tree where they perched and watched Celeste and Tegene demonstrate the purest essence of intimacy. It was a revelation to all, an expository declaration to the whole world. They were free, not captives, human, not chattel of warlords, healing not dying, a celebration of true love, not hatred.

They moved under the tree branch and let the waterfall cascade down on them. Their abandonment of innocence did not imply lack of purity but rather just the exact opposite, the full maturing of purity. Out of respect for each other and the moment, they didn't make love in the carnal sense but rose to a higher level of enlightenment, of healing, of wholeness, of feeling complete.

"Now that we have experienced the waterfall, I feel like I can bare myself, that I could run free, completely naked, naked in the sense I can bare myself, my full soul, and begin to dispense more of my feelings of shame, all my inequities," said Celeste.

"Even your outcries of righteous rage for the violation done to you? Even forgive yourself for carrying that baggage of shame that was never yours to begin with and beating up on yourself? Can you release yourself from the compulsion to prove yourself worthy because you feel that you were spoiled goods? Do you now realize that you are worthy already and always have been as much as anybody else who was not raped? Do you now see that Celeste is beautiful just the way she is?"

"Do you really feel that way—see me that way?"

"You are more beautiful than all the flowers and birds in my waterfall. You are the most beautiful thing in the world. And I don't love you merely because you are beautiful; rather, I see you as beautiful because I love you deeply, more deeply than I have ever loved any flesh-and-blood creature on God's green earth, more than anything under heaven. I am still searching for something, something more of a proper calling in life, but I know we both are. I know we will search for it together."

"You don't need to search for the waterfall anymore. My name is Okulu. It means born by or in the river. I am the river. I will be your waterfall. My loving water, the flow, will be the current, and over rapids, huge drops, and valleys in your life, I will be the waterfall. I will help comfort you and give you peace. I will help heal you as your love helps heal me. We will search out any destiny together."

"Yes, hold me. Hold me and let your love bathe me like a waterfall."

"Do you want me? You could take me now if you wanted to," she propositioned him.

"No, not now. There will be time for that later, a time when you will clearly know that I am not just taking you like they did to you; deep within your soul, you will know it. It will be more than special. Do you know what an epiphany is?"

"Yes."

"There has been a mystical epiphany here, what we have right now—an epiphany that we are experiencing. It is more fulfilling than sex, a more intimate love than mere sex alone could ever reach. I just … want … to … hold you—the first earthly love in my waterfall!"

She smiled. His respect overwhelmed her. She had not known this from any man before. They just embraced as the rain began to slacken. As the rain began to quit, the sun broke through the clouds, and splotches of blue began to veer through the gray. Egrets began to glide back over the pond, some lighting in water or on shore in search of food or drink. They looked up at the two, occasionally fluttering their wings as if to applaud, showing their approval. Rays of sunlight streamed through the sky and, as if to dance on raindrops, created a huge rainbow stretching across the horizon. Like a Noahic covenant, Celeste and Tegene embraced their own. Their life would eventually walk across their own rainbow to a life of joy. But the journey would not be free of obstacles to surmount, for no life journey is.

⋅⊙⊙⊙⋅

The next morning, Tegene awoke and walked outside where Celeste was already preparing the fire to fix breakfast. Outcries of anguish sounded from Obim Rock. Tegene quickly ran over and scaled the rock formation to the IDP camp atop it. A woman so distraught she collapsed in front of her hut was sobbing uncontrollably, screaming something about her children. She had three children, all boys in their teens. Marauders from the LRA had indeed been there. They had stolen the three to impress them into service. Camp officials came by and inspected the area. They tried to console her with the mythology that it wasn't the LRA. That despite Bartholomew Adenya's recent death, the LRA was miles away and at best the attack on Adenya must have been the act of stragglers. Perhaps the boys had just walked away or got lost and might make it back.

Tegene knew the LRA. He looked around and saw their signatures in various subtle ways that the officials would never pick up. "Don't tell her that!" Tegene shouted at them. "Besides, she knows it's not true and will be angry that you have lied to her. She knows full well what happened. The same thing that's been happening here for a long time now, and you know it! I know the LRA. I know the signs. They were here. Perhaps they still are. They sometimes use informants from the people in these camps. They sometimes work at random; sometimes they go after targeted people. She knows the LRA have her sons. I know it too. I once fought with them! They had abducted me too!"

The camp officials just stared at him and then turned and walked away. They could not perpetuate the illusion that all was safe when nobody bothered to hallucinate with them. So many knew about the raids, sending their children on the dangerous nightly trek to some perceived haven of refuge from Kony. It was folly to try to maintain the propaganda that the area was truly rid of him. Disgusted, Tegene turned away and held a confab with Alemayehu and Feleke. He discussed their exodus, which he now found to be imperative. If Kony's henchmen were indeed this close, it was just a matter of time before the intel got back to the LRA of their presence there. Then the next raid would be for the six of them.

As dusk came on, all six sat tensely around the campfire. They wondered what dangers the night would bring. Would there be another raid? Had the LRA already found out about them, and would they make a beeline for them? Tegene muttered something about the truck. He would go check on it and then come back. He walked over to the vehicle just to ensure that all was in good working order. They had already taken the ammo and weapons from the truck and stashed them in a few well-concealed but easily accessible locations around the compound.

LRA soldiers indeed were making another raid on the camp. Tegene heard muffled screams coming from the compound area. He ran quickly over to check on Feleke and Alemayehu, who were locked in an intense struggle with three LRA soldiers. Tegene dashed over to one spot where he had stored the weapons and grabbed an AK, outfitting it with a bayonet. He also grabbed a couple of ammo clips, loading one into the assault rifle and stashing the other one on his person. He set the gun on automatic fire and then sped over to help Alemayehu and Feleke. Feleke had just knifed his chief assailant, but the third began to attack him. Tegene bayoneted him in the back and then slung the rifle butt, ramming it into the remaining soldier who was locked in a struggle with Alemayehu. He no sooner turned around than two more entered the hut. Tegene opened fire and cut both of them down in their tracks.

"How about the girls? They okay, or have the LRA found them too?"

"Don't know. I think they are safe. The soldiers—I don't recognize any of them. They must have joined up with Kony after we left. However, they said that they were looking for you, though!" replied Feleke.

"Someone in the camp tipped them off—had to! How else would they know we were all here? They particularly want you though. They know who you are! They didn't have many nice things to say about you! They were pretty clear. We've got to go tonight, man, I'm telling you," added Alemayehu.

Just then, Miriam and Genevieve walked into the hut. They were safe. No one had touched them.

"I don't know what is going on with Celeste," said Genevieve. "She hasn't come out of the main hut! That's not a good sign!"

"Better go over there armed!" recommended Miriam.

Tegene pivoted out of the hut and then darted in the direction of the main hut. When he got there, he saw the worst sight possible, one he could only have seen in a nightmare. Two LRA henchmen were inside waiting for him, one with a firm grip on Celeste, fondling her, indeed proceeding to strip her bare. The other was against the wall holding an AK on both Mama and Celeste and looked up at him with a smile on his face. Tegene reset the gun on single shot.

"Tegene, Tegene, Tegene … where have you been so long? Haven't seen you in a while, or the whore. Okello was going to have her, he said, and then pass her onto us. That night we waited with great anticipation at the thought of having this one. She is in her prime! But then Okello never came back. In fact, we found him the next day dead in a ravine with his vehicle gone, and so were all of you! Tegene … what happened, I wonder, to our friend and comrade in arms, poor Okello? I mean … we know what happened to him. His throat was slit and a big hole in his chest, but the mystery remains as to how it happened and by whose hand? A witness says it was you!"

"What witness? If I was to do it, I wouldn't leave any! I'm a better soldier than both of you put together!" Tegene replied

"Me!" he said. "Now first I'm going make you watch as we do what we want with your little plaything! Then, well you know. But if you try to stop us, we kill her. If we just play with her and kill you, they all go free. Deal?"

Tegene looked at the soldier holding Celeste, who was terrified. He had a knife to her throat. The choice was to shoot him and risk getting shot from the other before he got his second shot off or die while she got raped. Celeste was everything. There were some things worth dying for. She was one of them.

"She's not a whore. Never was. She was a rape victim. No deal!"

He fired of a shot that took out the soldier holding Celeste. The other soldier fired a shot, wounding Tegene in the side. Tegene fired shots at him, hitting him in the leg, only to be shot himself in the upper chest, which spun him around, falling near Celeste.

"Wrong move. Now know as you die that I will be having a field day with her!" he yelled.

Tegene looked up and saw the stiletto she had used on Okello lying on the floor. He palmed it before the would-be assailant could see. As Kony's dog stumbled over to a screaming Celeste, getting ready to finish the job started by the other henchman, Tegene made one last heroic move. He threw himself onto Celeste, his back to her, facing upward at the dog who was already in the midst of pouncing on her. Tegene held onto the knife and then as the intended rapist fell, Tegene hit the button, ejecting the blade, driving it through the man's sternum into his lungs and heart. The man wheezed as blood spewed out of his mouth and chest. Then Tegene, with the last bit of strength left in him, tossed the bastard over to the side where he lay there, dead. Tefere just shuddered, gasping for his last breath. Celeste screamed as Alemayehu and Feleke came into the hut. Tegene lay on top of her, bleeding to death.

"I'll go get help!" said Alemayehu.

"No, I'm faster, I'll go. He doesn't have much time left!" said Feleke.

Feleke ran like the wind, wings on his feet. He flew to the medical tent where the doctors stayed. He notified them immediately. They were already up due to all of the commotion, particularly the sound of gunfire. They ran over to the hut as fast as they could with medical bags. They stood in the doorway of the hut, stunned as Celeste lay over Tegene's body sobbing.

"Move back. Let me in there!" said the doctor. He put his stethoscope to his heart and felt him still breathing. Then he cut off Tegene's shirt and observed the wounds. "He's still alive. We can't move him, so will have to treat him here. The wound in the side is a flesh wound. That one doesn't bother me. The chest wound, though—I don't know. I need more light. Can we get more light in here? Anybody have a torch?" The other doctor brought in a torch and beamed it down on Tegene.

"That chest wound is too high for the bullet to have hit the heart or the lungs. Hopefully the bullet didn't tumble and tear up the vital organs," the other doctor said.

The physicians went to work on Tegene. They pumped in some morphine to kill the pain. Tegene began passing out. The doctors removed the bullet from the chest. Fortunately it had not tumbled, and the vital organs were intact. The bullet in the side had gone clear through him. They worried about infection. They used some antibacterial salve on the wound but felt that this was not sufficient. They took an iron rod, heated it up in the fire, and poked it into the wound, cauterizing it the best they could, then stitched him up. There was a great deal of blood lost and nothing to be found for transfusions, not even plasma. The doctor made the sign of the cross on his forehead. "He's in God's hands now."

Celeste just sat by his side, weeping, but clinging to hope that her lover, indeed the only man she had ever loved, would pull through. She looked up to heaven and then back down on Tegene again. She prayed for his survival.

"God, you see us here suffering. Men did this not You, but please, I ask of You, please look down upon Your children with compassion! I have not been as You would have wanted, but what choice did I have? They say I was a whore, but wasn't Mary Magdalene, was not Rehab, whom You redeemed? Please, please God," she sobbed, "do You not still see something of Your daughter left alive in me that You can see fit to answer my aching prayer? Though I have not said some sort of sinner's prayer, I say this now, I will accept Your Son as my savior right now and lead this man to You, if You please, please give him back to me! Don't let him die, Lord. Please don't let him die on me, please, please. I beg of You, please!" She finished her prayer with sobs upon her fallen hero.

The doctor standing just outside with head bowed finished it for her. "Amen," he said softly. Then he walked away.

As the days past, Tegene moaned and groaned with fever, sometimes just writhing back and forth in a state of delirium. The doctors came by to check, finding Celeste evermore dutiful, bending over him tending to him. There was not much they could do without antibiotics. They were still waiting for another supply that government leaders and the UN had promised, but so far, no deliveries. Celeste continued to wipe his forehead, bathe him. and keep him cool in efforts to bring the fever down.

Finally, one morning when she was in prayer, holding his hand, she noticed him squeezing hers and rubbing her thumb with his. She looked up to see a slight smile on his face.

"Did you know that you snore in your sleep?" he asked.

"No, I don't, not me. I do not snore!"

"How would you know if you're asleep? You snore, I tell you, and rather loudly at that!"

"Not loud! Maybe a little—no, not even a little. I don't snore!" Celeste started laughing and crying at the same time. Her hero was alive!

"You do, but here's the deal. As long as you don't wake yourself up with it, I can live with it for the rest of my life."

"For the rest of your life, you say? Why, Tegene Tefere! What? You want to marry me or something? Do I have some say in this?"

"Probably not. Oh, I suppose so. You always find a way to get a say in everything else, even things you know nothing about, so yes, you have a say in this," he said with a smile. "We'll talk about it later. I have to go back to sleep now."

"Okay, you sleep. We'll talk about a lot of things," she replied. Then she kissed him on the cheek with joy. "Welcome back."

Chaos continued to swirl around northern Uganda, though the UPDF efforts were starting to show progress and signs of success. Kony made his retreat into the Sudan as Tegene began accelerating his charge into the healing process. Nobody made comment of any guns or trucks that just happened to be in the guy's possession, only that they had been heroic in thwarting another raiding attempt by the LRA on Obim. Even police in Gulu and the owner of the truck himself wrote it off to theft by the LRA. At last, Tegene could breathe a sigh of relief about that.

After discussing recent events amongst them, the six decided the best strategy was to try to head north to Ethiopia, to Axum, until the war was definitely over. Who knew when Kony would make a drive back into Uganda or whether there were desperate stragglers still running amok around the surrounding environs? Even Miriam's father thought this a good idea. Miriam and he discussed what at this point seemed to be her perceived calling into a ministry with him. However, she and the other five were at more risk than most, given they had already been with Kony and were now apparently targeted.

He also wondered, given her zeal and youth, how much was idealism not girded by a sense of realism that would have a price tag too high for his ministry to pay in the short run. She needed more time, training, and experience to season her present skills and instincts. Would she listen to her father or stubbornly try to compete with him? Her abduction had forced a distorted type of independency from home. She was too temperamental, but this would change with time and healing.

He particularly felt that she needed a quick exodus from Uganda and hoped Feleke could either provide for her or find a family that would take them at least until the madness was over.

Tegene, Feleke, and Alemayehu felt they could build lives with the girls on their own but were also aware that Africa wasn't too keen on youths their age getting married and starting families, particularly given their lives up until now. This wasn't Africa in the nineteenth century anymore. Certainly, the girls' families would not approve. They would insist on families or missionaries taking them in until they matured or reached legal age. Of course the major concern was assuring their immediate safety, which simply couldn't be done here.

Tegene sat in the driver's seat of the truck and weighed in on all of these issues. On the one hand, he wanted to marry Celeste, but that at least had to pay heed to tradition. He would have to ask her father's permission for her hand in marriage. With Bartholomew Adenya's death, this responsibility would be transferred over to her uncle, Geoffrey. On the other hand, there was also the issue of the bride price or dowry. How could he afford that? He had no trade except soldiering. To say the least, Geoffrey would not be too wild about the idea of Tegene saying, "I could steal enough to meet those terms!" One had to show the capacity to prosper or derive the bride price from honest labor and have some established position in life, which none of the guys had. Promises were made regarding some sort of future care regarding relatives or suitable people in Axum who could provide care, contacts that the three didn't have. Civil war in Ethiopia had either killed or dispersed what contacts they might have had to the four winds as wandering diaspora. Tegene, Feleke, and Alemayehu had no clue as to what they would find in Axum. Like so many places ravaged by war in Africa, home was no longer home anymore. It was going to be another trek into the unknown. However, as unknown as it was, it was still better than the known option of staying in Obim or Gulu on borrowed time. And sooner than later, time was going to run out. The unknown offered a better chance of survival than northern Uganda. After tearful good-byes, the reluctant pilgrims piled into the truck stocked with new, ample provisions and drove off, charting a course to a new uncertain destiny.

⟨⟨⟩⟩

The atmosphere in the truck was cheerful, with the occupants engaged in lighthearted banter highlighted by actual laughter. Celeste sat close to Tegene, as he could drive with one arm around her and one hand on the wheel. He only removed his left arm to shift down when they approached a town. They drove nonstop through Lira and Soroti and only stopped momentarily at Mbale to use the toilet and eat something before moving on to Tororo and across the border into Kenya.

Having dispensed with the guns, they could have no real problem crossing the border. It wasn't unusual to see someone eighteen employed as a truck driver, and Tegene looked much older than that. He had just turned seventeen but looked closer to twenty-one. They cleared the border and immediately took to the north, headed for Ethiopia and what they hoped would be sanctuary. As darkness came on, they stopped at Nyehururu. Tegene walked into a hotel and up to the night clerk to get a room for one. He had to wake him up from his drunken stupor. He went ahead and paid in advance. The night clerk just nodded his head, placed the money in a box below, handed him the room key, and went back to sleep. Moments later, the other five rushed quietly past him, and all headed up to the same room to economize. After catching a few hours of sleep, they all quietly slipped out the same way before the desk clerk awoke. They piled back into the van. "On to Ethiopia," muttered Tegene. Then they proceeded north to the border.

The Ethiopian border guards just saw Tegene as another truck driver completing a run to Uganda and just waved him through, not particularly concerned with the other passengers in the vehicle. Tegene breathed a sigh of relief. "Almost home," he said. He continued to drive straight through to Lalibela. "I know some people here. They hopefully will remember me and can put us up for the night," he said.

All nodded their heads nonchalantly in agreement. As long as there were no IDP camps or Kony in sight, it was just fine with them.

Tegene pulled up just outside of the excavation where the famous Church of St. George stood. It had been carved out of rock, mostly solid limestone, in the twelfth century. The church had been cut out in the shape of a cross and stood almost four stories high. They got out of the van and stood observing the wonder in front of them. The girls, having never been to Ethiopia before, marveled at the stone structure, its faded red, almost pink exterior paint giving way to dabs of yellow up to the stone brown roof. They took the tunnel below to enter the sacred house of God.

They walked into the church sanctuary. The atmosphere in the ancient temple of worship emanated a reverent mystical quality that stilled the soul, anointing it with a form of mystical charm, leaving them in awe. It was an environment of complete, total peace, something quite alien to them. Theirs had been an environment of hostility, and so tension-racked, they always walked around with a high level of stress, sometimes trying to sublimate it to the point of being relatively oblivious to the high current ever pulsating beneath the surface. But here that negative current disappeared, its generator shut off. Here it was quiet, peaceful. You could hear a pin drop.

An abba walked over to them, greeting them in Tigrean. Abba Lemuel (he is devoted to God) had been the chief abba there for twenty years. He looked deep into Tegene's eyes. "You have been away too long, my son, Tegene. Tell me, how have you been?"

"You remember me, Abba?" asked Tegene.

"Oh yes," replied the abba, "through the eyes. I have never seen eyes quite like yours. In that regard, I never really forget a face. You came here after your father had been murdered by the DERG, giving up his life to save you and your family. Though you were quite sad, there was an impeccable, unmistakably defiant look in your eyes and one of confidence—the look of a confident leader. That I could never forget."

"Much has happened since then. Much has changed in me. I am surprised you can see through all of the battle armor to see all of that," Tegene said.

"There has been much damage done, and I see much pain. But I also see signs of hope. I see through the eyes of the Holy Spirit. I can tell. And who are your friends?"

Tegene introduced them all to the abba and explained that they were fleeing from Kony and needed accommodations, at least for the night.

"You may stay as long as you like. We will care for you. You are headed back to Axum, you say? You will need someone, adults to care for you or at least provide for you. The authorities may not be comfortable with you on your own. None of you have reached majority age. Otherwise, you may be sent to some other IDP camp, possibly separated from each other, which you don't want."

"You could marry us," suggested Tegene.

The others just looked at him with wide-open eyes and then thought about it and shrugged their shoulders as if to say, "Yes, why not?"

"You are not old enough for that, given today's laws. Maybe a hundred years ago but not now. You want to get married, you say? Do you know what all is involved in sustaining a marriage?"

"Yes and yes. For all practical purposes, we have been through all of that, both during and after our abduction. We have been taking care of one another for a long time now, doing practically everything it would take to build a home, without the actual physical structure of one," Tegene answered. He then went on to explain everything they had been through.

The abba replied, "These things prepare you for a lot of life's twists and turns of a sort. But there is more to marriage than that. I am impressed as to what you have accomplished and what you have survived through. However, I still regret to inform you that, on the one hand, such a marriage would not be legal under current law. On the other hand, I don't think it would be a good idea for right now. You still have a lot of healing to do before you take that step, still ground for you to cover, more inner peace for you to rest on, to rest in. Then you will be whole enough to give of yourself and not simply be each other's rescuer in either the emotional or physical sense. More about that later. For now, have some queen cakes and coffee, and then we will find you suitable accommodations. Then we will sort through these things," the abba replied.

The six agreed. Their exodus from Kony had been exhausting, and now they finally saw light at the end of the tunnel. Taking the abba's suggestions, they all moved to another part of the church and sat down for coffee the traditional way: first the abol, and then they drank the second cup, the tona, and finally they had the bereka. The abba walked them outside the church and through the tunnel to the ground surface surrounding the church.

"We have a rest house of sorts we can accommodate you in for a while. Nice truck! Yours?" he asked, with a wink.

"It is now," replied Tegene.

The abba sighed, cleared his throat, and said, "Well, of course it is! No questions will be asked, given your circumstances. You've been through enough. Come, let's go. I get to sit in the front seat—right?"

They drove to the rest house, a type of hostel, and settled in for the night. Some women hired as cooks served up some ngira and wot. The exhausted sextet fell asleep in separate bunk beds as soon as their heads hit the pillows.

Tegene rose first, at dawn. He had problems sleeping much later than that. The rest continued to sleep. He took a bath, relishing the hot water, as it was the first real bath he had taken in over a week and the first hot bath since he could remember. A stack of towels had been provided, which lay on a shelf in the bathroom. The door opened just enough for a hand to reach in, laying his freshly washed and pressed clothes on a chair, then disappeared behind the door, closing it by the handle. Tegene was pleasantly surprised. *This is five-star luxury!* he thought. He felt outright pampered by the special treatment he and the others were accorded. He dried off, got dressed, and proceeded into the dining room where he found Abba Lemuel sitting at the table.

"Good morning, young Tegene! And how are you today?"

"Good. I appreciated the laundry and hot bath! It was very nice!"

"I'll bet it was quite luxurious given what you have been used to. Sit, sit and have some breakfast. And the others? How are they?"

"Still sleeping. Me, I can't sleep past dawn really."

"I am an early riser too. Tell me. This young girl, Celeste, you say you want to marry her?"

"Yes."

"Does she feel the same way?"

"More."

"Ah, is there another feeling—maybe pressure from her too?"

"Not really, Abba. But sometimes she hinted that she wanted me for life before I brought it up, just off of my deathbed. She has been more than clear on that since and clearly wants to hear me say it to her, that I love her, you know."

"That you love her? And have you?"

"In so many words."

"In so many words you say? I thought it only took three," mused the abba.

Tegene smiled rather sheepishly and then told the abba about everything, including the crystal waterfall experiences. The abba listened intently, showing great interest, particularly in the waterfall experiences and what they meant. He thought for a moment and began to speak, illuminating certain points about the topics Tegene and the others would need to hear.

"This crystal waterfall, as you put it, has more than some symbolic reference in your life. Of course water has been used for baptisms for thousands of years. It has more than a symbolic importance to us in the Orthodox faith. But what you have described is very deep, and you seek a very deep cleansing in your soul. You say you also stepped literally into an actual, physical waterfall and had some sort of spiritual experience or awakening of some kind?"

"Yes, near Murchison Falls in Uganda, after we went there following Father's death and before I was abducted by Kony and forced to kill most of my family," replied Tegene. "I keep walking out into the rain to try to reenact that, as if to keep cleansing myself over and over again."

"To cleanse yourself of what exactly?"

"The guilt. The guilt I feel from killing, starting with my uncle, or new father, his wives, my own mother. The guilt! I can't seem to get rid of the guilt!"

"You think this young girl, the river, and rivers often produce waterfalls—you think she is going to heal you, completely fulfill you and make you whole again?"

"I think maybe, but I know I love her and want her. I need her, and she needs me too. I know that much."

"Hmmmm, well, I have no doubt that there is a lot of emotional attraction there and need. And I won't say that it is or is not love, for I haven't talked to and observed the two of you long enough to determine that one way or another. But I can tell you this. She is not the river or waterfall that you require the most. You need the water of life to give life, particularly inside. However, she is someone who can be used by that true water of life to be one of its conduits, such that it can flow through you without being impeded so much after the point where you come to reconcile everything with that water's source. She is a helpmate, an aide to you in that process, and you to her as well, at the very least. I would like for you all to stay here for a while and talk with you about all of these matters. It appears that all six of you are paired up in a way that helps you fill the gaps, so to speak."

"Yes, that is true. Tell me, Abba, what is this water that you speak of?"

The abba opened up his Bible to a passage and handed it to Tegene. The passage was John 4:1–30, the story of Jesus at the well in which He revealed Himself as the Messiah to the Samarian woman and told of the water she could drink of and never thirst again. It was in reference to accepting Jesus and receiving salvation, where Jesus is seen as the living water of life. Tegene read the passage and closed the Bible. He handed it back to the abba and said solemnly, "I have thought long and hard about Jesus. When I was wounded, I remember Celeste crying out to God, saying she would accept His Son if God would not take me from her, and here I am. Still, I have much to wrestle with inside."

"I know. That is why you need to stay here for a while. You need time. Certainly you need more time before you make a huge step like marriage. You all need time. You should stay for at least a few weeks. We could accommodate you for that long here and then maybe make arrangements for you with contacts I have in Axum, if you have none."

Tegene nodded his head, and then a server entered the dining room with eggs and potatoes for breakfast. The abba blessed the food, and the two began to eat. Celeste entered the room, followed by the other four.

"Have you bathed yet?" Tegene asked them.

"No, not yet," responded Celeste. "But we did notice that our clothes were cleaned and pressed."

The others nodded their heads rather excitedly, showing their extreme gratitude.

"There is hot water!" said Tegene.

"And plenty of it for all of you," chimed in the abba.

"Hot water? Real hot water?" asked Miriam.

"It's been so long since we have had a hot bath. I feel like a queen!" said Genevieve.

"You are, and today you get to be treated like one," said Alemayehu.

The abba just smiled. "We will try to make your stay here as comfortable as possible. Why don't you go pamper yourselves with hot baths? After all, your clothes were all washed, dried, and pressed overnight. It would be a shame to have to put on clean clothes without a bath, and you will undoubtedly feel much better," he said.

All five agreed and individually took their turns in the bathroom in exquisite luxury!

After all had eaten breakfast, the abba escorted them about town and introduced them to the other abbas, those at St. George and the other churches at Lalibela.

"Long ago, the king of Ethiopia sought to recreate Jerusalem here. He structured the churches and landscape in an overall pattern to do so. The churches here are clustered into two groups, one representing the earthly Jerusalem and the other representing the heavenly Jerusalem. Then he had a trench dug, twenty-five meters by twenty-five meters by thirty meters, representing the River Jordan running in between the two Jerusalems. All of this has led both archeologists and architects alike to name this place the eighth wonder of the world."

The six marveled at all of the sights.

"Maybe some of that wonder will rub off on us and help us create better lives for ourselves," said Tegene. The others nodded in agreement.

"It will take a wonder of a different kind, the kind of wonder that breathed life in you when you practically had none, doing so in response to a heartfelt prayer," replied the abba.

This widened Celeste's eyes. "You told him about that? You heard it when I prayed for you?" she asked Tegene

"Yes, on both counts. I couldn't move. I was in and out of consciousness, but I heard it. And I told him. Why not? And who better to tell than him?" Tegene replied.

"True," she said. "I was meaning to talk with you about it all, but now that you know, it will be much easier."

"Yes and no," broke in the abba. "Certainly, there will be a lot to talk about concerning these things and many difficult matters and not about condemnation but about healing and pain, etc. There will be time for that later. For now, just relax a bit."

They all stayed at the hostel just relaxing for a few days. Then Abba Lemuel told them that arrangements had been made for them in Axum but that their new hosts would not be ready to receive them for at least two or three weeks. Until then, they would be welcome at the hostel in Lalibela.

Things were looking up for the first time in a long time. During their stay, the six began discussing matters with Abba Lemuel and some of the others at the Church of St. George.

Tegene spoke to Lemuel. "Abba, I want her, I want that living water. But so much anger builds up in me. I have tried to convert it all into a shield of armor to just try to tear my way through life. It's not anger at her but in general. At times, all feels so, so ..."

"Mechanical? Like you are just going through the motions?"

"Yes, something like that. It seems to block the flow of things like a state of paralysis inside. It has taken me a long time just to get this far. In terms of feelings for her, these things have been coming on stronger. But still, to let it all go and let it flow with her river—sometimes I can, and sometimes can't. It comes and goes."

"Your heart is heavily callused. You need to remove those calluses. You can't by yourself, by your own will. Only by His will alone can you do it. Tegene, my son, you present a tough case but not too tough for God. You need to completely submit your will to His and have confidence that He will steer you right. You need to totally submit your will to His—not in some form of public display but privately, in an honest environment on your own, where it will mean something—where it is real. You will need much prayer. Just to talk with God in a relaxed environment with no Celeste, nobody else save the Holy Trinity and you. If you want me there, okay. But I will not impose."

"I appreciate that, but, Abba, please explain some things to me. I feel I must know what to pray on. It should not be just some random bundle of words or thoughts, yet at the same time just reciting some written words by someone else won't work either. What do I say?"

"When you opened your heart to Him in the waterfall, things just flowed. You actually communicated from the spirit in total honesty. That would be a good place to start, to open yourself up like you did in the waterfall. Then just say what comes from the heart. Don't worry about trying to find the right words. One, God sees into your heart, and He will know what you are trying to say, and secondly, the words will come a lot quicker and easier the more you just talk with Him. There are a couple of things that are required, so to speak. You must first accept who Christ is, the only truly begotten Son of God. Accept Him as your only Lord and Savior and ask Him to forgive your sins—we all have to do that, by the way. Then, in prayer, submit totally to His will. You just let everything go into His hands and put your head in the lap that you can't see with the naked eye and just rest."

"Submit my will to His," replied Tegene thoughtfully.

"You may even have to ask His help with that to tear those calluses off of your heart. In a way, I think you are closer to that and God than you think, with what you described about the experience with Celeste in the rain, not to mention your near-death experience in the process of saving her life."

"Did we sin under that waterfall from the rain falling off of that tree branch?"

"Hmmm, not really," said the abba. "Some might get uptight about it, as they used to say, but me, not really. So you held each other naked in the rain. Do you know how many people run around naked with no clothes at all during and after a war, because of hate, stark-raving crazy? So you two did it out of love, but you didn't take her carnally, sexually, due to something more than mere respect, something quite more. Because you were both grasping something at a higher level, developing a truer sense of intimacy, indeed the foundation that true love is truly based upon, rather than what mere sexual relations alone provide. To get to that higher level, you had to go way deeper than mere sex alone. You were revealing yourselves inwardly and outwardly, both spiritually and physically to God in the most honest way. I see no sin in that," replied the abba. "But still, in your case, Tegene, you have become quite hardened in ways not healthy, and by His will alone will you be able to free yourself and make the journey back to wellness."

Tegene sat still for a moment and nodded his head silently. "Yes, I would need a rather disciplined strict lifestyle, no?"

"Tegene, Tegene, you have been so disciplined, so long. I think more you need to break away and let go to His will alone and let it fill you. Legalism is there as a lamp unto your feet. Sometimes you may want to cling to it, and you might find that helpful, but you need to remember it at best as a lamp, not a lamppost, and you need to be healed by His will and grace. The calluses will be removed from your hardened heart, and the chains will be removed. Now you don't live. You merely exist with those chains, beating up on yourself night and day. *That*, my son, is a sin," said the abba.

"Yes, that is a sin I have lived with for a long time. You have given me much to think about," said Tegene.

"Take your time, my son, and take as much time as you need, all of you, to sift through these things. Don't be in such haste to head back to Axum. Get things more settled inside you first and have a clearer perspective on what you want to do. Axum can wait. It has been there for over two thousand years. It will be there a bit longer for you to get there. All in good time."

Tegene sighed and felt more relieved. He had been living on the razor's edge too long. It was nice to be off of it and on some stable level or plateau in life for once. The rest felt the same way. One could tell by just looking at the relaxed atmosphere fostered by their growing sense of peace. It all produced an environment for inner reflection that they needed.

All six talked with the abbas occasionally, particularly with Abba Lemuel. They began the process of coming to terms with their past. Contemplative prayer was a major factor in helping them reach deep inside to reconcile their issues.

Alemayehu discussed the partnership-turned-romantic-relationship with Miriam in addition to her perceived calling to work with a ministry, particularly her father's. The abba nodded. He thought this was all admirable. Then Feleke told him about his relationship with Genevieve, of his interest in having, say ten acres, some cattle, and a nice house with indoor plumbing, if that came to the part of rural Africa he would eventually settle in. The abba smiled.

"I was a farmer raising crops and tending cows with my father growing up as a boy. It was most pleasant and very peaceful. But I discovered a new calling, and here I am," Abba Lemuel said.

Then he began to explain some things, interpreting things, imparting some much-needed wisdom to them all.

"You must understand that agape love flows from God and creates and heals through you as well as rains down heavenly rain. That rain that gives Tegene his real crystal waterfall, of which Celeste, the river, is a conduit of. That water flows through her and flows back, blessed by God's will from Tegene as well. You, Feleke, must see that agape in the form of grace, as God's grace abundantly blesses the land. The emphasis on grace, not punishment or mere legalism alone, is what you need for those rains to foster your resurrection. By that grace, you are resurrected from the dead zone your existence has been trapped in up till now to emerge into a new life. And it is through the grace that Miriam Akot becomes the rainy season in your life to facilitate that growth, and you hers. The grace endowed in you, Miriam, that living water of the rainy season you were born with. These character traits in you, Okulu, Akot, and Anyanyo, your parents could see because they were revealed by God. Whether they believed in Him or not, He revealed it to them. These things represent more than just the time of day or weather conditions of it or the season you were born in but the actual traits within you as instruments of God's love to be shared with someone else—someone like the guys you have found here. Alemayehu, you are looking for something new, you say. You need to become a new one in Christ, not just see a new dawn in Anyanyo, for it is only through the agape that flows through you two that truly brings out that new dawn and gives you the capacity to honestly see and appreciate it. It is the agape that flows through all of you as you become its conduits, conduits of His love, will, grace, and newness of life that makes for the marriages between you and makes the river flow to establish a communion of spirit and soul that provides a love with continuity. Put Christ at the center of your lives, and you will see the new future you want."

All six smiled. The abba hadn't written off their love for each other as mere childhood infatuation as they had feared he would. Instead, he had explained it in terms that made sense.

Over the next three weeks, they grew closer. All acknowledged that the abba was right. Then some people drove into Lalibela in a van from Axum. The abba met them, embraced them, and summoned the six to meet them.

"These are the people I told you about from Axum. This is Dawit, Amha Selassi, Dejen, and I don't know this young man. Who is this?"

Selassi responded, "He is Peter Ansulu VanHampton—Ansulu meaning "in His image"—Pete Jr. He is the son of a friend of ours who is back in the United States right now. Is everybody ready to go?"

The sextet packed up their belongings, got in the van, leaving their truck behind, and proceeded to Axum, leaving their past dreary existence behind as well.

Part 5

REDEMPTION

Abba Befikuda asked for a bottle of mineral water after drinking his cup of coffee for the bereka, "to avoid dehydration," he said. "Even though the last two cups, the tona and the bereka, are watered down in potency, it's still good to drink water to remain properly hydrated, particularly here in Africa. So, young gentlemen, what are your impressions from the three stories we have told you?" he asked.

Jamaal and Garret just stared rather blankly at the three oracles, who looked back at them with warm, understanding smiles.

"Wow, there's a lot there. I mean, like, there's a lot there to think about, a lot of impressions and thoughts going through my head right now. There are a lot of meanings to all of these stories that could take a lifetime to sort out, really," said Garret.

"Yeah, me too. I mean, you know, I see it the same way. Just trying to sift through all of this, whoa! I mean, you know this stuff is really deep and all. It'd take some time to really come up with a full understanding of it all," chimed in Jamaal.

"A full understanding of all of it, yes, and that may take more than a lifetime to get it all down. However, there are some basics that you can get. Let's talk about those," said Tsegaye.

"I mean, the way you describe and from what we have seen, Africa as a whole is a whole lot different than what I thought it was, a lot different than the way the Rastafaris claim it to be. It's been a real eye-opener," said Garret.

"Forget the Rastafaris. They are full of crap. They are Jamaicans who have lost their true roots in Africa. They know nothing about us, and we reject Rastafarianism right down the line!" said Addesu rather sternly.

"We kind of found that out from a bartender in Addis," said Jamaal. "But these stories, are they really true, or like, parables?"

"Both," answered Tsegaye.

The two nodded their heads and then opened the doors to probably the first real discussions about life and their issues in general they ever had. In the discussions, they revealed the true sources of their pain and illusions about life. It went back to their home life or the lack of one, their fathers, and failure to come to proper terms with it, not to mention acceptance by peers and Jamaal's life in the streets, etc.

"I mean, this thing about forgiveness—it's never easy. And I feel I've just been wandering for so long but going nowhere, because I can't seem to get past the past, if you know what I mean."

"Same with me," chimed in Jamaal.

"Now I think we are getting somewhere," said Tsegaye. "Forgiveness in such cases as yours in particular is never easy. But until you can reach back into your heart, mind, and soul and walk back through the catacombs of your mind and do it, you will never be free to walk in the present, much less proceed into the future. You certainly will not be able to open up any real route of intellectual, self, or spiritual discovery that you need to see a real path for a genuine pilgrimage of any kind. Remember what Abba Atatafe told James about forgiveness, about reconciling, not necessarily obliterating history. You need to free yourself, loosen your own chains. You should remember the points made by Abba Atatafe in the 'Abol,' particularly in cases of extreme abuse. You need to call on God's help to do that where you can't muster up the strength by your own flesh to do it."

The two nodded affirmatively. Then Abba Befikuda continued explaining the three parables' many meanings and how they related to Jamaal and Garret. The two, now ever respectful, asked several pointed questions, which the oracles answered, leading the two to conclusions they knew they had to embrace, and though still reluctant, they felt more comfortable about it than before.

"I think you first start with honesty," said Befikuda. "Think back to when I said one who lies merely seeks to hide the truth. This is often said, but that still implies that one is still cognizant of truth's existence in the first place. But one who tells half lies to cover greater lies no longer seeks to hide the truth but has conveniently forgotten where one put it and tries to blur lines of distinction so badly as to develop a spiritually lethal indifference toward the real things of value in life, preferring instead to walk in a void of moral anarchy, completely bankrupt of a genuine soul. What's being said here is that you must strip away as much of the false pretense as possible where you can deal with the terms of life more honestly, clearly—that is to say, you have to keep it real, as you say. Begin the process of sorting out the clutter and stuff in your life."

"All the excess baggage," broke in Addesu, "particularly that baggage that is yours and that which is actually somebody else's. What are false expectations imposed upon you as opposed to what you really want to be and who you really are?"

"Absolutely," responded Befikuda.

"From what you have said, neither of you two had much of a father in your lives, did you?" asked Befikuda.

"No. In fact my dad was like a gray ghost, more looking at Wall Street than at me. My mother was a raving alcoholic with her face in the booze all the time while getting down on me if I smoked pot! The old man, well, he just stared at three computer screens. When I wanted to discuss everything from sex to growing up in general, not to mention the church, he just said, 'See your mother,' and she was passed out drunk. They gave me cars, but you think that material possessions are so great? They're nothing, nothing but things for me to run away with and eventually wrap around a tree or telephone pole, which I tried doing a couple of times, trying to do myself in!" said Garret.

"Really, mean, like you actually tried to kill yourself? You never told me that!" said Jamaal. "Wait, dude, that nightmare you had on the plane? Is that what that was all about?"

"Yeah. And you know, like I didn't go into it because, like, I didn't know you well enough at that time. You know, you don't just open up with stuff like that with someone you don't know, but now I think, like things are different now, you know, with what we've all been going through and learning today. You ever try yourself? Be honest. I mean, that is what this is all about, like he said."

Jamaal thought long and hard and muttered, "Yeah, tried to overdose on heroin once. They took me to the hospital and all, and well, y'know, like here I am. What kind of car did you wreck?"

"Overdose on heroin? Isn't that what you were ripping your father for, why his life fell apart and left you? Whoa, dude, what prompted you to do the same thing if you resented your dad for doing it? And to answer your question, it was a Maserati."

"No kidding! Man, that's a sweet ride, kind of small though. How'd you make it out of there?"

"Wasn't too sweet when it hit the pole. The top was down, wasn't wearing a seatbelt, and I was thrown into a lake. Back-flopped into the water. Lucky! Would have broken my neck if I had hit land. Wasn't the only time. I thought about using a gun but didn't have the guts to pull the trigger."

"Man, they diagnose you with chronic depression or something?" asked an astonished Jamaal.

"They've diagnosed me with all kinds of things, and the medications have just made things worse. How about you?"

"They tried manic depressive, borderline personality disorder just to name a couple. You think these shrinks know what they're talking about?"

"No!" Garret responded. "I liked the part, Abba Befikuda, where you were talking about the battle scene with Kony's troops marching in. You know there doesn't have to be a war to see that the whole world is a mental institute and the lunatics are running the asylum!"

"Ditto. I mean, you know, it really seems that way sometimes. I mean, here some would say you had it all with the money, but in the long run, it don't mean nothin' if nobody's really there for you. I mean, my dad wasn't there. Heroin took him out of my life. He's in the Bronx somewhere, but I don't know where. But you got no one to love you, you got nothin', and sometimes that's the way it seems!" said Jamaal.

"God loves you. But sometimes young men like yourselves will have a hard time understanding that when you can't get anything from your earthly father. Satan tries to use that to paint a false picture and try to obscure your image of your heavenly Father through your earthly father's abandonment and demur your seeking a closer relationship to Him, indeed embracing Him as a loving Father who will not abandon you. Remember too, your fathers are human and are not beyond redemption. Neither are you," said Befikuda. "James Mecklenburg had problems with his father's loss, and Peter VanHampton didn't get along with his either. The child soldiers had to kill theirs. One of the things that the North Vietnamese soldier said rings true: 'Heal that schism before he dies.' If you don't, it will leave a chasm in your heart, a jagged hole that will grow and metastasize worse than a cancer and eat you alive. Your anger will only kill you, not your father or mother."

"Y'all talked about wars and stuff like that. Is there ever a moral cause to go to war?" asked Jamaal.

"Yes and no. Wars happen. To fight and react to them can be justified, but one has to remember the lessons taught, and they have far more overreaching implications than just war itself. You need to recall the discussion between Abai and James, not to mention the conversation between Nkomo and World Vision's personnel. More than some politically correct narrative, combatants must have a clearly defined pint of moral clarity. You have to envision a just society better than the one you war against, something to build toward, not merely tear down a system or thing you resent. Therefore, things don't just implode into a hodgepodge of blood and chaos for nothing. As this relates to you, examine your own temple. With your life badly cluttered by conflicting emotions, your visionary capability is obscured. This clutter swirls around from all of those unresolved issues, that emotional baggage mentioned earlier you have been lugging around all your life. Yes, there is a justification for wars, but first and foremost, you should examine the wars you have been fighting within you and in your immediate surroundings. To begin a real pilgrimage, you must embark on an inward journey and resolve those issues that cry out to you when you are prompted to wrap your car around a telephone pole or overdose on drugs, the same thing you crucify your father for. Only when you have resolved that are you truly capable of having the true prophet in you revealed and bringing the visionary in you alive to set real goals for yourselves. Then, if your journey takes you to someplace like here, you at least will be coming for all of the right reasons."

"Consider this also," said Tsegaye. "Until human beings first find peace in their own hearts, they are fools to think they can externalize it and produce peace between nations. Peace is not merely the absence of war but the development or restoration of justice. It is development that actualizes the potential and synergy of harmony that promotes growth. However, one has to be right with God in order to achieve that inner peace from which any true spiritual quickening process begins to spawn genuine enlightenment. Then and only then can one establish a righteous foundation to support any form of valid ideology, belief system, or decision-making paradigm. Without that, to quote Oginga Odinga of Kenya 'not yet *uhuru*.' Or to put it another way, not yet development. When Abai discusses this with James, he is clearly talking about something more than war, about James's whole sense of direction and orientation toward life itself."

Jamaal queried, "You talk about Africa's problems. The causes? Colonialism, the white man? No offense, Garret …"

"None taken," he replied.

"But y'all are talkin' as if a lot of this is due to y'all yourselves, like the brothers messed up their own continent."

"To a large extent, Africans have made a mess of things," Befikuda responded. "Certainly there is sufficient blame of colonialism for some things, and there have been those parties who have tried to exploit the situation, but in fact more exploitation has been committed by Africans than anyone else, and not even multinational corporations could pull off what mistakes they have made without indigenous pariahs who want to steal from their own people. We can tell you that Joseph Kony is not the product of so-called Western imperialism, and neither is tribalism, as tribalism goes back long before any white man discovered this place. There is no one real source of all the problems, except incompetency on everybody's part. There has been much water over the dam since colonialism, and the things that really threaten us today cannot be pegged solely on that or other foreign sources. The very existence of foreign aid itself has actually been a hindrance more than a help at times, regardless of what multinationals may or may not have taken out of this continent. Most of our problems today are our own doing, but most of the solutions will be our own doing as well. Our farmers have to be respected. They are intelligent people but need help, the type of help that will help foster many of their own entrepreneurial ideas, which I assure you they have despite what some development agencies or urbanites want to say. But there is no organized plot to keep Africa down by anyone. It is simply not an easy place to do business. Our infrastructure is lacking, largely because of our own officials and internal corruption. Not even slavery can be totally blamed on the white man, as many of our own African kings going back years engaged in the slave trade and sold many of our own to white slavers themselves. Today there are currently thousands of African Christians who are enslaved by black African Muslims in the Sudan. I think if we refer you back to some of the conversations by the World Vision people, a very responsible NGO out here, it will help put things in better context for you. Our leaders need to develop better game plans, plans that are set out on a real, valid premise with a clear focus as to what they want to accomplish and accomplish in the smallholder farmers' interest. Increase their income and you have what's called inventory burn-off in the larger cities. Commerce expands, and economic development rises evenly, and you have prosperity. Also, you must look at the focus on Christ, for He must be at the core of true freedom and nation building, regardless of what other religions say. The element of spiritually solid foundations is critically important, as here in Africa we must see some homogeneity in goal formation in order bring the conflicting tribes together to approach the concept of a national identity alone, much less embark on the building of nationhood itself. You say you are our brother, but are you really, Jamaal? Why, because you are black like us? That does not make you our brother, for Africa is not a country

Befikuda continued, "You are an estranged offspring of Africa. You are a form of diaspora. The voices of the ancestors are those of this continent, not slaves but free and proud people. To hear them, you must engage in rural development, work with our people and get to know them. You should also engage in prayer. Sometimes the voices of the ancestors are literal, those voices remembrances from the past that seem to speak out to us today, tossing a hint or two at the intuitive nature in us. Sometimes the voices are saying things we don't want to hear, things that we don't want to take responsibility for. But sometimes God opens up a channel to let us hear them. Who knows? Maybe they actually do speak to us in ways from heaven. You need to talk and work alongside our farmers and hear their stories, work with them like James Mecklenburg did," said Befikuda. "You need to penetrate into our culture and see the heart, mind, and soul of Africa. It really isn't as difficult as some claim."

"Man, that poem is beautiful, heavy, deep stuff. I'm beginning to rethink my whole gig on the documentary, on film, and the whole works," said Jamaal. "What does that mean, 'the brother's mountaintop'?"

"The brother is from the United States, referring to the one who had said he had seen the mountaintop," replied Befikuda.

"You mean Martin Luther King Jr.?" said Garret.

"He's the one. He understood. He is our brother," remarked Addesu. "In a way, we all will be striving to grasp that sacred Holy Grail called justice. We will get closer. But to see complete justice is almost to see perfection in this imperfect world. We will get closer, but to say that we will firmly grasp it—probably not in our lifetime, but we still strive for it and get better at it. That is why it is called the sacred Holy Grail."

"You keep talking about vision and Christ. How does that work again, and what's the relation to us?" asked Garret.

"Yeah, I've been thinkin' about that too," said Jamaal.

"Well, first you have to make the decision on your own to accept Jesus Christ as your only Lord and Savior. That is a strictly voluntary, conscientious decision that only you can make, but you have to honestly make it and mean it when you say the prayer or the prayer will be a vain prayer, as scripture calls it, something disingenuous that God will ignore which amounts to nothing more than parroting religious rhetoric, like you are just going through a ritual for no purpose," replied Addesu.

"Then you must pray to God, accepting His Son and Him, telling Him that you give your total life to Him. Admit that you are a sinner, as we all are, and ask forgiveness for your sins. Consider something else too. Ask for the baptism and indwelling of the Holy Spirit within you. When you repent you are actually turning away from what you are doing wrong and start doing what's right—the best you can. Nobody, particularly God, expects you to be perfect, but in the long run, you get better at overcoming your sinful nature by the grace of the Holy Spirit working in and through you," added Tsegaye.

"Then, over time, you find and feel amazing things happening, not the least of which is the tremendous weight of the burden of pain and guilt lifted from your shoulders," said Befikuda. "The visionary component comes out as your soul, heart, and then mind open up, just like Abba Atatafe told James. Just reflect on that and don't try to rush things. It will happen in time. Remember it was the Reverend—and I repeat, the Reverend—Dr. Martin Luther King who first knew God and was spiritually quickened to see the vision before he became the spearhead of the civil rights movement."

The oracles continued to explain concepts in ways the two could understand, continuing to answer questions from the young men who were maturing before their very eyes.

"Man, all this stuff is real deep. I know we've both learned a lot today," said Jamaal.

Garret nodded his head in approval.

Jamaal reached for another handful of popcorn. "You know that last story, the bereka, was incredible. I mean, we've heard about the child soldiers and all, but I got to tell you just hearing this, to try to see these kids coming back after all of that—pretty hard to believe. And God's love could heal that, but still those kids—hard to believe!"

Garret nodded his head, again in agreement. "It's real hard to believe," he said.

"You find it hard to believe largely because of the experiences you have gone through and then trying to compare that to the magnitude of what they have gone through," said Befikuda. "Well, you certainly see how well we are doing and see credibility in us, so you're going to have to believe it, because you see …"

Then all three oracles said together, "We are the three former child soldiers!"

"When we became free and saved, we became new people in Christ, and we decided to take on different names to match," said Befikuda. "That's not always done in Africa, but we felt that the experience was so special the situation merited it as a way to celebrate our new lives and freedom from Kony. I had to totally submit to God's will and thus went from Tegene Tefere to Befikuda, which means by His will alone."

"I had to concentrate on 'His grace is sufficient,' the most meaningful passage to me, and thus went from Feleke to Tsegaye, which means by His grace."

"In my case, I needed to focus on becoming a new one in Christ and hence went from Alemayehu to Addesu, which means a new one in Christ. In Africa, you do realize by now that names have meanings that are given to people who have either earned or possess those traits and distinctions," explained Addesu.

The two young men from America were stunned, sitting with their mouths gaping open in amazement. They had just heard what for all practical purposes was the story of the three oracles' lives. Then the oracles formally introduced their wives, Celeste, Genevieve, and Miriam respectively, who smiled at them while putting away the utensils.

"To lose one's parents is a terrible thing. Sometimes they are lost while still alive in the abandonment and emotional bankruptcy created in the home by various things. It is an imperfect world. You note that in the 'Tona,' the inanimate objects are given a life of their own to demonstrate a point and special dimensions of storytelling. Try as he might, the young man could not argue with the cabin and began to see that all was the real work of a divine voice stirring up the thoughts and memories within him that also revealed the most important aspects of the conflict, in addition to that contributed by his father—the anger and inadequacies he had developed and the conflict within himself. The schism was both parties' fault, but the inability to heal was due to both as well. Peter had to face himself and come to terms with himself and realize that the hate he harbored was hurting nobody but himself," said Befikuda. "First things first. You need to go back home and reconcile with your fathers."

The two agreed but wanted to stay a while in Ethiopia, at least until their visas expired to see more of the country and learn more from the oracles. They were at least embarking on a more valid track than before and one that could lead to more fruitful and productive lives.

⋰⋱⋰⋱

The oracles set them up with contacts in various locations around Ethiopia, contacts that would help them discover the real Ethiopia. Indeed, the in-depth look into the everyday lives of Africans, well off of the average tourist's beaten path, would unlock the genuine treasure of knowledge revealing the true Africa most would never see. The oracles traveled with them part of the way. Sometimes they left the two to discover on their own and just met them at some locations along the way. They experienced everything from smallholder farmers' coffee farms that also grow horticultural crops to larger coffee plantations. They got an in-depth look at small artisans and fabricators manufacturing everything from basic farm implements and appropriate technology to arts and crafts. They went to various restaurants where they were entertained by local musicians and dancers and spoke with painters and sculptors who showed them their work.

Garret exhibited an uncanny ability to relate to farmers, which surprised the oracles and Jamaal. Garret clearly connected in a way that seemed to reach out and touch their soul, and they, in turn, his. His capacity to relate to them appeared so natural one might even assume he grew up there. He closely observed a farmer named Adamu tilling what was to be a small vegetable field using a hand plough, a type of large hoe commonly seen throughout most of Africa, to till the soil. Garret also observed his wife doing the same, stopping occasionally to nurse her three-month-old child in the field and then wrap him up in a cloth around her neck and shoulders, suspending the child in a hammock close to his mother's heart to sleep while she picked up the plough and continued on. He looked on with admiration and then asked if he could lend a hand. Adamu smiled and agreed. Garret pitched in with gusto, tilling up the soil and planting seeds like an experienced farm hand, keeping up with the same pace as the farmer and his wife, to the amazement of all!

They walked over to another plot after finishing the first one, with Befikuda translating. Garret got on one knee and began inspecting the crops, examining the herbs grown and discussing their condition. He showed he was amazingly knowledgeable about all of the crops and horticultural in general. He asked detailed questions, which Adamu responded to, and then he made accurate suggestions. Then the two engaged in an in-depth, great conversation on agriculture in general, much to their delight. You could see Garret just come alive! He and Adamu got down and inspected the horticultural crops, and noting that they were extremely stressed due to lack of water, he spoke to him about problems meeting evapotranspiration rates and problems meeting the overall water requirements. Adamu nodded his head, affirming the situation, further amazed that the kid knew so much. He offered to take Garret around the rest of the six acres under cultivation. Garret's eyes began showing something besides the wanderlust he had come to Ethiopia with, actually reflecting an inner peace that few had ever seen in him.

He walked over to the patch of maize, pulled off one of the ears, bit off some of the kernels, and began chewing on them. He made several observations to the farmers regarding water deficiency, soil nutrients, and the need for more nitrogen in the soil to make up for the soil depletion caused by crops taking out the nutrients in their growth. They also discussed whether the time was right to consider irrigation or to wait to see if more rain would come, as the rainy season was not quite over yet.

"I'm actually an old hand at this," he said. "My grandpa Ben Holcomb had this farm just outside of West Lafayette, Indiana. That's also the home of Purdue University, the big agricultural school in Indiana. Some of my best days were on that farm before Grandpa died of a heart attack. Really shook me too! Also rocked my world when the farm got sold. It had been in the family for several generations. On the day of the sale, it was like I saw the ghosts of about five generations rise up and cast looks of grim disdain and grief when the deed and title changed hands. Farming's not a mere business. It's a lifestyle!"

"I know exactly what you mean," said Abba Befikuda. "I too grew up on a farm at first, not far from here with my father. We lost it too."

"Oh man, I'm sorry. Big loss, huh?"

"Definitely, and I extend my deepest sympathies to you too. I am seeing more of you now and am beginning to understand more about your loves and losses." Garret continued to squat down with the farmer, picking up a handful of the red-clay soil and letting it filter through his fingers. Inside he was thinking that this was gold! He smiled. He listened intently to the farmer. Garret noticed him running his hand over the ground as well. To engage with a farmer meant to engage with farming, and that meant a love for the land itself. That was necessary to interact going soul to soul.

"What did you say your name was? I'm sorry. I forgot in my passion for the farm and everything going on here."

Befikuda translated.

"Adamu," the man replied.

"It means man of the red-clay soil, like Adam in Genesis," said the abba.

Garret just beamed. My how fitting, for the man typified his namesake in every sense of the term! In Adamu, Garret could see more than a mere reflection of himself. He began to actually see himself and who he really was for the first time in a long time.

As the day came to an end, the sunset cast its radiant hues of color across the sky. Its beams of light pierced the clouds of ever-changing color and reached down to scour the land in a reverent caress, hallowing it, indeed consecrating the ground as if to ensure its bountiful promise. It spoke to Garret in a spiritual, mystical way, like when he looked out on the farm in Indiana. He knew in his heart the rains would come, the crops would grow, and the harvest would be abundant. Life would go on, but how well it would go on would depend on whether potential disciples would heed the message planted in his heart—to pursue development with a love and respect for the land and God's other children, those smallholder farmers, and promote their route to empowerment. He knew the decision he had to make. He nodded his head, smiled, and let out a subtle laugh. He had already dropped the fake Rasta accent. Now it was time to lose the dreadlocks as well.

ஐ௦ ௦ை

They traveled by matatu without the oracles to a number of places, from Gondar to Lalibela, eventually ending up back in Axum. Jamaal looked at Garret, still amazed at this guy's knowledge of farming and his ability to relate to farmers in the rural areas, the areas known to be more locked into the traditional mode and places where foreigners in general might have the hardest time trying to connect with people. Yet he did, better than Jamaal could. He just shook his head, still rather dazed. He asked Garret about it when he woke up from his catnap.

"I just relate to the land well, something all farmers have in common. I just suddenly felt at home, like some voice inside of me said this is what you want, not trying to be a reggae star or some Rastaman. To tell you the truth, I was never great at being a musician anyway. I saw not just something of Granddad, but I also saw myself in Adamu's eyes and how he and his wife work that land together, just like American farmers do. Oh, there're differences, but there is a common thread that those who work the land share. I can only tell you that I felt more fulfilled in being out there than I have felt in a long time. I just went soul to soul. You know what I'm saying?"

"Yeah, yeah, man, I do. I mean, like I didn't experience nothin' like that myself, but what you talkin' about, yeah. I think everybody is trying to experience that in one way or another. It was just amazing and beautiful to see you make that breakthrough."

"Dig that. And that's what it was too, a breakthrough. A real breakthrough! As soon as I get back home, I'm going to hitchhike or something to the old farm and talk to the guy we sold it to and like just look at it. I think that is where I am going to connect to a real life again!"

Jamaal just smiled and thought about Garret's revelation and stared out into space, wondering when he was going to get one of his own. *Patience, be patient*, he thought, remembering what Befikuda had said. *Keep your eyes open and your heart in God's hands. Some things you just have to wait for them to happen. You can't force something like this. That wouldn't work. It has to be a natural occurrence, and then you will see something in the long run and know it's real.*

"I'm happy for you, man," Jamaal said.

Garret just smiled and nodded, then held out his fist for the brotherhood bump.

"I still don't know how to deal with the dad issue though. I don't know for the life of me why he sold the farm. He seemed to be so happy there himself. Then he never seemed happy with anything else. Go figure," responded Garret.

"Maybe there was more to it than that. I mean, like, if he was happy with the farm and all, maybe there was some other stuff working behind the scenes or sumpthin'. I mean, I know it's going to be tough gettin' back together with dear ol' dad for both of us. But I think we're still going to have to do it, like they were talking about," said Jamaal.

Garret nodded his head and shrugged his shoulders as if to begrudgingly agree. Then he tried to get some more sleep.

Jamaal tried to knock off a bit too but found it difficult, not just from the bumpy ride of the matatu but also the thoughts of home that haunted him. Who was he? He still didn't know. The "film career" was a joke. He had just seized upon it from his admiration of Spike Lee, after he saw the movie *Malcom X* and observations of Spike at New York Knicks games. He thought he was cool. But this was no excuse for just jumping from one thing to another. He had been raised in the streets. The Rolling Stones aptly said it all regarding his life, being "born in a crossfire hurricane and howled at his ma' in the drivin' rain!" He hated his life. But there seemed to be something still inside him that was crying out to him for him to hold onto. If only he could get a grasp as to what it was. He admired Garret for his breakthrough. In fact, he was actually jealous of him for it.

They arrived in Axum and were promptly met by the oracles, who asked them how the trip had been to the other places, what they saw and learned. They all went to the coffeehouse for coffee. Celeste, Miriam, and Genevieve had fixed the place up with a couple of beds with fresh linens for the two to stay there while in Axum. After spending a few days with the oracles, Jamaal said he wanted to see a little of Addis's nightlife and hear some Ethio jazz. Befikuda recommended that they go to a place called Mama's Kitchen. It was a great jazz hangout that featured a lot of local artists and sometimes others from around the continent. Jamaal thanked him for the suggestion, saying both he and Garret looked forward to seeing Addis, a little modernity, and the music. The oracles laughed with them, recognizing that they needed to relax in a nice hotel like the Sheraton. Given that this was their first trip to Africa, they had probably had enough of the third world experience for now, and a little luxury wouldn't hurt. A couple of days later, the two pilgrims boarded a jumper flight back to Addis, waving good-bye to the oracles before taxing down the runway.

Befikuda contemplated all that had transpired with the two gentlemen from America. Indeed he pondered over all he had been through, not just with Garret and Jamaal but all of the other pilgrims who had come his way since his taking up the priesthood. In all cases, there was a commonality, where it was all the same. It was not some Old Testament relic that these people needed but the healing blood of a resurrected Jesus Christ. It was the huge step that the damned needed to take into the open, wide arms of Christ to become healed, to become the redeemed.

⁂

The plane arrived in Addis, and the two gathered their belongings from overhead compartments and proceeded to disembark. They collected the rest of their luggage from baggage claim and proceeded out of the airport.

"Taxi, mister? Taxi, mister … taxi, taxi? You guys remember me?" said a cabbie.

"Hey, look who's here, Garret," said Jamaal, "the same brother that picked us up when we first arrived! How you doing, man? What's up?"

"Hey, how are you? Yeah, why don't you take us to the Sheraton?" requested Garret.

"You got it, boss!" the cabbie replied.

"Say, you know a place called Mama's Kitchen?" asked Jamaal.

"Sure. I know every place in Addis. You want to go there?"

"Later, maybe tonight. Kind of tired from the flight. Tomorrow might be better. You want to hook up with us then?" replied Jamaal.

"Sure thing, boss! Tomorrow night would be a good one. They say King Sunny Ade' is going to be there jammin' with one of our most famous musicians, Mulatu Astatke. That would be a real performance to hear. They let some people onstage to play with them. Amateurs-meet-the-pros type thing."

"Oh, man, sounds cool. What do you think, Garret? The place to be or what?"

"Let's do it," Garret replied. "You know where we're at. Pick us up at, what, 7:00 tomorrow night?"

"Make it 6:00. You'll get a good seat then. The place starts jumpin' by 8:00. You might actually get to talk with them before the performance begins! They are very friendly, personable type people, not like some big stars," replied the cabbie.

"All the better!" said an enthusiastic Jamaal.

The cabbie took them to the Sheraton where the two checked in and immediately flopped on the beds in their rooms. The showers were like heaven. After a good meal in the restaurant, they retired for the night. They had no problems drifting off to sleep that night. Though their lives had been rocked with excitement and enlightening experiences, it was tiring. They cruised off to slumberland.

The next day, they mulled around the hotel, recovering from their experience. They discussed the events, things they'd seen and what they meant to them. They spoke briefly with the same bartender they had met the last time they were at the Sheraton.

Back in the room, Jamaal began fumbling with a rather long, hard leather case.

"Whatcha got there, man?" Garret asked.

"Aw, just a little something I always keep with me. Helps me relax," Jamaal replied.

Jamaal opened up the case to reveal a soprano sax.

"Oh, wow, man—you play? You never told me that!" said Garret.

"Yeah, well, it's been pretty personal. I wanted to find the right time," responded Jamaal.

"You gonna take that tonight?"

"Uh-huh."

Jamaal started blowing out some notes just to warm up a little and then launched into an eerie, mystical, wonderful jazz improv run that blew Garret away!

"Whooaaahhh, man, like you're really good, dude! Not like me—you're a real musician!" stammered Garret.

"You really think so?"

"Hell yeah! Definitely take it along tonight and get up on the stage when they call for the amateurs, man. But you ain't no amateur dude. You're a pro!"

Jamaal smiled and laughed. Somebody actually liked his music! He had been put down all his life, and now he was hearing some appreciation. His mom had hated the idea of him being a jazzman and put down everything he did musically, afraid he'd turn out to be like his father. In reality, she was suffocating his real gifts while she lived an illusionary existence in a cocaine stupor. He put the horn back in its case, nodded his head, and said, "We're off!"

Then the two left to meet the cabbie, who took them straight to Mama's Kitchen, which was to be more than a rendezvous with destiny. It would be a rendezvous with their shattered pasts.

They entered Mama's Kitchen and made their way to a table near the stage. Only one or two tables up front were left, about one-third of the whole place already filled. King Sunny Ade', Nigerian jazz icon, along with Mulatu Astatke, the jazz master from Ethiopia, mulled around on stage with the rest of Astatke's band. They began tuning up. Jamaal watched it all intently, his finger tapping on the table, looking more like he was fingering sax keys.

Suddenly Astatke stopped, saw Jamaal and his case, and peered deeply into his eyes as if he knew him, which startled Jamaal somewhat.

"I see we have another jazzman here with us tonight," Astatke said. He gestured toward Ade' to get his attention. The king of Nigerian jazz walked over to the center stage alongside Astatke, glanced at Jamaal, and then did a double take. Not seeing the sax case, Ade' asked him, "You play trumpet by any chance, my man?"

"No, soprano sax!" Jamaal replied, holding up the case.

"Ah, soprano sax, you say? That is good," Ade' said. Then, turning to Astatke, he said, "We don't have a soprano sax tonight in the band, do we?"

"No. Maybe this young man would like to join us tonight?" responded Astatke.

The whole audience sat breathlessly looking at Jamaal. Who was he? Who was this young man who merited such an address of the greatest renowned jazz artists to come out of Africa, icons whose reputations had spread far across the globe, making them famous on the world stage? They were astonished that he had captivated their attention.

Jamaal stammered nervously, "Yeah, I'd love to, if you really want to share your stage with me. I mean, like, you guys are such great pros, and I'm just …"

Astatke cut him off. "You are a jazz great ready to happen. Come, come up here. Don't be bashful. You will probably not be the only one tonight. Besides, I don't know why, but for some reason your face has a look of familiarity about it. Come up here. Warm up and show us something."

Jamaal, wide-eyed, walked up on the stage with his sax. He was eager now, wanting to jump into it, the fire of desire to play burning hotter than ever. He actually loved playing and felt that special spark of excitement every time he touched his horn, like all passionate musicians feel, as this was a gift not just a passion that had to come out and flourish for him to be whole. The release from his sax was a greater and more satisfying experience for his healthy, emotional well-being than any release from sex.

Garret just stared in amazement, noting the crowd's reaction. Looking around, he just thought, *What the hell?* He looked straight ahead to see the two jazz icons still looking at Jamaal with curious smiles.

Jamaal began blowing a few notes out. No need to tune; he'd already done that. He then let loose with some jazz melodies and went improv, his sound gliding through the night air. He then returned to what sounded like a song theme, which was a totally original piece. He played for about three to five minutes and quit, totally mystifying the jazz greats!

"What's your name, son?" asked Mulatu.

"Jamaal Abdul Meriweather, from New York City," he replied.

"Meriweather? Meriweather, you say?" asked Ade'. "Please stay up on stage with us. Then later we'll talk."

Mulatu agreed. He turned around, seeing the rest of the band in place, looked at his watch, then up at Jamaal. "Just follow us. I'm sure you can," he said.

"I know your music well. I've got all of your albums and yours too, Mr. Ade'," Jamaal replied.

The two older men smiled. Then Mulatu kicked off the first number. Jamaal flew through the song effortlessly. His music flowed in a perfect complement to that of the older jazz greats. His music danced with it, sometimes dancing upon it, dancing past any inhibitions that might prompt others to demur approaching this intriguing, seductive genre of music. He was clearly unrestrained, unlike so many others from Western culture who fail to breach ethnocentric walls, leaving them incapable of understanding, feeling, or fully appreciating Ethio jazz. On the contrary, his sound flowed through cross-cultural barriers on rivers that shined, not hampered at all by the Ethio jazz modals, not bothered by the dark-turned-brighter sounds of the strange, minor twists with the flat sixth and then hitting a bright sharp seventh, which gave Ethiopian jazz part of its unusual tonality. He was unhampered by the rhythms, the African polyrhythmic sensibility often featuring sixes against fours and three against twos. Sometimes the bass line would be in six and the drums in four, pulsating a symphony in rhythm that swung in syncopation, making it all work. This led British jazz pianist Alexander Hawkins to say, "If you told the dancers that, they'd fall over. But don't tell them, and they're fine."

It all flowed like a river with major bends and turns leaving straight form but not getting wedged on the sandbars, navigating a perfect course through to the end. On many songs, the music took the listener on an eerie, seductive sojourn down a seemingly endless path of a two-toned chord. It was the perfect combination of the traditional Ethiopian music with modern American jazz forms, incorporating the outside world into the innermost soul of Ethiopian music. The crowd danced through the night feverishly.

Jamaal's music seemed to float on light and flash into brilliant hues revealed in the notes and tonality. Indeed, it seemed to reveal light, broadcasting the full spectrum in its sound: the deep purples, dark blues, indigo, occasionally mixed with shades of green as the tones weaved in and through each song. Then suddenly they would explode with flashes of vivid reds, magenta, oranges, yellows, and gleaming silver as the horns, particularly Jamaal's soprano sax, blasted into shrill high notes for accents, taking the music and the crowd through the stratosphere! It was a rhapsody of emotions pouring through jazzmen's improvisation, becoming a spiritual conduit that cascaded a delightfully eerie mysticism upon the entire crowd. Jamaal's music featured an array of colors and light so intriguing, his music was to light what Monet's paintings were to same with oils and acrylics. True artistry cuts through walls of cultural division.

As he played, he released more than a passion from deep within himself, from deep within his soul. He had at last found the key to unlocking that vault where that inner thing he had been grasping for in futility for so long was hidden. Indeed, in playing on stage that night, he was releasing himself. He more than played. His music, like Ethio jazz, was a mix of the functional and spiritual dimensions of music. It was as if his music was a spiritual word of knowledge from God that Pentecostals claim to receive when "praying in the spirit." However, he prayed through his horn. Like the blast that brought down the walls of Jericho, his music brought down the walls inside of him that had enslaved his soul, revealing a clear path to redemption. His music was his prayer that reached out to heaven and touched the very heart of God—jazz's greatest fan!

The grand finale brought the crowd roaring to its feet. After the introductions of each to the applause of the listeners, King Sunny Ade',

Mulatu Astatke, and Jamaal embraced in a three-way hug. Garret collapsed in a chair with an Ethiopian beauty on each arm asking him if he wanted to go party with them afterward. He just laughed in delirium and said, "Maybe the next time I'm in Ethiopia. Got to pack tomorrow for a flight back to the US." They quickly agreed to help. He just laughed and shook his head, looking up at Jamaal. Both were thinking that nobody back home was going to believe this, much less relate to it!

After it was all over, Ade', Mulatu, and the two pilgrims sat down to talk and relax. Mulatu and Sunny were anxious to talk about a topic aside from how well the night had gone.

"Your name is Jamaal Meriweather, and you say you're from New York?" Mulatu asked. "Is that your real name, the one you were born with, because you definitely remind me of someone?"

"Your style reminds me of John Coltrane, but there is also a distinct pure tone and approach to music that reminds of someone else," broke in Ade'.

"Well, my birth name was Clarence Meriweather Jr., but I didn't like my dad much, in fact hardly knew him, so I changed it on my own. My legal name on my passport and all still says Clarence Jr.," he replied.

"But you still refer to your last name as Meriweather. Why?" asked Mulatu.

"Oh, I don't know. I guess there's something there I still try to connect with. Until tonight, I wasn't sure what it was, but I guess it's the promise he made to me when I was three, that I was going to grow up to be a jazzman someday. And then there are the memories, the good ones I still cling to. I guess there is still a place in my heart for him alongside all that anger," he responded.

"So, you're Gabe's boy, you're Lil' Gabe!" said Ade'. "We both know your father. He's a great jazz musician."

"Why does everybody call him Gabe and me Lil' Gabe? What's up with all that? And how in the world do you know my father?" Jamaal asked.

"Because that's his name. Yours too! Clarence Gabriel Meriweather, and you are Clarence Gabriel Meriweather Jr. You didn't know that? You didn't know you had a middle name?" replied Mulatu.

"Nobody told me," Jamaal replied. "I guess that was another one of dear old Mom's tricks to try to remove him completely from my mind, identity, and world."

"We referred to your dad only by Gabe because of the way he played, like Gabriel blowin' that horn," said Ade' with a warm smile.

"Yeah, man, he was good. The tone so pure and clear," said Mulatu. "To answer your other question, I studied at the famous Berkelee College of Music in Boston in '63. I did a lot of giggin' in the bars in Boston and New York, eventually moving to New York for a while. That's where I met your dad. Jammed with him, Dizzy Gillespie, and Miles Davis on stage. One of the best experiences of my life. Gabe was very much interested in the whole free jazz movement in the early sixties as a freer form of expression. Later, he read Haley's *Roots* and got into the whole find-your-roots thing. That brought him over to Africa, which is where he met up with Sunny. He went to Nigeria first, just to check out Lagos, and then came here, as somebody, his grandfather I think it was, had told him they came from Ethiopia."

"So that's why!" exclaimed Jamaal.

"So that's why what, dude?" Garret asked.

"He had this map of Ethiopia on the wall with a pin stuck in Axum. I was fascinated by that map. It had all kinds of colorful pictures of elephants, lions, and stuff. Mom tried to tear it down when he left, but I raised such a fuss, kicking, crying, and screaming, and she gave up and left it up there. I developed my own fascination with Ethiopia, but deep down inside I always wondered what his was."

"Maybe, deep down, that's really what brought you here—trying to follow your father's footsteps as a way of reconnecting? I think that is something maybe you still want to do, maybe why you still call yourself Meriweather?" suggested Mulatu. "Even if you couldn't find him physically, maybe you could find him in a way you could at least cope with."

Jamaal just looked straight down. He tried to fight back the emotion swelling up inside him but couldn't. Tears began to stream down his face, and he bawled out, "I actually don't hate him. I love him! Why didn't he come home that night? Why did he leave us like that? My life has been hell since then!"

Mulatu put his arm around him and said, "He couldn't come home that night. He was hospitalized. I won't go into why, but when your mother found out why, she went crazy and divorced him. When he finally got out of the hospital, he desperately tried to find you. But she blocked his every attempt, as did Human Services once they took you out of her home and put you in foster care."

"We heard all about it," said Ade'. "Try not to be too hard on him. He was far from perfect. You know about the heroin, but there's none of us who haven't fallen short of the kingdom of God and need forgiveness and redemption. I guarantee you, losing you ripped a huge hole in his heart."

Jamaal just sat stunned and ordered another whiskey. The bartender just looked up at him and then at Mulatu. Jamaal had already had a lot.

Mulatu looked up at the bartender and said, "It's okay. It's medicinal—trust me!"

"Well, he came over here lookin' for his roots. Tell me, what did he find?" asked Jamaal.

"I don't know all of it. He'll tell you, and you must reconcile with him. Your ancestors do come from Ethiopia, Axum in fact, but you are not Ethiopian. You still have to go through real rite of passage. On this continent, it is a sin to disrespect one's elders, much less harbor this schism with your father. If you want to really come to Africa, you first have to go inward, inside yourself and then through your father, reconciling it as if to come back through his soul and the souls of your ancestors. I'm not talking about any New Age channeling bullshit. I'm talking about the love and unity through which you develop more of an understanding of your ancestors and in that way start the journey back home. Then when you come back, and you will, I'm sure, you will be one of us," said Mulatu.

Turning to Garret, he asked him, "You say you're Garret Holcomb Jr. from Indianapolis? Are you the son of Garret Holcomb, the rich philanthropist from there?"

"Philanthropist? My dad?" Garret replied.

"Yes, yes, Garret Holcomb, the man who funds several NGOs in Africa. We know him well!" remarked Ade'.

Both Garret and Jamaal sat stunned, looking straight at the two and then looked at each other. They just shook their heads in disbelief.

"Looks like both of you have some fence mending to do, as you say in America, when you go back home," said Mulatu.

"They do indeed. However, I, for one, am bushed! It is time we go to bed. Let's meet tomorrow at the Sheraton for lunch, and we'll talk some more," Ade' said.

They all agreed and then parted ways for the night.

After passing out at the Sheraton, both got up the next day, met with Ade' and Astatke, and then prepared to pack for an early flight home. It was a 4:30 a.m. flight. The familiar cabbie picked them up and dropped them off at the airport.

"See you when you come back. You know you will. Africa is a beautiful woman singing a song for you to return. You can't resist her!" he said.

The two nodded their heads, laughed, and then proceeded into the terminal, knowing that he was right. But first they had to return home and face a lot more than they had left.

⋅ༀ ༀ⋅

Garret walked out of the airport in Indianapolis and just stood on the sidewalk for a moment. He didn't want to go home. In fact he had no idea of whether anybody there knew he had even left in the first place. He knew what he wanted to do. He got a taxi to the bus station and took the first bus to West Lafayette. From there, he just walked. He walked past Purdue University, glancing at the buildings with a smile, past convenience stores, and headed for the edge of town. Once he got there, he stuck out his thumb to hitch a ride to a place where he once found serenity, a little place right off the intersection of Highways 52 and 231. It had been the Holcomb place.

Along the way, he gazed out at the Indiana countryside. It was autumn, the most beautiful time of the year in Indiana. *Observing classic monuments such as rural America's barns from the side of the road, or an old classic farmhouse constructed long ago, projects more than our history,* he thought. They stand out, dotting an emerald-green countryside graced by golden sunrays from an autumn sky, a scene punctuated by trees donning the season's colors, prompting one to more than wax nostalgically. *These are our cathedrals in rural America,* he thought, *symbolic of a noble work ethic and fierce independency in people who built this state, indeed cut it out of the sod years ago.*

That gutsy determinism found in the agricultural sector served not only as the bedrock for decent values but spawned an agricultural industry that paid the bills for the rest of the state long before the construction of steel mills. The heart of rural America's values is a moral, ethical soul that seems to be sadly absent in other parts of country. It's in the people who he saw as biblically defined "salt": substantial, nourishing, as in salt of the earth. He remembered the words of Alexis de Tocqueville and felt that this place was the epitome of de Tocqueville's observation: "America is great because America is good. And when America ceases to be good, then she shall cease to be great." That goodness he found going through rural America and looking into its churches, the same type of little white churches and chapels Garret saw in the distance.

Indiana was not a mere track of land between a couple of longitudinal lines, rivers, and a big lake. And it couldn't be found by merely looking at a Rand McNally map. Indiana was a brilliant gem of innovation that rested in the heart and soul of good people here. Garret found that spirit within himself, even though he had to go to Ethiopia to find it. The trip got him away from the family dysfunction that obscured his vision to see it, but it also got him back home. No matter how far he traveled or how far he roamed, there would still be a little place in him called Indiana. In that regard, this ol' country boy wasn't ever leavin' home. For the same reason, he hadn't really left Africa either. It was all just fine with him. At last he was at peace. He just smiled, looking out the window.

He got out at the intersection of the two highways and walked up to the old homestead. He knocked on the door. Jed Slocum, the man they had sold it to, opened the door.

"Can I help you?" he asked.

"I'm Garret Holcomb Jr. You bought this farm from my father years ago when Grandpa died. You remember me?"

"Yes, yes, son, come on in. How are you?" he replied.

The two had some iced tea and talked. Jed was a great farmer but not a good businessman and was having trouble with the farm, managing costs and such. He told Garret that his dad had been picking up payments on the farm for at least five years, much to Garret's surprise.

Garret told him about the trip to Ethiopia, the farms, and how he felt he had finally found himself. He wanted to just stay at the farm for a while, recuperate from jet lag and just think a while, lending a hand if Jed needed one. Jed agreed, saying that he could always use an extra hand. They had a room already available for him, as Jed's kids had already left home.

"Your dad know your back?"

"No. I don't know as he ever knew I left."

"He knew. Told me about it too. You'd better call him. Your Grandpa Williams died while you were gone. He was lookin' for you. Say, I need to go into Indianapolis for a few days, leavin' tomorrow. I can give you a ride."

Garret sat motionless but not overly emotional. He had never connected with his grandfather or anybody on his mom's side of the family. Grandpa Williams was worse than his dad at being distant. "Yeah, there's a lot of things I need to talk to Dad about," he said.

The next day, Jed drove Garret back to the palatial estate of the Holcomb family but not before Garret stopped off at the local barbershop and got a haircut. As his father opened the door, he was shocked at his son's appearance.

"Garret, what happened to you? This is a new look. I thought you joined up with the Rastas in Jamaica? You look clean-cut. I'm impressed!" said Garret senior.

"Dad, let's just talk without the yelling this time," he replied. Then he threw his arms around his father and hugged him. His father was startled by the new Garret.

He smiled and said, "Yeah, sure, son. It's been a while."

The two sat down and talked for hours. Things rolled out that the two had to confront. Then Garret asked about his grandfather's death. His dad just looked out in space for a moment.

"Yeah, he died of a heart attack. If you're going to ask me if I'm torn up about it, no, I'm not. In fact, I couldn't stand him. His interference caused most of the problems around here. His philandering and jet-set lifestyle, never being there for your mother, opened the door for her excessive partying and eventual alcoholism. Her mom just saw the marriage as one of convenience and played around too. Of course, your mom could have chosen better ways to deal with it. Her choice to drink was her own responsibility. She's recognized that, become a Christian, and is in a twelve-step program. She's been sober for about the last three months, since you left. As for me, I'm through with the financial business, Wall Street, all of it. Not that that is necessarily bad as some people claim, but it was rammed down my throat. Hell, I wanted to get a master's degree in agricultural economics and go to work for USAID or the World Bank or something like that that would get me back to Africa," he replied.

"Back to Africa? Somebody over there told me you had been funding all these NGOs out there. Why didn't you ever tell me?"

"Because you seemed to talk with Jack Williams more than me, and there was no way I could. Look, the dialogue shutdown was a two-way street. Jack Williams told me that there was no way I was going to take his little princess to those 'shitholes,' as he called them in Africa. If I was going to marry her, which I desperately wanted to do at the time, not to mention the fact that we thought she was pregnant then, I was to work with him and make a lot of money, living in plastic land, which I must say I actually hated. This whole thing ain't me, boy. Hell, I didn't know what to do, so I got an MBA, went to work for him, and became very good at it. Turns out your mom wasn't even pregnant but wanted to get married just to get away from him. Boy, did that backfire! If he had known I still pursued interests in Africa, he'd have found ways to screw everything up. He didn't even like the fact that I came from the farm, didn't think I was good enough for his debutante daughter, and he really put pressure on me to sell the farm when Dad died. Said I'd never go back to the farm."

"So that's why everything has been so dysfunctional around here! I never really liked the guy either!"

"Well, it's been a lot of things. It wasn't too late to correct one thing. I got out of the business, liquidated all my holdings, except for a few accounts to keep a balanced portfolio and cash for the proverbial rainy day, and either liquidated or placed all of the inheritance in a special account. We're worth a lot now—I mean a lot. I'm in the process of setting up for-profit and nonprofit development organizations to go back into Africa. Did you know I was a Peace Corp volunteer in Kenya? Saw Ethiopia, Sudan, Uganda, Tanzania. Love that place!"

"Well, Dad, I really connected with the farmers out there. Hey, listen, this is what I want to do."

Garret explained his desire to go to Purdue and double major in agronomy and agricultural economics. He wanted to go back to Africa and work with the farmers. He also explained about Slocum's financial woes.

"I'm already aware of Jed's problems. I'm going to buy the farm back and keep him on as a production manager. Guy's great at disking fields but not too good with the financial end. I'll handle that. You say he's agreed to let you stay out there for a while? Look, if you're serious about this, I'll spring for college. I'll even buy you another car so you can commute. Just don't wreck this one. In fact, I'm buying you a Ford pickup, not a Maserati!"

"Don't worry. I don't have those issues anymore. Yes, on the issue of staying at the old place, we even talked about a long-term stay while I went to school. I'd really rather live on the farm than in the dorms. They're a zoo, and I don't need any more partying. Time to get serious."

His father smiled. "Maybe we can both work the farm and the development NGOs together, father and son. What do you say? We maybe can try a new beginning, start over?" he suggested.

"Yeah, a new beginning. It's already started in me. Yeah, sounds great, Dad."

"Welcome home, son."

"Good to be back, Dad."

⁊⊙ ⊙⊱

Jamaal stepped out of JFK International and hailed a cab. He fumbled with a slip of paper in his pocket. It was his father's last-known address that Mulatu Astatke had. His father had moved to Brooklyn from the Bronx. Jamaal just shook thinking about it—going to his house and facing his father for the first time in years.

A cabbie pulled up.

"Where to, man?" the cabbie asked.

Jamaal gave the address to the cabbie, who nodded his head and reached back, opening the back door for Jamaal to get in. Jamaal sat in the back, almost hoping that the address was wrong or old, that maybe his father had moved on. He had such high anxiety he didn't know whether he could face this scene or not.

He sucked up the courage to go through with it as the cab pulled up to the brownstone row house in Brooklyn. Jamaal paid him, gathered his bags, and walked up the steps. He rang the doorbell and just looked around at the neighborhood, his heart racing out of control like he was having a heart attack. A moment later, a woman about in her midfifties answered the door.

"May I help you?" she asked.

"Does Clarence Gabriel Meriweather Sr. still live here? If so, is he home?" Jamaal asked.

"Yes, he still lives here, and he's home. May I ask who's calling on him and the reason, young man?"

"I'm … I'm Jamaal, uh … I mean," he stammered and then took a deep breath. "I'm Clarence Gabriel Meriweather Jr. He's my father."

The woman's eyes widened with shock and surprise. Jamaal, now Clarence Jr.'s, words sucked the air out of her lungs!

"So, you're Lil' Gabe. Only you aren't so little anymore! You're all grown up now! Your father's talked about you a lot. Wait here, I'll go get him. Gabe, Gabe—someone here to see you, honey!" she hollered.

She walked into the kitchen where Gabe Sr. was preparing a sandwich.

"Did you hear me? I said someone's here to talk to you."

"Yeah, yeah, I heard you. Just a minute," he responded.

"I think that you really want to drop what you are doing and go see this man, now … seriously! Believe me, you really want to do this!"

He looked at her with raised eyebrows. "Well, who is he?"

"I think you need to go find out for yourself."

He shrugged his shoulders and walked through the living room to the front door to see the "stranger." At last, the two had come face-to-face.

"Can I help you?" Senior said.

Gabe Jr. just looked at him a moment, observing his hair, which had turned from salt and pepper to snow white with age. "I'm Lil' Gabe. I'm your son, Dad."

Gabe Sr. stood paralyzed for a moment and then shook his head almost in disbelief and stammered out, "After all these years, I … I … I don't know what to say, where to even start. How—how did you even find me? I'm glad that you did, honest I am, but how?" He reached out, arms outstretched to embrace his son, but Gabe Jr. just responded by extending his hand.

"It's … it's a little soon for that. Don't be insulted or anything. It's just that I'm not sure as I'm ready for all of that. I mean, I had such anxiety just coming here," he said. "I just came back from Ethiopia. Mulatu Astatke gave me this as your last-known address."

"You talked to Mulatu? How the hell is he?"

"He's doin' fine. I jammed with him and King Sunny Ade' in Addis. They told me practically everything about you going to the hospital, but he wouldn't say why. I understand things a bit better now, but still, growing up without you, without parents—in the Bronx! Man, that was a nightmare of living hell! Messed me up pretty bad."

"I know, I know. It had to be tough. I know the Bronx myself. I tried to see you. Heaven knows I tried, but well, you know all that too. Well, come on in, come on into the living room. Those your bags out there? Let me give you a hand. You have to be tired. You can't just leave stuff like that out on the streets, not in this city! You want something to eat? We'll get you some grub. My wife just made some fresh greens and all."

"That'd be cool."

Senior grabbed the bags, and the two walked into the living room. Charlotte came in and set up some TV trays, then went back and forth to the kitchen and living room, bringing in plates of food with sandwiches, greens, potato salad, and baked beans, just to name a few delicacies Gabe Jr. was ready to jump into! Then she came back out with a tray holding a pitcher of iced tea and two ice-filled glasses and set it down on the round coffee table between the two.

"Now, y'all say the blessin'! Ain't gonna have no unblessed food in my house! And include a prayer for yourselves, because ya'll gonna need the Lord's help in this one, I think," she said with a smile. "Thank Him for the reunion and see this as a blessin', not something to be afraid of."

Senior prayed. Then they dove into the food. Gabe Jr. was famished, not to mention exhausted, suffering jet lag. He thanked Charlotte for the food. Senior nodded his head to her, showing his gratitude, his mouth already full.

She walked back to the kitchen. "I'll just leave you two alone now. I know that you have a lot to catch up on," she said.

They held off the heavy dialogue until they were finished. Then it began. Junior expressed his anguish, how he'd grown up hating his dad and not feeling much love for his mother either. He talked about how life had been growing up in the Bronx streets, encountering the gangs, drug dealers, junkies, prostitutes, hustlers, not to mention the abuse in the foster home system. But, he said, he still retained a place in his heart for Senior in the midst of all the swirling anger and pain. He told him he learned how to play the saxophone and jammed with Ade' and Astatke. It was there that things began to come together and he could begin to make some sense of it all. Then he stopped, as if time froze.

"I don't really hate you, Dad … in fact, I love you. I'm just really, really hurtin', y'know? Really, really hurtin' bad!"

Tears began to flow down his cheeks again. Junior made the first move, getting up and knocking over the TV tray, rushing, arms outstretched toward his father. Senior embraced the opportunity and met him halfway with a bear hug. The two just shook as they embraced.

"Daddy, Daddy, I wanted you back so bad! I couldn't figure out why you left! I thought it was me! I thought you didn't want me anymore!"

"No, no, no, son! I wanted you in the worst way! It was torture for me too!"

The two just hugged and cried for what seemed like an eternity. Then they sat down, and Senior began filling in all the missing details that Astatke and Ade' had left out.

"That night I left, I was scared. We were playing in a syndicate-owned club. The night before, I walked back to pick up something of mine near the office, and I saw something that I wasn't supposed to see. They didn't know I saw at first, but it got back to them that I was a witness. Even though I didn't know they knew I was a witness, the next night when I left to play the gig, I was still scared because you don't mess with the mafia! Well … you know I had a heroin problem back then. They had been my suppliers. An easy way to make the witness disappear was to give me a 100 percent pure solution of smack, where I had only been used to cut stuff, about 50 percent pure at best. I overdosed in the alleyway that night and damn near died. Miles Davis found me and rushed me to a hospital and then paid for my rehab. I mean, by the mob's figurin', whose gonna investigate just another dead heroin junkie in the streets of New York? Happens all the time. Fortunately for me, Miles found me. Also fortunate for me, the feds busted the place. Turns out the bartender was undercover. They didn't even need me for a witness. The mob guys who did know about me got killed in the fire fight during the raid! So I was safe from everybody but your mama. She went berserk! Hated me anyway. This was a convenient excuse to not only get a divorce but convince 'Inhuman Services' not to tell me where you were after they pulled you from her place."

"If only I could have known. And here all these years, I thought that you had just abandoned us."

""Nah, nah, son. Just the exact opposite. Look, it was my fault that I was a junkie, and I am sorry for that. But I always wanted to be with you. I got cleaned up. Been going to Narcotics Anonymous meetings regularly. Been sober for years now."

Junior reached down to his horn case, opened it, and pulled out the map of Ethiopia.

"Remember this? I just went to Axum too!"

"You still got that? I can't believe you still held onto it after all these years!"

"Some treasures you just don't toss away. I know our ancestors are from there. But y'know I think our current history between us is more important, at least for now. I can hear about the rest later."

Senior agreed and offered Junior a place to stay. They had a spare bedroom. He would be welcome as long as he wanted to stay. Junior quickly took him up on it. He didn't have any place else to go anyway. Then Charlotte walked into the room holding two Yankees tickets to the game with Boston the next afternoon.

"Gabe got these for us. But I think that you two ought to go on and use the opportunity to get better reacquainted." The two men beamed, as they had grown up great fans of the Bronx Bombers. Junior's eyes started to go. He was spent. Charlotte led him up to his room where he collapsed on the bed and fell asleep immediately.

The next day, the two men hustled off to the ballpark, dad and son, peanuts, popcorn, and crackerjacks—the whole works. It was an exciting game. Then in the bottom of the ninth with the Yankees down 7–4, bases loaded, Alex A-Rod Rodriguez stepped up to the plate. The count went down to three and two. Then suddenly A-Rod took a hard swing at a ninety-five-mile-per-hour fastball and hammered it so hard he almost parked it in another time zone! It was a walk-off grand-slam homerun that drove the crowd wild! Father and son jumped up and down hugging each other, cheering wildly! Junior thought, *If New York and the Yankees could forgive A-Rod for his earlier transgressions, I could at least look past my father's.*

On the way home, Senior suggested, "Son, I have this gig tonight. Why don't you come along. You say you're a sax man? Any good?" he teased.

"That's what they say," Junior replied.

"Of course you are. You're my son!" Senior laughed.

"Sounds great, Dad. Let's do it!"

They grabbed a bite to eat at home and then rode to a jazz joint in Manhattan. Senior introduced his son to the rest of the band. They were delighted to see the two reunited and to have Gabe Jr on stage with them. The band played, and the two sounds blended together like there had never been a schism.

After a while, Senior turned to Junior and said, "We had a great time today, didn't we? I mean, there's still a whole lot of healin' to do, I know, but at least we got us a great, new start, don't we, son?"

"Yeah, yeah, we do, Dad!"

"I mean we saw the game and all. And ol' A-Rod hit that grand slam! You know, playin' music with you has always been my dream. Looks like A'Rod ain't the only one hittin' a grand slam today, is he, son?"

"Nah, Dad. I think we hit one today too!"

The piano player said, "Okay, let's hit it and git it, one more before break!" He counted off the time, and the band took off playing "Big Swing Face" by Buddy Rich.

As Gabe Jr. played, he thought, *Relationships should be a lot like jazz. Jazz, like, takes you down a big river, only the river's not without twists, turns, and bends, because jazz will leave straight form a lot and incorporate all kinds of polyrhythms. But if you don't get stuck on the sandbars, no matter what delta jazz is gonna take you to, you know, it's gonna be some place beautiful!* The thought made him smile as he continued on playing throughout the night.

TRUE DIRECTIONS

An affiliate of Tarcher Perigee

OUR MISSION

Tarcher Perigee's mission has always been to publish
books that contain great ideas. Why? Because:

GREAT LIVES BEGIN WITH GREAT IDEAS

At Tarcher Perigee, we recognize that many talented authors, speakers,
educators, and thought-leaders share this mission and deserve to be published –
many more than Tarcher Perigee can reasonably publish ourselves. True
Directions is ideal for authors and books that increase awareness, raise
consciousness, and inspire others to live their ideals and passions.

Like Tarcher Perigee, True Directions books are designed to do three things:
inspire, inform, and motivate.

Thus, True Directions is an ideal way for these important voices to
bring their messages of hope, healing, and help to the world.

Every book published by True Directions– whether it is non-fiction, memoir,
novel, poetry or children's book – continues Tarcher Perigee's mission to publish
works that bring positive change in the world. We invite you to join our mission.

For more information, see the True Directions website:

www.iUniverse.com/TrueDirections/SignUp

Be a part of Tarcher Perigee's community to bring positive change in this
world! See exclusive author videos, discover new and exciting books, learn
about upcoming events, connect with author blogs and websites, and more!
www.tarcherbooks.com

TRUE DIRECTIONS
AN AFFILIATE OF TARCHER PERIGEE